Angels, Sinners and Madmen

by

Cate Masters

This is a work of fiction. Names, characters, places, and incidents are either the product of the author's imagination or are used fictitiously, and any resemblance to actual persons living or dead, business establishments, events, or locales, is entirely coincidental.

Angels, Sinners and Madmen

COPYRIGHT © 2023 by Cate Masters

Cover Art by *Tina Lynn Stout*

The Wild Rose Press, Inc.
PO Box 708
Adams Basin, NY 14410-0708
Visit us at www.thewildrosepress.com

Publishing History
First Edition, 2023
Trade Paperback ISBN 978-1-5092-4921-3
Digital ISBN 978-1-5092-4922-0

Published in the United States of America

Beneath the surface, the tumultuous waves and winds were obliterated by the slow, otherworldly atmosphere where peace reigned equally alongside horror. He aimed for the first sinking body—a woman. Liam would have a laugh if he rescued a female first. Yet Sam had other reasons: weaker-limbed, women proved less likely to save themselves than men, and their saturated skirts became heavy, making the effort to swim doubly hard.

He swam toward the light blue fabric, sinking faster than usual. Kicking hard, the girl ploughed deeper, her hands plunging ahead. Her fall must have confused her into swimming downward rather than toward the surface. Such confusion was common in shipwrecks. He slipped his arm around her slim waist.

She turned, her eyes wide, and pushed at his hands. Her golden hair swirled in cascades, as magical as a woman of the deep. No mermaid ever looked so angry— or so determined.

He tightened his grip and pointed up.

Her hair swirled as she shook her head and pointed down.

Sam followed the direction of her finger. The turbid sea revealed nothing beyond churning debris.

She broke loose from him. Her foot caught him in the stomach, forcing a burst of bubbles from his mouth.

Precious air lost. He had to move fast. He locked his grip across her ribs and labored upward. She twisted beneath his arm and kicked at his legs, making the journey to the surface an arduous one.

Dedication

To Gary,
for enduring the angel and madman in me

Chapter One

The *Elizabeth Rose* sliced through the waves of the Atlantic, creating a diamond-bright spray of shimmering gold in the morning sun's rays, bright beneath dark clouds.

A fleeting treasure to behold.

To Livvie Collins, standing at the helm, all of life seemed to be a treasure, but so fleeting. She intended to experience it to the fullest.

In the seas ahead, hundreds of silver fish dotted the waters. They parted for the ship, some leaping from the sea. Some skimmed along the surface, their translucent fins extended like wings. A few bumped into the ship's sides. Others rose higher and glided in the air.

One floated alongside the deck rail and landed at her feet. "Oh, poor fellow." She bent for a closer inspection. Another fish, and then another, thudded on board around her.

"Miss!" someone called.

She met Peter's friendly gaze, his grip steady on her elbow. He guided her to the side, dozens of fish raining around them.

"Get down." He crouched, tugged her to the side and held the rail to shield her. His lean frame belied its sinew. His ease of movement showed his strength, a grace she'd noticed watching him when he scaled the mast to the lookout tower or helped haul up the sails.

She focused on the strange sight beyond him and tried to ignore his musky scent, the result of hard labor and no bath facilities. Father would have frowned upon her for allowing such intimacy with someone she hardly knew.

Father was gone now. She alone steered the rudder of her destiny—until she reached Wendell's house, at least. Her brother would no doubt attempt to assert his opinion above her own. When the ship made port at New Orleans, he would find her unwilling to relinquish her freedom.

"What are they?" she asked.

Peter angled toward her. Up close, his dark eyes shone even more warmly. "Flying fish. Harmless enough, unless you step in their path."

"Flying fish! How incredible." She craned to see past him, delighting in the winged creatures. So beautiful, she hoped to capture every detail in her journal later.

"They don't really fly," he said. "See how they spread their fins to catch the wind, much the same as our ship's sails."

The number of wayward fish had dwindled to an occasional flop onto the ship.

Peter eased to a stand and peered over the rail. "It's safe now." He stepped back and extended his hand toward her.

Rising, she slid her palm across his, its coarseness pricking her senses to life. "They aren't very good navigators."

A smile lit his face. "Cook loves them. The crew, too—it's less work for us when the food supply presents itself."

"And without any argument. Oh, who could eat such a magical creature?" Akin to something out of a fairy tale, the way they'd appeared in the air. She couldn't wait to see her brother's face when she told him. He, of course, would tell her to stop dreaming, a favorite admonishment of his before he moved south.

"Magic or not, they're delicious." Peter gently squeezed her hand.

At home, Livvie might have blushed at such boldness and released him before her father's quick eye could glower in warning. Here, there was no one to see, and she would not take offense at an innocent gesture.

Good-natured banter filled the air as several of the crew scooped fish up in their arms, carrying them to a barrel.

A familiar high-pitched voice called, "Olivia, are you all right? I heard a terrible noise."

She withdrew from Peter's grasp to face the stern figure of Martha Locke, crow-like in her widow's dress. "I'm fine, Mrs. Locke. The noise was only dinner, delivering itself to ship's cook."

Ducking his head, Peter grinned at her.

Mrs. Locke gripped the rail, picking her way toward them, daintily stepping over the wriggling fish. She clutched her side and fanned herself with her handkerchief. "You shouldn't stand so close to the edge. You could have toppled overboard."

"Peter saw to my safety." She curtsied in jest. "Thank you, kind sir." Her gratitude extended beyond her safety. She would cherish the memory of his gallantry.

He bowed. "My pleasure, milady."

Mrs. Locke's wide eyes narrowed, no doubt owing

to his enthusiastic tone.

Peter bent to retrieve a flopping fish and walked backward, his gaze locked on hers.

She reached out. "Careful, Peter."

Slipping on a fish, he landed on his derriere, legs splayed.

A mate looked from him to Livvie and guffawed. "Aye, careful, lad. Ye'll get yourself in a slippery mess."

Livvie understood the double entendre all too well, yet no embarrassment tainted her good mood. Peter was a friend, nothing more. Once they landed, he'd sail off, and she'd travel on to New Orleans. Until then, he provided interesting company, and she was sure he felt the same.

He caught the fish again and carried it to the barrel.

She hid her smile behind her hand. Her spirit hadn't felt so light in a year, since before her father had grown ill.

Mrs. Locke clutched her arm. "See, I told you it's not safe. Come below, where you will be secure."

The rocking of the boat beneath Livvie's feet didn't frighten her. The sensation was not dissimilar to riding her horse, which she loved to do with abandon. Although much larger than her beautiful gelding, the surge of the ship's rise and fall reminded her of the steady canter of her beloved Swedish Warmblood.

Mustering what she hoped was a reassuring pleasantness, she turned to Mrs. Locke. "It's unbearably dark below. I much prefer the open view from here."

Peering out across the bow, Mrs. Locke muttered, "I feel faint." Her eyes fluttered, and she swooned with a low moan.

Livvie linked arms with her. "Hold tight to me. I'll

take you below."

The widow shuffled across the deck as though her feet were encased in leaden boots. "The rocking of the waves, the howling wind—it terrifies me, all of it. I fear we will be lost to the sea." Her grip on Livvie's arm tightened enough to leave a mark.

Livvie pried Mrs. Locke's fingers loose and patted them. "Nonsense. We'll make port soon. Until then, you must keep your mind occupied. Worrying is useless."

"All I have left is worry in my life," the older woman moaned. "My happiness is past. My beloved Andrew is gone. I will only be a burden to my poor son." Her voice broke, and she held her handkerchief to her mouth.

Livvie adopted a tone her father would have used. "I'm sure that's not true, Mrs. Locke. You have many happy, useful days ahead. Engage yourself in worthwhile pursuits, and happiness will return." Those words rang empty to her now.

Mrs. Locke sighed. "You are too young to understand my dire situation."

She steered the woman down the steep steps, toward her bedding. No use telling the old biddy she herself was in no better a position. All she loved she had left behind. Her brother and his wife were opening their home to her, yet Livvie suspected their expectation was for her to marry—and soon—to relieve them of her presence.

To calm Mrs. Locke, Livvie sat beside her, though she soon grew uneasy. The gloom of the lower hold infected her, its still, dank air suffocating her. No wonder the widow was half-mad with worry, always retreating to this dim haven. The closed-in hold assaulted Livvie's senses and quashed her hopes. "Where is your book? I shall read to you."

Her hands shaking, Mrs. Locke handed her the Nathaniel Hawthorne novel, *The House of Seven Gables*.

Livvie opened to the page bookmarked by an embroidered strip of fabric and read aloud. The cadence of the words soon lulled Mrs. Locke, her breaths softening to flutters.

The words enflamed Livvie's senses and fueled her desire to capture a reader within her own stories. In New York, she'd penned two novels, praised well enough by her best friend, though on reflection, she'd realized her writing lacked the most necessary aspect—experience. Embarking on this journey opened up a new world, a world she fervently desired to explore—without the binding oversight of a man. Unless, of course, the man happened to be an editor providing guidance with her stories. Before making sail, Livvie had carefully wrapped her latest novel, pressing a kiss to its pages before sealing the package. It should have reached Kenneth Randall by now, a renowned publisher. Hopefully soon her publisher.

****

A dim light cast a gray pall throughout the hold. Morning must have dawned, though Livvie had no idea what the hour might be. She arose quietly so as not to disturb Mrs. Locke, whose tiny snores sounded akin to a piglet's.

Livvie went up to the helm to lean against the rail, letting the wind riffle through her hair. It exhilarated her to stand there, the open vista of the world spread before her, but today, the wide skies loomed heavy, and their dark clouds reached into the ocean as if to cut off the ship's path. Aroused by the sharp winds, the seas frothed, offering not even a porpoise to entertain her in leaping from the water in playful bounds.

One new bit of scenery had appeared overnight. Land.

For a long while, she stood there, weighing the good points versus the bad. Land meant release from the ship, but to what? Had the publisher received her novel? Adored it? Abhorred it? Oh, if only mail could reach ships at sea.

Soft huffs signaled Mrs. Locke's inevitable approach. "Do come away from there, Olivia. The ship rocks like a cradle this morn."

"I will in a bit." Did the woman think Livvie under her charge? She longed to escape Mrs. Locke's clinging embrace. If only the widow would attach herself to someone else. Unfortunately, the other two dozen passengers consisted of couples and families. Aside from Mrs. Locke, Livvie was the only other single female aboard.

Releasing a long sigh, Mrs. Locke cast her gaze heavenward. "Yesterday's glorious sunlight struck the deck prism and illuminated below enough to read. This poor light makes it impossible to sew this morning. I would love to have your pleasant company to help pass the time."

Livvie's sympathetic ear had already drawn out Martha Locke's life story. She couldn't imagine what was left to tell. Mrs. Locke had lost her husband when his carriage overturned and his neck snapped, killing him instantly. Forced to leave her Boston home, the woman was headed for St. Louis to live with her son. Her constant frights had grown tedious. The widow startled at every creak of timber or snap of sailcloth.

Once again, Livvie found herself in the role of

comforter and caretaker, a less difficult role to assume when she imagined the woman to be her own mother, lost ten years earlier to pneumonia. Until her father's death, Livvie had been his caretaker as well.

Mrs. Locke's fears of sailing hadn't tainted Livvie's love of it. In New York, her father had taken her sailing on his schooner since she was old enough to walk. For both women, this trip proved their first time on a tall ship. The glorious billowing sails overhead filled Livvie with an indefinable yearning.

On the deck above, Captain Richard Pierce stood and pointed a brass telescope to the horizon.

"I would like to speak to the captain. I shall come below afterward, I promise."

Her smile feeble, Mrs. Locke turned in a wobble and made her way to the descending steps.

Livvie crossed the main deck and climbed up the steps there. "Ahoy, Captain Pierce. Where are we now?"

The captain collapsed his looking glass. "Mornin', Miss Collins. According to my calculations, we are off the coast of southern Florida."

"I see." Her voice fell as flat as her hopes.

"You're not eager to land ashore?" The captain's amusement showed plainly in his arched brows and suppressed smile.

She drew herself tall. "I prefer sailing—the wind in my hair, the absolute freedom of the wide ocean."

He shook his head, chuckling. "You're the first woman to say so."

She crossed her arms over her chest, as much to appear steadfast as to steady herself against the increasing winds. "Perhaps I should captain my own boat." What an adventure story that would make!

Her remark drew a hearty laugh from the captain. "Aye, I'll retire so you can captain the *Elizabeth Rose*."

"Why name ships after women, Captain?" In her limited experience, men proved fickle, but she couldn't imagine competing against the grace and beauty of a tall ship.

"Not all are." Captain Pierce leaned against the rail. "I imagine it's because, for us sailors, our lives are bound to the ship, much the same as other men are bound to their wives. It's a means of comforting ourselves, I suppose. You'll forget the ship when you get to New Orleans."

Not likely. Her writing would ensure that. "I suppose I should go below and see how Mrs. Locke is faring. Thank you, Captain."

"Aye, best you stay below awhile." The teasing had left his voice.

She paused at the stair. "Why?"

He set his mouth in a grim line. "There's a storm ahead. The seas may soon be rough."

In the few minutes they'd been speaking, dark, roiling clouds had blackened the skies.

"Oh, dear." She would be holding the pail for Mrs. Locke, whose feeble stomach did not abide rough waters. She took her leave of the captain, descending the steep steps to stroll below. The stench of sweat and sickness stung her nostrils, more depressing than the dank atmosphere.

Even in the dim light, Mrs. Locke's sallow skin and sunken eyes warned of impending illness. She held her shawl tight, her gaze fixed on the glass prism hanging from the ceiling as if she could will it to disperse more light.

Sitting beside her, Livvie placed her hand atop the older woman's trembling shoulder. "Tell me more about your son."

A wan smile crossed her face. "Thomas is strong and kind. His blacksmithing business keeps him very busy. If only he could have met you before marrying." She patted Livvie's hand. "You are exactly the kind of girl I hoped to have as a daughter-in-law."

Pity the poor wife of Thomas, having to meet the widow's strict standards.

The ship seesawed upward, then sharply down. Livvie captured their belongings before they slid away, and piled them in her lap and in Mrs. Locke's, who teetered back and forth.

She attempted a brave front. "Don't fret. The *Elizabeth Rose* will carry us safely to our destination."

Whimpering, Mrs. Locke nodded. In the shadows, the others huddled in tight groups.

"Do Thomas and his wife have any children?" If Livvie could engage the woman in a subject dear to her heart, perhaps they could weather the storm without sickness.

"One—a little girl." The woman squealed as the ship rocked. Akin to the flying fish, it rose beneath them. Upon its return to the sea, the deafening crash resounded through the hold.

Livvie held her tighter. Mrs. Locke's fear began to infect her. "What's her name?"

The stern reared upward, faltering in its descent.

Mrs. Locke opened her mouth to reply, but halted. A loud, eerie groan echoed through the ship like a woman's sad cry of desperation. The *Elizabeth Rose* shifted sideways in a disorienting whoosh, too quickly to have been caused by the rudder. The ship must have caught on something—what could it have struck at this distance from shore?

A loud crack traveled along the ship's sides. Near the helm, wood splintered, and water bled through its wound in a spray. Mrs. Locke's scream mingled with others. People scattered.

Livvie took hold of her arm and tugged her upright. "We must get up top. Now."

The older woman rooted her feet in place, stiffened by panic. Livvie pulled hard. Short bursts of screaming interrupted Mrs. Locke's constant moans. The wood continued to collapse inward, and the stream of invading water became a waterfall.

Livvie dragged her toward the stairs. "Climb to the top. Quickly." She set the woman's hands on the rail. Mrs. Locke stared in horror at the advancing water swirling across the hold's floor. A man shoved ahead of her and helped another woman up.

"Martha, we must go now." Livvie couldn't leave her below. It would mean certain death. At least up top they had a fighting chance. To rouse her from the grip of terror, she slapped the woman's cheek. "Climb up, now!"

Nodding, Mrs. Locke took hold of the rail and set one foot on the step. Livvie followed close. The woman's shaking limbs were too slow for those behind, who yelled in anger and fear for them to move faster. The cluster grew.

Despite prodding, the widow resisted all urgings to hurry.

Livvie glanced back. "She's going as fast as she can."

Mrs. Locke screeched when the ship tilted crazily up, and then drifted down. Her steps became increasingly more halting. As they neared the top deck, water surged across the deck and down the stairs, drenching their clothing.

Many hands pushed at Livvie's back, crushing her against Mrs. Locke. "Get up top, Martha—now!"

At the top step, Livvie gave a final shove at Martha's back, and she fell across the drenched planks. The gale-force wind tossed waves over the rail and across the unnaturally angled ship.

Livvie dragged Mrs. Locke to her feet. "We must take hold of the mast." Panic mounted inside her, but she swallowed it back and focused on steadying Martha.

The ship lunged upward. Livvie's boot slipped on the slick wood. Wind-driven spray lashed her face. People scrambled to take hold of whatever was nearest, their screams heightening her fear. All along the rail, men and women clung, some holding crying children. Relentless waves drew sputtered moans and screams from all, soaked through to the bone.

The captain's voice carried over their heads. "Take down the remaining sail, men! Look lively!"

Livvie clutched Mrs. Locke's waist, pulling her along the slippery planks. Someone grabbed Livvie's waist.

Peter's body warmed hers. "I'll help you," he yelled against the gale's roar.

His strong arms comforted Livvie while he propelled them to the mast, a rope dangling from his outstretched hand. "Take hold. Don't let go for anything." His wet hair hung in wisps around his face.

Livvie placed the rope in Mrs. Locke's fingers, then

strengthened her hold on it.

Peter yelled, "I'll check back in a while. I have to go—"

The ship lurched sideways. His arms and legs flailing, Peter skidded to the rail, his gaze locked on Livvie's. Her hand shot toward him, reaching as far as she dared, though it was no use. For an eternal moment, gravity pinned him against the side. Another sharp tilt of the ship, and he flipped over its side. Churning waves swallowed him.

The sight dumbfounded her. For a moment, her lungs could take in no air. She let out a cry and whispered, "Peter."

Another man followed Peter's awful path. A girl descended to the sea without a scream, her face frozen in shock.

The deck shuddered, and Livvie clutched Mrs. Locke. The hold must be filling up with water. The ship seemed somehow unable to move past whatever barrier had captured it.

Uttering constant, high-pitched cries, Mrs. Locke clutched the rope, her eyes glazed with panic.

A great groan filled Livvie's ears, and the *Elizabeth Rose* rolled on her side. Livvie lost her foothold on the planks and clung to the mast as it lowered toward the sea. The tilting deck tossed men and women downward, their screams silenced when they plunged into the water. The very axis of the world had tilted.

Livvie's grasp of Mrs. Locke gave way. The woman floated down through the air until she landed in the water, small as a raindrop. A splash flew up around the outline of her form, and she disappeared.

The mast split from its base in a loud crack.

Clutching the rope, she hung above the water, rising to meet her. Through the driving rain, a fleet of shadows bobbed across the white-capped waves toward the ship like phantoms coming to claim the victims.

Unable to sustain her grip, one hand gave out, and then the other. Dreamlike, Livvie sailed down into the jagged waves. The water closing around her erased the awful sounds of screams and chaos. A terrible peace settled over her until long shadows passed overhead. Forms jettisoned into the sea above her, bubbles exploding around them like cannonballs. Death sought her in the shadows. Even owing Hell as penance, she wouldn't give herself over without a fight.

Chapter Two

The Florida cut ahead of another schooner along the reef. Samuel Langhorne grimaced against the lashing rain, silently urging the vessel onward. The boat's mascot, Barnaby, sat beside him, his long black fur and ears pinned by the force of the wind. The schooner neared the tall ship as it fell to its side, bucking in its death throes, its magnificence lost in tattered sails and broken planks.

Sam clasped his mate Liam's hand in triumph when *The Florida* reached the ailing ship first. Now no one would challenge Captain Howe for the title of Wrecking Master, in charge of the salvage operation.

Captain Howe shouted orders to the men. Other schooners arrived and positioned around *The Florida,* a show of acknowledgment.

"Wonder what her cargo is?" Sam called to Liam over the howling wind.

Liam checked the life lines were secure. "I'm hoping for a cargo of gold, meself."

Fortune carried a burden of its own, requiring careful looking after. To Sam, wealth represented a liability, causing others to react differently to its owner. Causing women to see the gifts he might give them rather than the man himself.

Best to use it up while he still had his youth and could enjoy its benefits.

Sam scanned the surface waters for signs of life. "Like the captain says, passengers first."

"Aye, I know ye'll be first to reach the females." Liam peered at him, grinning.

"You can't blame a lonely man in need of company. Right, Barnaby?" Sam laughed and patted the dog's head.

At the captain's urging, divers jumped into the choppy waves.

Sam tagged Jasper's shoulder when he leaned against the rail. "A bottle of rum."

Jasper's wide smile filled his black face. "Ready whenever you are, partner."

Filling his lungs with a reserve of air, Sam plunged into the white-capped sea. If he lost Jasper's bet, he'd gladly buy him two bottles. The game—who could save more people than the other—provided less gratification than the deed itself. The element of challenge made their task no more fun.

Beneath the surface, the tumultuous waves and winds were obliterated by the slow, otherworldly atmosphere where peace reigned equally alongside horror. He aimed for the first sinking body—a woman. Liam would have a laugh if he rescued a female first. Yet Sam had other reasons: weaker-limbed, women proved less likely to save themselves than men, and their saturated skirts became heavy, making the effort to swim doubly hard.

He swam toward the light blue fabric, sinking faster than usual. Kicking hard, the girl ploughed deeper, her hands plunging ahead. Her fall must have confused her into swimming downward rather than toward the surface. Such confusion was common in shipwrecks. He slipped his arm around her slim waist.

She turned, her eyes wide, and pushed at his hands. Her golden hair swirled in cascades, as magical as a woman of the deep. No mermaid ever looked so angry— or so determined.

He tightened his grip and pointed up.

Her hair swirled as she shook her head and pointed down.

Sam followed the direction of her finger. The turbid sea revealed nothing beyond churning debris.

She broke loose from him. Her foot caught him in the stomach, forcing a burst of bubbles from his mouth.

Precious air lost. He had to move fast. He locked his grip across her ribs and labored upward. She twisted beneath his arm and kicked at his legs, making the journey to the surface an arduous one. He'd never encountered anyone so intent on drowning. She wasn't going to bring him to the depths alongside her.

Struggling against her flailing, he broke through the surface exhaling a forceful gasp. "I need help with this one!"

Liam appeared at the rail. "Jasper, assistance, please."

Still wet from his dive, Jasper leaned over and glanced back to the girl. In the spring, he'd saved an older woman from sinking to Davy Jones' locker. She'd complained bitterly of the indignance of having to endure the touch of a Black. Jasper had grown reluctant to assist any woman since.

Liam took hold beneath her arms, but lost his grasp to her struggles. "Well, come on."

Jasper reached down for her other arm. Together, they hauled her into the boat, gasping and crying. And kicking.

The moment her feet touched the deck, she bent herself over the side of the boat toward Sam. "What are you doing? You must go back and find her." Her chest heaved, her lips parted by the effort of refilling her lungs.

A strangely mesmerizing sight. In the choppy seas, he nearly forgot to tread water until Liam extended a hand overboard.

Sam grabbed it and flung his leg over the rail. "Find who?" He climbed into the schooner and plopped to the floor.

She coughed to regain the oxygen she'd lost beneath the sea. Her glare bore into him. "Mrs. Locke. She fell into the water just before I did. I was trying to save her, but you dragged me up here. Why did you stop me?"

"*I* saved *you*!" Ungrateful wench. Why couldn't he have happened across one of the others huddling on board? Silent and shivering, they made no complaint against Jasper or Liam.

Yet something about the girl struck him hard. Her honey-colored tresses and tawny brown eyes, even turned on him in anger, made his blood churn in a whirlpool. Her wet dress clung to her curves, stirring something deep inside him. She was nothing short of magnificent. Ripe for the plucking. Sam might volunteer for the honor, but he preferred labors of love. He suspected she would simply be a labor, but oh, what a tempting one.

"I didn't need to be saved. Mrs. Locke did." She bent over him, and droplets fell onto his skin. "She's drowning! Please, please go back for her!"

Her cries barely penetrated the haze in his mind. All at once, he was aware of every part of her: the way she wrapped her long hair around her hand to tame it, the fire in her eyes that sparked something in him, something that swarmed like bees through his blood.

To clear his mind, he pushed himself up and away from the rail. "I'll dive again in a moment. As soon as I'm able."

She clutched his arm, her grip electric. Alarmed, he shook her off, but the sensation remained.

"You can't leave her down there. She can't swim. You must go save her!"

Jasper grinned at Sam and dove off the boat. When she clasped her hands and stared after the other wrecker, an unfamiliar discomfort pricked at Sam. Disappointment? No, he'd made himself immune to it. Especially regarding females, who proved more prone to inflicting it.

Sam's lungs ached from the effort of breathing. Damn Jasper—outdoing him already.

Liam paid little notice. He likely had mentally marked the moment of Jasper's dive and was counting off seconds. In such rough seas, the men sometimes had to rescue their crew mates. If Jasper ran into trouble below, they'd pull him up. With or without the prized woman.

The schooner rocked, and the girl stumbled to the side of the boat. "At least someone on board has the courage to do what's right." Her body moved in concert to the rhythm of the waves, a siren song for a wrecker who hadn't known the company of a woman in many months. The sea sprayed across her, the wind riffling her long hair, yet neither seemed to distract her. She focused solely on the submerged line.

Clenching his jaw, Sam cursed the waves and the

rocking boat. He forced himself to look away, to picture Jasper diving deeper, searching.

She fixed her fear-filled gaze on him. "Shouldn't he be back by now?"

Her guile bedeviled him.

"Soon." He turned away to signal Liam of his impending dive.

Worry clouded her face. "It's been minutes. She couldn't possibly—"

A searing gasp sounded, and Jasper broke the surface and took hold of the life line. His head bobbing in the waves, his words came in short bursts. "Have to…work on…this one."

Sam reached overboard to reel in Jasper and the woman. "Sit back. Away from the side."

The girl pushed closer. "I want to—"

"Move now." He had no time for her scolding. Not while Jasper needed help.

Her nostrils flared as she retreated and swiped a tear from her cheek.

The woman lay limp, unmoving in Jasper's arms. Sam crouched to get hold of her. Her arms flopped upward when he grabbed beneath them. Liam came to his side, and the boat tilted while they leaned over to take hold of her. Sam released his grasp once they'd cleared the side to grab Jasper. With one pull, he lunged onto the deck.

Liam laid the woman on her back, and pressed his hand against her stomach. Sam knelt by her head. Water spilled out of her mouth. Droplets sputtered as she coughed.

Sam glanced up at the girl. Her distress erased his triumph.

"This isn't Martha Locke." Her lip trembled, and she looked out over the sea.

An icy chill passed across him. "I'm going down." He nodded to Jahner Lang, who took his place propping up the woman's shoulders.

Sam inhaled deep breaths, holding the air in his lungs as he dove. He plunged farther toward the larger ship in hopes of finding other survivors. The rough waters could have carried the woman adrift.

The deeper he swam, the more pressure built in his lungs. It was not in Sam's nature to give up. Plenty of time later to haul up whatever the ship carried in its hold. People couldn't wait. If another wrecking crew hadn't already rescued her, the woman had likely drowned.

A form came into sight. He plunged toward it. A woman. He swiveled her shoulders to turn her. Her wide eyes stared ahead lifelessly.

A movement caught his eye. He dove yet farther, his lungs aching for air. A man drifted in the murky depths. He twitched—a sign of life. Sam grasped him beneath his arms and swam upward. Nearly as tall as Sam, yet more slight of build, the man's unmoving weight made him seem heavier when Sam reached for the surface. He clamped his jaw shut, fighting the urge to inhale.

His hand broke through the water and caught the side of the schooner. His chest heaved in an effort to refill with much-needed oxygen. Liam and Jasper took the man by the shoulders and pulled him up, and Sam dragged himself aboard.

Liam pumped the man's stomach. Water burbled from his mouth. The fortyish man gave no other response.

Sam turned to Liam. "I'll take one more dive. There

may yet be some alive."

Jasper rose and stepped between them. "You just came up. I'll go."

Sam glanced at the girl huddled on the other side of the schooner. Her dejected face pricked his determination. "I'll go."

Jasper laid a hand on his shoulder. "We both will." His dark eyes conveyed his concern. He would watch out for Sam.

Together, they climbed over the rail to dive, this time aiming outward of the ship.

Debris drifted through the depths. The storm churned silt up from the bottom, clouding his view. He swam toward a shadowy form. It turned out to be a split plank, yellow fabric caught in its splinters. At the sight of two dresses suspended at the surface like jellyfish, Sam pushed upward. The women screamed in hysterics as he broke through.

He took hold of the piece of wood to which they clung. "Ladies, hold tight. I'll take you to safety."

Adjusting their holds, they nodded.

After giving the rope a yank to signal to Liam, Sam took hold of one end of the wood, tugging the women toward *The Florida*. Their weight doubled the laborious journey. Their hands often slipped loose, their frequent cries piercing Sam's ears. Divers from other ships must have passed them over in favor of those beneath.

Finally reaching the ship's side, his muscles burned. Jahner helped Liam draw the women up from the water. Exhaustion robbing his strength, Sam flung a leg over the side and hung there.

The scene repeated on the surrounding schooners: men diving, hauling up men, women, and children. *The*

Florida held more than a dozen people clinging to one another in small groups. Their faces registered shock, exhaustion, relief, and sadness.

Sam's chest heaved. He looked over at the girl, still huddled on the other side, her arms around Barnaby's neck. Wiping her eyes, she stared at the two women. A heaviness washed over him. Neither of these women was the one she sought. He'd failed.

Laboring for breaths, Sam watched for Jasper. His shadowy form came into view just before he broke through the surface holding a man about their own age.

When they hauled the two aboard, the girl gasped, rushing toward them. "Amos!"

The man looked in her direction.

She fell to her knees beside him. "Have you seen Peter?"

Amos groaned, closing his eyes. "Gone."

Her breath caught in her throat. Stricken, she blinked back tears as she shrank away. Two lost; one for certain.

Captain Howe called Liam, Sam, and Jasper to his side. "Is it worth going down once more?"

Sam wiped his brow. "I saw only one other. Already drowned." He glanced at the girl.

She covered her mouth with her hand.

Jasper stared at the roiling seas. "Anyone still beneath will be also."

His voice weighted by dread, Liam said, "Aye, I believe so too."

The captain set his jaw. "Right. Let's get these people to shore before we start on the cargo."

The group broke. Liam called to those on board to go below for safety's sake. "We'll get you to shore as swiftly as the storm allows."

The girl rose and went to Liam. "Please," she implored. "Isn't it possible to continue the search?"

"Captain's orders. We must get you all ashore." He stepped to her side.

She matched his step in a tense dance. "Can't I stay?" Her feet planted securely on the boat, she maintained her balance in the rough sea as well as any wrecker.

Liam nudged her arm toward the entrance to below. "Sorry, miss. We need the room for new passengers. And you need to rest."

She slipped her arm from his grasp. "I need to find Martha Locke."

"You may find her ashore ahead of you." Liam's tone grew less solicitous. "Now get below."

Unmoving, she stared at him, her eyes glazed in shock.

"Captain's orders," he repeated insistently.

Her glance toward shore moved Sam. The wind whipped her wet hair behind her shoulder. Her stern grace gave her the countenance of a warrior princess strategizing her next move, though she had no option except to follow orders. Her gaze met Sam's almost instinctively, and his insides buzzed like a hive again. Prickling heat stung him.

She folded her arms across her wet bosom. Despite the schooner's bobbing in the waves, her stride never broke.

The Florida turned toward shore, where the only hope now lay for finding her companion.

Chapter Three

Sam squinted against the morning sun. The only traces of the previous day's storm were the still-turbid seas and the remains of the *Elizabeth Rose*. The bilged wreck hung on the reef, its battered shell beyond hope of salvage. The sun rose behind the ship's silhouette, breaking through fading patches of clouds to reveal the brilliant blue sky beyond.

Captain Pierce had been rescued by another schooner. He consented to allow Captain Howe to salvage the cargo of pewter dishes and mugs, lumber, and whiskey. As he announced the last, a cheer went up on *The Florida.*

The three men designated as *The Florida*'s deep divers dove one by one into the shattered hold of the sunken ship. One of the designated skin divers, Sam would follow Isum into the water, Jasper close on their heels. All recognized Jasper as the wrecker's best diver.

Liam stood at the rail. "When you're ready."

Gulping in air, Jasper nodded at Sam and Isum. They stepped off the side of the schooner and plunged beneath the surface.

Divers from ten other wrecker schooners helped salvage the goods. The lumber they left for last because it would require a more unified effort.

Several personal trunks had smashed open, so they hauled up miscellaneous jewelry, clothing, and personal effects in sacks. They dove again and again into the waters beneath the ship. After six hours, Sam's body felt as wrecked as the *Elizabeth Rose*. The captain called for a halt, recognizing they'd strained their muscles to the breaking point.

Sam dropped to the floor, exhausted. The motion of Lewis Pinder's hand slipping a brooch into his pocket caught his eye. Pinder looked about with narrowed eyes. Sam glanced away before Pinder could notice. The man's slow work habits always irritated Sam. Deliberately slow, so as not to do his own fair share of the work. Today wasn't the first time Pinder had taken more than his allotted share of the salvage. Pinder the pilferer, Liam called him, though without malice. Sam couldn't make the same claim to good-natured tolerance. He'd like nothing better than to see the man pay for his crimes. Not all, he suspected, would prove petty. Earlier, Pinder had admired the fine makers' marks on the pewter ware, raising Sam's suspicions.

At the end of the day, the schooner off-loaded its haul to a horse-drawn wagon on the beach.

Sam wiped the sweat from his brow, pushing a crate toward Liam. "Any word of the girl?"

Grunting, Liam shoved the crate off the rail. "What girl? We hauled in quite a few."

Sam jumped down and lifted the other end. "The first one. Looking for the older woman."

Puffing his breaths, Liam set the crate on the wagon. "The captain may know where she's staying. Why?"

Sam dragged his sleeve across his brow. "Just curious, is all. Wondered whether the other survived or not."

Arching his brow, Liam smiled. "Ye don't usually

take such an interest in the well-being of the passengers."

Sam drew himself taller. "My first concern is always for the passengers."

"Especially the young, pretty ones." Liam winked.

With a grin, Sam agreed, "She is, at that."

"Ah, another conquest for the great Samuel Langhorne." Liam clasped his friend's shoulder.

A rush of anger made Sam shrug the hand away. "No."

Liam's surprise matched Sam's own. He couldn't explain the nature of his curiosity. The previous night had passed awash in dreams of her: Sam plunging into the water, finding her there, and instead of pushing him away, she enfolded him in her arms. When their lips met, they floated in the churning seas. Sam was smothering in her kiss, yet still, he held tight. He'd awakened with a drowning man's gasp.

Lying in the darkness on the rocking schooner only brought vivid images of her, holding to the sides, her body swaying with the sea's rhythm, echoing Sam's fervent desire to press his body against hers in that same ebb and flow, hypnotic and intense.

Sam adjusted the crate on the wagon. "I'm simply curious, as I said."

Liam stacked another box on the wagon. "All right. Don't get so testy."

"I wouldn't be if you didn't make me so." Hell. Sam hadn't intended to be so curt.

Liam's eyes twinkled as he wiped sweat from his brow. "Are you certain it's not something else agitating you?"

"Yes, I'm certain." Something unfamiliar twisted inside him, something besides shame at exhibiting his bad mood to Liam, who'd always been a steady buoy for Sam in troubled times. Why should he take offense at his teasing? Any other time, it would have rung true.

This time, Sam wasn't so sure. Something about the girl tugged at him. Her willfulness in not wanting to be rescued; her stubborn insistence that they find her companion. A beauty that, combined with her youthful innocence, would attract any man. He sensed a depth beneath her surface. Like the sea, she held untold surprises. He had an undeniable urge to throw caution to the winds. Dive deep to unearth her treasures.

Like his dream, those treasures might prove his undoing.

"Let's just get these things to the warehouse, all right?"

Liam set a hand on his hip. "Why the hurry?"

"I have a terrible need." Sam set another crate on the wagon.

Liam's eyes widened.

Sam grinned. "For an ale. And something to eat. I'm starving."

Jasper pulled the last crate from the schooner. "I could eat a shark."

"A whale," called Jahner, jumping from the schooner to the beach. The wagon jerked, its wheels stuck in the sand. Jasper and Isum set their shoulders to the rear of the wagon, heaving it forth.

Liam raised an eyebrow. "Aye, an ale it is." He walked alongside the wagon.

As Sam fell in step, their talk turned to the value of the goods salvaged and what their shares might total.

"The tonnage of the lumber will bring up the shares," Isum said, enthusiasm shining in his face.

Like the other deep divers, Sam would receive a larger share because of the greater risk he endured. He usually enjoyed speculating on what he would earn. Part of the reason he became a wrecker was to earn as much wealth as he could, only to squander most of it. The practice was almost a ritual, a kind of bleak homage to the life he'd left behind in Philadelphia, to burn away bad memories.

Walking up the short stretch of sand toward town, the discussion faded to Sam's ears as the vivid image of the girl returned.

Yes, an ale would wash away his foolish notions— beneath the water, her long hair making a golden crown, fanning around her head. That sharp gaze and even sharper tongue. Her wet dress clinging to her curves, the most tantalizing sight he'd ever beheld. More surprising was her strong will, her loyalty to her traveling companion. So strong, she willingly had put herself in harm's way to ensure her friend's safety—a rare quality. He'd known few other women who would have done the same. None in Philadelphia.

Laughter broke through his thoughts. They were outside the warehouse. Following the other men, Sam lifted a crate to carry it inside. The wagon soon stood empty, and the crew dispersed. Liam sang an Irish song, the words growing unrecognizable as his brogue thickened, as it always did in songs of home. Sam walked a pace behind, lost in his own head. No girl had so bewitched him, not since Helen had entranced him in her silken web—so soft, yet treacherous. He could not—no, would not—sacrifice his soul for any other woman.

Sam had arrived at Key West infected by a bitterness against women. He was glad for their small numbers on the island. Here, females were already wives or betrothed to be wives. The transients he rescued sometimes tempted him. He had needs, after all.

Only twice before had he been moved enough to attempt to get to know them. The first, Maryellen, was a widow en route to Texas. Her nerves proved too frail. Every gust of wind filled her eyes with fear of another storm. Her clinging nature quickly turned his feelings sour. When she sailed away in tears, he prayed the ship would not wreck again to cause an extension of her stay.

Next, Victoria crashed into his life. An Englishwoman of indefinite nobility, her fine manners and pale beauty at first made her seem unlikely. The fire in her eyes when she looked at Sam revealed another nature which easily lured him into her arms. Liam had warned him against her, but Sam didn't listen. He came home to find her in his cabin, tearing the place apart. She denied her treachery, pleading she only wanted him. What she really wanted was his money. The bitterness of the realization soured him for a long time. He had no desire to be in the company of any woman. For whatever reason, he always attracted the kind who wanted not him but only what he could give them.

The few Key West women—such as Millie and Annie—who were still single, he found easy to ignore. If the choice existed between Annie and a goat, Sam would choose the goat. Its bleat sounded less annoying than Annie's cackling laughter or braying voice. While attractive enough, Millie tempted him little because of Liam's affections for her. More so because Millie constantly tested her powers of persuasion over men. She had the same wandering eye Helen had.

Helen—beautiful Helen. Named for the pious saint,

so proclaimed her parents. Sam thought her akin to Helen of Troy—enchanting, enticing. Her magnificent beauty stunned men and women alike. The face that launched a thousand ships. He could not have known, upon proposing, how she would launch his own ship to a new world.

After he'd won her, the victory tasted sweet. The sweetness ended there. She grew into a yawning cavern of need—always more, more, more. At first, the challenge entranced him. Her methods of convincing him to get what she wanted brought him to thrilling heights. Once she obtained what she wanted, she cooled, until the next sparkling thing caught her eye. Eventually, he saw her methods as too practiced. She'd spent a lifetime honing her womanly wiles to get her own way. No one, he'd later learned, could ever adore her as much as she adored herself.

The satisfaction he felt in her arms, too, proved short-lived. He could never seem to hold her attention for long. When she cast him an inviting look, he would be drawn to her as though under a spell. While in her embrace, a certain detachment struck him about her. Her movements seemed smooth, timed to perfection, yet left him sensing she'd choreographed them, that he'd been merely a player in her scheme. She might hold him close, but her gaze drifted away, always to another. She would never be satisfied by any man. He almost pitied the poor fool who took her from him. Like the infamous Helen of Troy, she invited destruction to all who surrounded her.

Yes, squandering his earnings felt like sweet revenge. When he couldn't spend it fast enough, he shared his money with Liam, who squirreled it away.

Inside the groggery, Sam stood next to the bar.

Winking, Liam set a glass of whiskey in front of him. "This will clear your head."

Sam lifted the glass to Liam's. "Here's to my mates from *The Florida.*"

A cheer went up, followed by the clinking of glasses all around. The men tilted their drinks to their mouths. Sam did the same. He laughed when the others laughed, though he had no idea about what. Try as he might to concentrate on the conversation, Sam grew more lost than ever. He lost count of the ales he downed. The harder he tried to steer his thoughts away from her, the stronger the sensation of being pulled below, to the silence and peace and beauty of the deep, where a girl waited offering open arms and soft lips, whose soothing murmurs were a salve to his aching heart.

Chapter Four

In a haze that may have been twilight or dawn, Livvie stood beside Peter at the ship's rail. All around them, flying fish leaped. The air grew thick with them, and she reached for Peter's hand. Suddenly, he disappeared behind a curtain of fish. Panic filled her. A cold fin slapped against her head, and the horizon tilted. For a long time, she fell and fell, until strong arms encircled her, guiding her gently upward. Into safety and sunlight. Its warmth penetrated her skin and burned where his chest pressed into her back, his fingers splayed against her ribs. Turning her head, she meant to thank Peter, but instead met the heated gaze of another. "You," she said, not surprised at all.

A rooster's crow startled her. "That's not the cry of Mother Carey's chickens."

"No," he said. "You're not at sea now. You're home."

At another rooster's crow, Livvie's eyes flew open. Sunlight flooded through a tall window. For a moment, she lay in the unfamiliar bed, in a room she didn't know. Not home at all. Somehow, the idea disappointed her. She had no home, after all. Yet his arms made her feel at home. Something she hadn't thought possible.

Pushing the bed linens aside, she hastened to the desk, pulled sheets of paper from the drawer and a silver-nibbed pen. Closing her eyes, she summoned the dream, all its glorious moments and unexpected rapture. In this pseudo dream state, she dipped nib into ink and wrote in a feverish rush, though time was of no consequence here.

****

Pain pounded through Sam's head as each thud landed on his door. Outside his cabin, Liam called, "Arise, young Samuel. Let's be off. We've lumber yet to haul. Samuel?" The door shook with the force of Liam's fist against it.

Sam's pillow bit into his cheek, hard as encrusted sand pebbles. His skull threatened to split wide open. "Stop that infernal racket. I'm coming."

Releasing a moan, he rolled out of bed. He'd managed to get his shoes off last night, nothing else. A change of shirt was all he needed; today's sweaty work would be rinsed from his clothes with each dive. His crew mates would smell worse, he bargained.

He dragged his boots on and opened the door. The sun blinded him. Such brilliance occurred only following a storm, the gales having swept the sky clear of clouds.

Shielding his eyes, Sam groaned. "Oh, hell, why did I drink so much?"

"Shake it off. Let's go." Liam's gruff voice broke his catatonic stance, his friend already trudging down the street toward the dock.

To fortify himself, Sam filled his lungs, following in Liam's wake to the schooner.

The Florida sailed to the wreck, its crew readying the pulleys. Sam's muscles ached, though he'd long ago grown used to the strain of working nonstop for days. Unlike the previous day, the topside crew would do the heavy lifting today—literally. Sam, Jasper, and Isum dove carrying grapple hooks and clamps to fasten to the stacks of lumber. As soon as they'd secured the line, one gave a tug so the others could haul it up. The divers swam to the top to catch their breath. By the time the crew retrieved the lumber, they were ready to go down again.

Sam went through the day by rote, performing his tasks by habit or instinct. Not until late in the day, after the crew had finished hauling up the last of the lumber, did his mind fully clear.

The Florida pointed toward shore, the last of the wreckers to leave the site. Captain Howe went below to his cabin. The day's heavy labor had taken its toll on the crew. All looked toward shore wearing bag-lined eyes, bodies slumped as though already in repose.

Sam stood at the rail not far from the entrance to the lower deck, staring at the horizon. Making sure no one watched, he slipped down the stairs. The captain's door stood open. Out of respect, Sam knocked on its frame.

Captain Howe turned from his desk. "Come."

Sam stepped into his cabin. The space was modest, for a captain's dwelling: a bunk attached to the wall, a small table beside the bunk. A desk on the opposite wall, nearly as large as the bunk, held ledgers, maps, and papers.

Gathering the papers scattered across his desk, the captain placed them inside the lidded bin for safekeeping. "Good work today, Samuel. As always."

Sam gave a nod. "Thank you, sir."

"What's on your mind?"

"I wanted to inquire about the passengers, Captain. Might you know which boardinghouses put them up?"

Captain Howe's gaze pierced Sam in inquiry. "Oh, the usual. The Dixons took in the couple and their young girl. A few are staying at Mrs. Armbrister's. The

Crowells have two families, an older woman, plus a young girl—pretty, she is. I believe you brought her up first." His eyes narrowed at her mention, perhaps divining Sam's intention.

Yes. Exactly the information he sought. Sam struggled to maintain his casual demeanor. "The young woman looking for her matronly companion? So they found her."

The captain stood. "I believe the crew of the *Brilliant* found her. Half-dead, she was, but they got her breathing."

Some of the day's tension left Sam's muscles. If the woman had died, or not been found at all, the girl would never have forgiven him. He shouldn't assign so much importance to it, except she would.

Where women were concerned, Sam spoke to no one of his personal business. A girl might talk of him, how he brought her to the beach at night; he never revealed such things to anyone. Except perhaps Liam. Even so, he gave only sparse details. His private life was not for discussion by his mates.

Sam read the captain's stance as a sign the meeting had ended. The schooner would land ashore any minute. "Excellent. I'd wondered. The girl insisted so fervently on finding her. So they're at the Crowells? They're on Duvall Street, aren't they?" His tongue moved too fast, faster than his mind could work. He never spoke so much. He certainly avoided nonsense of the ilk that now flowed from his mouth.

The captain fixed him with a speculative stare. "Yes, I believe so."

Sam gave a nod. "Very good." He stepped to the door to make a hasty exit. No one so much as glanced his way when he eased against the rail as though he'd been there all along. The schooner approached the docks, and the crew lowered the sails. Jahner manipulated the rudder so *The Florida* glided sideways. Sam jumped onto the dock beside another man to halt the boat, knotting it to its slip for the night.

The captain's guarded reaction to his questioning, followed by Liam's teasing remarks, kept Sam from wandering past the Crowell boarding house after they went ashore.

Instead, he walked to the groggery alongside Liam. Soon after they arrived, Millie linked her arms around Liam's neck. Like a noose—tightening around his mate's purse string. Liam was more than willing to share.

Annie sashayed toward him, her grin lopsided. He set his coins on the counter and then strolled outside.

Sam stretched his aching limbs. "Time to go, Barnaby."

The dog leapt to its feet, falling in step, tail wagging like a metronome.

The day's humidity hadn't lessened and would hold sleep at bay. Rather than heading toward Conchtown, where wreckers' cabins lined the street in tight rows, he was lured by the salty ocean scent to the narrow beach. Feeling the sand beneath his boots, he slowed his pace to view, through the limbs of the red mangrove, a crescent moon hung above the horizon. He stepped atop the tree's tangled roots that appeared to tiptoe along the water's edge. He leaned back, inhaling the sweet night air, perfumed by plumeria blossoms.

The sea undulated toward shore, endlessly swelling, cresting, falling like the sighing surrender of a lover. Its unpredictability demanded clarity of thought, an immediate response to its force. Unlike his former life in Philadelphia, it required no forethought, no planning, no scheming or devising—such planning proved useless against such an opponent. It forced Sam to abandon his schooling. There could be no fallback position, no secondary level of victory. The sea demanded her due, and always collected it. The exhilaration of acting with precision in the face of extraordinary odds fortified his sustained efforts while diving. His every sense sharpened, not by fear, but in rising to the challenge, recognizing that responding inadequately to that challenge would cost him—possibly his life. The sea wanted his full attention. He willingly gave it.

Tempered by awe and respect, the thrill of unleashing his skill against the rages of a storm only served to fuel his desire to go against it again and again, though no victor could ever be declared. He knew better than to claim victory over the sea, for she could snatch it back at any time.

After he'd begun wrecking, Sam would have accepted without blame the sea's demand for his all, even if rendered in his death. The thrill, the challenge, of acting in each moment against such a force drew his senses to unimaginable heights, soaring like a sea bird. Some men had been able to sustain their wrecking careers for decades, though many others met sudden, untimely deaths. Drownings. Shark attacks. Accidents involving equipment. Did they lose their focus for one moment too long, the sea sweeping in to claim her booty?

Barnaby's barking roused him.

"What's wrong, boy?" He stepped along the roots to where the dog stood in the water, snapping at something beneath. Barnaby gave a yelp, jumping away.

"Ho, now. Did you find a crab? I'll wager its claw found you." Peering into the shallows, he saw the prize. Using great care, he grabbed its shell to lift it. "Tomorrow we feast! Come on, let's go home."

Holding the crab at arm's length, he strode to his cabin. He put the sea creature in a bucket. After filling a bowl for Barnaby along with his wash basin, Sam stripped. He lay in bed, the dog stretched on the floor beside him.

Despite his walk, sleep eluded him. The night sounds amplified his thoughts of the girl. He should make sure she'd fared all right, dissuade her worry before she embarked on a new ship. He hadn't even learned her name.

****

"Olivia." The soft moan echoed down the hall.

Stifling a sigh, Livvie tucked the pages into the drawer. "Coming, Martha." How relieved she'd been to find Mrs. Locke at the Crowells' boarding house, alive and well, with hardly even a bruise to show for their struggle. The doctor had declared the widow in fair health, even if her mental state remained more fragile after the shock. Hysteria overtook Mrs. Locke in the middle of the night, dissipating when Livvie read to her. From the boarding house bookshelves, she'd selected the first installment of *Bleak House*, by Charles Dickens. Someone, according to the proprietress, had saved the twenty publications during a shipwreck, only to later die. In New York, Livvie had already read the first seven installments. After Mrs. Locke's pleading, she began again at the first. The intricate plot clearly overwhelmed the distraught woman, who fell into a fitful sleep after a

39

few pages. Livvie took the opportunity to tiptoe away from the room back to her own.

A soft knock sounded at her door. The housekeeper entered carrying Livvie's dress. "It's dry now, Miss Olivia. I washed it and mended a tear or two."

"You're so kind, Florie. Thank you."

The woman laid it on the bed. "No need to thank me. I do as I'm told."

"I appreciate it all the same."

Florie turned. "I best go. Don't know how I'll do all my chores before nightfall."

"Isn't there anyone to help?"

"Oh, no, miss. I have to hurry to the market. Miz Crowell will be angry if all the best fruits are sold. She don't like to hear about my sore feet."

"I'll go." Livvie clutched the bed post.

The housekeeper hesitated near the door. "No, no. You're not even dressed."

"I will be. In two minutes. Oh, please, Florie, I need to get away for a while." Before Martha awoke, and her soft pleadings tied her to her bedside.

"Well…" The woman bit her lip.

Seeing her opportunity, Livvie stripped off the nightgown. Wriggling into her dress, she bent for her shoes.

Florie chuckled. "Let me help you button up. We can't have you rushing off half undone."

More than half undone, Livvie wanted to say. Too much had happened these few months. The shipwreck had stripped her of her last hold on the past. All her belongings, all her regrets; the sinking ship had cracked open the world to reveal a new place, one of untold history. One she wanted to explore.

****

Sam walked to the market in the square. Visitors often found oranges a rare treat, so he went to a table laden with fruit. He'd bring her the best oranges she'd ever tasted.

He smiled at the rotund woman behind the table. "Good morning, Mrs. Simmendinger. How's Ullrich?"

"He's home, suffering a touch of the gout today."

"Sorry to hear it. Hope he's well soon." From the corner of his eye, he caught a glimmer of gold shining in the morning sun. He lifted his head, stilling at the vision in the street.

The girl. The sun appeared to favor her, to gather around her in concentrated illumination. The rays kissed her skin, outlined her features in softness. The light blue of her dress glowed like a cornflower in summer, glorious in its peak. Her hair fell thicker than he'd imagined, flowing in long waves to the middle of her back. She walked toward him, looking left and right at the market wagons or tables, her bearing as regal as a princess.

Her gaze swept across him and snapped back. Mouth agape, she slowed uncertainly.

He held up a hand in a wave, afraid to call out for fear his voice would fail him. He could be at her side in five long strides, but he held back. A thickness filled his throat. His thoughts scattered as though swept clean by the brush of her skirt's hem. When her gaze met his again, his heart leapt against his ribs.

She ducked her head, walking to the fruit stand where he stood, clutching a small basket in front of her. She nodded to Sam. To Mrs. Simmendinger, she said, "May I have fifteen oranges? Twenty lemons, too."

The woman crossed her arms over her chest. "Pick which you want."

The girl's slight took him aback. He might well have been invisible to her.

He stepped to her side. "Hello."

Selecting an orange, she glanced at him, placing it in her basket. "Hello." She squeezed another, set it down.

Momentarily flustered by her abruptness, Sam persisted. "How are you?"

"Fine, thank you." Dropping the last orange into her basket, she moved to his other side, where the lemons crowded in bushels.

Perhaps she didn't recognize him. Shock was common in rescued folk, particularly women. He bent to bring himself to her eye level. "Do you not remember me? I'm the one who—"

Her gaze flicked to his. "Who brought me ashore, yes." After a moment's pause, she added, "Thank you." She held out the coins to Mrs. Simmendinger. "Good day." She turned, her strides long for a genteel girl.

He followed, confused and intrigued by her rebuff. "I hear they found your companion. She's doing well, I hope?"

The girl's gait had equal purpose and grace. "She had quite a shock. However, the doctor says she'll be fine."

"Good, I'm glad to hear it." The woman's death would have been a permanent barrier between them, yet now provided a link. A tenuous link, still, a link nonetheless.

She appeared intent on not looking at him, nor breaking her stride.

Hadn't he used the right mix of concern and

sympathy in asking about her friend? He'd practiced several versions. How could she show no gratitude? At least, a bit of interest, as other women did.

"I'm Samuel Langhorne."

"Pleased to make your acquaintance." Her pace increased slightly. Sunlight filtered through the coconut palm trees lining the streets. The rays glinted off her hair, turning her honey-colored tresses brilliant.

She turned her head his way, only to look down the street before crossing.

He doubled his pace to step in front of her. "Might I be so bold as to ask your name?"

Her tawny eyes searched his briefly. "Olivia Collins."

Such stiff treatment stung. Perhaps she suffered from shyness. Or perhaps she sought to increase his attentions with her lack of interest.

He'd play along. "You're looking very well today, Miss Collins. I'm glad you are as fit as ever. And as fast." His chuckle came out breathlessly. He could dive four fathoms repeatedly for six hours but wasn't accustomed to walks at such a pace.

Halting, she whirled to face him. "I'm sorry, Mr. Langhorne. I don't mean to be rude. Mrs. Crowell's expecting me back. I shouldn't dawdle." Her light brown eyes, fringed by long, dark lashes, bore into his bearing with no pretense of flirting.

Speechless, he glanced away. The Crowells' Boarding House sign hanging above the porch entryway re-oriented him. That was why she'd stopped. They stood outside her temporary place of residence.

She wanted him to leave.

"Of course. Maybe I could stop by later, to visit?"

"I don't know…" Her wide eyes had the look of a trapped animal searching for an escape.

He knew the look. He'd affected it many times himself when conversing with the opposite sex. Women he wanted to avoid.

"To make certain you're both fine. You and…Martha Locke, wasn't it?" Including her friend's name surely would calm her fears. Waiting those few seconds for her response, he arranged a line of arguments in his head should she refuse him.

Straightening, she looked him in the eye. "All right. I'll let Mrs. Crowell know to expect you."

It wasn't Mrs. Crowell he wanted to visit. "Very well. I'll see you tonight."

A lightheadedness overtook him. He stepped backward, already anticipating tonight.

Turning abruptly, she walked down the stone path alongside the house. Strong-willed as a filly, her movements as graceful, even if less dainty than other ladies. Perhaps she hadn't been broken to the school of feminine wiles yet, though she wasn't so young as he'd first perceived. Maybe nineteen or twenty. Luscious as a ripe orange. He nearly drooled at the thought of peeling her stiff outer skin away to reveal the sweet and tangy flesh beneath, aching to be tasted.

Tonight.

A sense of victory struck him. He'd spend the night sitting on the sofa beside Olivia Collins, sipping lemonade in Mrs. Crowell's parlor. Such a mundane activity would usually seem torturous. If it led to even a touch of her skin, the torture would be sweet.

****

Livvie forced herself not to glance back, to continue

following the stone walkway that curled around the main house to the small outbuilding that served as the summer kitchen. She was sure he'd still be standing there, watching her.

The past two nights, she'd relived the shipwreck in nightmares. The chaos of the ship bucking its passengers off one by one, like a wild mustang. The horror of seeing Peter disappear forever, coupled with her terror at being unable to find Martha Locke, of finding herself utterly alone. Her movements slowed by the turbulent seas. The strong grip of hands at her waist, the sight of him—coming for her, and her alone—a sea god intent on plucking a pearl from the waters.

In her dreams, she swirled into his arms, clinging to him. Each upward thrust rippled his muscles and resonated inside her, drew her closer so by the time they broke through the surface, she required his touch more than air. His arm tightened against her ribs, his hand atop her beating heart while he carried her to shore. The waves pushed them to the sand, chest to chest, legs tangled. His voice low, murmuring her name like a prayer, like salvation: *Livvie, Livvie;* the weight of his body against hers somehow freeing rather than trapping her.

She awoke from each dream breathless, shoving aside the bed sheets, her skin dampened by sweat not owing to the heat of the night, but from within herself.

No one except her father had ever called her that name. Hearing it from his lips, even in a dream, was like finding home in this strange, strange place.

Seeing him at the market had made her head light. She could not trust her own thoughts. He showered his insistent attentions in too practiced a manner. She had no desire to be the target of any man's conquest for sport alone. Determined not to give him the satisfaction of a backward glance, she forged ahead toward the summer kitchen house.

Lilting humming sounded within.

Following it, Livvie pushed open the door. "Hello, Florie."

The warm tones of the Cuban woman's mocha skin glowed when she smiled. "Miss Olivia. Back so soon?"

Going about her duties, Florie sang, rhythmic tunes matching the stroke of the knife while she cut. Her movements across the kitchen house floor became swirling dance steps. As though having to cook for ten people each day were no chore at all.

Livvie set the basket on the table, sorry to add to Florie's work. "I hoped to return before the heat set in. It's such a lovely day."

"Mmm-hmm. Goin' to be a beautiful day." Florie glanced out the window.

Apparently the sunshine-filled view was enough to satisfy her. The only time she spent outside was in walking between the small outbuilding and the main house to deliver meals.

Livvie rested her hands atop the table, watching Florie slice the fruit. "Do you enjoy any hobbies, Florie? Besides preparing excellent meals?"

Florie's sharp knife halved the lemons with speed, releasing their citrusy scent. "What do you mean, Miss Olivia?" She squeezed the juice from the lemons into a pitcher.

"What do you do when you're not cooking for the Crowells and their boarders?"

"I take care of Mr. O'Hanlan." By her matter-of-fact

tone, the woman didn't understand the question.

"What about you? Is there nothing you do for yourself?"

The housekeeper gave a whooping laugh. "This is what I do for myself."

Livvie wanted to take the woman by her shoulders, ask if she never walked outside just to feel the sunshine warm her face, to stand by the ocean just to feel its vastness stretch far away to unimaginable places.

The cook must have sensed her confusion. "I come from Havana many years ago, Miss Olivia. My family was poor, too poor to feed nine young ones. I met Mr. O'Hanlan when I was years younger than you. He promised to take care of me. He has, so I take care of him too. I made him quit the wrecking business. Now he's much happier sponge fishing. Much safer, too, and a good living. Because we both work, we can help my family back in Havana. All my brothers and sisters are married now with their own families. Gives me a good feeling to know we still all depend on one another." Humming, she stirred the lemonade.

Florie's circumstances were beyond Livvie's comprehension. The woman who'd kept house for her father while she was growing up never took pleasure in her work. Livvie was sure her father had treated her better than the Crowells treated Florie.

The confines of the kitchen constricted Livvie's nerves. "I should go check on Martha."

The woman wiped her hands on her apron. "If you'd like to bring the lemonade, it's ready."

"Thank you, Florie."

A wide smile crossed her face. "No need to thank me, Miss Olivia. It's what I'm paid to do."

"You deserve thanks for doing it so well."

Her joyous laugh filled the kitchen house. "You go on now, Miss Olivia. You'll fill my head with nonsense."

At a loss to explain how her praise was far from nonsense, Livvie lifted the pitcher. "I will see you later."

Florie's rich voice echoed through the windows while Livvie strolled the walkway to the house. The song's peculiar beat intrigued Livvie, made her wish to hear it rendered by musical instruments, though she guessed even those would be beyond her limited experience of pianos, violins, and guitars.

In the parlor, Mrs. Crowell looked up from her sewing, clucking her tongue. "Why did Florie have you carry the lemonade inside?"

"I offered to bring it. I was coming in anyway."

Mrs. Crowell pursed her lips. "We pay the woman to work, Miss Collins. You are not obliged to assist her."

"I'm happy to do anything I can to assist any of you. To repay your kindnesses." She stressed the last word, hoping the lady would recognize its inclusive meaning.

"We are a boarding house. We earn our living by our kindnesses." Mrs. Crowell's tone suggested just the opposite. Did no one in Key West act except for financial gain? Perhaps Mrs. Crowell suspected Livvie's actions were intended as a ploy to reduce her six-dollar-a-week payment for her stay.

"I'll bring some to Mrs. Locke, if you don't mind." Hurrying into the kitchen, she opened the cabinet.

Mrs. Crowell's voice floated through the hallway. "If you please, I'd like a glass, also."

Biting her tongue, Livvie poured two glasses. She carried one back to the parlor.

Mrs. Crowell's tight smile held no graciousness. "If

Florie had brought it inside, I would have had her bring me some."

Forcing a smile, Livvie resolved not to remind the woman of her status: a paying guest, not a servant. "I'll be upstairs."

She climbed the staircase. The second door from the end stood closed. Perhaps Martha still slept, though it must be nigh on nine o'clock. She rapped gently on the door. Within, the bed creaked.

Huffing an exaggerated sigh, Mrs. Locke answered, "Yes?"

"It's Olivia. I have some lemonade for you." She half-hoped Martha would send her away.

"Come in, dear," came her strained reply.

No escape just yet. Livvie opened the door.

Mrs. Locke lifted herself higher on her pillows. The sheer curtain surrounding her bed was still closed, like the window curtains.

The hot air stifled Livvie. She left the door ajar. "A nice breeze is blowing. Shall I open your windows further?"

"Oh, no. I can't abide the mosquitoes. They're awful, the largest monsters I've ever seen."

Suppressing a laugh, Livvie set the glass on the night table. If mosquitoes were the worst monsters Martha had ever encountered, she should count herself among the lucky. "Are you well this morning?"

Martha gave a long sigh. "I suppose I'm improving."

An unease grew within her. Though not as dark, the close air reminded Livvie of the ship's hold. "Is there anything I can get for you?"

Mrs. Locke fanned herself. "A little something to

eat, perhaps. Is there any fruit?"

She started for the door. "I will ask Florie."

The woman's energy multiplied. "No, wait. Please sit. Talk a bit first."

Livvie sat in the cane chair, folding her hands in her lap. And waited.

Sighing loudly, Martha stared at the wall.

Livvie would not sit in silence. "I ran into Mr. Langhorne this morning."

The woman's gaze drifted to Livvie's. "Who?"

"The man who brought me up from the depths. I told you about him." She wouldn't mind talking about him more. To make him seem more real. Less like a dream.

Exhaling, Martha leaned against her pillows. "Where on earth did you see him?"

"At the market. I went for fruit."

"You had an escort, I hope." Mrs. Locke's voice sounded flat, her eyes accusing.

"No. Florie was busy. Mrs. Crowell hadn't yet come downstairs." Silly details, not relating to what she'd begun to say.

"Surely you didn't speak to him. Not while alone."

Her disapproving tone riled Livvie.

"Of course I spoke to him. Mr. Langhorne asked about you."

Martha's eyes widened in alarm. "Me? I've never met the man."

Livvie kept her voice even. "No, although he knew I was looking for you. He was relieved to hear you were well."

Her voice weakened. "As well as can be."

She brightened her tone. "He asked if he could visit later."

Martha closed her eyes. "You declined, I'm sure."

Tired of sitting, Livvie stood, pacing toward the window. "Not at all. Mr. Langhorne was very kind to ask."

Mrs. Locke's eyes flew wide. Her voice shook, increasing in pitch. "Those ruffians are not to be trusted, Olivia. You must realize that."

Ruffians. Living free and wild, as Livvie yearned to do. "They saved our lives, Martha."

The widow's clipped words shot from the netted bed like musket balls. "Yes, so they could get to their true aim of our cargo."

She stared out the window. "That's not true. Even Mrs. Crowell says the wreckers value life above all else." The lady of the house gave compliments sparingly, Livvie had already learned.

"I don't mean to upset you, dear. Mrs. Crowell's opinion of the wreckers is much lower. They are nothing more than looters, preying on others' misfortunes when ships are ruined."

Livvie turned. "Who do you suppose would have saved us, if not them, Mrs. Locke? The crew's loyalties lie with the ship, not its passengers. We would surely have drowned without the help of the wreckers." Her tone grew as clipped as Mrs. Locke's.

"Oh, dear, now I've upset you." The woman's timidity riled Livvie more than her tainted opinions. Martha's look of suffering came too easily upon finding herself in a bad position.

She smoothed her skirt. "Don't be silly."

Martha's strained voice soured the atmosphere. "So you'll let Mr. Langhorne know we cannot entertain any visitors tonight?"

Livvie would not be dictated to. Not yet, at least. Certainly not by someone she barely knew. "If you are unable to rise to the occasion, I shall meet him myself."

Martha's weakness disappeared. "Olivia, it isn't proper. Mr. Langhorne can have no other intention than to dishonor you."

She whirled to face the bed, and the woman hiding within. "Mrs. Locke, I am well able to maintain my honor. Mr. Langhorne may be handsome, but he's lacking inner depth. He is no temptation to me. However, while we are in Key West, it's our duty to be gracious guests. I owe him at least that much, in return for my life. Even if he was only doing his job." She suspected he carried out the rescue much like any of his other duties—lacking much care.

Men such as Samuel Langhorne were plentiful in any location. The ape of a man gawked at her as though she were no more than market wares, available to the highest bidder.

The same look Elijah Foster, her father's partner, gave her when he'd come to dinner, or she'd visited Father's office. The comments Mr. Foster uttered so breathlessly once her father left the room had disgusted Livvie. She made no pretense about making allowances for him. He may have been her father's partner; he would never be Livvie's. After her father's death, he'd proposed swiftly, displaying no great dignity. Perhaps he assumed her destitute, lacking any other option. Had he known of Father's encouragement to use her intelligence for better pursuits than a loveless marriage, Mr. Foster may have reconsidered his proposal.

Samuel Langhorne might be younger and more appealing; still, Livvie wanted more from life than to spend her days in a summer kitchen house while her husband sailed out on the open sea with his mates. She would never be anyone's servant save her own.

Martha's lips trembled into a weak smile. "Would you ask Florie for some fruit? Then perhaps you might read the newspaper to me?"

"All right, Martha. You might try coming downstairs to sit awhile. Or outside on the porch. The fresh air would do us both good." Certainly Livvie preferred the outdoors to the confines of a darkened room.

"Maybe tomorrow, dear. I don't believe I'm up to it yet."

Livvie held in her thoughts. The woman was never up to anything she didn't want to do.

"I'll return soon." Frustration filled her at the notion of spending the afternoon in Martha's room. She'd have to find excuses for constant errands. Martha's presence on the ship had proven more confining than the vessel itself. Livvie couldn't allow herself to be trapped in the small bedroom until their next voyage.

Descending the stairs, she vowed never to let herself become so weak she'd depend on others, or so needling that her constant whining manipulated their actions.

****

Morning wore on into afternoon. Livvie read the *Key West Enquirer* aloud by Martha's bedside. The woman lay listlessly, appearing unmoved by any news account other than to remark occasionally what a peculiar place Key West was.

Its peculiarity held particular appeal for Livvie. Its lack of daily structure lent an air of lawlessness, except regarding wrecking procedures. Held to strict accountability for his own crew as well as those he hired, the captain deigned Wrecking Master followed a myriad of rules, during and after the salvage operation. All wreckers abided by the decisions of Judge William Marvin, presiding over the District Court of the United States for the Southern District of Florida, stationed in the town for the sole purpose of deciding wrecking cases.

As afternoon gave over to evening, Livvie found herself looking forward to Mr. Langhorne's visit. His presence would provide a different face, a handsome one at that.

Something in the way he looked at her, as though she were the only one who could fulfill his longings, stirred her. A practiced look, to be sure—one he'd no doubt affected for use on other women. She had no intention of allowing him to bolster his ego using her affections. Besides, soon she would receive word on the arrival of the next ship. The one that would deliver her into her brother's obligation.

Chapter Five

After jumping onto the beach from the rowboat, Sam helped haul it up. "Look lively. Come, Barnaby." The dog leaped onto the frothy sand.

"What's the hurry?" Liam stood.

"I am a busy man, Liam." The lowering sun would sink past the horizon in a few hours. This evening should provide an excellent view of the Gulf Stream's cloud bank. A view he intended to share with Livvie.

His mate chuckled. "Busy leading yourself astray. Keep me company at the groggery instead."

"Not tonight. I have promises to keep."

"And to break, eh?" Liam lifted the front of the boat over his head. "Take care not to break yer own heart in the process."

Sam shouldered the end of the boat. "My heart is not part of the bargain."

Trudging inland, Liam shouted a laugh. "I've seen yer face when ye look at her, Samuel. Yer puppy-dog eyes, beggin' for attention."

He'd have to guard his emotions more carefully. "The only puppy-dog eyes here belong to Barnaby. Eh, boy?"

At the sound of his name, the hound woofed, bounding to Sam's side.

The men set the boat near a cluster of palm trees. The unwritten wrecker's code ensured its safe haven until morning because it bore the mark of the *Elizabeth Rose* name. Should a ship go down, they'd return sooner. An unlikely event, given the calm of both sea and skies, unless an inexperienced crew manned the helm.

Liam set his hands at his waist. "Give yerself a fightin' chance. Take a bath."

Sam winked. "As good as done. And clean clothes to boot."

Liam clucked his tongue. "I hope the girl knows how lucky she is."

"I'll be sure to remind her."

Liam's steady, inscrutable gaze gave Sam pause. The two joked about the similarities of storms and lovemaking—getting caught up in the height of the moment, not knowing what the aftermath might bring. The girl had preoccupied Sam's thoughts: how her wet clothes clung to her alluring form, her hair cascading in waves. Like a siren song, he heard her whispers in the night, imagined her soft touch against his skin. Other women had distracted him before, briefly, and perhaps not with the same intensity, but Sam knew the cure. A good dousing of her would quench his thirst. And then he could forget her, like all the rest.

The fact she acted less than obliging toward him only made it a more interesting challenge. He would tame the tempest she wrought upon him. The sooner the better, so he could purge her from his system.

Liam held a hand to his stomach. "I'm starvin'. Let's go eat."

They walked to Groll's Groggery. Wreckers filled nearly all the tables, a common enough occurrence between shipwrecks, with little else to do.

The cook set three steaming plates on a table where

some of *The Brilliant*'s crew sat.

Sniffing, Liam leaned toward their meals. "Green turtle?"

Lipp Reichert hoisted a spoonful to his mouth. "Caught it yesterday, we did. Cook should have plenty left. It weighed a good three hundred pounds." Lipp looked at his crew mate, Adam Stroh.

Stroh nodded. "Three fifty, I'd venture."

Liam's eyes lit up when he turned to Sam. "Hurry and tell cook we want four servings." He grasped Sam's shoulders, pushing him toward the bar.

"There's only two of us." Sam studied his friend, but had no clue what he might be up to.

Liam's response came quickly. "I'll eat three, if ye can't handle two."

"I have no wish to eat so much tonight. I must leave soon, remember?"

"Fine. Order three. I have plenty of time to linger." Liam halted at the high-pitched laughter coming from the other side of the room. "Then I'll have enough to share."

Ah, now Sam understood. Millie. He'd warned Liam she'd be his downfall. Liam always responded that he hoped so.

Sam called to the cook for three orders of turtle and two ales. He leaned on the counter while Liam watched her.

Millie sat on the lap of a burly wrecker from another schooner, her low-cut dress providing a clear view to all of her ample cleavage. Her gaze meeting Liam's, she whispered in the wrecker's ear. He guffawed. Pushing herself up, she swished through the tables toward them.

If only she'd marry. Leave Liam alone. Not likely, given she enticed so many men to shower their attentions upon her, along with anything else she wanted. She did give more of her time to Liam than anyone else—but not before casting inviting looks at Sam.

Perhaps his own conceit made him suspect she tried to make him jealous through Liam. Sam had no use for her, or any other woman who would allow herself to be used by so many men. She made no pretense about it, at least. Still, he preferred females who had an air of innocence—such as Miss Collins. Wooing her would be worth the untarnished prize.

He handed the mug of ale to Liam, tugging him toward two open seats at a table occupied by other wreckers, including Jahner Lang from *The Florida*. Giggling, Millie bent over Liam's shoulder, nearly spilling her breasts from the bustier. Dragging her lips across Liam's ear, her gaze bore into Sam's.

He turned to Jahner to remark about the fair weather.

Stepping between the chairs, Millie bumped her rear into his arm. "Pardon, sweetie." She nestled onto Liam's lap.

Flashing a tight grin, Sam scooted his chair away.

The cook carried three plates to the table. Liam held up two fingers. Millie squealed after he said one was for her.

Sam downed spoonfuls of turtle with ale. After he'd emptied his mug, he whistled. When Barnaby trotted in, Sam set the plate on the floor.

Liam groaned. "Oh, the tragedy! Giving such excellent food to a dog."

Sam chuckled. "Barnaby worked hard. He deserves a good meal."

The dog licked the plate clean. Standing, Sam lifted it from the floor. "I'll say good night."

"Aren't you well?" Millie pouted.

Liam guffawed. "He will be soon. Eh, Sam?"

Jahner winked. "See you tomorrow."

"Unless he's still busy." Adam lifted his mug to his lips.

Sam set his plate and mug on the bar. Digging money from his pocket, he set it beneath the plate. "Good night." Giving a wave, he walked out the open door. Barnaby followed.

They walked down Duvall Street toward Conchtown, where Sam's home stood near the outskirts. Nothing more than a shack, really. Good enough for now. A space to store his clothes and gear, a bed to come home to, when *The Florida* had no need for its crew. He'd prefer a place farther away. He'd make the move later, after he amassed enough money to buy a patch of land. Liam's ways must be rubbing off on him.

He poured water into his washing basin and then stripped to clean the sweat from him. His pants were worn, yet clean. He buttoned his white shirt, rolled up the sleeves midway, and smoothed back his hair.

"Not bad, eh, Barnaby? Let's go." When he opened the door, the dog trotted through.

Walking down the street, he heard a low whistle. A man leaned from a second floor window. "Who's the lucky girl, Sam?"

"Wouldn't you like to know?" Unmarried females rarely stayed single for long in Key West. Competition was fierce. No doubt others would soon call on Miss Collins, if they hadn't already.

He stayed to the wooden sidewalk to keep the dust from his clothes. He wanted to give Mrs. Crowell no cause to complain about him tracking dirt onto her carpets. After jogging up the steps to the home, he knocked. Too late, he remembered: he'd meant to buy flowers.

Panting, Barnaby flopped onto the porch.

The door opened a few inches. Florie's wide eyes peered from within.

He smiled. "Evening, Mrs. O'Hanlan. Is Miss Collins about?"

She eased the door open. "Mr. Langhorne. Please come in. I'll let her know you're here."

He stepped into the foyer. No lamp had been lit in the parlor. A light shone in the dining room down the hall. Upstairs, floorboards creaked.

"Have a seat, please." Florie sashayed down the hallway, rather than upstairs, as he'd expected. Maybe she'd warned them of his impending visit. No doubt the woman would soon return to tell him she'd fallen unexpectedly ill. No point in sitting. He studied the portrait on the interior wall, as best he could in the gathering shadows of evening. A stern-looking man sat beside a woman, an expressionless girl standing between. Most likely the Crowells and their daughter, Anne, now grown, possessing a daughter of her own.

Footsteps clicked down the hallway. He turned, expecting to see Florie's apologetic face asking him to leave.

The half-light illuminated the girl's features. The vision of loveliness made Sam's pulse surge.

"Mr. Langhorne. What are you doing in the dark?" She held a hand against the archway.

The inviting pose tantalized him. He imagined himself sliding his arm in the open space between her raised arm and her slim waist, his other winding behind her knees to carry her upstairs to bed.

"Waiting for you." His soft, throaty tone—his own siren song—appeared to hold her in check in the shadows.

Ducking her head, she crossed the room to the table. "I'm very sorry. I'll light the lamp. This parlor grows dim too early." She struck a wooden match, holding it to the oil light. "Please, have a seat."

He perched on the end of the sofa, leaving plenty of room for her to sit next to him.

The soft yellow glow of the lamp across her face captured his full attention. An image appeared in his mind of her loosening the ribbon in her hair, shaking it free. Of his fingers loosening the buttons of her dress… No, Miss Collins would never allow such intimacies so quickly. Breaking this filly would require finesse, a gentle touch. Sam would have to rein himself in, take his time with this girl. How many weeks did he have before she sailed away again?

She sat in the chair by the window. "Would you care for something to drink?"

He glanced away to clear his mind. "No, thank you. I dined with Liam—Mr. Byrne. You may not remember him." He flashed a smile. He was talking too fast, saying nothing.

"Yes, of course. From *The Florida*."

"Yes." She remembered. Usually, shipwreck victims were insulated in shock, numb to their surroundings, wanting only to return safely to shore.

Twining her fingers in her lap, she appeared stiff as the portrait on the wall. "Is Mr. Byrne well?"

Sam shifted in his seat. "Very. Thank you." If only he'd had whiskey instead of ale. Something stronger might have loosened his tongue. He'd imagined this moment so often today that being here now seemed more like a dream. A dream rapidly deteriorating into a nightmare.

She dabbed her handkerchief to her brow. "I don't know if I could ever get used to this heat."

"It's cooler outside now the sun's setting." Outdoors, perhaps he wouldn't feel others lurked out of sight, listening. Florie's gossip spread faster than a heat wave.

Straightening her back, Miss Collins appeared less comfortable than he. "I'm afraid Mrs. Locke isn't up to company."

"Who?" He'd watched her lips move, let the words flow past him. Her lips looked like pale rosebuds soft with dew, certainly sweet with nectar.

Her mouth twitched, yet no smile appeared. "Martha Locke. You inquired about her this morning?" She met his gaze in mock challenge.

"Mrs. Locke, yes. I'm sorry to hear it." He tried to make his face a mask of sympathy and concern, rather than elation.

"I'll tell her so." Suppressed laughter edged her voice. More serious, she turned, haltingly adding, "I was remiss in not thanking you earlier."

"For what?"

Her expression blanked. "For saving my life."

"It's my job." A pleasure best described as work, for her sake. Lucky for him no other wrecker had found her first.

Her eyes narrowed for a moment. Gradually her features smoothed. "In any case, I am grateful." Rigidness returned to her spine.

He'd upset her. He struggled to discern a reasonable explanation. None came to mind.

Their conversation had run aground. She cast glances about the room. It would only be a matter of minutes before she made some excuse, and he would have to take his leave.

Barking erupted on the porch. She rose and went to the window. "Did you bring Barnaby?"

"Yes, sorry. I'm afraid he's insisting I keep my promise to play fetch on the beach. Would you care to join us?"

She glanced at him. "To play fetch?"

A silly question, possibly insulting. Most females would rather sew, or sip their tea while complaining of the weather.

"Unless you object to throwing a stick for a dog. He needs his exercise while he's ashore."

"I wouldn't want to deprive Barnaby of his play."

"So you'll come?" Surprise heightened the intense pleasure washing over him.

After a moment's hesitation, she stepped to the hallway. "I'll tell Mrs. Crowell I'll be gone a short while."

A short while. Unless he could take her mind off the passing time.

****

The setting sun sent glimmering rays atop the sea as its waters rolled across the sand and then fell back. The sand sighed at each wave's crawling retreat, like a lover exhilarated by its touch. Gulls drifted over their heads like marionettes worked invisibly by angels. Their cries, mingled with the rush of the waves, instigated an unfamiliar yearning within Livvie. Her heart swelling in her bosom, and she had the urge to run, arms flung wide open.

Chasing birds from the sea line, Barnaby barked. She would give anything to join in the chase.

Sam hastened across the sand toward the south.

Livvie couldn't help but laugh. "Are you in a hurry, Mr. Langhorne?"

"No more than you were this morning, Miss Collins." He cast a teasing look back. "Actually, there's something I want to show you."

She glanced toward the retreating boarding house. Perhaps she'd acted too hastily in accepting his invitation. If his intents turned lecherous, no one would hear her cries for help so far away. No one had questioned her leaving without a chaperone—another heady freedom—yet, who here cared for her welfare?

Halting, his mouth opened, curling in a half smile. "No need to worry. I believe you will enjoy this."

The playfulness and challenge in his voice made her hike her skirt, scurrying to catch up. No chaperone also meant more freedom to be herself. In Sam's presence, she did not feel the need to be otherwise.

"I'm sure you say that to many a female, Mr. Langhorne." Lifting her chin, she strode past. "Well, come along then."

He jogged to her side. "Only a little farther. Have your apology at the ready." Squinting, he looked out to sea. "Ah…there."

When she followed the direction of his pointing finger, he stood closer than necessary to ensure she missed nothing. Was this part of his job, too, she wondered—entertaining those he'd rescued?

Clouds gathered offshore, a rising fog bank.

Thickening, the clouds caught the sun's rays while it sank below the horizon, gilding its edges a glowing silver-gray.

Her breath caught in her chest at its eerie loveliness. "What is it?"

The sunset alighted upon his tanned face. "The Gulf Stream's way of saying good night."

She tilted her head toward his, letting the magic of the moment wash over her. Part of it was his nearness, the warmth of him as strong as the sun. "Rather a romantic notion, Mr. Langhorne. I'm surprised at you."

His dark eyes caught the spark of the last light of day. "Not at all, Miss Collins. It's purely scientific. While mists are rare in this area, the Gulf Stream's current contains warm waters. The fog forms due to the temperature difference after the sun departs. It is, however, one of my favorite times of day."

"Very interesting. And beautiful." She inhaled deeply, taking in the salted air. "The sea is so fickle. Making kindling of a magnificent ship one day, now as beautiful and alluring as could be."

"She's a harsh mistress sometimes."

"Mistress?" His echo of Captain Pierce's notion that sailors were wed to the sea confounded her. Were all sailors daft?

"She's our first duty. And great love. She tempts us like a siren; we cannot resist her call."

"The sea speaks to you?" She failed to hold back her sarcasm.

His soft tone held no defensiveness. "In many ways, yes. Speaks to me, sings to me, sends out signals. It's a hard schooling to learn her signs, yet worth every lesson." He whistled for Barnaby, far down the beach.

The dog bounded back, mouth wide as if in laughter.

She bent to scratch his ears. "Barnaby seems to share your love of the ocean. Does he not grow restless on board ship?"

"He loves sea and shore alike. Wherever we go, he goes." His pocket yielded the stick he'd taken from the Crowells' yard. He tossed it hard, and it sailed through the air, Barnaby chasing it.

She strolled along. "A loyal mascot. However, can your lives be fulfilled by a dog and an elusive mistress?"

Sam laughed. "No, not always. We need the company of a female as well."

Livvie grunted in acknowledgement, wondering the depths of the company to which he referred. A walk on the beach was fine, but Mr. Langhorne would get no more from her.

"Females appear to be a bit scarce on the island. How do men meet companions?"

"A few brought wives when they moved here—the judge, some of the attorneys. Their daughters have many suitors, and often marry young. Some wreckers meet women in Havana and then bring them to live here. Others are from passing ships."

"From ships? You mean, wrecked ships?"

He ducked his head shyly. "Yes."

She gulped back indignation. "Truly? Women who are shipwrecked marry their rescuers?"

He furrowed his brows. "Many do, yes. In fact, several years ago, according to the newspaper, about twenty women aboard a vessel all married wreckers, including a German woman along with her six daughters. The ship became known as the 'ship of brides.'"

"How do you know?" She tucked a stray strand of

hair behind her ear.

"Know what?"

"Of the newspaper account?"

"I read it, of course." Though he smiled, his brows twitched together.

"Oh." She turned her head to hide her embarrassment. She'd assumed he was illiterate because he made his living by his brawn rather than his mind. To cover her gaffe, she hastily added, "That's terrible."

"Why is it terrible? They'd lost all their possessions, had nowhere to go. The men provided good homes for their wives."

"They could hardly have had time to acquaint themselves properly."

"Rescuing a girl provides for a rather intimate acquaintance, wouldn't you say?" His low voice was meant to tease her, she suspected. He looked at her with expectancy, perhaps suggesting they had been intimate beneath the sea.

Straightening to her full height, she walked on. "Under forced circumstances. And only the briefest of intimacy." One not likely to be repeated. Not in her case. "What about you, Mr. Langhorne? Are you looking for a bride on one of the unfortunate ships?" She suspected not. Handsome men such as he always seemed inclined to want a wide array of women, rather than just one. They used women up and then tossed them away like rags. By the time they moved on, the women *looked* like old rags, worn from overuse—and useless to any other man. Livvie intended to make her own way in the world.

"Not I. Several have tried to reel me into marriage." He gave an arrogant laugh. "I have no interest in settling down."

A haughty chuckle escaped her. "A woman would have to be a fool to marry someone who worked such a dangerous job, never knowing whether he'd be home at night. Whether he was out in the company of other women. A woman is a fool to marry at all." The last she said more to herself than to him. The bonds of marriage equaled those of slavery.

The wreckers' homes she'd seen in Conchtown appeared to be shanties, jammed up against one another lining the street, the sound of drunken, raucous laughter providing an evening's company. She could not imagine herself living there.

Removing the stick Barnaby held in his teeth, Sam pitched it ahead, sending the dog running. "I suppose you're telling me you're not interested in marriage either?"

Had she stayed in New York and married Mr. Foster, she would have had servants, yes, although her wifely duties would extend beyond overseeing the staff to entertaining at endless dinner parties. Even those mindless affairs would have been preferable to what followed in the bedroom. The thought of his yellowish, picket-like teeth above beady eyes leering at her, not to mention those clammy hands on her skin, made her shudder in revulsion.

"Certainly not." If Wendell didn't pressure her too quickly, her brother's home would provide a safe haven in which to stay while she searched for some means of employment. At least until her greatest love, writing, could bring in enough for her to support herself. If other women could make a living penning novels, she would be able to rely on her talent. Until she gained a following, she could take in sewing, or find some other means.

His shoulder bumped hers. "We should spend more time together, then."

"Why?"

His touch had an unnerving way of agitating her, setting her nerves at attention. Most unsettling was she didn't know whether she wanted to slap him or slide her hand across the contour of his chest.

"I like a girl who's independent. Who knows what she wants." His gaze lingered on her lips.

For a moment, the warmth of his breath mesmerized her, washing across her face so invitingly tender. She had an urge to feel the same warmth across all of her, and imagined herself opening to him, wrapping around him. His lips parted, and he drew closer.

Like the whale before it swallowed Jonah. She would be lost if she allowed herself to be so enraptured.

"And what she doesn't want." She slipped away before his mouth could touch hers. "Good night, Mr. Langhorne."

His lips might entice her, but she knew better than to believe he wouldn't hesitate to entice the next woman he saved from a watery grave.

Oh, no, not for Mr. Langhorne. Even if he were to offer marriage—a proposal she would not encourage—his kiss would be too brief.

According to Mrs. Crowell, wreckers took too much pleasure in drinking and brawling while not at sea, seeking rough recreation as reward for their hard work.

Still, his dark eyes drew her in and invited exploration. As did the rest of him. He awakened unfamiliar feelings, an unfurling of something she'd closed off for too long. Now, she yearned to know.

She glanced back.

Hands on his hips, he stood on the beach and watched her. The sun lowered to the sea behind him, alighting it in liquid flame. His figure stood out in dark relief against it.

Something similar lit within her, too, when he looked at her. For a moment, the strength of his allure made her forget herself, and she paused.

He dropped his arms, poised to run to her.

The realization both thrilled and alarmed her, for the same reason. She turned and ran all the way to the Crowells', the sand slowing her footfalls until she reached the street. She'd forgotten how much she loved to run in her younger years.

Florie stepped out of the summer kitchen and down the path. "Goodness, Miss Olivia. Are you all right?"

"Yes, thank you, Florie. Simply getting a little exercise." Her breathlessness exhilarated her.

Florie's wide-eyed gaze skimmed across her. "You ran like the devil himself chased you."

She wasn't far off the mark. Mr. Langhorne presented a definite temptation toward sin. "No, I was out for a walk, and—"

"Where's your gentleman friend?"

"He had to go."

Her eager tone hinted at a thirst for gossip. "Was there a shipwreck?"

"No, nothing like that." The subject became too labored. "Is there any lemonade?"

"I brought a pitcher inside a little while ago. Should be some left. I'll go see."

"No, thank you. I don't want to hold you up."

"I have to say good night to Mrs. Crowell anyway, Miss Olivia. Let me fetch you a glass. You look in sore need of refreshment." Groaning, Florie stepped onto the back porch. "My lumbago's acting up today."

"You should go home and rest."

Florie waved her off. "Rest? I got my laundry to do. And cooking for Mr. O'Hanlan yet. Sometimes I wish he was still a wrecker, so I could have some time to myself."

Livvie followed her inside. "I thought he stopped being a wrecker because you asked him to?"

"Sure enough. I wanted to know he'd be alive at the end of the day."

"How lovely." Reassuring to find one couple, at least, still living happily together.

"Yes, I shouldn't complain. He works very hard." She poured lemonade into a glass and held it out.

Livvie sipped. "You both do. I admire you for keeping your independence."

She chuckled. "My independence? Child, I work to keep us out of debt." In a hoarse whisper, she added, "If Mr. O'Hanlan were still a wrecker, I would live as leisurely a life as Mrs. Crowell." She resumed her normal tone. "Now he's too old for such work. I want to keep my husband healthy."

Florie waddled down the hallway to the parlor.

Livvie drank while the housekeeper said good night to Mrs. Crowell, who grilled her about what she'd completed during the day. Florie answered each question, showing the same good nature as always.

Walking back to the kitchen—Florie never used the front door, at Mrs. Crowell's request—she smiled. "Good night, Miss Olivia."

"Have a lovely evening."

Her lilting tone sailed through the air. "I will."

How could she say that, when more work awaited?

Livvie would feel more useful if she could contribute, certainly, although such long hours of mindless cooking and cleaning would exhaust her. Florie met each task with a smile and a song.

And her husband had given up his livelihood for her. Instead of diminishing their love, their sacrifices appeared to enrich it.

Livvie trudged upstairs, imagining what it might be like to keep a house for a man. For instance, Sam Langhorne. A brute, for sure, yet his intelligence surprised her, at least matching her own. His unique way of thinking intrigued her. What would it be like to awaken each day beside him? To cook for him, clean for him? Would he repay her in kindness? The most respected men of society sometimes proved themselves anything but civilized when it came to their husbandly duties. Many deemed marrying for love as foolish, yet how much more foolish to marry for money and be treated as another possession?

Or worse, cast aside like a useless object.

In New York, rumors had spread about her father's sister, Marjorie. She'd married Judge Walsh, who apparently judged his wife inferior to himself—and lashed out at her using his tongue and the back of his hand. Powerless to help, Livvie and her father despaired each year as Aunt Marjorie withered away more. Livvie had thought she would disappear entirely, perhaps by design, or necessity. Judge Walsh took care of that for her. One day, a black carriage pulled away from their home, a woman shrieking inside. Her aunt was never seen again—except by the caretakers at the lunatic asylum. Judge Walsh remarried a year later, and the new Mrs. Walsh, younger by fifteen years, was with child when Livvie left home. She hoped the asylum would not hold a succession of the judge's discarded wives.

No marriage of any kind was worth that sort of torture.

Chapter Six

The sliced fruit and fresh bread made the breakfast table festive. Livvie sat opposite Mrs. Locke, whom she had cajoled into joining the group. The widow's sallow complexion appeared the only dim spot around the table. The other *Elizabeth Rose* passengers made it easy to ignore Martha's sighs and whining complaints.

John and Pearl Henry, a couple in their early twenties, spoke gently to one another, touching frequently, possibly to remind themselves they had indeed survived. Tom and Elizabeth Clift preoccupied themselves tending to their sons Wilson and Curtis, whose wide, dark eyes reminded Livvie of poor Peter.

Mrs. Crowell, as ever, kept watch over her housekeeper. "Please begin clearing, Florie."

"Yes, ma'am." The woman removed the Clift boys' cleaned plates.

"And after you're through, I need you to run some errands for me." Mrs. Crowell dabbed a napkin to her mouth.

Livvie handed her empty plate to Florie. "What sort of errands?"

Mrs. Crowell rested her hands on the table. "I'm in need of thread and mending tape."

"From the dry goods store? I would be happy to go." She couldn't bear the thought of spending another morning cooped in Martha's room reading to her while the woman lazed about.

Mrs. Crowell looked from Livvie to Florie, who aimed her wide eyes at Livvie.

Livvie placed her napkin on the table. "I would appreciate the exercise. I'm eager to post a letter to my brother, too. The sooner I contact him, the sooner he can send payment for my stay here."

"Well…" Mrs. Crowell pressed her lips together. "I suppose it would be all right."

Mrs. Locke chirped like an injured bird. "Surely you can't wander the streets alone."

"Why not?" Livvie's attempt to keep her tone light failed. The widow tried to anchor Livvie, when she wanted most to wander.

"Unescorted?" Martha Locke apparently was not one to back down in the face of trespasses against society.

"Key West is quite safe, I assure you." Mrs. Crowell pushed her chair from the table. "I used to walk to town myself, before my arthritis reduced my freedoms."

Freedom, yes. Although the tall windows stood open, Livvie couldn't spend her days confined within this house, or any other. The walls closed in on her, the view beyond the window frame beckoned. To hear Mrs. Crowell express the same sentiment surprised Livvie.

Livvie rose from the table. "I'll get my letter."

Climbing the stairs, the implications of the letter became more clear. Wendell would not refuse her the money for her stay here, but posting the letter would reveal her situation. Her whereabouts. Silly to want to keep her status a mystery, yet there was a certain freedom in that as well. She felt reluctant to give it up.

She descended the stairs and followed the voices of

Mrs. Crowell and Florie into the kitchen.

Bent over the counter composing a list, Mrs. Crowell glanced up and halted her writing. "Oh, and I suppose we'll need more paper. I always keep a supply on hand for guests, and we've been running low. You'll be wanting a stamp, so that's another three cents." She made a half-sigh, half-hum and continued writing. Finishing, she stood straight and held the paper to Livvie. "I've signed it, so the cashier will know it's all right to add the total to our tab. We've been customers for years."

Livvie scanned the list: thread, mending tape, paper, stamps. "Any particular color thread?" She stalled, gauging whether to ask for yet more paper. The atmosphere in Key West inspired her to write, and she'd already used the supply of paper in her room.

"No, white is fine. Be certain to remember the amount so I can update my ledger." Mrs. Crowell's sideways glance contained more than a concern for her accounting. "Did you need something else?"

Not one to blush easily, Livvie felt the tinge of heat in her cheeks. "Would it be possible to obtain an additional supply of paper for me? I promise to reimburse you in full—or, my brother will, rather. And for the postage, of course."

Mrs. Crowell studied her. "You write a great deal."

Again, Livvie's face flushed warm. "It's my calling. I hope to publish my novel someday."

The women stilled, and Livvie grew more uncomfortable when they focused their attentions solely on her.

Mrs. Crowell's mouth turned downward. Her refusal was certain to follow. "I suppose it would be all right."

Joy swelled within her. "Thank you. I'll be going." Taking the basket from the counter, she nearly sprang through the back door onto the porch and bounded down the steps.

Finally, open space. The expansive sky held only a few thin white clouds, too high to cause a care. Every part of the horizon stretched beyond her sight, making it easy to forget the island was so tiny.

Homes dotted the tree-lined street until it opened to the business district. Inside the tall windows of Whelan's Dry Goods Store hung sail cloth and rope. Anchors and other nautical necessities unfamiliar to Livvie occupied one side of the store. After wandering several aisles, she found the sewing items. One spool of white thread appeared thick enough to sew stitches in horse hide. While she examined it, a movement caught her eye, and the back of her neck prickled.

She glanced up to see Sam Langhorne stroll in. As he walked toward her, his smile widened, and his gaze wandered freely across her, sending heated pinpricks across her skin.

He sauntered closer, his movements panther-like in their grace. "Good morning."

The prickles traveled from her neck down her spine, deepening along their inward path. She held the mending tape across her chest to hide her quickening breath. "Hello, Mr. Langhorne. What brings you here?"

He stepped closer, his eyes bright. "Our schooner suffered a battering during the storm. I'm charged with mending the sails and am in need of some strong thread." His fingers closed around hers. "I see you have what I need."

Her voice failed her. "Pardon?" she whispered.

"The thread." He slipped the spool from her hand. "Are you mending sails today also?"

Disappointment surprised her. "Mrs. Crowell sent me here for sewing thread."

From the display, he selected a smaller one and held it up. "I suspect she meant this type."

Warmth crawled up her neck. "I'm not much of a seamstress, Mr. Langhorne."

"You aren't joining Mrs. Crowell's sewing circle?" He clucked his tongue. "I thought women enjoyed passing the time that way." His brown eyes sparkled. Stubble shadowed his jaw and chin, framing his mouth.

She forced her gaze away when she found herself staring too long, wondering how his rough face would feel against hers. She pretended renewed interest in the threads. "I've little experience in that area."

He leaned an elbow against the display and looked up at her. "Ah. Your passels of servants took care of your sewing for you, eh? And here I was hoping you might come lend a hand." Grinning in a teasing way, he searched her face intensely, as though trying to divine the truth.

She lifted her chin. "After my mother's death, my father hired a housekeeper. I'm afraid I wasn't an ideal charge. I spent more time with Sir Galahad than at home." Never had she wanted to be one of the primping girls who practiced domestic skills in hopes of enticing a husband, or took more interest in their appearance than anything else. Now she felt deficient in womanly skills. Sam Langhorne made her feel more deficient. Since their last encounter, she'd dreamed of practicing womanly skills on him.

He pressed his lips tight. "Your own knight in

shining armor?"

So he knew of King Arthur. How, she wondered?

"My horse, Mr. Langhorne." Something tightened in her chest while he held her gaze, so she scanned the mending tapes and selected one, hoping he wouldn't correct her.

He straightened and stood closer than propriety allowed. "I see. You're full of surprises."

His nearness warmed her skin. She stepped away and forced a light tone. "And you, as well. You're a man of many talents, apparently—sewing, salvaging, sailing. Is there anything you can't do?"

"I'm sure there is. Nothing comes to mind." His low voice rumbled like an approaching storm, one of searing lightning and drenching rains.

Livvie had always been fascinated by such storms, and the thought of Sam tearing at her clothes like a gale made her shiver.

"A typical male affliction." The newspaper tucked beneath his arm caught her eye. She tilted her head to read the banner. "Is that a Philadelphia newspaper?"

He held it out for her to see. "Yes, my brother sends it to me now and again, thinking he'll taunt me into coming home. His letter said this edition had an interesting article on the wrecking industry."

"You're from Philadelphia?" She'd imagined him a farm boy, perhaps, from some obscure place providing no outlet for his energy. What else would propel a man to travel far from home to become a wrecker?

His tone fell flat. "Born and raised there." He inserted the newspaper in its resting place beneath his arm.

"What made you come here?" Surely Philadelphia

had entertainments similar to those in New York. Perhaps his occupation—maybe a blacksmith—didn't allow time for social events. Judging by the abundant muscles on his lean frame, he'd worked hard all his life.

He leaned in dangerously close. "Why don't you let me walk you home so we can continue our conversation?"

No ready excuse came to mind to refuse him. Nor did she want to.

Barking erupted outside.

Straightening, he muttered, "Can't stay out of trouble for one minute. Excuse me." He strode to the entrance, yelling, "Barnaby!"

The ruckus ceased. She waited for him to walk in again, aim his warm smile at her, but waited in vain. Feeling conspicuous, she pretended to examine other goods, moving toward the window. A few passersby walked the streets. Sam was not among them.

Frustration coiled within her. Men were so easily led astray. Sam Langhorne was no exception. Perhaps she'd best not spend any more time with him. Seeing him only inspired more thoughts of him. Such unbidden thoughts confused her. He would only bring trouble, of that she felt certain.

At the counter, she asked for paper. After the man tallied the items, he waited. After a moment, she realized she'd forgotten to inform him of the charge to the Crowell account, so produced the signed list. He gave a curt nod, then bent to write in a ledger book. Noting the amount, she thanked him, putting the items into her basket.

A hot breeze wafted through the open door. Reluctantly, she walked toward it. Another boring day at the Crowell home lay ahead. She stepped outside to take in the breeze.

Sam leaned against the wall, his brow knit, reading the newspaper. Glancing up, the lines of care on his face erased. The glint of the sun gave his dark hair a sheen. At his feet, Barnaby lifted his head.

"You're here." Something effervesced deep inside her, bubbling up to entwine in her breath.

Jumping up, Barnaby nuzzled against her. She crouched to scratch his face.

"I said I'd walk you home. Did you forget so soon?" The breeze ruffled his white shirt, pressing it against his well-defined chest.

"No, I…" Words escaped her, though his warm smile indicated they were unnecessary.

Ducking his head, he pushed away from the wall to stand in front of her. "Shall we?"

She rose. "Yes." Uttering the sole word opened up a wild array of possibilities. She would have to use it more carefully in the future. He held her gaze in such a way that not looking away could imply *yes* without speaking the word. Yet she did not wish to look away.

"I must post a letter."

Sam scrutinized the envelope she held.

Hastily, she added, "To my brother." Revealing the addressee to be her brother would have no effect on Mr. Langhorne, even if part of her wanted it to. Why else would she have said it?

The midmorning sun blazed harshly. Perhaps the heat affected her brain, addling it so she behaved so differently from her usual self. Since leaving New York, she'd acted in a manner inconsistent with her girlish self. Perhaps that Livvie no longer existed. She may very well have been lost at sea, long before the *Elizabeth Rose* wrecked.

A flicker of something akin to relief crossed Sam's face. "This way, then." He touched her elbow and led her farther into town.

The detour would extend her errand, along with their walk. She followed none too quickly. He pointed out the Customs House.

The letter deposited, she lifted her hand, shielding her eyes from the sun. "How do you stand this heat every day?"

"Come. There's a quicker route. More shaded, too." He nodded toward a street leading away.

The street appeared to lead to the opposite side of the island. She wouldn't argue its direction.

"Not by much. Why do trees grow so sparsely? And so oddly shaped?" She kept her pace slow, not wanting to arrive at the Crowells' too soon.

His pace grew even more leisurely. "You're right; we should plant more trees in town. There is an abundance of trees on neighboring islands."

"Do you travel to other islands often?" Florie complained of the wreckers' drinking binges between salvage operations. Livvie wondered how Sam might occupy his time.

"Yes, to hunt turtles or whatever else we can find." Sweat caused his shirt to cling to him.

To divert her attention from his shapely form, she asked, "Such as?"

"Depends on our needs. Deer for venison. Pelicans, if we're in need of new pouches. Shells to sell to collectors."

His hobbies sounded innocent as a boy's, yet his

knowing smile led her to believe hunting and fishing were not his only pursuits. Acutely aware of his presence beside her, she suspected he had the same effect on other females. "It sounds like your days are very full, Mr. Langhorne."

He halted, his gaze intense. "Will you never call me Sam? I may be older than you, but not so old as to warrant such formality."

His sudden seriousness took her by surprise. Using his name implied an informality—a familiarity—she wasn't quite ready to allow. But then again, he'd brought her up from the depths, his strong arms leaving an indelible impression on her skin, one she felt even now. How much more familiar could one get? "Sam."

He continued walking. "Thank you, Livvie."

He said it naturally, as though he'd called her that all her life.

She glanced behind them, and then ahead. These streets were new to her. The houses appeared larger, maintained better than those on Duval Street, at least at the end where the Crowells' boarding house stood.

"This is not a quicker route. In fact, I believe it will lengthen our walk."

He pressed his lips together. "Hmm. Is that a fact?"

The stern look she tried to affect gave way to a smile. "So. Tell me about Philadelphia."

"It's a bustling metropolis where small-minded people live." His tone had a sharper edge, and he avoided her gaze.

"City life doesn't suit you?" Livvie's curiosity got the better of her, one of her father's chief complaints.

"Not when I could be here instead. The choice between spending my days there, devising means to outwit others, or here, in the glorious sunshine, my life mine to live as I see fit—well, it was the easiest choice I've ever made."

"What do you mean, outwitting others? Were you a thief?"

He laughed. "In a manner of speaking."

So willing to share certain parts of himself, so reticent to share others. What secrets, she wondered, did Samuel Langhorne hide?

She scrutinized him. "You are a puzzle." More like a Pandora's box, and the temptation to open it grew.

He lowered his head, his smile sly. "Puzzles can provide many hours of enjoyment." His arm brushed hers as they walked. Beside them, Barnaby woofed, perhaps catching the excitement in the air.

To hide her grin, she turned away. Did his ego know no bounds? "What did the article say? What you were reading earlier?"

The teasing left his voice. "Yes, another diatribe against us. Full of lies, or worse, romanticizing the wrecking business."

"What sort of lies?" She could imagine the romanticized version. Man saves girl, they fall in love… The stories of the ship of brides he'd described in portent.

He spoke quickly, decidedly. "Rumors have circulated in the north of unscrupulous wreckers who place lights along the beach to lure boats toward shore, causing them to wreck on the reef. The obvious argument is that any captain worth his salt would know such a small light could not possibly be a lighthouse. Key West has enough wrecks to keep us all busy. We have no need to cause any."

"Why did you leave Philadelphia?" Had he been threatened with jail?

He shrugged. "I hated feeling trapped in my life. Isn't that why you left New York?"

"My father died. I had nowhere to go except my brother's home in New Orleans." The memory of her father's death still stung, almost equally to the prospect of what awaited her.

"I suspect you could have married to stay there." His intense gaze bore into her.

"Marry for convenience?" She hadn't meant to snap so. "I would have felt trapped in my life too."

At this answer, his lips parted, his gaze flicking to hers. They walked a short while in silence. "What will you do in New Orleans?"

The question she dreaded to learn the answer to herself. "I hope to make enough of a living from my writing."

His mouth agape in a half smile, he regarded her. "What do you write?"

A blush of heat crept up her neck. "Novels." He could not possibly understand the drive to write.

"I see. Women's stories."

"You make it sound so petty. Such novels are highly valued for their authentic portrayal of life in these times."

"Life in general? Or focused more narrowly on…other aspects?"

His focus on these aspects flustered her. "Yes, I write about relationships. Of course, there are some romantic aspects because it's part of everyday life."

"Ah. So you write fiction."

His leering smile unnerved her.

Despite her effort to remain calm, her voice

increased in pitch in relation to her frustration. "I hope to portray one's entire life, not merely the romance. I do know a little."

"I'm sure you do."

"Don't be so condescending."

"All right. If you find you cannot make a living by your writing, what then?"

What did he aim to suggest? An embarrassment? To insinuate she wrote poorly? "I don't know. I can find some sort of work. I don't intend to burden my brother and his wife forever." Tears stung at her eyes, so she blinked them away. She would not allow herself to be so weak. Nor show any weakness to him. Why did he have to ruin every encounter?

They rounded the corner onto Duval Street. When the Crowell house came into view, their pace slowed further.

She steadied her voice, forcing a polite tone. "Might I borrow your newspaper? I would love to read news from up north."

He halted. "On one condition."

His serious tone took her aback. "What is it?"

"You allow me to visit you tonight." He stood so close, their shadows on the ground appeared as one.

"I don't know. Mrs. Crowell might object." She didn't know why she said it. Mrs. Crowell had no say over her comings and goings.

"So?" His gaze held a challenge.

"She was kind enough to take me on when I'm destitute. I've written my brother for the money. However, she cannot know for sure I will pay her. Her respect ensures she will not throw me out."

The excuse held no weight of truth, sounding flimsy

even to her. Still, she couldn't admit his company rendered her unable to trust her own decisions. His presence made her feel vibrant, alive in every sense. Unexpected bursts of energy made her want to run giddy along the beach, knowing he would follow.

Sam set a foot on the stone walkway. "I will lend you my newspaper. Upon my return tonight, you may tell me to leave, or invite me to stay." He proffered the newspaper.

She slid it from his grasp. "All right. I'll see you tonight."

He flashed a smile. "Until tonight."

Chapter Seven

Sam hurried back to Whelan's Dry Goods Store for the supplies, continuing from there on to the dock. When the crew complained of his lateness, he gave no excuse, instead joking that the time gave them additional rest. Liam cocked an eyebrow, but said nothing. Sam went about his chores, whistling while mending the tattered sail. He strove to engage himself in every conversation, but his thoughts returned to Livvie again and again.

Liam side-eyed Sam. "Why are you in such a good mood?"

Sam squinted. "The day is fair, the company is enchanting. Why shouldn't I be?" He could think of more enchanting company. Since Livvie had told him of her writing pursuits, his imagination ran wild. What sort of stories did she write? He had to read them. Tonight, he'd ask to borrow them.

Liam grumbled. "If the day were not fair, we would be making profits."

"We cannot salvage every day. Variety, Liam. Have you not heard it is the spice of life?" Although Sam loved the challenge of the wrecking business, he treasured days such as these more than gold. Especially considering the prospect of seeing Livvie again this evening.

Liam snipped the knotted thread. "I've a hankering for a different kind of spice. And I suspect ye do as well."

He stood, pulling the sail taut to test his stitches. His

mending held, and his work was finished. "I hanker for some supper. How about you?" Sam wouldn't let Liam's prying sour his mood.

Jahner Lang straightened from his task. "Are you going to the groggery? I'll join you."

Liam extended his hand in a gracious sweep. "By all means. Let's have a party."

Sam gave an inward groan. A large gathering would delay dinner. Perhaps he could slip a few extra dollars to hurry his meal ahead of the others. All day, he'd aimed to finish work so he could retrieve his newspaper from Livvie. Discuss the news, perhaps take another walk. Just the two of them.

After wreckers from another schooner joined them on their walk to town, Sam's high spirits deserted him.

They arrived at the groggery and filled two tables. Sam fetched a pitcher from the bar and ordered the fish special. "And hurry, can you?"

Liam slapped his shoulder. "What's yer hurry? Have a beer to wet yer whistle."

Sam held his impatience in check, though not without a struggle. "I'm hungry."

Liam leaned toward him. "I know that look, Sam Langhorne. It's not fish ye're hungry for."

Raucous laughter filled the nearby table.

Sam held up a hand to the bartender. "Keep an eye on this one. He'll drain your kegs if you let him."

"Ye'll be helping me, won't ye?" Liam teased.

Sam resigned himself to a lengthy verbal sparring. "Not tonight. I have to catch up on my reading."

"Really? What are ye reading, now?" He bellowed with a theatrical flair, capturing all the men's attention.

Any attitude beyond casualness would invite further

teasing. "The newspaper my brother sent." He winked at Jahner, who guffawed.

Liam widened his eyes. "It contains urgent news, does it?"

"I won't know unless I read it, will I?" Sam gulped his beer.

The cook set Sam's plate before him, and other men called out their orders. A reprieve, however temporary.

Looking at each man around the table to engage his audience, Liam said, "I thought perhaps ye might be payin' a visit to a certain little lady."

The men sing-songed a low *oooo* in concert. Now Sam would have no peace. He shoveled a forkful of fish into his mouth and chewed fast.

"Which one?" asked Jahner.

"Not Joanna Lavery, is it? Because I intend to visit her myself." The smile left Adam Stroh's face, and he lifted his mug to his mouth.

"No," Liam teased. "She's younger. And prettier."

Lipp Reichert turned to Liam. "The companion of the hag?" The crew of *The Brilliant* still laughed about the older woman's constant moaning.

Jasper's clipped Bahamian accent cut above the din. "Olivia Collins. Isn't that her name?"

"She's something." A faraway look haunted Jacob Preston. "A bit feisty." The younger man, a crewman from *The Brilliant*, drained his ale.

His eyes flashed too bright for Sam's liking. "How do you know?"

Jacob met his gaze. "I spoke to her a few times. She almost cut me off at the knees."

Sam recognized the hunger in Jacob's eyes—the same hunger Liam described in his own. "She can be testy, yes."

"Ye're going to visit her nonetheless." Liam's eyes twinkled with glee.

"Yes." Sam ate as hastily as he dared.

Jahner laughed. "You always did love a challenge, Sam."

"The higher the challenge, the greater the reward. Eh, Sam?" Liam nudged him.

"You'll get no reward from her." Bitterness edged Jacob's tone.

Sam grunted in agreement, eying the boy warily. Jacob would vie for Livvie's affections again. Of that, Sam was certain.

After he finished his meal, Liam insisted on buying a round of whiskey. Not Sam's drink of choice, but he couldn't refuse. Not the first, at least. Liam poured a second before Sam had the chance to decline.

The sunlight faded from the sky. Sam drained his glass and turned it over on the table. "That's it, I'm done."

"Off so soon?" Liam said in mock surprise.

He'd have been off sooner if it weren't for his friend. He smacked Liam's shoulder. "See you in the morning." The whiskey hit him while he walked. His gut burned, and his nerves went fluid. He needed a good splash of cold water. And fresh clothing. He would take care of the rest himself.

Chapter Eight

The light shifted through the bedroom window, fading as the sun dipped lower. Livvie moved her chair closer so she could read the newspaper without lighting a lamp, but the words on the page scarcely penetrated her thoughts.

Where was he? Had he forgotten? Or had he stopped at the groggery to carouse with his mates? Her father had warned her that a lady could never depend on a man to keep his promise. Sam Langhorne was living proof.

The three knocks at the front door echoed up the stairs to her room and set her heart to pounding. She folded the newspaper and stood to smooth her hair in front of the mirror.

Downstairs, Florie lumbered through the hall, mumbling. The door creaked open, and Florie's voice mingled with Sam's. Livvie hurried back to her chair and pretended to read. Footsteps thudded up the stairs, and Florie stood in the doorway. "Mr. Langhorne's downstairs for you."

Livvie affected a look of surprise. "Oh, thank you, Florie. I'll be right down."

Hesitating, Florie glanced at Livvie's newspaper and smiled. "I'll tell him."

After she'd gone, Livvie realized she held the newspaper upside down. She threw it on the bed and followed the housekeeper down the steps. "Never mind,

Florie. I'll tell him myself."

Sighing, Florie headed to the kitchen.

Sam stood peering at the painting on the opposite wall. Turning, his face lit up. "Good evening, Livvie."

She affected a lofty air. "Mr. Langhorne. You always seem to be in the dark."

He stepped toward her. "It does appear to be the case."

"Let's go sit on the porch where it's cooler." Away from prying gazes. She opened the front door. "Did you bring Barnaby?"

"Not tonight, no." He followed her to the bench and sat beside her. "He stayed aboard." His breath smelled of whiskey.

"I see."

His mouth spread in a lopsided smile. "We all share him, though he belongs to Captain Howe. So I have the night to myself." He studied her while he spoke.

"I understand." She'd assumed incorrectly that he owned the dog. Barnaby appeared so taken by Sam. Apparently, he thought a dog would infringe on his freedom. Barnaby had misplaced his loyalties. She wouldn't make the same mistake.

His smile filled his face. "I had a feeling you would." He eased closer, his gaze intent on her.

She drew away. "I meant I'm very sad for you."

His brows twitched. "Why?"

She held back a laugh. "You cannot even commit to a dog."

His eyes blazed. "That's not so—"

"Can I get you a glass of lemonade?" She moved farther down the bench.

"No, thank you." He inched closer.

The heat of the evening amplified the stench of alcohol emanating from his breath.

"I hope you didn't interrupt your evening for me," she said.

He cocked his head. "What do you mean?"

"I wondered whether you'd forgotten. You've been drinking, apparently." She gazed down the street, where lamplight flickered in windows of the houses lining it, interrupted by sparse trees. The halting strains of a piano sounded, probably a child practicing.

"Liam—Mr. Byrne—insisted on buying rounds at dinner."

Typical of a man to blame another for his own actions. She glanced away, disappointed.

"A friend of yours was there," he added.

Confused, she searched his face—a mask of innocence. "A friend of mine?" Her friends lived in New York, not here.

"Jacob Preston."

From his tone, she should know him. No one came to mind. "Who?"

His gaze pierced hers. "A crewman from *The Brilliant*. He said he'd spoken to you several times."

She sensed anxiety beneath his light tone—in the way he held himself so still, awaiting her response. "I don't know who you mean."

Inclining his chin, he watched her lips. "Young, a bit cocky. Handsome, or so he likes to think."

"Oh, yes." He hadn't introduced himself, only stepped in her path wearing a confident smile. She'd made quick work of his conceit and hadn't given him another thought. She didn't include cockiness among the traits she admired.

Sam straightened, his pleasant demeanor turned serious. "So, he did speak to you?"

"Briefly, yes." She searched his face. "Why?"

His breathy laugh held no humor. "He's not to be trusted."

"Trusted how?"

He bent toward her and lowered his voice. "He has a terrible reputation. If I were you, I would—"

"Thankfully, you are not me." Men could sometimes be worse gossips than women, turning on one another like dogs in a pack of strays. Yet, let one catch a scent, and they all headed off together. "And I am perfectly capable of making my own decisions."

"I'm sure you are. However, you're unfamiliar with people here." His tone reminded her of her father's partner's when he intimated how lucky she would be to have him for a husband.

She bristled. "And you intend to set me straight, I suppose?"

He chuckled. "Well…"

Standing abruptly, she stepped to the rail. "You presume too much, Mr. Langhorne." He had no right to decide with whom she kept company, or called a friend. Must every man, even one of little means, be so controlling?

The sparkle left his eyes. "I'm only looking out for your best interests."

"Yes, I'm sure it's what all men tell themselves." Indignity prickled the small hairs along her neck. Saving her life allowed him no additional privileges. She owed him nothing beyond courtesy, and now, perhaps not even that. She tilted her head. "I wonder what advice Mr. Preston might give me about you."

His lips thinned. "Surely you've no intention of asking such a question."

She folded her arms across her chest. "And why not?"

His nostrils flared as he stood. "Careful what games you play, young miss. And with whom."

Anger swirled her blood faster at his condescending tone. "It's late. I'm going inside. I'm sure you can catch up to your drinking partners if you hurry."

His eyes flashed in the gathering darkness. "Yes, and they're more companionable." He descended the steps without bidding further adieu.

She stomped inside and slammed the front door behind her. The audacity! Men believed they were granted the power to control women, to decide who was an acceptable social partner and who was not. She would renew her previous caution regarding men in general, and Mr. Langhorne in particular. No man would decide the least detail of her life without her permission.

Chapter Nine

Pale stars faded into the lightening skies, a blaze of orange and gold rimming the horizon. Standing at the *Florida*'s bow, the breeze washed over Sam as he scanned the reef for any sign of a distressed ship on their morning patrol. Heat would thicken the air soon enough. He loved this time of morning, when the world was still and the day was new.

Usually, anyway. If today ended anything like the past four days, it promised to be aggravating, lengthened by repeated reflection on his last conversation with Livvie. Such a headstrong girl. Likely to get herself in trouble. He would have been glad to be the one to help her find trouble, yet each time he remembered her stubbornness, anger overtook him again. He crawled to no woman, especially one so obviously lacking in female skills. Owing to her sparse experience, her writing must pale in comparison to reality. Even fiction required a basis in truth. Another thing she knew little about, apparently.

In his experience, all women resorted to their own strategies to get what they wanted. But what did she want? Apparently not him. The idea stung him more deeply each time it came.

He grew distantly aware of a presence beside him.

"Stop brooding." Liam leaned his elbows on the rail. "Ye're depressing even me."

Sam set his boot atop a nearby crate. "I'm not brooding. I'm thinking."

His friend grunted. "Don't think too hard. Ye look about ready to strain yerself."

"No chance." The knot in Sam's mind loosened. Liam's easy nature always had such an effect. "Besides, I don't believe it's possible to depress you."

"Not today. Not when we'll be having sand fish."

"True, mate." A delicacy, to be sure. If he couldn't have one sort of delicacy, he'd indulge in another. Their planned trip to Sand Key this afternoon would ease his tangled thoughts.

The *Florida* set course for shore. Sam leaped to the dock and tied the boat to its post. A girl in a blue dress at the edge of the dock caught his attention. A breeze blew her golden hair behind her shoulder as she turned.

Livvie.

His heart leapt against his ribs.

She met his gaze and looked away uncertainly.

Sam called over his shoulder, "I'll be right back." He strolled toward her. "What brings you to town?" After their last exchange, he was certain it wasn't him.

She clutched the handle of her basket. "Running errands for Mrs. Crowell. It's such a beautiful day. I couldn't bear to be inside."

Errands in town. He wouldn't ask what led her to the docks—to do so would tempt another outburst. "Captain Howe has invited several people to supper at Sand Key. Why don't you come along?"

Barnaby bounded from the schooner and down the dock.

She bent to scratch his head. "Hello. Are you sailing today too?"

"Yes, we can't leave our mascot behind." Perhaps Barnaby could convince her, if Sam could not.

She stood, cupped her hand over her eyes and scanned the horizon. "Where is Sand Key?"

Not an outright "no," at least. "It's a beautiful island. If the wind is strong, it's less than an hour's sail."

She hesitated. "Who else is going?"

He held his hands at his hips. "A few of the townspeople. Doctor Meade and his wife. We'll be having sand fish, a rare treat."

The mention of the doctor appeared to put her at ease. "It sounds lovely. However, the captain didn't invite me." Disappointment weighted her voice.

The hope that she wanted to go lifted his spirits. "I'm inviting you. Captain Howe welcomes any and all. If it will make you feel better, I'll ask him now."

Her golden-brown eyes searched his. "Are you sure? I don't want to impose."

"Wait here." He jogged back to the schooner and climbed aboard. The captain was in his cabin, the door closed. Sam knocked.

"Enter."

He pushed open the door. "Sorry for the interruption, Captain. I wondered whether you might allow another visitor to accompany us to Sand Key."

Captain Howe continued to write. "Who?"

"Miss Olivia Collins. She's from the *Elizabeth Rose*."

"Is she a friend of the doctor's?" the captain asked absently.

"No, sir. Of mine." Sam fought to steady his breath. He'd never made such a request before, although other crewmen had.

The captain turned with a look of surprise. "Oh. All right."

"Thank you, sir." He waited for the captain to excuse him, though he wanted to burst from the cabin.

Captain Howe assessed him. "I expect you to be on your best behavior and not neglect your duties."

Sam forced a serious look. "Yes, sir."

"Close the door on your way out."

Sam took the stairs three at a time, and then slowed approaching her. "Captain says he's happy to have you along."

Without hesitation, she asked, "What time do you leave?"

His reply came as quickly. "Two o'clock."

She smiled. "I'll see you at two, then."

An ache and a thrill crowded Sam's chest. "Good."

She walked toward town, looking back once to wave. Holding up a hand, he knew he should move away, to not let her know he still watched. No, he wouldn't disguise himself behind maneuvers, nor hide behind pretense. He stood his ground, hoping she would turn again.

A hand clasped his shoulder. "Have ye turned to salt in the sun? Or perhaps the vision blinded ye?" Liam teased.

"The vision?"

Liam widened his eyes, fluttering his fingers in feigned awe. "Of loveliness."

Sam would not allow his mood to be darkened. "Ah. Not yet." He would not admit to even his best friend his inability to focus on anyone else in her company.

Chapter Ten

As she walked to the schooner, the heat of midafternoon caused Livvie's dress to cling uncomfortably. The same dress she wore every day. If only she had thought to grab her bag before the *Elizabeth Rose* sank. She'd lost her favorite dress, along with her mother's pearl-and-sapphire necklace. The last was irreplaceable. Father would not have forgiven her.

Upon spying her, Sam strode from behind the captain's cabin. Climbing from the deck, his gaze swept across her. "Hello."

"I'm not too early, I hope." Impatience had niggled at her ever since his invitation, until she could wait no longer.

Beneath his sailor's cap, his smile appeared brilliant. "Not at all."

A carriage stopped at the end of the dock. A man stepped out, then helped a woman to the ground. Captain Howe climbed onto the dock to greet them.

Sam touched Livvie's arm. "Come, I'll introduce you." He stepped toward the small group. "I'd like you to meet Olivia Collins. This is Captain Howe. Dr. Meade. Mrs. Meade."

The doctor's wife smiled. "Please, call me Lorena." She extended a slim hand.

Her weak grip did not surprise Livvie.

Livvie inclined her head. "I'm pleased to meet you,

Lorena."

Barnaby barked from the upper deck.

Captain Howe turned. "Have you met Barnaby?"

"I have indeed. A fine mascot."

The captain gestured toward the *Florida.* "Shall we?"

The Meades strolled to the schooner, and the doctor helped his wife aboard.

Sam paused at the edge of the dock. "You should put on your hat."

"I don't have a hat." She'd plaited her hair in a loose braid to discourage tangles. The hat she'd carried in her suitcase belonged to her mother, too precious to wear, nonetheless lost to the sea.

"The sun will damage your fair skin." Frowning, he scanned her from head to toe.

"I will stay in shade. Now let's go." She climbed aboard unassisted.

Mrs. Meade urged Livvie to sit near her. She did so while the crew readied to sail. Barnaby trotted over, and she bent to scratch his cheeks.

Fanning her face, Mrs. Meade groaned. "Ugh, he smells awful."

"Perhaps he'll have a swim today, eh, boy?" She patted his head.

The ship was soon underway. As they glided away from the dock, Livvie stood by the rail, the wind in her face.

Sam joined her. "Are you enjoying the voyage?"

She inclined her head to the sun. "I envy you being able to sail in such a fast schooner."

"Yes, there's nothing like it. Unless, of course, we lose our tail wind."

No chance today. The sails billowed full.

Biting his lip, he glanced over.

"What?" she asked.

He leaned close. "I've been meaning to ask…would you lend me your stories to read?"

Apprehension made her tense. The writings she'd carried in her satchel rested now at the bottom of the sea. Only one, barely begun, sat in the desk drawer in her room. "I haven't yet had enough time to recreate those I lost in the shipwreck. I have some pages started, although they're full of crossed-off lines or revisions. Hardly worth looking at yet."

"I'd still love to read them." His dark eyes held no pretense.

"All right. I'll bring you what I have finished."

His sincere delight astonished her.

"I look forward to it." Glancing back, he murmured, "Captain'll have my head if I don't get back to my duties." Giving a wink, he strolled off.

They soon landed at Sand Key, an island so tiny each end was visible at once.

Sam helped her from the boat. "There are beautiful shells, if you care to look for them while we fish."

"Really?" The sun blazed brilliant against the sand, making it difficult to see. "Yes, I may." She gave him an obliging smile.

"Here, you'd better take my cap." He removed it and set it atop her head.

"Yes, it does shield my eyes from the sun a bit. Thank you."

He appeared to restrain whatever thoughts he had. He gave a slight nod before joining the other men. After netting several buckets of sand fish, Vernon, the cook, said he had enough for their lunch. The men dove beneath the water to cool off, the dog in their midst.

She wandered down the shoreline, soon spying a large shell in the wet sand. She lifted it to study its pearlescent interior winding inward. It was so beautiful she hated to set it down. After finding two more, she clustered them together on the beach. She couldn't wait to show Sam, even if he'd probably mock her girlish enthusiasm. He'd likely long forgotten about natural treasures. At finding a fourth, the largest yet, she let out a cry. Turning to look for Sam, her skin flashed hot. He lumbered from the waves, his half-unbuttoned shirt clinging to the contours of his chest. Mesmerized, she clutched the shell, unable to look away. His head glistened in the sun, water dripping from his hair and face. She wanted to catch the drops on her tongue. She imagined peeling away his shirt to taste the salty skin beneath.

He ran a hand through his hair. "I see you found some."

"What?" Her thoughts floated away.

One side of his mouth hitched up in a half-smile. "The seashell."

She must clear her mind, not allow this perfect day to carry her away.

"Oh. Yes, I found several. They're fascinating." She led him to the others.

"Beautiful." He ran his finger lightly across the peaked edges.

His description surprised her. She hadn't wanted to use the word for fear he'd think her a dreamer. A strange yearning filled her when the rest of the men emerged from the waves. "The water looks lovely." Its clear aqua depths glistened like nothing she'd ever seen. If only she could go for a swim too.

He nodded toward the ocean. "You could wade in a bit. Cool your feet in the waves."

She would have to guard her thoughts more closely. He read them too easily. Still, the invitation tempted her enough to check the whereabouts of the rest of their party. The crew were headed for the cook, busy preparing the fish. The captain's group appeared to be engrossed in conversation around the fire.

A sensation came over Livvie the likes of which she hadn't felt since childhood. Total abandon. Freedom. Here, she could act however she pleased without fear of suffering societal disapproval. She took off her boots, threw them away from the foamy wet sand, and then stepped in. The water was warm, deliciously refreshing.

Sam rested against his elbows on the beach near her shells. "Watch for jellyfish. They sting."

Down the beach, the others conversed jovially, paying no attention to Livvie and Sam. Even Barnaby nosed through the sand yards away. She found a branch and broke off a twig. "Fetch, Barnaby." She tossed it into the waves.

The dog bounded into the water, chomped onto the stick, and paddled back to shore. Livvie waded farther into the ocean with each toss. Barnaby's barking grew incessant.

"Livvie," Sam called. "What's wrong with Barnaby?"

She turned back to him. "I don't know."

Sam shielded his eyes, then leapt up, his face a mask of horror.

Barnaby hadn't returned with the stick. She whirled

to search for him.

A large fin zigzagged in approach. A porpoise? The waves obstructed her view. She'd overheard the *Elizabeth Rose* crew speak of porpoises saving sailors, but Barnaby's barks held no playfulness.

Sam yelled from the beach. "No!" His arms and legs pumped wildly. He charged into the water, sending great splashes in all directions. "Get back!"

She stepped toward the beach. "What's going on? I don't—"

Barnaby lunged beneath the ocean.

"No, Barnaby!" Diving beneath a wave, Sam swam past her.

"…understand," she finished. Dread crawled across her skin like fire ants.

The fin veered in their direction. The gray shape headed straight for Sam. Through the clear water, its wide, flat head came into view. Too wide to be a porpoise's.

Sam's head bobbed in the water. He glanced back while Barnaby paddled toward it. "No, go back! No, Barnaby."

Her breath caught in her throat. "Sam, look out!"

The creature closed in. Leaning back in the water, Sam landed both feet hard on its snout. It veered sharply away, but came back just as quickly.

The dog circled back, barking furiously.

"Barnaby!" Sam reached for the dog's tail, missing it by inches.

The dog yelped. In a second, he disappeared beneath the water. Sudden turbulence shook the surface.

The water washed red.

Sam swam reckless as a madman, not stopping when

he reached her.

"Wait—" The wind left her as his arm hooked around her waist and dragged her inland.

"Hurry, Livvie. To shore!" His cry garbled in the waves.

He jerked her uncomfortably, and she found herself unable to assist his effort.

"I'm trying," she tried to say, but caught a mouthful of salt water. She coughed and sputtered.

The depths receded. As Sam's feet touched bottom, they lurched ahead. She tripped on her wet skirts, their weight cumbersome as she tried to find her footing, but the waves helped push them ashore.

She glanced at the fearsome monster. Its fin sliced the water as it raced along. She clutched Sam's neck while he freed them from the waves. The shark turned sharply away, the fin disappearing beneath the surface.

Sam did not release her until they were well away from the water.

The crew ran toward them. "Are you all right?"

She collapsed to the hot sand, barely able to breathe as she watched the shark's movements in horror. It appeared to patrol the area, changing direction in an instant. "Barnaby…"

In unison, the men turned to the ocean in horror.

"Barnaby's gone?" Liam asked in a ragged voice.

"I couldn't…" Sam peered out at the spot where their mascot had lost his life, saving his. "I couldn't save him."

Liam's sudden cry of anguish pierced Livvie through and through. He bent over as if he'd been punched.

Livvie wiped a tear from her cheek. "I'm so sorry. I

had no idea."

Sam hung his head. "You couldn't have known."

"It's all my fault." Why had she been so foolish? She should never have gone in the water. Never thrown the stick into the waves for Barnaby to fetch.

Captain Howe heaved a breath. "No, Miss Collins. Sharks are a constant danger. Always on the hunt. It happened upon us by chance."

"Or the men's splashes might have attracted it," Doctor Meade offered.

Their attempts to clear her of blame did not hearten her. Poor, dear Barnaby! Would Sam ever forgive her?

"God bless Barnaby. He gave his own life to save yours." Liam's eyes glittered with tears.

Sam sat motionless, his mouth set in a grim line, his face expressionless, cold.

Sniffing, Captain Howe hurried to compose himself. "We're lucky no one else got hurt. It goes without saying—no more swimming today. For anyone." He broke from the group, trudging away. The group followed in pairs, all headed for the fire. Jasper threw his arm around Liam's quaking shoulder, steering him toward the others.

Despair overshadowed the bright sunshine.

Her lip trembled. "I could have gotten you killed." Shivers passed through her. She looked away, over the white sand bordering aquamarine waters. Such treachery lurked in paradise.

In a sober tone, he added, "Or been killed."

"I owe you twice for my life."

"You owe me nothing, Livvie. Barnaby saved us both." His voice failed him at the last word.

"Oh, God, poor Barnaby." She drew her knees to her

chest, sobbing freely.

He inched closer. "Shhh. There now." He pulled her to his chest. His skin next to hers felt like hot coals.

"Sam," she whispered. "I'm all aflame."

"Oh, Livvie. Me, too." He eased nearer, his shoulder pressing into hers.

She pushed at his chest, sucking air through her teeth. "No—truly. My skin is burning. I'm on fire."

"Oh my." He pressed a finger to her arm. A white spot appeared, fading slowly. "You have quite a burn."

"A burn?" Impossible. She'd never been one to succumb to any element of weather.

"From the sun. I hoped it late enough in the day so it wouldn't affect you, but your skin is too fair." He winced. "I'm afraid you'll be in pain for a few days."

By the light of the setting sun, her arms showed a reddish tint. Nothing too harsh. Her pain could not be compared to the tragedy of losing Barnaby. "It's not so terrible. We should join the others."

Pushing herself up, she walked to her boots, shook the sand from them, and sat to put them on. To show her ankles anywhere else would have branded her a trollop, yet here, no one mentioned it. Sam certainly didn't seem to mind.

He dug at the sand absently. Making no pretense of hiding his gaze, he watched while she first pulled on one boot, and then the other. It was the most sensual experience she'd ever had. The weight of his gaze slowed her movements, imagining his hands helping her slip each delicate foot into the leather and tug the shoe onto the arch of her foot. She laced the strings slowly up her foot, struggling midway up.

He rose slowly and strolled toward her, his gaze

locked on hers. Orange and pink swirls of clouds glowed in the sky behind him, a beautiful backdrop against his muscled body.

Glancing up, the sunset playing across the sky shone in his eyes.

A heady sensation overtook her, a wooziness that didn't calm her unsteady breaths.

He bent before her. She was sure if he touched her, the warmth of his hands would leave an imprint on her skin.

His low, soft voice seemed to catch in his throat. "Allow me." Slowly, he tied her boot laces. After he finished, he gave a sharp intake of breath. "There. That should hold." The intensity of his gaze pierced hers.

"Thank you." Her breath carried away her voice. Her heart pounded against her breast so hard, he must be able to see it.

He was right. She had no experience in matters of the heart. Her reaction to his touch proved it.

"My pleasure." Rising, he extended his hand.

Sliding her palm across his, she arose with the heady feeling of being drawn into the depth of sky stretching beyond.

Isum's voice broke through. "Supper's ready." Cupping his hands to his mouth, he stood. "For those who are hungry." He strained toward them, worry plain in his face.

She steadied her breath. "We should join the others."

He held her gaze a moment. "All right."

His tone revealed the same reluctance she felt.

Their slow steps brought them to the group.

Livvie settled next to the doctor's wife.

The cook scooped fish from the pan onto plates. Liam held the plate to Captain Howe, who insisted the first go to Mrs. Meade. After the doctor received his plate, Liam served Livvie hers.

"Thank you." She accepted the dish. Whether her body would accept food after such a fright, she didn't know. Each time she thought of Barnaby, her stomach clenched anew.

Sam squatted near the fire. "Don't sit too close. It'll irritate your skin."

Dr. Meade pierced fish onto his fork. "He's right. You're already burnt. The fire will only add to it."

Her smile held no mirth. "No need to worry. This is not the first time I've endured such a burn. My father took me in his boat many a time while I was a girl."

Sam pressed his lips together. "Ah, so you're acquainted with the malady. Still, the Florida sun holds a greater intensity than up north." His skin, too, had a sun-kissed glow, bringing his handsome features into relief.

The doctor sipped from his cup. "If you need a salve tomorrow, send your servant to my office."

"Thank you," she said. "The Crowells' cook is very good at preparing ointments also."

"The island has a wealth of plants." Mrs. Meade chewed daintily. She smiled politely at Sam, some unspoken suspicion in her gaze.

Liam shoved the food around his plate. After he set it down half-eaten, the cook did not complain. Barnaby's death had robbed Livvie's appetite as well.

Sam and the other crew members helped Cook clean up afterwards, and then they pushed off for Key West. The evening sky's colors faded to gray.

Mrs. Meade smiled. "I'll do my best to quell any gossip, Olivia."

She tilted her head. "Why should there be any gossip at all?" Could they only think of such small talk, after such a horrible day?

Dr. Meade harrumphed. "Key West is a small place." He smiled. "Luckily, you didn't go off alone with these wreckers of reportedly ill repute."

Her mouth dropped open. "Their poor reputation is not deserved."

Captain Howe chuckled. "You're quite right, Miss Collins. Perhaps you could inform others upon your return to civilization."

"Yes. Civilization." Along with all its dear trappings. She wished he hadn't reminded her.

Sam leaned against the opposite side of the boat. "Don't worry. Word will never reach your brother's ears of our outing."

Liam gave a great sigh. "Many things happen in Key West of which the outside world never learns." He hadn't so much as grinned since the shark took the dog.

Her heart ached to console him. Of Sam, she couldn't quite discern his state of mind. He'd turned quiet, too, going about his tasks stone-faced.

She leaned on the rail. Such a fateful day. Its bright promise snatched away by a shark. She shuddered to think of what might have happened had Sam not come to her rescue. If only she'd recognized the danger earlier, she might have saved Barnaby.

The sky darkened to deep indigo. A glint caught her eye where the schooner sliced through the water. She gasped. "What's that?"

Captain Howe moved next to her. "That, my dear, is

phosphorescence."

Entranced, she could not look away. "I've never seen anything so magical."

The boat stirred up the tiny light-giving sea creatures along the reef, turning the water luminous in their wake.

The doctor harrumphed. "It's hardly magical."

"To one who's never seen it before, it is. Like you're opening the door to a treasure beneath the glassy surface of the sea." She would not be dissuaded from her poetic nature. At times, she held onto childish notions others her age had long abandoned. Sometimes, such as today on the beach, her childlike ignorance brought her into the path of danger.

Still, she was glad to have a quick mind and an active curiosity that served to educate her.

The schooner neared the wharf, and Sam helped lower the sails and secure them. Jumping onto the dock, Liam and Jahner tied the boat to its posts. As the *Florida* jerked to a stop, Doctor Meade climbed out. Captain Howe assisted Mrs. Meade.

Hitching her skirt, Livvie climbed up. Sam took her arm to guide her. Though she needed no assistance, she thanked him.

He murmured, "If you give me a moment, I'll walk you home."

"All right."

Mrs. Meade turned to Livvie when Sam went aboard. "We would be happy to give you a ride in our carriage."

She gave a polite smile. "I prefer to walk, thank you." If her reputation was to be in doubt, she could do no further harm by allowing Sam to walk her home.

Although they weren't so snobbish as New York's society people, she much preferred Sam's easy company to theirs.

"Thank you again, Captain, for a lovely outing." Mr. Meade shook hands with the captain, who bowed to Mrs. Meade.

Bidding good night, Livvie stood on the dock, gazing out over the sea.

The conversation between Sam and Liam was unintelligible, but their easy tones conveyed their close friendship. After moving about the deck to finish their tasks, Sam followed Liam onto the dock.

"A lovely evening to you, Miss Collins." Liam nodded.

"Thank you, Mr. Byrne. The same to you."

"Don't let this scoundrel bedevil you." Walking away, he held up a hand, whistling softly.

"Don't worry, I won't," was Livvie's quiet reply, directing her comment to Sam, approaching her.

Cocking his jaw, he watched Liam walk away. Letting out a half-breath, half-laugh, he stood beside her.

Facing the open sea, she sighed. "It's incredible how calm it can be. After seeing how terrible its storms are." A full moon hovered at the horizon, its light growing stronger in contrast to the fading daylight.

"We have the best and the worst of weather here." His expression proved unreadable—a mixture of appreciation, awe—and yearning.

Livvie wondered if Sam was akin to those sailors in love with the sea, not needing a life on shore. How could any man live such a lonely life? "Tonight's beauty almost makes me forget the ugly storm."

He grunted, appearing to be lost in rumination.

They stood in silence a few moments. She shouldn't be speaking of weather at such a time. Of course his mind was elsewhere.

She shivered. "I suppose I should be getting back, or Mrs. Meade will inform Mrs. Crowell of my loitering."

He laid a hand on the small of her back as they turned toward town.

"The old biddies gossip because they've nothing better to do."

"I'm well acquainted with gossip." How she despised it. Along with the small-minded people who engaged in it.

He gave her his full attention. "How so?"

Realizing she'd given him an improper impression, she hurried to correct it. "After my mother died, my father followed rather unorthodox methods of raising me. The pastor and his wife visited often, concerned for my well-being. We were not churchgoers."

He grunted appreciatively. "Always deemed a cry for help up north."

Something about his knowing look raised her curiosity. "So you're acquainted with gossip too?"

His face hardened for a moment, and his eyes glazed. If she'd touched a nerve, he hid it well.

"At least in Key West, we can ignore it more easily. We wreckers are much more forgiving of one another because we're all sinners."

A shiver passed over her, whether from his nearness or the night air, she didn't want to know. "I don't believe it."

He threw his head back in a laugh. "Believe it, Livvie—sinners and madmen. Oh, we're saintly enough while we're rescuing others, I admit. The times between

115

shipwrecks tempt even the most angelic of us toward sin."

The growl in his voice gave her a thrill to imagine such a handsome angel sinning in the most pleasurable way. She glanced away to break from his spell. "What do you do to fill the time?"

He strolled easily beside her. "Crews patrol the reef every morning for wrecks. If there are none, we're free to hunt, or fish, or go turtling. We sail to Havana for supplies. If the time drags on too long, fights become common."

"Oh, dear." Mrs. Crowell had spoken of wreckers' fights. Livvie had dismissed it as idle talk.

Sam lifted his face to the stars. "Liam says he's going to buy a plantation, get out of wrecking. He claims too many others are in it now to make it profitable."

"You disagree?"

"No, I believe he's right. More men arrive each month looking to make their fortune. Some men have centered their entire lives around wrecking. I don't yet know if I will or not. Liam's idea is very smart. I may have to follow it."

"You'd compete at farming?" Men were impossible, always aiming to best one another at everything they did.

"Not at all. I'd plant alternate crops. There are plenty of possibilities."

"Would you miss the wrecking life?" Perhaps the labor of farming would yield greater reward, or at least a more lasting satisfaction.

"It's gotten in my blood, but many things can satisfy a man's soul." He leaned his head toward hers.

She stifled a grin. Sam was never one to miss a taunt, to try to instill in her the recklessness he must feel. Safest not to acknowledge it. "So do you think you'll get another dog?"

He inhaled sharply. "It's up to the captain."

"What about you?"

"I don't understand."

"You loved Barnaby. Surely you'll miss him."

He stiffened. "I'm sure we all will."

"Why not get a dog for yourself?"

"What? No. It's not possible."

"Of course it is." She found it hard to believe he hadn't considered it. The way he coddled Barnaby, fed him, petted him—he must have loved him.

"No," he said sharply, and then softened his tone. "Let's not discuss it any further."

His rebuke stung. "I'm sorry." Sorry he apparently considered even owning a dog too much of an intrusion on his personal life. She rubbed her arms. "The night air has a chill to it."

"I suspected as much." He halted, his hand light on her arm.

"What?" Her pulse raced.

Moonlight dappled his face, and he stepped close. The air hung heavy with unspoken words, emotions she could not name, too tangled to sort.

He held his palm to her cheek. "Your skin's burned."

If not by the sun, her cheeks burned now at his touch. "Really, you must stop worrying. I'll be fine." The urge to discover the real meaning of love renewed itself. Caution struggled against it and finally restrained her.

His hand drifted away, leaving a tingling trail in its wake.

The boarding house stood less than half a block

away. Close enough to run to. Or run from without being seen.

She shivered. "I should be going." She turned too abruptly. "Thank you again for inviting me."

He gave a nod. "Thank you for joining us."

For a moment, she stood, her gaze locked on his. The pale glow of the lamp inside softened his features. His full lips parted when she glanced at them, her heart quickening. She imagined how he might take hold of her, his mouth insistent upon hers.

Her voice failed her as she whispered, "Good night."

After rushing to the house, she hurried up the steps without looking back. Maybe Florie had spoken the truth when she said the devil himself chased after her.

Chapter Eleven

The morning's sail along the reef revealed no ships in need of aid. Again. After a long night of bedeviling thoughts of Livvie, Sam needed a distraction. Even now, miles from shore, he felt drawn to her.

Liam said something. Sam only heard the last word: think. His brain desperately needed a reprieve from thinking. He knew of no cure.

"Well?" Liam asked.

"What?"Sam pretended an interest.

"What do you think? Do you want to go hunting today?" Liam set his hands on his hips. "Or perhaps we'd be in more danger in your company. You're likely to shoot one of us."

"You're mad. I'm an excellent shot."

"Yes, when you're not blinded by love." His loud cackle infected the rest of the crew to echo it.

"If I'm not back in time, go without me." Sam cleaned up in a hurry, and walked at a quick clip to the boarding house.

Mrs. Crowell opened the door only a few inches, her quick gaze traveling his length and displaying palpable distaste.

"Morning, Mrs. Crowell. Is Miss Collins busy?"

"Wait here. She's not feeling well and may not be up to seeing anyone." By her tone, he gathered she meant especially not him.

He summoned his best smile. "Thank you kindly, Mrs. Crowell. I'll wait while you ask her."

Her thin lips and arched eyebrow signaled disapproval. Her husband made a good living as a merchant, equally profiting from the wreckers' livelihood. Still, the woman had a ready scowl for any wrecker approaching her home. Sam hoped her tales of wanton wreckers hadn't tainted Livvie. Enough rumors swirled from this town like schools of piranhas— warning of wreckers' thievery, of their plotting against ships to cause their ruin. None of it true. Well, little of it. Sam couldn't deny some of his crewmates lacked equal scruples for all salvaged goods. Lewis Pinder being an exception, even petty thievery seemed scarce. None would commit major crimes against others.

The creak of the door caused him to turn. Livvie stepped onto the porch, and surprise burst from him in a laugh. He disguised it by coughing and covering his mouth with his hand.

Her face, bosom, and arms glowed red like an angry sun. Her bright eyes shone like starlit amber. The sun had been kinder to her hair, which glinted gold among her honey-colored tresses, giving her an angelic appearance. An angry angel.

She put her fists to her hips. "You needn't hide your mirth. I know what I look like."

He cleared his throat. "I would never take pleasure in your pain."

"But you'll relieve yourself of fault. You did, after all, warn me."

"I should have protected you. I share equal blame." At her frown, he added, "More blame, since I've experienced the Florida sun's effects."

She turned away abruptly and held the railing, her bright red skin contrasted against the white paint. "My stubbornness is to blame. I release you from any guilt."

The pain in her tone urged him toward her, along the rail. "I cannot forgive myself unless you allow me to make it up to you."

"Do you have a different salve than the awful stuff Mrs. Crowell gave me? I smell like a rotten greenhouse."

He sniffed. "No, not nearly so awful. I'm afraid I can't offer anything better than Mrs. Crowell's ointment."

"Then what?" She eyed him warily.

"Come to the dance Saturday."

She winced. "Dance? I can barely move without flinching."

He kept his tone even to calm her, like a skittish filly. "You'll feel much better by Saturday. The salve aids in healing and eases the burn."

Her sharp exhale told him boredom had already set in, being confined indoors. Her leg twitched in impatience, or to ease pent-up energy. If she weren't suffering from a stinging burn, he would take her to the beach and let her unleash her energies on him.

She pressed her lips together and stared ahead, and he knew she would accept. He did his best to hide his elation.

Her bosom rose as she took in a breath. "Where is this dance?"

"In the town hall. Mr. Simmendinger is a master accordion player, and Mr. Caruthers plays a lively violin also."

"I haven't been to a dance in two years." A wistfulness hung in her voice. "The only gown I have is the one I'm wearing."

"It's lovely. Like its owner." Sam's tongue loosened uncontrollably in her presence. He made a silent vow to hold it from now on. Or put it to better purposes.

"It's a mended rag, torn in so many places." She smoothed her skirt as if to erase the tears. "If only I'd been able to save my mother's necklace. Its beautiful pearls and sapphires would steal the attention away from my shameful garment."

Pearls and sapphires? Hadn't he glimpsed such a necklace in Pinder's hands? Tomorrow, he'd ask. Bribe the weasel, if he had to. He'd love to see Livvie's delight when he returned it to her. She might even repay him with her own special kindness.

"No one will be looking at your gown, Livvie." His greatest fear was that the other men would be imagining her without any garment.

Her head snapped up. "Because they'll be laughing at my bright orange skin—yes, I know."

Frustration exited him in a sigh. "What I meant was that your loveliness will distract them."

Her eyes flicked expectantly. Never a good thing. He lightened his tone. "It will be a night to remember. Good music, dancing, food. And excellent company, if you're with me."

She gave a laugh. "Is that so?"

"I will make sure you have a wonderful time, to make up for the agony you've suffered." He had every hope for it. After the dance.

"You make it difficult to refuse," she said softly.

He gripped the rail to keep himself from reaching for her. "Good. Then I will come by at eight."

"Eight? Isn't that rather late to start?"

"Not in the Keys. To dance any earlier might cause a lady to faint from the heat."

She squared her shoulders. "I have never fainted, Mr. Langhorne."

He smiled. "Or suffered a sunburn." He ran a finger up her forearm, faintly grazing her skin, the heat of her rising to his touch.

Her gaze followed the movement, and their heads inclined toward each other. Both raised their glances at the same moment. The heat from her skin was nothing compared to the heat that washed over him. If she weren't suffering, he'd be sorely tempted to taste those parched lips, draw her flaming body to his, and quench both their needs.

At the creak of the door, she stepped away and turned.

Mrs. Crowell glared. "Perhaps you'd care for some lemonade, Mr. Langhorne?"

The woman's sardonic tone discouraged him enough.

He straightened. "No, thank you, ma'am. I must say good night."

"So soon?" Livvie whirled to face him.

Her disappointment heartened him, and made him more eager for Saturday's approach. "I'm afraid I have business tonight that cannot wait."

"What business?"

Curiosity appeared to drive her question rather than prying, he was relieved to note. He could not abide a suspicious female.

"Turtling. We hunt by moonlight." He nodded. "I hope you're feeling better soon."

"I'm sure I will be. Thank you. Enjoy your turtling

expedition."

The yearning in her voice made him long to invite her. Maybe some night when Mrs. Crowell wasn't hovering like an old crow.

The proprietress waited until he descended the porch stairs. "Good night, Mr. Langhorne."

He paused to touch two fingers to his forehead in salute. Once she turned, he smiled and winked at Livvie.

Her face flushed and she smiled.

Mrs. Crowell croaked, "Are you coming along, Miss Collins?"

"In a moment."

He walked backward, and she watched. The further he walked, the stronger the urge washed over him to return to her.

All in good time. Only that thought allowed him to turn, finally, and stride to town.

Chapter Twelve

Liam hunched over the bar and slammed the shot glass on the counter. "Another whiskey."

Sam clasped his shoulder. "You started without me."

"Did ye expect otherwise?" Liam surveyed him like something looked different. "Where have ye been, my boy?" He lifted the refilled glass to his lips.

Sam leaned onto the counter and signaled the bartender. "I paid a visit to Miss Collins."

Sputtering, Liam set down his glass. "Miss Collins again?"

"Yes. She'd exposed herself the other day. I wanted—"

"Exposed herself, eh? Ye told me ye only walked her home." Liam nudged his elbow into Sam's side.

Sam's thoughts were tangled enough without any help from Liam. "Her fair skin overreacted to the southern sun, as I suspected."

"Did ye apply a special salve, eh?" Liam narrowed his eyes and arched his brows in expectation.

Sam thanked the bartender, who set an ale in front of him. He would not answer his friend's lewd suggestion.

Liam clucked his tongue. "Ye be careful, lad. Ye'll soon be the one who's caught—in a soft net. Don't be fooled. The threads of those nets never loosen." His eyes glittered, no doubt imagining Sam's sins.

The cool beer soothed Sam's palate and his spirit. "No woman's wiles have trapped me yet, my friend."

Liam's throaty chuckle gave Sam pause, uncertain whether his joke amused him, or some perceived blindness.

"Tonight ye'll be safe from the reaches of all females. Finish yer ale, and we'll be off. We're wasting moonlight."

Sam raised his glass. Moonlight was better spent on other pursuits besides turtling, but he wouldn't inspire Liam's teasing by saying so. "We must fulfill Captain Howe's promise to Mayor Worthington for venison and turtle for the feast." He tilted the glass to his lips. Tomorrow, they would hunt Key deer—smaller than the deer up north, their meat every bit as tasty. A day in the wilds of the Keys would distract him from imaginings of Livvie. The week had been too slow, allowing too much idle contemplation. A day away would provide relief, a quiet space to renew his pledge of personal freedom. "Excellent."

****

The sloop hit the sand, and Sam, Jasper, Liam, and Jahner grabbed its sides and hauled it up away from the water. The full moon lit the beach like early morning.

After the men had walked a few yards, Liam pointed. "Tracks."

"Our timing couldn't have been better," Jahner said. "The nest must be close by."

They followed the indentations to a crescent-shaped mark, indicating where the turtle had swiveled, its hind shell gouging into the sand. The Conchs had taught them long ago to look for these signs, only visible before the

126

tide or wind erased them.

"Let's dig." Liam dropped to his knees and scooped away sand.

Jasper grasped Jahner's arm and looked down the beach. "Look, there's another."

They ran after it like wild men. Jasper ran along the water line to cut off its escape. Jahner circled behind. They set upon it, and after a struggle punctuated by shouted curses, turned it over, giving a chorus of whoops as they stood.

Sam laughed and helped Liam uncover the nest. "Impressive. Not many can turn a turtle heading for water. Let's hope our luck is equally good tomorrow."

"Jasper has the strength of three men. And he's not much for humor, so I don't test our friendship by taunting."

Sam chuckled. "I noticed. You save your taunts for me." His fingers found the smooth, round eggs. "Here's the first sixty or so. How many beneath?"

After removing the top eggs, they found a second layer of more than one hundred.

"Like buried treasure, they are." Liam cupped three in his palms. "And more to be had. Come on." He walked toward the two men and their prize. "Careful she doesn't get away from you—she's trying to turn herself."

The turtle craned its neck against the sand, lifting itself, and failing in each attempt.

"Place the coral rock beneath its head to take away her leverage."

Jahner set the coral under the turtle to discourage any further effort to flee. They followed its trail to the nest and dug up the eggs. Jasper stood guard over the turtle while they gathered eggs.

A pang of guilt crept over Sam while they robbed the nest within sight of the flailing turtle. He never wanted to feel so helpless, so utterly beyond hope, or so overwhelmed by despair that death itself was preferable to suffering through another day. When he left Philadelphia, he'd vowed never to experience that again.

The reminder washed his preoccupation with Livvie away, allowing him a night's rest before rising early for the hunt. His renewed focus sharpened his aim as he raised his rifle to his shoulder. His bullet felled one of the three deer they brought back. Lifting the doe's head, its light brown eye—full of accusation, innocence and beauty—seared into his brain, mingling with images of Livvie: standing so close to him on the porch, walking beside him through the streets of night. Trusting. Waiting.

"Anything wrong?" Liam looked at Sam as though he were a madman.

"No." He laid the deer's head down carefully. They tied its legs onto a pole. Sam made sure to take up the front so he could not see its face, only feel its weight while he walked.

Chapter Thirteen

Livvie no longer resembled a boiled lobster. Patches of white skin flaked from her arms, neck, and forehead, although Florie's soothing balm lessened the peeling. On her walks into town, she'd noticed few others whose skin hadn't been tinged bronze by the sun, and so felt less out of place.

When Sam arrived at her door, her heart fluttered like a swarm of hummingbirds as she descended the stairs. She wasn't quite sure if it was because she would be free of the oppressive scrutiny of the Crowells, and the clinging whines of Mrs. Locke, or because of Sam.

Or the dance. She so eagerly anticipated tonight. Florie had helped her fix her hair, sweeping the sides up into a barrette and adorning it with three plumeria blooms. In the heat, their fragrance filled the bedroom. Mrs. Locke would think her a harlot. Livvie giggled. Let the old woman think what she would. Tonight, Livvie intended to dance.

Florie opened the door. He'd taken obvious pains to comb his hair and wear good clothes, and his gaze went immediately to Livvie, oblivious to anyone else. He crossed the threshold the instant her foot touched the landing, as if he sensed her eagerness. Or felt it himself.

Mrs. Crowell stepped into the hallway and raised her chin. "These affairs can be rather raucous. Take good care of Olivia."

His sideways glance sent a shiver through Livvie. "I will, Mrs. Crowell. Have no fear."

"Good night." She swept out the door before the woman could say another discouraging word.

He laughed and caught up to her. "Reserve some energy for dancing, Livvie."

"You will dance with me, won't you?" She had energy to spare. If she didn't exhaust it dancing, she feared the headiness of the evening would cause her to lose her head—or worse.

"Of course." His mouth opened in a half-smile.

"Then worry about your own stamina. I can dance till morning."

His gaze crawled across her appraisingly while they walked. "May I say you look especially lovely tonight?"

She straightened her shoulders. "Yes, you may." To distract his attention from her faded dress, she held her head high and exuded the grace of a princess. Tattered royalty she may be. In Key West, few people truly judged. Oh, they wagged their tongues for sport, but even Mrs. Crowell turned a blind eye to the goings-on in town, for the most part. Livvie suspected the woman's stated concern sprang from a business, rather than a personal, nature. Patronage at the boarding house might suffer if one of its guests came to harm.

"I'm happy to return the compliment." She forced herself to look ahead, sensing his intense attention. His dark eyes could draw her in too easily, distract her toward musings best ventured into after solemn vows. Silently, she pledged to end the evening with her honor intact.

Key West's town hall doors were thrown wide to the evening. Music mingled with laughter to echo through the streets. Lanterns strung from posts added to the festive air.

"Sounds like there's quite a crowd." Her insides twinged, imagining herself in his arms—soon to be not a dream, but very real.

Sam matched her stride. "I expect everyone in town will be here."

"Except Mrs. Crowell or Mrs. Locke."

He took her arm as they neared the doors. "Thank heaven for small favors."

"Oh, it's marvelous."

Men and women moved in pairs across the dance floor while others stood at the edge, clapping or cheering. Not the sober, somber dances of New York. Skirts swirled, feet flew to the merry rhythm of the accordion and violin. Although she'd never before witnessed such dances, she longed to try them.

Sliding his arm around her waist, he pulled her into the crowd. "Let's dance."

"I don't know how." Despite her protest, she entwined her fingers in his.

He drew her close, his mouth at her ear. "Then you'll learn." He swept her onto the crowded dance floor.

Not even attempting to mask her pleasure, she laughed, trying to follow the other women, who whirled about, swirling around their partners. He grabbed her hand, raised it above her head, and she twirled beneath it. She followed his gentle nudges that hinted at which direction she should move. After three such dances, she had trouble catching her breath.

He held her hands, his mouth open in a smile. "Shall we sit one out? Get a drink?"

She tucked a stray strand of hair into place. "Yes. I'd love a drink."

"Ah, there's Liam." He led her to the table where his mate sat, a woman draped about his shoulders.

Liam's companion flashed a provocative smile. "Hello, Sam."

When Sam held out a chair, Livvie sat. "Millie, this is Olivia Collins."

Livvie nodded. "Pleased to meet you."

Sam leaned over Livvie's shoulder. "What would you like to drink?"

Even in the heat of the night, his breath felt warm and sweet on her face. She might rather gaze into his dark eyes a little longer. "I don't know. Is there any punch?"

Millie tittered, whispering in Liam's ear.

Sam chuckled. "I'll see if there's any." He straightened. "Anyone else?"

Millie held out her glass. "You know what I like, honey. Whiskey."

Livvie couldn't help staring. Millie hardly looked old enough to drink whiskey, let alone flirt with a man easily twice her age.

"Are ye enjoying yer stay in Key West?" Liam asked.

"Yes, thank you."

"You leaving soon?" Millie leaned her elbow against Liam's shoulder. Her cool gaze cut through the humid night.

A stubbornness came over Livvie. She could inform this brazen girl she'd likely be gone within weeks. Millie would have to wait for Sam awhile longer. "I'm not sure. It all depends." On what, she'd not reveal.

Arching a brow, Millie's eyes narrowed.

In smug satisfaction, Livvie leaned back against her chair.

Sam walked through the throng, balancing two smaller glasses against a tall beer mug, conversing amiably with those he passed. Throughout, he kept his gaze on her, like a guiding star.

A feeling rose within Livvie, the likes of which she'd never experienced. She might have been reeling him in, drawing him toward her. The lights, the noise, the crowds faded away. Sam approached, his gaze locked on hers. She had the sensation of being underwater again. Everything else seemed in a haze, fading from existence.

He placed the drinks on the table. When he finally sat beside her, the sensation heightened as his hand swept lightly across her back.

"Sip it slowly, Livvie. It's a little stronger than you're used to." He ducked his head, his look stern, like she were a schoolgirl.

The tang of the drink refreshed her palate. "It's delicious. What's in it?"

"Jamaican spirits, mainly—along with caracoa, eggs, some other ingredients. It'll sneak up on you if you're not careful."

Millie's high-pitched titters cut through the music. "Drink up, sweetie. It's good for what ails you. Or perhaps you, Sam. I'd wager the young miss will be paying a visit to Conchtown tonight."

With a leering smile, Liam murmured in her ear as his hand crept across her waist along the bottom of her breast.

Tensing, Livvie forced her gaze to the dance floor. She gulped the last of her drink as she stood. "Let's dance."

"In a minute." Sam rested his elbows against the tabletop.

She pulled on his sleeve. "Sam."

His resolute smile did not match his clipped tone. "I'd like to finish my drink."

Millie's sultry gaze went to Sam while Liam nuzzled her neck. "Sam, the lassie wants you."

Livvie shot her a hateful look. Millie smiled, the gleam in her eye equally loathsome.

Sam tilted the glass to his lips. "I said in a minute." He patted the chair. "Sit."

Bile rose in Livvie's throat. No man commanded her like a dog. "I'm getting another drink." Turning too quickly, she bumped a chair. Millie's lilting giggle fueled her anger.

Sam would follow any minute, as she'd asked. She was sure of it. She couldn't endure Millie's vile presence any longer.

At the punch bowl, she refilled her glass, gulped it down, all the while stealing glances at the table where Sam sat. The men were engrossed in conversation, while Millie appeared more interested in Livvie's whereabouts.

Livvie sipped until she'd emptied her glass. She refilled it again. The dancers all looked so graceful, so exhilarated by one another. The thrill of feeling Sam's touch upon her had been too fleeting. Likewise his attentions.

A young man strode toward her, his eyes bright. "You look lonely."

"I am." A glance at Sam made her regret her hasty response. She'd rather be sitting beside him.

"Care to dance?" the young man asked.

Why had Sam not followed? "I shouldn't."

"Why not? Maybe it will spur more attention from your escort."

He had a point. Why not indeed? "All right, I'd love to."

The young man guided her through the crowd to the dance floor, whirled her against him and led her in a lively dance.

She stumbled along, unable to match his movements. Other dancers bumped into her, and glared at her in disdain.

The song ended none too soon. Her head spun, and she fanned at her face. "It's so warm in here."

"Let's go outside, then." His voice buzzed at her ear, his arm clenched her waist.

The closeness of the hall made her blink, caused the lantern light to swarm. She realized she was walking, and that he held her too close. Her feet trampled atop his. His hold was too high on her waist. Pushing failed to budge it.

His voice sounded kind, even if he gripped her tightly. "You're a wee bit unsteady, miss. Let me help you."

"I should go back." Where was Sam?

"Not yet." They cleared the doorway. He dragged her sharply to the side, along the building. At the end, where the shadows were deepest, he pinned her against the wall.

Her shoulders thumped against the wooden slats. Alarm brought clarity to her head. "What are you doing?"

"I have a cure for your loneliness." He pressed harder against her, cupping her derriere. "You don't remember me, do you?" His face nearly touched hers when he spoke, his tone held no sweetness.

"What? No. Let me go." She squirmed, fear building when his grip tightened.

He locked his hips against hers. "Jacob. Jacob Preston. We met a few times in town."

Her alarm ratcheted higher. "Leave me alone."

He thrust his knees between her legs. "Not just yet, pretty girl. I've wanted to do this since I first saw you." His lips raked against her neck. He hissed at her ear, "You won't forget me again."

Shock somehow loosened her muscles. Panic made her uncoordinated. She shoved at him. "You're disgusting. Let me go."

His mean laugh seared through her. Terror overwhelmed her as he tugged her skirt up. The feel of his fingers along her bare thigh made her scream, a high-pitched noise that surprised even her.

Clamping a palm tight across her mouth, he clucked his tongue. "You and I are going to spend the night together." His grip firm, he moved behind to drag her. "You're going to make me very happy."

"Livvie?" Sam called.

Jacob clamped tighter against her mouth. She managed to open her lips, and widen her jaw enough to chomp into his calloused skin.

His agonized cry spurred her to action. She whirled to face him and jerked her knee upward, hard into his crotch. With a surprised grunt, he doubled over. When his grasp loosened, she stumbled away.

Footsteps thudded in the darkness. "Livvie, where are you?"

Jacob lunged for her and dragged her backward.

"Stay out of this, Langhorne. She's leaving with me."

Sam's outline shone against the backlighting. "Not if she doesn't want to, Preston. If you let her go now, I'll spare you further agony."

Fury overwhelmed her senses. Clenching her teeth, she twisted in his grip. "Let me go." She stomped her heel atop Jacob's foot. His grasp loosened. Clamping her hands together, she whirled, swinging her fists to land against what felt like his jaw.

Groaning, Jacob tumbled backward, thudding to the ground.

Two men rounded the corner. One asked, "What's going on?"

Struggling to his feet, Jacob called, "Lutz, I need help."

Sam grabbed Livvie's arm. "Time to go, dearest." He steered her toward the street. "Gentlemen, relax. It's a misunderstanding. Nothing more."

Their pace slowing, one asked, "Sam?"

"Yes, Lutz. My girl and I were just leaving."

"She's my girl." Jacob lunged toward them.

Livvie gasped, clinging to Sam.

"What's going on?" The two men closed in.

Sam backed her toward the street. "The girl came here as my guest. I'm duty bound to see her home. Go about your business."

"Is that the truth, miss?"

"Yes." Livvie's voice shook. "Sam is my escort. This awful man tried to force himself on me."

Sam squeezed her arm. "Shh, darling. It's all over now. Let's go home."

The men followed. "Yes. Take her home, Sam."

"I am."

"If she goes to your home, we'll know she's yours. Then no one will bother her again. Isn't that true, Jacob?"

Jacob's eyes flashed in anger.

Lutz spoke slower. "Jacob, isn't that true?"

"Yes," came his angry reply.

"Thank you, gentlemen. It was a pleasure to run into you tonight." Sam turned, his arm tight around Livvie. "Say nothing," he whispered.

From behind him, Lutz said, "We'll make sure you get home safely."

Sam walked steadily ahead. "No need for that. We're fine."

The houses along these streets appeared little better than shacks, hardly any space between. They must be in Conchtown, where the wreckers lived.

"Your girl's a bit drunk," said the other man. "If she refuses you, we'll be there to step in."

Sam waved them off. "Like I said, no need. I'm perfectly sober."

Lutz gave a throaty laugh. "Sober, willing, and able."

"That's me." Hastening his pace, Sam whisked her down the dark street.

Through a blur of tears, her heart pounding, Livvie did her best to keep up until they arrived at a small dwelling.

He pushed open the door and nudged her in behind him as he turned. "Here we are. I bid you good night, gentlemen."

The third man guffawed. "Turning in already, Sam?"

"Not quite yet." After closing the door, he moved to the window.

In the darkness, only his silhouette was visible. "Are they gone?" she whispered.

"No. Looks like they're making themselves cozy. We'll have to stay put for awhile."

"Where are we?" She could see no other shapes or objects to give her any clues.

"My place."

"Oh." She backed away.

Exhaling sharply, he pulled the tattered curtain closed. "You might as well make yourself comfortable."

His footsteps neared, and then he grazed past her. A match flared to life as he touched it to a candle wick and then replaced the glass covering. Sitting on the bed, he ran his hand through his hair, his glance a silent accusation.

A dull ache throbbed at her temples. "Sam, I'm sorry."

"How did this happen?" The whisper hissed from him.

"I don't know. He asked me to dance. I said yes. The room closed in on me, so he took me outside. For fresh air, I thought."

His lips formed a thin line. "How much punch did you have?"

Livvie tried to recall. The one Sam brought her, another at the table. Then another. She hung her head. "I meant no harm."

He stared at the floor. "That won't budge them from their post."

Hugging herself, she glanced at the window. To think of them outside, waiting—watching—humiliated her. "What do we do?"

He shrugged. "We wait."

A different sort of panic took root. "How long?"

"Until they give up, or pass out, or fall asleep." He tugged a boot from his foot, and it thudded to the floor. "Are you going to stand there all night?"

The other boot dropped.

The memory of Jacob's rough touch returned, too raw. Too vivid. Tears stung her eyes.

In a moment, he was holding her, rocking her. "Shh, it's all right." Leaning away, he smoothed her hair, his eyes warm.

She wanted to say she was fine, but again she felt Jacob's unwanted hand defiling her skin. Her lip trembling, she blubbered, unable to contain herself any longer.

He held her head against his chest. "Don't cry. I won't let anyone hurt you."

Clutching his shirt, she let her tears flow freely. Tears she'd held back for months, since her father's death left her abandoned, at the will of his partner. The uncertainty of the journey, her brush with death—she cried not for herself, but for all those on board. For young Peter, whose sweet youth was cut short.

He slowly backed to the bed, drawing her down in its soft cushion. The sheets smelled of him, a heady scent that quieted her tears. A powerful urgency filled her, like a snake writhing inside her, a pulsing need to entwine her limbs around his. She pressed closer, moving her lips along his neck. His skin intoxicated her more than the punch. Instinctively, her mouth sought his.

He groaned, and his moist lips closed on hers; his tongue caressed hers. She whimpered urgently, clutching him as if overtaken by madness.

His moans became words as he cupped her face.

"No. Livvie. You've had too much to drink." He fell against the pillows, releasing an anguished groan.

She lifted herself above him. "Sam, this is what you wanted, isn't it?" She unfastened the barrette, her hair falling past her shoulders. "I want you, too. Take me."

The tortured look in his face melted. He pulled her to him and his lips sought hers. His roughness thrilled her. Not like earlier, when Jacob had forced his lust upon her. Now she instigated it willfully, skillfully, like a trained courtesan. Any doubts she harbored about her skill concerning men dissolved. She moved her body along his, stoking the fire already burning out of control. A puppet master she was, with Sam her puppet, moving according to her instructions, as communicated through her touch. She arched her neck up to entice him to cover the length of it in kisses. She arched her back, offering her breasts. His breath trembling, his lips touched her bosom in a reverence akin to worship. The power of these unspoken commands filled her with excitement and tenderness, a deeper yearning than she thought possible to fill.

Her breaths became more labored; the writhing inside her intensified. The churning in her belly moved upward. Gripping the headboard, she groaned, though not in pleasure. Her vision blurred as the room swam. "Oh, no."

He paused, chest heaving. "Livvie?"

"Oh, no." When she closed her eyes, the room spiraled.

He slipped from beneath her. "Livvie, are you all right?"

She was about to say no, she didn't think so. Her gut burning, she held a hand to her watering mouth.

He scrambled off the bed and dragged her out the door just in time. She bent over, spasms of sickness washing over her. He held her hair, his other hand holding her up.

Cackles of laughter erupted across the street. "Sam, your girl is trying to tell you something."

The humiliation of it made her groan. Each time she emptied her stomach, the three men laughed and hooted as though it were the funniest thing they'd ever seen.

When she coughed, Sam's voice was in her ear. "Better?" She nodded.

"Any more?" he whispered.

"I don't think so."

The men cheered. "Give her another round, Langhorne."

He tugged her inside to the bed. "I'll get you some water."

Her muscles hung limp on her frame, unwilling to do her bidding. Her head felt like a bowl full of sloshing, swirling water.

A glass appeared in front of her face. "Drink as much as you can."

Like an obedient child, she gulped. The churning quelled. Behind her, the mattress bumped with his weight.

Exhaling a long sigh, he drew her down. "That's right. Rest awhile."

"I have to return to the boarding house," she murmured into his shirt. His warmth comforted her, so she nestled into him.

"You will, in awhile. Now rest."

Her eyes drifted shut, and darkness enveloped her.

Chapter Fourteen

Sharp murmurs split the night. Sam knit his brow before he opened his eyes. The evening's events came to light in his mind, and he relaxed into his pillow.

Livvie.

He rolled to his side and curled his arm against her, snuggling his face into her shoulder.

"No," she murmured, "you can't."

"Livvie?" he whispered.

"Papa." Relief edged her whisper. "Don't leave me." She gasped, and sobs shook her shoulders.

"Livvie, wake up." He kept his voice soft and low, so as not to frighten her. "You're having a bad dream. You're all right." The night's events must have shaken her to the core. Murderous thoughts overtook him when he imagined Jacob's hands on her.

Shifting away, her murmurs grew frantic.

Sam sensed her mounting panic. "Livvie? It's Sam. Remember?" He should have kept the candle lit.

Her head lifted slowly toward him. "Sam?"

"Yes. You're safe." He eased his grip. His worry that she might scream faded.

She clutched his shirt and sobbed into it.

"What's wrong?" He cradled her, yet not so tightly as to cause her worry.

She whispered, "My father's gone. I'm all alone."

He smoothed her hair. "No, you're not. You have

me."

Her crying halted abruptly, and she tensed. "What am I doing here?"

"You were struck ill."

"Oh, no. What time is it?" Too quickly, she sat up, groaning and holding a hand to her head.

He stroked her back. "Take it slow."

"I have to get back. Mrs. Crowell will…"

"Will what? She has no authority over you." He hoped she wasn't still too drunk to see reason.

"I cannot shame her household like this." She seemed to speak more to herself than to him.

"You did nothing shameful. Except drink like a sailor." He chuckled. "And fight like one. Remind me never to get on your bad side."

"This isn't funny." She stood in the darkness but wobbled back to the bed.

"I'll get you back safely. First I must put on my boots." He sat up and ran his hand through his hair.

"Oh, my." She steadied herself at the bedpost.

"What's wrong?" He'd hoped her stomach had settled, though readied himself to grab her and lunge for the door if needed.

"I was sick." She angled toward him. "And I was in your bed. With you. And—oh, no."

"Nothing happened, Livvie." His fingers searched out one boot and then the other. His foot wouldn't fit into the second. *Livvie's*. After finding his other boot, he located hers and lined them up beneath the bed.

"I remember more than nothing." Her tone held more wonder than accusation. "We…and you held me."

More than nothing, though less than he desired. The little taste had instilled an insatiable desire for more.

"Your chastity was preserved, milady."

"No one will believe that. My reputation will be ruined. Even my brother won't want me in his house."

"This is Key West, love. Like I told you, many things happen here the world never learns. If you hurry and put your boots on, no one will learn of this, especially not your brother."

She hoisted herself straight and grabbed the bed post. "My head is about to rupture."

"I'll help you." Bending on one knee, he clasped her calf and lifted her leg. If the indiscretion horrified her, she kept mum. He tugged her boot on and laced it, and then set to the other.

She clung to the bedpost as if it were a life ring. "I will never drink punch again. What was it, anyway?"

He stood. "Camperou. I warned you it would sneak up on you. The caracoa masks the Jamaican spirits."

"Caracoa. That's why it was so sweet. Until later, when it wasn't."

"Up you go." He slung her arm around his waist and held it there while he lifted her and dragged her to the door. "Mind the step." He hobbled outside, pulling her along.

"Ugh, what's that smell?"

He stifled a laugh. "You should recognize it. It came from you." He made sure to pass it swiftly, so as not to inspire a recurrence. "Shh," he whispered. "You'll wake your audience."

She turned her head away. "You must think I'm a terrible fool."

Something twinged inside him at her confession of humility. "No more than the rest of us."

Her feet dragged along.

As many times as he lifted her up, she sank again. "Are you all right?"

She nodded.

"We're going to have to do better than this, Livvie, if you want to be home before dawn."

"I'm sorry."

"I should be the one apologizing. I should never have kept you so late."

"It's my own fault, all of it. If I hadn't been angry at you, I wouldn't have drunk so much punch, or danced with that man, and certainly never have allowed him to bring me outside. If you hadn't come along when you did…"

"You might have seriously hurt Preston." She packed quite the wallop, from what he'd seen.

The Crowell house loomed in the night, quiet and dark. He pulled her onto the porch.

"Where is your room?" he whispered.

"Upstairs, to the rear."

Of course, it couldn't have been located in a more convenient location. Not a first-floor bedroom, nor near the steps.

He released his hold. She swayed and held her head. In her condition, she might not make it up the steps without rousing the household.

He cupped her face. "I'm going to carry you."

"What? No."

"It's your best chance of not disturbing the Crowells. No arguing. Or talking." He scooped her into his arms, and she linked her arms around his neck.

Inside the house, darkness overwhelmed all obstacles, no shapes visible. At least he'd been inside before and knew where the staircase lay. A straight climb to the second floor, and then left to the end, hopefully encountering no tables or lamps to break along the way.

Loud snores echoed down the hall. Another thing in their favor. The noise would mask any creaking stairs or floor boards.

He tiptoed the best he could up each step. The creak of bedsprings halted him, and her arms tightened around his neck. The snores continued, so he did, too. They reached the top without incident. The rail guided his steps—slow steps, because he couldn't see the end of the hall, and they would only find it by bumping into it.

One arm dropped from his neck and slid along the wall. Her other arm's grip on him tightened, and he stopped. She reached down to turn the doorknob, and a breeze wafted over them as she eased open the door. In three steps, his legs bumped the bed, and he set her atop it.

Her hold around his neck tightened. "Sam."

A door creaked open down the hall. "Olivia. Is that you?'

"Yes, Martha. Go back to sleep."

Shuffling footsteps neared. "I thought I heard someone."

"Only me." Livvie pushed the bedcovers down and lay against the pillows.

Sam crept around the bed, feeling his way along. He dropped silently to his hands and knees beside it, trying to gauge how far the window was, wondering what might lie beneath it to break his fall.

Martha continued her inquiry. "You were out in the hall?"

Livvie's sickly tone was not rehearsed. "I haven't felt well tonight. I've made several trips out back." She pulled a sheet across her.

"Using no lantern?"

"I didn't want to wake anyone. I'm sorry if I disturbed you."

Martha stood in the doorway holding a candle. "I could have used some assistance with the night pan."

"I'm not well, Martha. You should not come in."

"What is that smell?"

"I told you. I've been ill. I must have eaten something that upset my stomach."

"Well, young lady, that's what happens when you attend public outings in a dubious part of town."

"I must get some sleep. Good night, Martha. Please close the door. I forgot on my last trip."

The woman drew back her head and studied Livvie. "Good night."

The door clicked shut. A long exhale came from the bed, followed by the rustling of covers.

"Sam?" Her whisper came from directly above him.

He reached up and caught a strand of hair. Her hand closed around his, and he pushed himself up and leaned against the bed, kneeling.

His finger found her jaw, and traced along it. "Why were you angry earlier?"

"Because," she whispered.

Typical female reply, but it made him smile. "That's not a reason."

"I wanted you to dance, but you wouldn't. And that trollop gave me nasty looks, though she looked at you nicely enough."

A thrill went through him. "You're jealous."

"No!"

He held his finger against her lips. "Shhh." He lifted

her chin and pressed his nose to hers. "You are."

"You only want me to be jealous." Easing closer, her soft lips moved slowly against his.

His blood raced through his veins and pounded in his ears. Her skin was warm against his, and she held him so sweetly, his head clutched in her hands. Her words echoed in his head: *You only want me to be jealous.* Their calculating seductiveness stung him. He hadn't thought her capable of such manipulation. Perhaps her inexperience had led him to believe it, and all women were destined to flaunt their wiles as weapons as they aged. He pulled away.

When she leaned closer, he backed farther.

"What's wrong?" she whispered.

"I have to go." Pale pink light rimmed the horizon. Liam would be knocking at his door to rouse him.

She reached for him. "Now? Can't you stay a little longer?"

"Why? Haven't you tired of toying with me yet?" Though he'd meant it to insult her, he tensed while awaiting her response. The horizon brightened, and its pinkish orange glow suffused through the window.

She released a breath. "You knew my stay here was only temporary. I think you were the one toying with me."

Certainly, he had begun with that intention. Her pretty face and her bold spirit that dared him to challenge her both enticed him. Yet all the while, she'd surprised him at every turn. Matched his challenges, surpassed his expectations. Made him yearn for more.

Soon, she would be gone.

"When are you leaving?"

"I'm awaiting word from my brother. I expect he'll

book my passage on the next available ship."

"I see." The disappointment in his tone surprised even him. He wanted her to go, didn't he? She threatened his peace of mind. His way of life.

Her head lifted from the bed as her eyes searched his in the half-light.

"Livvie." Emotions struggled against one another— lust, affection, sorrow, regret. He wiped his hand across his mouth. Better to say nothing than to make promises that would return to haunt him in all their obstinate forms.

"I must be off." Rising, he stepped lightly to the window. Mr. Crowell's snores had grown lighter, so he must be close to waking. To be caught inside the house would cause an uproar that would come back upon him like a fifty-foot wave.

"I'll see you out." She crept from the bed.

He waved at her to stay. She shoo'd him on after opening a drawer.

The doorknob made no noise as he turned it, so he eased the door open. She clutched the back of his shirt, matching his steps so the footfalls sounded as one set shuffling down the hall, and then the steps.

She took his hand, tugging him down the hall to the back door. Opening it, he paused against its creak. When she pushed it open quickly, they darted outside. He stepped off the back stair, turning at her touch.

"What?" he whispered.

She slipped her arms around his neck. "This." Pressing her lips to his, her body fell against him, their heights evened by the single stair.

Their kiss was slow and delicious, making Sam forget his duties. Birds called in the trees, as yellow and orange clouds brightened the sky.

Finally, he lifted his lips from hers.

She clung to him. "Sam."

Although he tried to let his thoughts drift, to revel in the pleasant sensation giving no consideration to what was to come, his conscience wrestled with his emotions. "Hmm?"

She leaned away to look at him, her hands soft on his cheeks. "You could have taken me tonight, willingly. But you didn't."

He couldn't divine whether her voice held more disappointment or wonder. Definitely too much seriousness, so he forced a light air. "If you had been ill all over me, you'd have bruised my ego irreparably."

"I don't think that's the reason."

Before he could concoct a better excuse, she took hold of his head. "You are a good man. A wonderful man."

"No, Livvie. If that's what you see, you're looking at the wrong man. I'm a sinner. A simple wrecker. That's all I aim to be." The simpler his life, the better. His initial intention in coming here, yet here he was, complicating things.

Ducking her head, she pressed papers into his hand. "Here."

"What's this?" One look told him: her story. He'd meant to ask again, but he hadn't found the right time.

"Just some pages of my story. But I'll want your honest opinion." She wrapped her arms around his neck. "Come back tonight." She kissed his cheek, jaw, and ear.

He drew his lips across her ear. "We sail to Havana today. I won't be back until tomorrow, maybe the day after."

Easing away, she searched his face, her fingers splayed along his cheeks.

He studied her expression while it changed from sadness to disbelief to something like frustration. He opened his mouth, ready to tell her he'd see her soon, as soon as he returned. It was what she wanted to hear, he thought. What he wanted to say. But promises were sticky as honey, and sweetness soon separated from them, leaving only blandness and boredom. He could not be held to his word, except for his word to the *Florida*. His livelihood and lifestyle—it held no place for a woman.

He clenched his teeth to keep from betraying himself and slid his hands down her back to her waist, holding her a moment longer so he could take her all in. With a quick kiss, he said goodbye, then strode down the side path to Duvall Street. The rising sun cast a long shadow before him when he walked seaward.

Chapter Fifteen

The *Florida* caught a tail wind and reached Havana as the sun set.

Captain Howe stood at the rail. "Set anchor. We've arrived too late. We'll make port in the morning." He looked toward the mahogany-planked wharf lining the port, where Spanish man-of-war ships were moored beside smaller boats. Too crowded to navigate safely past sundown, incoming vessels were barred until the next day.

Liam settled beside Sam on the deck. "Too bad we left so late."

Sam worked a nautical knot. "We can make an early start tomorrow."

"But tonight we're deprived of Havana's beauties and excellent spirits."

"All the less for Millie to be angry about after we return."

"Millie will be touched by yer concern." Liam's smile faded. "I suspect she's not at home embroidering while I'm gone."

Sam was relieved the conversation centered on Liam's love life and not his own. "She's popular. Free to do whatever she chooses."

Liam held his hands on his knees. "As am I."

Sam wouldn't point out that Millie was one of a handful of available women in Key West. "She does take to you, though."

"Most of the time." Liam knit his brows and stared off at nothing in particular.

"She's not beholden to you. You always said you preferred it so, correct?"

"I have. Now I'm considering other options."

His friend's admission took Sam by surprise. "Such as?"

Liam slid his gaze to Sam. "I'm not getting any younger, my boy. A man likes to put down roots when the time is right."

"You're joking." His friend had celebrated his forty-second birthday over the summer by out-drinking every man in the groggery and had been the first to report to the *Florida* the next day. While in Key West, he favored Millie's companionship. In Havana, he slathered his charms on every willing woman. He'd always spoken of marriage as a condition of weak-minded men.

Liam stood. "Where's Cook and our supper?"

Sam stared open-mouthed, unsure of what to make of the sudden change of topic and mood.

"I'll go see." Liam strode toward the entrance to the lower hold and disappeared below. He returned some time later to announce dinner and went below again.

Sam stowed the ropes away and pushed himself up. He walked downstairs, filled his plate with fish, and ate alongside the crew. He talked and joked as usual, all the while feeling he stood outside himself, watching his own actions. Not until he settled on deck atop his bedroll and lay beneath the stars did the strange sensation leave him.

The four stars of the Southern Cross spread wide above him. A navigation point for sailors, the constellation indicated their location. Nonetheless, Sam felt lost in the vast interior of himself, devoid of definitive markers except those jagged edges imprinted by his past. Experiences best forgotten, unless their memory served as warning to avoid similar pitfalls.

Sam was not a praying man. He felt no need to attend Sunday services. Not while he could look out his window at the great expanse of shifting sea and skies, consumed by such a calm that could only come from the great beyond. Not while he could sail to another island, untouched by humans, to sense the stillness beyond the rush of water or the calling of birds. Beyond the great stillness came the hum of the universe in its intricate motions, like the workings of an immense clock moving in its own particular rhythm. The silence beneath which was layered the murmur of the heavens, the hushed whisperings of another realm, a realm unknown, yet familiar. He had never spoken such thoughts to anyone, but the insistent longing to share it with Livvie now surprised him. To open himself up in that way would be to invite another catastrophe of the heart.

Havana's lights reflected on the water. As the sky darkened, the glow rose toward the heavens, full of music, laughter, and the everyday sounds of people's lives. Sounds that, tonight, echoed through the hollow ache inside him for hours.

****

Clouds cut the heat of the day, worsened by the paved stone streets. Sam walked beside Liam along the narrow street, too narrow for pedestrians, cargo-laden mules and those odd-looking carriages called *volantes*. The wreckers were obliged to duck into the large carriageway constructed in a building to allow a *volante* to pass. The driver raised his whip to the horse's flank repeatedly.

Liam aimed a disapproving glare at the driver. "I'm thankful not to be a horse on this island."

"Or any other," Sam joked. He'd never been much of a horseman, but the constant lashings the *volante* rig horses received at the hands of the drivers made him flinch.

When it rolled away, they stepped behind it.

"Jasper said we missed the lottery by a day," Liam said.

"Mmm. Too bad." The monthly Havana lottery incited a frenzy among its citizens. Sam was not sorry to have missed the excitement.

"Shall we join the nightly promenade to the governor's palace? Perhaps we can find some pretty Havana girls who'll let us join their parade."

"If you'd like."

Liam cast an appraising eye on Sam. "Yer enthusiasm for Cuba has waned, I fear."

"Not at all. I said we can go if you like."

Grumbling, Liam waved away the argument.

Already, music floated through the streets.

Fearing the verbal backlash sure to follow, Sam said, "We can cut through this way to be ahead of them."

Liam held back when Sam veered down a side street.

"Well come on. You don't want the captain-general to have all the beautiful girls, do you?" If nothing else, a pretty girl's smile would divert Liam's attention from Sam.

Liam followed begrudgingly until they reached the intersecting street. The crowd came into view, laughing and singing as they marched or rode. His tentative grin opened into a full-fledged smile as females of every age passed.

Liam fell into step beside a woman who batted her eyes, ducking her chin in an alluring fashion. Sam filed in behind, glad to be rid of Liam's glare.

A merchant led a mule-drawn wagon loaded with sea shells at the end of the promenade. Sam stepped out of the crowd to wait for it. He picked up a basket constructed entirely of shells. The man called out its price, a bit steeper than Sam had anticipated. The thought of Livvie's face as he presented it to her made him dig out the coins, handing them to the merchant. Navigating through the dips and swells of the moving crowd, he made his way to his former position behind Liam. The parade came to a stop outside the palace.

Laughing, Liam sang off-key, clapping, his face close to the woman's. He glanced at Sam, his gaze flicking to the basket at Sam's hip. Sam jerked his head toward the quay where the schooner was docked. Liam turned his back to him until the music ended.

Sam stepped to his side. "It's nearly sunset. We can't be late."

Frowning, Liam bowed to kiss the woman's hand, and lingered there.

"We must go now." Sam nodded to the woman, forcing a curt smile.

"Hold up, now, I'm coming." Liam jogged to his side. "I'd have liked a bit more time with that one."

Sam grunted in agreement, though he'd felt no sentiment resembling his friend's on this trip. Women had smiled at him in that certain way, several very beautiful women, in fact, yet he had no desire to accept their unspoken invitations. Their warmth only made him think more of Livvie.

As much as he wanted to break away from her, his heartstrings pulled him back double. She was headstrong as a mule. Such a temperament was necessary for life in the Keys, where sharp-toothed dangers lurked in shallow waters or crawled on poisonous pincers along branches, where people needed strong backs to stand against tide and wind.

Love—he knew nothing of it, really. All affairs of the heart appeared transient, shifting like the tides from one shore to another. Women themselves were transient, as changeable as the tide. And less predictable.

The basket would make a nice keepsake. The vision of her boarding a ship made him realize: she was leaving. Soon. The realization had him feeling hollow as the sails, holding nothing more substantial than air.

"Feeling all right, Samuel?" Liam slapped his back.

"Nothing a drink wouldn't heal. You did gather everything on your list, didn't you?"

"Aye, I have all I need. Same as always."

Sam wondered if that were true but thought better of asking. Liam would laugh at him, call him a lovesick fool. And he might be right.

Chapter Sixteen

An hour before sunrise, the *Florida* followed its daily duty, sailing along the outlying reef. Sam leaned against the rail, his gaze aimed outward, while his thoughts raged inward. Sleep had eluded him again last night. Today his mood plummeted. Not even Liam's humor could raise it, so his friend had taken leave of his sour company. Losing Barnaby had made Sam acutely aware of his helplessness against the forces of nature. Not the least of which was the intense churning Livvie stirred within him. She might have been Aphrodite herself, plucked from a shell like a perfect pearl, instead of a shipwrecked girl caught in the foamy mouth of the sea.

Jasper stood with Isum at the bow, surveying the horizon.

Straightening, Isum strained against the rail. "A ship."

Sam roused from his place to join them. The ship's sails had been lowered. Likely it had run aground on the reef.

Captain Howe strode to the bow. "Aye. Set the rudder, Jahner. She may be in need of assistance."

The *Florida* raced ahead, then dropped anchor alongside the ship. Captain Howe hailed the ship's captain, who invited him aboard. Howe returned looking dismayed. "We're obliged to wait, men. The captain refuses our aid."

"He'll soon change his mind," Liam said.

Hopefully sooner rather than later, Sam thought. He had a bad feeling about this job. Stubborn captains may have been a boon to masters of industry, but they were a bane to wreckers. Their poor decisions sometimes cost more than time.

For two days, the *Florida* waited with five other wrecker schooners while the ship's crew tried various methods to free it from the reef. On the third day, when the ship's captain signaled, Captain Howe went aboard again. Returning this time, he yelled, "We've work to do, men. Look alive."

The crew gathered around. "There's cotton in the lower hold. We'll salvage it first; much of it's not yet underwater. I went below, heartened to see it's accessible by stair."

"Any other cargo?" Jasper asked.

"Corn and grain are below, to the aft," Captain Howe said.

The men needed no further instructions. All flew into action like cogs of a well-maintained machine.

A stream of men converged on the ship from the *Florida*, while other wreckers drew nearer. The stairway to the lower hold wasn't wide enough to allow to and fro movement, so the men moved in a group going below and then climbing back up.

Carrying up the cotton, Sam joked to Liam, "I'll almost feel guilty being paid for such easy work."

The fair weather contributed to the rest of the crew's high spirits. They brought bale after bale up from below to be offloaded to the schooner. When cotton filled the wrecker, it hoisted sail to Key West, and another wrecker maneuvered alongside the ship in its place.

"It hardly seems like work, eh?" Liam held his face up to the sun.

As the *Florida* came to shore, Isum jumped out, running to the warehouse to fetch the horse and wagon. The Conch's long muscular legs made him the crew's fastest runner.

After some minutes, the wagon came into view. Sam joined the others in readying the cargo for offloading. While the Conch backed the wagon toward the boat, the men formed a line to hand down cotton. Once the wagon could hold no more, Isum clicked to the horse. The wheels had sunk slightly into the sand, so five men pushed the back to boost it from its place. Sam walked alongside with Liam, the others following to the warehouse.

Liam announced the cargo of the ship to the warehouse caretaker. After the clerk noted it in the register, the men removed the cotton to the specified corner.

While Sam lifted a container from the wagon, a passing buggy caught his eye. Livvie rode in the back beside Mrs. Locke.

He stepped toward the carriage. "Hello."

Turning, Livvie met his gaze, smiling. "Mr. Langhorne." She touched the driver's arm, and the buggy stopped.

Wiping his sleeve across his sweaty brow, Sam strode to the buggy. "Good afternoon, Miss Collins, Mrs. Locke. What brings you here?"

"We grew concerned about the ship. Are its passengers all right?"

"Oh, yes. They should be arriving soon. The captain

finally allowed us to assist him. We're removing the cargo now, in hopes we can budge her off the reef once she's lighter. They can get underway again if there's no damage."

"What a relief for everyone. You, too, I imagine."

He took heart when relief showed in Livvie's face as well. For three days, he hadn't called on her; she must have wondered why. In all that time, he hadn't had a proper chance to read her pages, either. He needed solitude for that. The boat's close quarters had provided none.

"Waiting was beginning to get tiresome." He might have told her she occupied his thoughts every minute. For once, the old biddy's presence aided him.

The Conch whistled, steering the wagon toward shore.

Sam touched his fingers to his forehead in salute. "Duty calls. Good to see you, ladies. This area will get busy very soon. I recommend not lingering."

"No, we had no intention of lingering." Mrs. Locke pursed her lips.

Livvie smiled. "Thank you, Mr. Langhorne. Take care."

He caught up to the wagon, hopping inside next to Liam.

"The girl appears everywhere you are lately, Sam. Some coincidence, eh?"

"She was concerned about the ship's passengers."

"Mm, yes. I'm certain there's nothing more to her visit." Liam's feigned innocence could not hide his mirth.

Sam turned away to hide his grin. Her gaze held such concern, such warmth, he found it infectious. The warmth took root deep inside him. He glanced back. The buggy moved along slowly. Livvie looked his way. Sunlight illuminated her face, her beautiful lips turned up in a smile. For him.

The sight arrested him. Not since Helen had a woman bewitched him so. Casting all hesitancy aside, he hoped this job would go quickly. He planned to pay a visit soon. Very soon.

****

After returning to the wreck, the men busied themselves in menial tasks while they waited their turn alongside the tall ship. The schooner's tightly run operation was no accident. The crew busied themselves tying knots and keeping the schooner in top shape.

By midmorning the next day, all the cotton had been offloaded to the warehouse. Captain Howe grew more irritated watching the ship turning on the reef. He'd complained many times of foolish commanders who caused more damage than necessary by hesitating to accept help. Water now leaked into the ship's lower holds. Captain Howe ordered the men to move quickly to remove the remaining corn and grain. Dark clouds gathered, and the winds had sharply increased. An ill portent.

"This will require more of our skills, men." Captain drew a crude map to show where the goods lay below. "With any luck, our weather will hold until we've finished. Let's move quickly."

Sam reached for the grapple hook.

Jasper tugged it away. "I'll go first. You can go later, when the storm hits."

"Ah, you're so considerate." Sam smacked his diving mate's wide shoulder.

Jasper slipped into the water carrying the hooked line. Divers from each wrecker plunged beneath the surface soon after.

Sam waited by the line, feeling uneasy. Tendrils of lightning blazed from distant clouds. "Looks like we're in for it."

"Like Jasper said, we'll be below during the storm. He'll have to keep the ship steady above." Liam's light tone belied his worry.

The wait grew too long, and Sam's feeling of foreboding grew. "Shouldn't they be up? None have yet come up, have they?"

Liam narrowed his eyes and scanned the other schooners. "I had the same thought." He turned to Sam. "We should ready to go below, just in case."

A tug on the line signaled Jasper was ready to come up. Liam moved to the pulley and cranked the handle. The rope jerked wildly. The tugs grew in frequency and intensity.

"Something's wrong." Liam cranked faster.

Sam rushed to the side and searched for any sign of the diver. There was none.

"I'm not waiting any longer." He dove over the side and aimed for a dark figure. Jasper's arms and legs flailed, and he swam crazily, legs and arms splayed in every direction except up. Sam grabbed his arm to signal he was there to help. Slipping his arm around Jasper's chest, he pumped his legs and free arm to get him to the surface quickly. The huge man's weight slowed Sam considerably, until Jasper followed his movements and aimed upward.

Gasping, Sam grabbed for the boat when they burst through the water. "Someone help him in."

Two men reached overboard to haul Jasper aboard. Scrabbling onto the schooner, he sat, bracing himself against the deck, his eyes wide and wild.

Captain Howe pushed through the gathering crowd. "What happened down there?"

Jasper jerked his head toward the captain, though looked beyond. "Captain?"

Captain Howe's gaze intensified. "Yes, of course, it's me, Jasper. What went on below?"

Trembling, Jasper lowered his gaze, looking at nothing. "I found the opening, right where you said it would be. The others swam toward it at the same time. The first came out quick, waving like a madman, holding his head. I went next. As soon as I got inside, my eyes burned like they were on fire."

Shouts sounded from two other boats. "They're blind! They're blind!"

Terror shot through Sam. He glanced at Liam, whose grimace betrayed the same horror.

Captain Howe crouched next to Jasper. "Good God, man. Are you blind?"

Tears welled in Jasper's wide eyes. "Yes, sir. I am."

The captain touched his shoulder. "Get him below. See what you can do."

"Now what, sir?"

"I must confer with the ship's captain. The cargo should have been corn and linens. Unless the dyes leaked…." Captain Howe's face twisted into a grim mask. He strode away, calling for Jahner to bring the schooner alongside the wreck.

Tension filled the air. The men watched their captain go aboard hailing the other officer. The two men talked, their faces stern, their movements stiff. The ship's captain flailed his arms while Captain Howe shook his head.

Beyond, lightning streaked through roiling clouds, closing in fast.

"Bloody hell. He wants us to go back down." Dread flattened Liam's voice.

"Impossible. We'd send more men to their doom. It's not even a risk—every man who dove is now blind. For what? Ruined corn? Washed-out linens?"

"I know." Liam set his gaze on Sam. "Still, a contract is a contract. Captain may have no choice."

"The circumstances warrant a change in the contract. Certainly Captain Howe knows Judge Marvin would recognize that."

Liam's brows twitched. "We'll see."

Captain Howe's look of dread reboarding the *Florida* spoke volumes. "We have to give it one more try." He called to the first mate, "Spread the word. One more dive. Using utmost caution."

Through cupped hands, the first mate yelled to the nearest schooner. The word echoed from wrecker to wrecker. Each crew met the news in wide-eyed amazement or uncertainty.

Sam stepped forth. "I'll go."

The captain's response was quick. "No." He pointed to Isum. "Ready yourself. At the first sign of trouble, return to the *Florida*."

Isum's wide eyes held fear and hatred.

Sam touched the captain's sleeve. "But Captain, I have more experience."

Captain Howe glared at him. "Are you challenging my command, Mr. Langhorne?"

Sam stepped back. "No, sir."

"Assist your mate and keep quiet."

Sam sneered, "Yes, sir."

Captain Howe hesitated, his gaze boring into Sam. Sam kept his attention ahead, wiping the emotion from his face the best he could.

Bearing the somberness of a man approaching the gallows, Isum readied himself. His dignity and grace while he plunged into the water filled Sam with sorrowful pride.

Bending over the side, he whispered urgent pleas for him to return quickly. The seconds ticked by like hours. Tension made Sam's breath more ragged. "Come on, Isum."

Liam came to Sam's side. "Any sign of him?"

"Not yet."

They waited together.

Finally, the rope jerked.

Liam pointed. "There." Before Sam could respond, Liam dove into the water, landing at the man's side to help him to the boat.

Grabbing Isum, Sam drew him up.

Isum gasped, falling to the deck. Rubbing his eyes, he shook his head.

Captain Howe stood over him. "Are you all right, man?" Hope edged his stern tone.

Isum blinked rapidly. "The water burned my eyes, so I closed them. I tried to feel my way back out. I couldn't, so I had to open them to find my way."

"Are you blind?"

His gaze jerked from man to man. "I see shapes." His voice shook. "All I see are shapes."

As divers returned to the other boats, the cry arose again: "They're blind! They're blind!"

Sam clenched his teeth. The crew should not have been put in harm's way. His blood boiled at the injustice.

"Take him below. See what you can do for him." Captain Howe's steady gaze met Sam's. "That's all. I'll inform the ship's captain there's no more we can do. When I return, we head for shore."

After the wrecker pulled aside the ship, Captain Howe boarded. The two captains argued. Howe came back to the *Florida*, his internal struggle obvious in his abrupt movements. "The captain chooses to stay. Cast off."

Sam exchanged a knowing glance with Liam.

"But the storm—" Jahner said.

"I told him he was putting his crew at risk. We'll return later to offer assistance again. It's all I can do for now. We must tend to our wounded."

One by one, the boats turned to shore. The gusting winds hastened their journey to the wharf. Two or three men from each schooner had to be pulled to the dock, their arms helplessly outstretched, their wide eyes unseeing.

Sam sickened at the sight. He helped secure the schooner.

Captain gave word for three of the boats to return to the ship after taking care of their crews.

Liam slapped Sam's back. "We need a trip to the groggery. What do you say?"

He nodded. "An extended trip."

The two walked in solemn silence across the docks and into the street. Rain pelted their backs, barely penetrating Sam's consciousness.

All the wreckers were apparently of one mind. The groggery's crowd grew to capacity.

Sam signaled the bartender. "Two whiskeys, please."

Liam grunted. "No, no. Not by the glass today. Send a bottle over." Pulling a chair away from a table, he plopped into it.

"You're right. By the glass would take too long." Sam's chair scraped across the floor, and he sat.

Three other wreckers joined them, as sullen-looking as Sam felt.

Jahner emptied his glass. "Doc's got his hands full today."

"Think he can help them?" someone asked.

"Maybe. If Isum wasn't blinded completely, there may be hope for some sight to return, at least."

Blinded. Jasper's life ruined in less than five minutes. Better he'd have drowned than been blinded.

Or better Sam had. The guilt weighed on him greater than a tall ship itself.

While the others continued their banter, it barely registered in Sam's mind.

"Perhaps he'll see again. Depends on the damage."

"What caused it?"

"Fermented corn, I heard."

"And dyes. Cargo sat too long underwater."

"If he hadn't kept us waiting so long, we could have cleared his hold without disaster."

"Maybe the captain didn't divulge all the cargo below."

"I hope the ship crumbles to pieces on the reef. And its captain too."

"No man deserves death, even one so stupid."

"His crew deserve better, for sure."

"Captain Howe did his best to persuade him. The

pig-headed goat wouldn't budge."

Afternoon became evening, which bled to night. The storm howled outside, battering the windows. The men held their places and awaited word from Captain Howe. The bartender stayed busy filling drink orders long past midnight.

Sam turned to bleary-eyed Liam. "My vision's been affected too." And his speech. His words slurred together almost nonsensically.

"Eh?" Liam grunted, trying to lift his gaze. "Time to go," he mumbled and pushed himself to a wobbly stand.

Sam raised his head. "Need a hand?" he tried to say, but the resulting sound garbled into nonsense.

Waving him off, Liam weaved his way through tables to the door. He fumbled the door open, steadying himself against the door jamb. Although a breeze blew in, the rain appeared to have stopped. He shuffled outside and was gone.

Sam rested his head against his arm.

Someone shook his shoulder. "Let's go, lad. We're closing."

He raised his head and waved in recognition.

The bartender moved from table to table, rousing drunken patrons. One by one, they rose and stumbled out. One fell to the floor, and another dragged him by his shoulders.

Sam inhaled and laid his palms on the tabletop. His head felt overfilled with sloshing, disconnected brains. His senses functioned enough to see a half-full bottle of whiskey still on the table, and he held it like a rudder and steered himself outside.

The wind refreshed his senses, but he couldn't go home yet. He wandered back toward the wharf and leaned against a palm tree, where he slid down to the sand.

Reddish yellow light rimmed the horizon. "Red sky at night, sailor's delight. Red sky at morning, sailors take warning." He chuckled. "Too late for warnings."

Light bled across the wide sky and the outline of the foundered ship emerged, rocking while waves struck it again and again against the reef.

"Too late for warnings," he whispered.

Chapter Seventeen

Livvie dressed early and went downstairs. Snatches of song drifted from the back of the house, and she walked down the hallway into the kitchen. Florie bustled about, humming.

"Morning, Florie. I'm going for a walk." She headed for the door.

Florie worked a rag against the counter. "So early, miss?"

"Yes. I'm concerned about the ship. I'm going to try to learn how it fared in the storm last night."

Wide-eyed, Florie waved the rag. "Oh, I heard the wreckers came up blind from their dive."

"What?" Fear iced Livvie's spine. "Surely not all."

"Some from each boat. 'Bout twenty, in all."

She clutched the door handle. "What about Sam— Mr. Langhorne?"

The housekeeper wiped her hands against her apron. "I didn't hear his name mentioned. Most were coloreds. The ones who do the deep diving."

Livvie's thoughts raced. Sam was among those who dove deep. Panic welled up, threatening to choke her.

Florie chattered on, oblivious to Livvie's despair. "The storm kept me awake most of the night. All that booming."

Livvie hadn't been able to sleep, either. Not for fear of the lightning. She'd worried about Sam. And now that worry continued, with urgency. "Is there anything you need from the market while I'm out?"

"You're a sweet child. No, I went yesterday before the storm and brought enough back for three days."

Livvie pulled open the door. "Would you tell Mrs. Crowell, then? I don't believe she's up yet."

"The storm probably kept her up too. I'll tell her. You be careful now."

"Thank you, Florie. I will." She stepped into the morning sunshine. The usual sense of freedom eluded her, replaced by a sense of foreboding. She had to find Sam.

Her footsteps echoed along the wet streets littered by grit. Inside the homes she passed, faint movement appeared through windows, people beginning their days. Farther into town, a few carts squeaked along the streets near the market. She turned toward the wharf. The *Florida* floated at its dock. A few crew men slept on the deck, caps covering their faces. Sam was not among them.

On the reef beyond, the ship listed to the left. Three schooners were moored nearby.

What a wretched business, having to wait helplessly nearby and watch a ship be dashed to pieces.

She sighed, not knowing whether Sam might be aboard one of those schooners. Waiting here would be useless. Hours or a day might pass before anything happened.

She turned and headed back toward town, halting at the sight of a figure slumped against a tree on the beach. As she approached, his familiarity grew. "Sam." She hurried to him. "Sam!"

Grumbling, he waved her away.

"Sam, it's me. Olivia." When he didn't respond, she said more forcefully, "It's Livvie."

He squinted up at her, his face absent his usual ready smile. "Livvie." He looked out over the sea, to where the ship rocked against the reef.

She laid her hand on his shoulder. "Are you all right?"

He gave a bitter laugh. "Yeah, fine. I can see all too well." He swiped his arm across his forehead.

Relief swept over her. So he wasn't blinded. She crouched beside him. "Have you slept at all?"

Even sitting, he wobbled. "Noooo. We're waiting. The ship's captain might decide he needs us. Might need more men to throw themselves to their doom."

Her grip tightened. "Sam, what happened?" He'd had a long night of drinking, to be sure. Not in celebration. Something terrible hung in the air, some unspoken threat.

At her touch, he dropped his chin to his chest and held a hand to his forehead. "Twenty men," he muttered. "Twenty men sacrificed themselves for that bloody stupid captain."

She gasped. "Oh, my God. Did all twenty men die?"

"Worse. They're blind." He turned to her, his reddened eyes blazing. "Do you know what's the worst part, Livvie? It should have been me." His voice broke in anguish. "It should have been me."

"No, don't say that." Her skin chilled at the thought.

"It's true. I wanted to go down. Jasper stepped ahead of me. He came up blind, same as all the divers on the other boats. Captain Howe said we had to make another dive, but sent Isum instead. Do you know why?"

Dread filled her. She didn't want to hear the

explanation. "No. Tell me."

His smile, like his voice, cracked. "Because the Conches are always sent first when it's most dangerous."

Shocked, she sputtered, "But you said they're free men."

"Free," he spat the word. "They're still slaves to money. If they refuse to dive, they lose their jobs."

"How awful!" Even here, no justice existed.

Sam pressed his lips together, his bleary eyes wetted by tears.

"Let's go. I'm taking you home. You can't sit here all night and day."

He turned to her, his smile lopsided. "You're taking me home? Aren't you afraid I'll take advantage of you?"

She grabbed his arm. "Let's go. To your feet."

He grabbed the whiskey bottle and held it up. "Empty." He sounded surprised and devastated.

"We'll get you some water to drink. Maybe some coffee later. All right?" She tugged. "Up."

He snorted. "You're mighty bossy." Peering up, he swayed.

"When I need to be, yes. Come on." She pulled, using all her might.

Grabbing her, he struggled up from the ground.

She toppled under his weight. "The tree. Hold onto the tree."

He finally managed to straighten his legs—for the most part. He belched loudly. "'Scuse me."

"I hope we can do this," she said, more to herself than to him.

He held up a hand. "One second." He took a deep breath and straightened his spine. "Oh, never sleep against a tree."

"Or drink an entire bottle of whiskey." She held his waist and chest. "Let's try this."

He stumbled ahead. "Liam."

"What about him?" She glanced down the narrow strip of sand for a body, hoping not to see one.

"He wanted to help me finish it off."

Relief washed over her. "I see. And where is Liam?"

He swiped at the air. "Home. Hours ago."

"You should have gone home too."

"Couldn't. Had to keep watch."

His shortened sentences seemed to help him focus on walking. His steadfast pace surprised her.

"Someone else will watch now. You must rest."

"Yes, Livvie, dearest." He chuckled, looking down at her, his brows knit. "Why are you here?"

"I'm helping you home."

Half a smile crossed his lips. "You came looking for me."

Since it wasn't a question, she didn't deny it. "Let's get you to bed."

He gasped. "Why, I'm shocked, Miss Collins. You're a brazen hussy."

She flashed a weak smile at a passing man. "No more talking, Mr. Langhorne. Just walk."

He winced. "You won't allow me any fun, will you?"

"Not at my expense."

His feet stopped as though mired in quicksand. "I would never hurt you."

"Come on, Sam. Keep moving." Her shoves were useless.

"You know I would never hurt you, don't you, Livvie?"

His desperate pleading touched her, and she struggled to keep her voice even. "Yes, Sam. I know. Please walk."

He shuffled on. "You wound me."

"I'm sorry."

Their stumbling steps finally brought them to Sam's door.

"Do you have a key?" she asked.

"I don't lock it." He reached for the doorknob and pulled her inside.

She helped him to the bed. "I'll get you some water."

He clutched her skirt. "You won't leave me, will you?"

She peeled his fingers away. "I'm simply getting you some water."

His other hand grasped the fabric again. "Say you'll stay."

To deny him in this sad condition would be cruel.

She softened her voice. "Sam." Her heart ached, seeing him so vulnerable, in such pain. She laid her palm against his cheek, and he nuzzled into it. She yearned to take him in her arms, tell him it would be all right. Instead, she gently pushed him back onto the pillows.

He gave a long exhale and rested his forearm across his eyes.

She untied his boots and tugged them away, then his socks.

She poured a glass of water from the carafe on his dresser and brought it to him. "Here, drink a bit."

He raised his arm, grabbing her wrist. "Sit by me."

Her nerves tightened, every inch of her aware of him. "All right." She perched at the edge of the bed, by his legs. Outside, someone called to someone else, and she tensed. If anyone were to catch her here, gossip would surely follow her. Possibly all the way to New Orleans.

His grip tightened. "Closer."

She tried to hide her nervousness while she inched nearer, until he loosened his hold.

"There." His smile lazy, he relaxed against the pillow.

She presented the glass. "Drink."

His fingers entwined through hers around the glass. "Will you kiss me if I do?" He held her gaze. His tousled hair and unshaven face should have repelled her, yet instead held a strange attraction. She found it difficult to resist him. "Not today. Your breath smells too heavily of whiskey."

He took the cup and rested it against his chest, studying it. His gaze flicked to hers. "If not today, perhaps tomorrow?"

She suppressed a smile. "Maybe."

"Maybe." His eyes shone, and he brought the cup to his lips. Emitting a jagged sigh, he eased down on the pillow. "Maybe." He placed the cup on his ribs. "Events prevented me from reading your pages. I'm sorry."

"No need to apologize." Her story seemed flimsy in comparison to what had transpired these past few days.

"I intend to read them. And I will." His eyes drifted shut.

"I know. Get some rest." She slipped the glass from his grasp, smoothed his hair against his forehead, and eased upward.

He grabbed her hand and dragged it across his lips.

Her mouth dropped open at the touch of his stubbly

whiskers. They scraped her skin, leaving their mark deep inside.

"You said you'd stay." He cradled her palm to his chest.

"I can't." Despite her effort, mounting fear crept into her voice.

His face looked as angelic as a little boy. "Just until I fall asleep. I won't be able to sleep unless you're here." His gaze holding hers, he squeezed her hand.

His sincerity melted her heart. "All right. Until you fall asleep."

He swallowed hard. "Good." His eyes fluttered shut.

Watching him lie there, a tenderness welled within her. The horrors of the previous day still lay evident in his knit brow, his firm grasp. Even roughened from lack of sleep, his striking features, his long-lashed eyes and full mouth, took away her breath. He was beautiful. His nose widened at the nostrils, slightly flared, sometimes giving him an annoyed appearance. She ached to trace her finger along the curve of his full lips, wishing she could feel those lips against her own. While sober, this time, so she could fully remember it. Hazy memory didn't allow her to relive it properly beyond the overwhelming sensation. Whether caused by the drink, or Sam, she couldn't be sure.

She'd allowed two other boys to kiss her in her lifetime. One had less experience than she, if his slapping kiss were any indication. The second had barely touched his lips to hers before his fingers wandered too far up from her waist; she'd pushed him away and then run. For once, she wanted to know the touch of a man who knew what he was doing, who would know how to arouse her. Unless her dreams had embroidered upon the memory, he certainly had the other night.

He'd spoken correctly when he said her writing about relationships would be a fiction. She knew nothing firsthand, however much she longed to. Since meeting Sam, such thoughts grew to vivid imaginings, consuming all ration and reason.

Sam clutched her like a lifeline, his strong grip warming her.

The feelings rising up were unlike any she'd ever experienced. While his breath evened out, hers grew more rapid. Her fingers fluttered across his chiseled chest, to his navel.

He turned his head. The sound he gave—half moan, half sigh—sounded an intimate signal, inviting her to curl next to him. His breathing deepened. When his shirt fell open, his revealed skin aroused more than her curiosity.

A loud snore snapped from him as he rolled away, releasing her. She was free.

She told herself to leave now, before she allowed herself to get into deeper trouble than she'd ever known.

The narrowness of his waist invited her touch, her kiss to his hip. Oh, such sweet trouble it would be.

Easing from the bed, she pressed her lips to his forehead. "Sleep well, Sam."

Opening the door, she paused to look at him. How easy it would be to stay.

Footsteps outside reminded her of the precarious situation. She shut the door until they passed, glancing out the window before opening it again.

"Maybe tomorrow, Sam." The door clicked shut behind her. She cut down a side path to the next street and headed home.

****

Time had stretched immeasurably since Livvie had left this morning. She walked to the kitchen house, where Florie sang in loopy rhythm. The cook would be able to give her an idea of the time and whether anyone had asked after her.

She pushed open the door. "Hello, Florie."

Florie's smile quickly faded. "Miss Collins. Are you all right?"

"Yes, I'm fine. Why do you ask?"

Narrowing her eyes, Florie appraised her. "You look different somehow. Did something happen?"

"No. I ran into Mr. Langhorne. He was rather ill. I had to get a friend to bring him home." Her earlier feeling of treading in precarious territory returned. This subject could only lead to more questions. She had to change it. Now. "He'd been waiting all night for the ship's captain to signal for help. Apparently they never did. At least all of the twenty wreckers who were blinded survived. Such terrible news."

Florie's sharp gaze penetrated uneasily. "Mmm. Are you sure there's nothing else?"

The woman's uncanny senses picked up on Livvie's excitement.

"I'm disturbed to hear such awful tidings, of course. Has Mrs. Crowell been out?"

"Yes. It's nearly lunchtime. You missed breakfast."

"I wasn't hungry." Although her stomach fluttered, her hunger was definitely not for food.

"You're not going to eat? I made a special chicken salad, very light and delicious."

Livvie could always divert the cook's attention by speaking of food. "Yes, I'll have lunch. May I assist you?"

Florie waved a dish rag at her. "No, you'll get me in trouble with Mrs. Crowell again. You go on inside and wash up."

Walking up the stone path, everything looked different. Florie was right. She felt far removed from the girl who'd left a few hours earlier, as if another dimension had opened to her. She had glimpsed that which so many authors wrote with such authority. The key now was to learn to navigate the new territory.

Chapter Eighteen

Pounding on the door startled Sam from sleep. He jerked upward. The pounding in his head worsened.

"Go away." He fell back to the pillow.

The door muffled Liam's rough voice. "If you want to keep your job, you'll get up now. Awake or no, we've work to do." Muttering, he added, "If the sorry-assed lad can't take his liquor, he shouldn't drink."

Blinking, Sam sat up. His eyes felt drier than the Sahara; an unnamable ick lined his mouth. "Liam."

"What?"

Rolling off the bed, he shuffled to the door. Outside, Liam sat on the doorstep, holding his head in his hands.

Sam chuckled, but immediately stopped when it caused his head to almost burst. "I'm not the only one suffering."

"Aye, misery loves company. Let's go." Liam sat, unmoving.

"I'm coming. Let me put on my boots." He shuffled back to the bed, reaching for the spot on the floor where his boots usually sat. He found only empty air. Strange. He always set his boots exactly there, so he could find them no matter what condition he was in. When he bent further to look for them, the lightness in his head made him sway.

Liam grumbled outside.

"Hold on. I can't find my boots. I don't understand

where…" Realization struck him. He hadn't been the one to take off his boots.

His memory of yesterday returned in bits. Livvie finding him at the beach. Helping him walk home, acting as his crutch. Sitting at his bedside. The last memory he had was of holding her hand, asking her to stay. Ah, hell. Had he really been so pathetic? Yet she had stayed.

A wave of renewal washed over him, refreshing Sam from the inside out.

Clattering came from the doorway. Liam lurched against the door jamb. "What in the name of all that's good and holy are ye doing just sitting there, grinning like a fool? Have ye lost yer mind?"

"Not my mind. Perhaps another part of me." To say any more to Liam was to invite ridicule. "And my boots."

"Are ye daft? They're right there." He pointed.

Sam followed his finger. "Ah. So they are." He bent to retrieve them, and his earlier nausea hardly registered. All he felt was Livvie's touch, her brushing away his hair, soothing his brow.

Liam set his fists at his hips. "If ye move any slower, we'll arrive in time to go home."

"Patience is a virtue, Liam." A virtue Liam did not possess. Sam loved to remind him anyway.

"Virtue." Liam spat the word. "Of the seven virtues, I've only Prudence and Fortitude left, my boy. I never claim more."

"And it's balanced evenly by the seven sins. You're only guilty of Lust and Gluttony. Perhaps an occasional Sloth, though it's well earned."

Liam set his steely gaze on Sam. The previous day's alcohol had diluted its intensity. "Yer looking to invoke Wrath also. Yer lucky I have no energy for it today."

Sam chuckled and tugged on his boots. He exhaled and set his hands on his knees. "I've no energy for work, but I suppose we're bound by duty." He stood, raking his fingers through his hair.

Walking into the sunlight outside, they both groaned, and shielded their eyes.

"All right, my friend," Sam said. "Let's go see whether the good captain has come to his senses and will let us put his ship to rights."

"It's not the ship I'm worried about. It's whether its captain will cause trouble for the *Florida*."

"Surely, he's come to his senses by now. To send any more men below would be ludicrous. Blind men cannot salvage goods."

Liam growled, "The ship's captain doesn't care about our men. His interest lies in his contract, and his own duty to deliver the goods."

Sam's legal texts held the key. "The contract was signed assuming the ship would arrive safely. All the conditions have changed since he put his signature to it."

Liam's narrow-eyed look crawled across Sam. "Spoken like a man of the law."

"The only law I follow is common sense, which dictates valuing lives above goods. It's the wrecker creed, is it not?" Sam hid his legal training from his colleagues. He had no desire to return to a courtroom, and even less desire to be treated differently from what he wanted to be—a wrecker.

Liam grunted. "Aye. But the captain no doubt has his own creed and keeps to it."

They walked past the warehouses. The wide doors stood open, the only two men in sight idly talking. When one saw them approaching, he leaned closer to the other and whispered something.

Sam said, "It's unusually quiet today."

"Too quiet. I have an uneasy feeling."

They stepped onto the wharf. The *Florida* sat secured to the dock, and they climbed aboard.

Liam asked, "What's going on? Any word about the wreck?"

Jahner sat on a crate, tying knots. "The *Florida* has been ordered to stand down."

Sam tensed. "What do you mean?"

Jahner set his jaw. "The captain lodged a complaint against Captain Howe. Said he failed to fulfill his end of the bargain as Wrecking Master when he deserted, so-called."

"Hogwash." Liam spat over the rail.

"Judge Marvin signed an order against the *Florida*. We're not allowed to assist any wrecking operation until he decides one way or the other."

"This is outrageous." Sam balled his hands into fists.

"Though it may be unfair, we're bound by it."

Sam persisted. "Where's Captain Howe? Has he hired an attorney?"

Jahner shrugged. "Haven't seen him today. I expect he's at home."

The captain never sat idly. He must be doing something—meeting lawyers, reviewing the relevant documents. Something. Anything. Not merely waiting for a judge to decide his fate.

Judge William Marvin had a reputation for fairness, for the most part. Occasionally, he made unseemly decisions. After review, most were equitable. Sam had read the judge's Treatise on the Law of Wreck and Salvage and admired his forthright interpretation. The only decision Sam ever grew angry about was Judge Marvin's decree that the slaves on a shipwreck were property, ordering they be returned to their "rightful" owner. Rightful. As if any man could own another. The notion made Sam's blood boil.

"Any idea when the judge's decision is due?" Sam asked.

Jahner shook his head. "The first mate said to keep the *Florida* in top shape until we get word. Once we get the go-ahead, we sail straightaway."

"*If* we get the go-ahead." Something didn't feel right. All too often, justice was determined by who had the better connections, and the fuller purse, rather than adhering to its virtue.

"All of Key West knows Captain Howe is a righteous man guided by unerring judgment." He couldn't understand how the judge had reached such a decision, unless it was merely a tactic to appease the ship's captain.

"Let's hope the good judge shares our opinion." Liam lit his pipe.

Sam couldn't sit tying knots today. He grabbed the mop and bucket. At least swabbing the decks would work his muscles and hopefully quiet the nagging thoughts in his head.

The harsh afternoon sun softened to evening light, and Sam allowed himself to rest. He'd worked yesterday's drink from his system, except for a slight ache in his head. Food and water would remedy that.

"What do you say to some dinner?" He leaned against the rail next to Liam.

His friend stared out over the reef where the ship sat. Several wrecking schooners floated nearby.

"Yes. I suppose we've outlived our usefulness here."

They walked to the groggery and sat at a table. Liam ordered beer. Sam wanted milk. And bread, fried eggs, and pork. His body cried for good food to help it heal the effects of too much alcohol.

After he'd eaten, weariness set into his bones. "I believe I'll get back to my bed and continue where I left off this morning."

Smirking, Liam asked, "Will ye be continuing alone?"

Sam pressed his lips together. "Most certainly."

Liam lowered his voice. "I wasn't so certain today. I stayed outside, thinking ye might be entertaining someone. I heard ye had a visitor."

Sam leaned toward him to whisper, "She only helped me to bed. She didn't stay long enough for anything else."

A sly smile crept across Liam's face.

Sam insisted, "It's true. I don't want her reputation sullied. Not on my account."

Liam winked. "Ye're a true gentleman, Sam." Disappointment tinged his tone.

Sam chuckled. "Not a willing one. I'd like nothing better than to bed her."

"What's stopping ye?"

"I can't rob her of her virginity." Much as he'd love to. Much as he dreamed of it.

"And why not? She'll be gone soon enough. Unless she's thinking of staying on."

The thought of Livvie leaving seared his gut like a red-hot poker. "No. I don't expect she would stay."

"Ye're awfully disappointed, I see."

"No," Sam snapped. He couldn't bear Liam thinking him so weak.

Liam clucked his tongue. "Sam. Don't try to fool a fool. I know a lovesick man when I see one." His intimate tone indicated his acceptance of Sam's condition, forlorn though he may be.

"Now who's daft? Lovesick." Sam forced a chuckle.

Liam's eyebrows furrowed. "So, ye're saying ye're not in love with her?"

"Absolutely not."

"But ye'd love to bed her."

"Well, sure. Who wouldn't?"

"'Tis true. Ye're not the only one." His flippant tone belied the trap he set.

Anger boiled to Sam's surface. "Who else?" He knew all too well. Jacob Preston. The young prig considered himself the cock of the walk. Sam's fists clenched, wishing he were choking the lad. Ach, it would do no good.

Liam leaned away to study him. "Ah, Sam. The worst kind of fool is the kind who fools himself." His kindly expression bordered on pity.

"What? No, you've got it wrong." He failed to summon resoluteness.

Liam held up a hand. "I'll say no more. I can see arguing is of no use."

"There's nothing to argue about." And if there were, Sam wouldn't argue it with Liam.

His tone fluttering like a sail, Liam said, "Of course. In a few weeks, she'll be gone. Forgotten. And she'll forget ye too."

"Do you think she will?"

Liam grasped his shoulder. "My boy, she will unless

ye cause her not to." He winked and laughed from deep in his throat.

"Aye." Sam played along, grinning through the stab of pain. Livvie would sail off, without any consideration of him.

Chapter Nineteen

Sam said goodnight to Liam and had every intention of going home. Before he needed sleep, he also required something to quell the restlessness churning within him. He found himself walking toward the residential streets. Toward the Crowell boarding house.

The hour approached nine. Too late to call. He was in no condition anyway. He should have bathed, and freshened his clothing. The stench of two days sweat clung to him. He hadn't noticed until now. He must appear no better than a street urchin.

He stood away from the house. A light in the parlor shone, and Mrs. Crowell sat holding an embroidery hoop, working a needle in and out, chattering away. Mr. Crowell read a newspaper in a chair opposite and nodded occasionally, otherwise taking no part in the conversation.

A light upstairs revealed nothing. Frustrated by his inability to locate her, Sam moved on silent feet along the border of the yard. Night had not yet fallen completely, and the lights inside the house would mask his figure well enough. He strained to see the second floor bedrooms in the back of the house. All sat in darkness save one window, where a lace curtain shifted, illuminated by a lamp. Could it be Livvie's room? She loved to read—

"Sam."

He froze, only his gaze moved to the back porch. He hadn't considered she might be outside. "Good evening, Livvie."

She walked to the rail. "What are you doing here?" Her voice trembled in delight, or perhaps astonishment.

He could only guess what she must be thinking of him. "I wanted to come by to thank you."

"For what?" She descended the stairs using steps silent as his.

"For your kindness yesterday." He cringed when she approached and hoped the fragrance of the night air would cover his own foul smell.

She glanced back at the house, lowering her voice to a whisper. "I did nothing. Are you feeling well?"

Embarrassed, he glanced away. "Yes, better, thank you. Please don't diminish your actions. What you did was certainly not nothing. You went out of your way to help me. I might have sprawled helpless on the beach all day if you hadn't come to my rescue." He shuddered to think how repulsive he must have looked, a whiskey bottle his only companion.

"One rescue deserves another in turn. I was merely fulfilling my obligation."

A pang of disappointment surged through him. "You've no obligation to me, Livvie." Although meant it to reassure her, the words came out sharper than he intended. He didn't want her to remain in his company because of some perceived debt. He wanted her to be with him because she wanted to. Because he made her want to.

She drew back and searched his face. "No. I suppose not." The hurt in her voice surprised him.

He yearned to reach for her, to hold her. Her beauty

captivated him, made him feel a pauper to her royalty. If only he'd thought to make himself presentable.

Mrs. Locke's whine echoed through the hallway. "Olivia? Where are you?"

Livvie gasped. "Don't move." She ran back to the porch and opened the door. "I'm enjoying the cool night air, thank you. Can I do anything for you?"

Mrs. Locke's wavering tone echoed from within. "No, of course not, dear. I wanted to be sure you hadn't wandered off."

"I couldn't sleep. I may go for a short walk. It's such a lovely evening." She glanced at Sam.

His heart skipped a beat. He moved behind a coconut palm in case the biddy should become curious. He hurriedly raked his hands through his hair, wiped his mouth on his sleeve, and smoothed the wrinkles in his shirt.

"If you do, take care not to walk too far. I'm turning in for the night. My arthritis has acted up something terrible today."

The woman's strained sigh sounded loud enough for the neighbors to hear.

"Good night." Livvie waited while the woman shuffled away before tiptoeing across the porch and down the steps. She crossed the yard. "Quickly. Before she thinks of something else." She clutched Sam's arm using both hands.

Her touch sent a thrill through him. "We're going for a walk, I take it?"

"Yes." She lifted her chin. "You can assure my safety from the rabble."

"You're quite safe on these streets. Even at night. Although the people of Key West have their vices, there's been no murder or other crime on the island. Not since the Seminoles attacked years ago."

"The Seminole Indians? What happened?" Her wide eyes flashed in the half-darkness.

"You needn't worry. The Seminoles were driven out in 1840, sixteen years ago. They haven't returned since. They likely still live on the mainland somewhere."

"But they attacked people here?" Her voice held less fear than excitement.

"Occasionally, if an encounter went awry. The Seminoles have a different set of rules and customs, and many times people here offended them without realizing. And they're a very territorial tribe. They slaughtered quite a few of the residents of Indian Key. The military came to their aid. Too late for many."

"How terrible."

Sam might have felt a fool telling this to any other woman. In Livvie's company, his tongue wagged too freely. Her keen curiosity drew it from him. All subjects interested her. Perhaps he could stretch this walk to greater lengths by reciting more history.

"They did us a favor in one way, at least."

"How so?"

"They ruined Captain Jacob Housman's business. His dishonest dealings gave us wreckers a bad reputation. He built his own empire on Indian Key, even a warehouse and dry goods store. He bribed customers to inform him first of shipwrecks, even when the delay further endangered the ship."

"How ironic that he was ruined by the Indians."

"Yes, I suppose. Newspaper accounts of his unscrupulous methods turned many northerners against us. Houseman even petitioned for Monroe County to be split, and so the middle and upper Keys became part of Dade County."

"To what advantage?"

This response surprised him. And thrilled him. She had a fine mind and was not afraid to show it.

"His own. In doing so, he removed himself from the jurisdiction of the Key West wrecking court. He was a shrewd businessman, shrewd in all the worst ways. For nearly twenty years, he skirted the trade laws."

"If the Seminoles didn't kill him, what happened to him?"

Sam hesitated before responding. The answer would repulse her, so he kept it brief. And vague, to conceal Housman had been crushed between two boats. "He came to a bad end on a salvage mission. After he died, wreckers were determined to repair our reputation. Some newspaper accounts still get it wrong. Visitors to Key West are always surprised at the tight control judges have over us."

"Not surprising at all. The law serves those in power, and those in power serve themselves before all else."

"You'd make an excellent lawyer, Livvie."

This remark seemed to vex her, and her tone sounded venomous. "If women were allowed to be lawyers."

Sam had no argument. He'd known quite a few women whose intelligence far surpassed their husbands or brothers, yet their opinions were not valued.

When she spoke again, she sounded wistful. "I should like to have seen a Seminole Indian. At least, from a distance."

"Yes, we invaded their territory in settling here.

They hunted and fished here long before outsiders came. Not only from the northern states. Plenty of Spaniards, Cubans, and Bahamians—the Conchs—lived here before we Americans took over."

"The Conchs are the very tall ones with the light brown skin? Why come here, when the Bahama islands are so beautiful?"

"Same as us. For the wrecking trade."

"Incredible. We always hear of the great wilderness out west. Why is there never talk of the wilderness to our south? I never dreamed such a wild paradise existed."

"Paradise?" He laughed in delight. Few women described Key West in such manner. Most complained of the preponderance of large mosquitoes, the scarcity of social events, and even scarcer opportunities to shop for niceties rather than necessities.

"Yes. Don't you think it is?"

"Of course I do. It's why I'm here. But paradise is not without its hazards."

"But you said the Seminoles were gone."

"Other dangers remain. Alligators. Scorpions. Sharks. Just to name a few."

"Alligators?"

"Sometimes fifteen feet long—boasting the longest snout you've ever seen. Long enough to swallow a child."

She gasped. "Oh, my."

"On other Key islands, panthers prey on deer. And unwitting people." He hadn't done so much teasing since his brother was a little boy, quaking in their bed at Sam's tales. "Ah, I'm talking too much."

"No, I'm very interested to learn about Key West. Such a strange place, like something in a fairy tale."

"The place can seem magical." The creatures were the least magical part of the island. The ever-changing colors of the sky and sea captivated his heart. He could never be happy anywhere else after living here. His work hardly seemed a job, and the freedom of his days was more valuable than any payment. The companionship of his mates equaled that of his family.

"I'll be sorry to leave." The husky tone of her voice conveyed the depths of her sorrow.

He wished she hadn't broken the spell by mentioning it. "When do you go?"

"I should learn soon. I'm in no hurry, really. I'm sure my brother and his wife aren't either."

"Why do you say that?"

"I will be a burden to them. They'll no doubt arrange for me to meet many of New Orleans' eligible society bachelors."

He had no doubt bachelors would call on Livvie soon after her arrival, and not at her brother's bidding. Her dance card would be filled at every ball. Other men would hold her. Try to kiss her.

Imagining such scenes made his blood boil. He found himself unable to rein in his frustration. "Is that what you want? To marry a wealthy gentleman who will provide you shelter and security?"

Her tone sounded every bit as accusatory. "No, it's not what I want. I have no intention of marrying."

"Why not?" He couldn't keep himself from challenging her to see what she would say.

Her eyes caught the lamplight of a nearby house. "Happily ever after might be commonplace in fairy tales, but I've yet to find proof of its existence in real life."

"I believe you're wrong." He would not accept she

spoke from her heart. Before she'd arrived, he might have said the same thing. Now he wanted to believe in the possibility, at least.

A blush tinged her cheeks, even in the near-darkness. "Don't be ridiculous. You're a grown man. You're telling me you think love can last a lifetime?"

"More than one. Were your parents not proof?"

"I told you my mother died long ago."

"But your father never remarried, did he?"

"No."

"Is that not proof enough?"

"I refuse to hold onto childish notions."

"Again, I ask you—why not? Isn't it exciting to indulge yourself? Doesn't it make your heart feel as though it's soaring like a sea bird? Or drifting on the ocean's swells?"

Her voice wavered. "Yes."

He said more passionately than he intended, "So there's no reason to stop."

A look of resolve smoothed her face. "Not for you. You're a man."

"Nonsense. I will not validate your argument that a woman must live by a man's rules. Don't you have a head of your own? Desires of your own?"

"Of course, but—"

"If you lived here, you could sail to an island, swim however long you wished, or run along the beach. No one would scold you or challenge you. You would have your own freedom." He'd never argued anything with more conviction. More hope.

His words penetrated her deeply, he knew, by her silence, by her reflective nature.

"If only it were so."

He halted and grasped her arm. "It is, Livvie." What was he doing? Trying to convince her to stay? She stared up at him in surprise. And expectation.

He released his grip. If she stayed, she would claim his argument had convinced her. And he would be obligated to provide for her. No real freedom existed without obligations. "You can live however you please. You need no one else's approval."

She waited, immobile. All they'd left unspoken roiled in the air between them. He could offer her nothing except heartache and disappointment.

He would not lead her to believe otherwise. Yet he might entice her on other grounds. "Nor do you require anyone's support. You said you wanted to earn your own living. Where better than here in Key West, where there are no such restrictions?"

The bright expectancy faded from her face. Her nostrils flared, and she pressed her lips into a thin line. "I must return."

For a moment, he thought she meant to her brother's house. To civilization.

She held his gaze briefly, abruptly pivoting toward the direction from which they'd come. To the Crowells'.

Her skirt flounced, she walked so hastily.

"I'll accompany you." He followed, unsure of what else to say.

"You needn't bother. You said it was safe." Her voice trembled.

He jogged to her side. "Are you angry at me?"

Her pace increased. "No. I'm angry at myself."

"Why?"Sam hurried to keep up. She had a long stride for a female.

She folded her arms across her chest and walked on.

"For entertaining frivolous notions."

His heart leapt in his chest and struck against his ribs like a trapped bird. "What notions?" He reached for her arm.

She jerked away from his touch. "Oh, stop it, Sam. I'm not going to say any more."

Her refusal to look at him encouraged him. She cared more than she would admit. "I'm sorry if I've upset you."

She knit her brows. "I told you I'm not upset at you."

"Why do you scold me, then?" He hoped to keep her from going home by engaging her in another argument.

"I don't wish to speak of it any more, please."

"All right. We'll walk along in silence. Amiable companions."

She snorted.

"You disagree we're amiable?"

"You're really enjoying yourself, aren't you? You use words so cleverly, you think you can trip me up."

"I would never try to trip you." Sam hoped his attempt at lightheartedness would lighten her spirit too.

"If you're trying to make me admit my feelings to you, you're wasting your time."

"Admit what? I was talking about the love of childish play."

"Because you know how much I long to be free. Like you." Frustration and yearning filled her voice.

He touched her arm to slow her, ease her mind. "Livvie, you are free. Free to do as you choose."

She pulled from his grasp. "There can never be true freedom for any woman, Sam. You're well aware of the restrictions."

"Restrictions of what? Society? We pay no mind to

those here, Livvie. We live however we please."

She whirled to face him. "Oh, and the women here live however they please also? Do as they wish?"

"Of course."

Her arms flailed, and her words tumbled from her mouth. "Their days aren't filled by cooking and cleaning and tasks and chores?"

He softened his voice, hoping his calm would soothe her. "Livvie, any person's life contains those. How you spend the remainder of your day—who you spend it with—is yours to choose. Anyone has that prerogative."

Glaring, she pressed her lips tight and let out a ragged breath. "Good night, Sam."

"Good night, Livvie." He waited until she crossed the yard and climbed the steps. She turned back, hesitating, and light from inside the house illuminated her face. Her lips parted.

His muscles coiled, ready to spring toward her at the mention of her slightest desire.

After a moment, she dropped her chin to her chest and went inside.

His powers of persuasion had failed him. Had he lost his talents as a litigator? He was sure he hadn't. Yet Livvie deflected his arguments. Perhaps she'd sensed his own hesitation. While his heart yearned to give her everything, his logical brain held back, insisting it was too soon. He could sense her yearning to believe in what he said, yet something held her back.

Fear. The distance she'd put between them must have been brought on by her fear. Of what? The unknown? Him?

She had good reason to fear him. If she stayed, he would have her in his bed in a wink. Having no father or brother to protect her, she would come all too willingly.

And then what?

His steps halting, he backed away down the street. The parlor light blinked off, and the house fell dark except for a light shining from a second floor window.

A light beckoned him to watch while she undressed, and while she brushed out her long honey-colored hair.

Oh, he must be careful, or he would become tangled in her web. Such a delicious web it was! But so very sticky, it would entangle him in every way.

He turned and walked toward his cabin. The night had not intoxicated him beyond all reason. Like Livvie, he was not willing to relinquish his freedom.

Chapter Twenty

After a night of much-needed rest, Sam's mood improved. The ship still hung on the reef, and Jasper and Isum's absences posed a sore reminder of their fates. The men lingered aboard the *Florida*, performing needless tasks while awaiting Judge Marvin's decree. Captain Howe dismissed them. If he harbored any guilt, he hid it well.

Sam strolled through Conchtown. The afternoon sun blazed in the sky, hanging low like a torch aiming for his skin alone. Jahner sat on his stoop, whistling "The Wrecker's Song."

"Are you trying to bring on a storm?" Sam teased. Sailors' superstitions held strong here. How a whistle could summon a storm, he couldn't guess, though some swore by it.

Jahner grinned. "That's the idea."

"I'll join you, then." Sam whistled along. He waved and walked on toward the lookout tower.

From up above, Liam called, "Who's whistling?"

"Me."

"Stop. Your off-key racket will cause a storm to knock me from my post."

"At least you'll be cooler." Sam set his foot on the first step.

"Wait. Before you come up." Liam moved away from the side and shuffled through things above. He reappeared holding his switchel bag. "Fill this up, will you? I'm dry." He dropped it.

Sam snatched it from the air and stepped back. "Anything else?"

"Yes. An orange or two."

Sam chuckled. Liam's love of oranges caused the crew to tease him, though he was not one to abide teasing. His bad reaction fueled more taunts for a while, but Liam put an end to them by squishing an orange in the face of a taunter.

Sam strode to the market and purchased three oranges. He could use one himself this hot day. Back at his cabin, he mixed a bath of switchel water from molasses and vinegar. He filled Liam's switchel bag and his own, went back to the tower, and climbed the staircase angled around its long legs.

He stepped onto the deck of the tower. "What's the news?"

"None. No sight of anything interesting. Unless ye count the two in the cabin over there." Liam turned back toward town and aimed his eyeglass to the homes.

Sam clucked his tongue. "Liam, I'm surprised at you."

Feigning indignation, Liam said, "They should close the shutters if they're going to undress in the middle of the day."

"Maybe they thought being on the second floor protected them from prying eyes."

Liam chuckled. "Not while I'm up here."

Sam handed the bag to him. "Here. Cool yourself off. Your switchel pouch is looking rather shabby."

"Yes, on our next hunting trip, I'm going to find a pelican willing to give up his pouch." Liam drank, and then smacked his lips.

"Or a turtle willing to give himself up for dinner." Sam pulled the core from his orange.

"Ye have a knack for turtling. A fine eye for hunting, too."

Sam heaved a relaxed breath. "When I tire of wrecking, that's what I'll do. Hunt and fish. Maybe become a sponger."

"Not much excitement in sponging, even if the money's steady. I tell ye, we should buy a nice bit of land to farm."

Sam chuckled. "You? A farmer?" They'd had this conversation before, always in jest. These days, Liam argued more forcefully.

Liam pulled himself straight. "Why, yes. I've farming in me blood. I was going to offer you a partnership. I'll reconsider if yer going to look down on it."

"No, I don't look down on it. Farming's an excellent idea. It would leave enough time for hunting and turtling. Along with other pursuits." Sam guessed his friend might spend more than his spare time at the last, and Sam knew with whom.

Liam held up his pouch in cheers. "My thoughts exactly." While he drank, he looked Sam over. "Are ye tired of wrecking already?"

"Not tired, exactly." Sam leaned on the side. "Restless, I suppose. The excitement has lost its luster. Lately, I feel there's something missing."

Though smiling, Liam groaned. "I think I know what it is."

"What?" Sam turned to him in hopes of his friend's sage insight. He couldn't put his finger on why he didn't look forward to salvaging shipwrecks. The pay was good, he loved Key West—its unpredictability, even its ungodly heat. The island satisfied something deep in his soul, yet a yearning remained.

"A woman, ye fool. A companion to share the good alongside the bad."

Sam winced. "I'm not ready to marry."

Liam's shoulder nudged his. "I wager ye'll change your mind after a certain little lady's ship arrives to take her away."

"What? You're out of your gourd."

"Am I?" He eyed Sam. "I've seen the way ye look at her."

"I look at her no differently than anyone else." Only for a hundred times longer than he looked at other women.

"Ye look like a lovesick schoolboy whenever she's near."

"You're insane." Denying Liam might convince himself, too, but he doubted it.

Liam sputtered. "I won't debate that. All I'll say is, I know what I see."

Though Sam tried to laugh it off, he couldn't. The sight of Livvie made his insides twist. An invisible winch connected him to her; he was drawn in without thought or warning.

He set his jaw. "I couldn't be what she needs."

"What are ye talking about? Ye've all the standard equipment. Ye know how to use it, too." Liam's elbow nudged Sam's side.

"I know that part would be good." His voice trailed off. "Incredible, in fact."

Liam laughed. "So what's stopping ye?"

"She needs someone she can depend on. Not someone like me." He didn't know if he could trust anyone, even Livvie, to keep safe his heart.

"No, not someone *like* ye. You. She's crazy about ye too."

"She's young and impressionable."

Liam cocked his head. "Are ye her uncle? She's the perfect age. Ripe for the picking."

The picking was not the problem. Sam had been more than ready since the moment he saw her beneath the waves. Something had clicked into place, shifting the universe slightly. He'd known when his arm encircled her waist that she would fit against him as though molded for him alone.

Liam leaned in close. "Not every woman is a shrew like Helen."

"Every woman I choose seems to be."

"Ye can't let the past stop ye from having what might be very good in your future."

"I can't give myself freely as you do." Not to someone like Livvie, whose acceptance or rejection mattered too much.

From down below came another slow whistle.

"Now who's trying to raise a storm?" Liam peered over the side. A wide smile crossed his face. "Ah. So it's you."

Sam leaned next to Liam.

Millie looked up, her hips swaying. Looking down from the tower afforded a generous view of her ample cleavage. "Hello, boys. I thought you might need some company."

"Yes, I'm in need of entertaining company. Sam's boring me to death."

Giggling, she disappeared up the stairs.

Sam turned to Liam. "She can't come up here."

"Why not?" Pursing his lips, Liam screwed up his face like an old biddy.

"What if she falls?"

"I'll keep hold of her." Liam winked. "I am in need of giving myself freely. It's been a week. A very long week. "

Sam flinched as she screeched on her ascent. He bent alongside Liam toward the stair opening. She hitched her skirt high and labored upward. "Almost there. Are you ready for me?"

"I'm ready, darlin'."

When she came within his grasp, Liam slipped his arm around her.

She squealed. When her feet touched the floor, she swirled in Liam's hold to face him. "Thank you."

Liam widened his eyes. "I will. Soon."

On tiptoe, she pressed her lips to his, and then turned to Sam. "Why, hello, Sam."

"Millie." Sam went back to his orange, gazing out over the sea.

Her laughter joined Liam's throaty chuckles, the smacking sound of lips.

Sam tried to ignore it, peeling the last section of orange.

Liam cleared his throat. "Don't ye have somewhere else yer needed?"

"Can't I finish my orange first?"

"Here, I'll give ye mine."

Sam winced. "No, keep it. Soon it will be all the balls you'll have remaining."

Giving a delighted squeal, Millie slapped Sam's

shoulder. Liam growled, nuzzling her neck. Her eyes pierced his, and in them a fire burned for more than Liam.

Sam pitched the remains of his orange. "All right. Will I see you later at the groggery?"

Liam grinned. "If I'm not tied up otherwise."

Sam held up a hand, not wishing those images to remain in his head. "Fine. I know when I'm not wanted."

"Oh, Sam. Never say such a thing." Millie's breathy voice matched her smoldering stare.

Anger flared up. How could she flirt so brazenly while Liam's fingers inched toward her breasts, and his mouth too? He would never understand the female mind.

"Don't forget to come up for air once in awhile to look out." Squatting, Sam lifted the hatch. "You're lucky no eyeglass can spy you here."

"Exactly." A gritty chuckle issued from Liam.

"Bye." Millie batted her eyes.

Sam glared at her before climbing down. Footsteps shuffled overhead while he descended. A loud thump shook the tower. She gave a husky laugh, and then more shuffling sounded. Liam's appreciative groans and her sighing moans carried from above.

Sam couldn't help but laugh as their cavorting grew louder, more intense. He smiled at a Conch, who stared wide-eyed at the tower. "Afternoon."

The man looked from him to the tower.

"I wouldn't go up if I were you. Not for, oh, an hour at least."

After a few whiskeys, Liam often boasted of his virility, thrusting lovemaking pointers on an unwilling Sam. According to Liam's accounts, he took his time both before and after because ladies appreciated his extended affections. Many times, attentions afterward led to a second round—a slower, more deliberate act. It made women feel more appreciated, while making them appreciate him all the more. Their ecstasy was heightened by its very slowness, he said.

Sam had never felt the need to satiate a woman so thoroughly before, although he certainly thought about applying the method to Livvie. The constancy of those thoughts often necessitated an urgent need to relieve himself. He didn't. He preferred to allow the delicious ecstasy to build until she herself released it for him.

After he went to his cabin, the air inside was too still, too hot even for reading.

The shell basket sat on the floor beside his dresser. Lifting it, he brushed the dust from its sides.

He'd bought it for her. He should give it to her. Today.

His heart turned over in his chest thinking of her fingers tracing along the shells, of the basket sitting in her room. A gift to cause her to think of him while she unbuttoned her dress and removed her bloomers.

A gift was more than a gesture of good will. Such a gift might imply more than a token. She might look at the basket and infer that he held tender feelings for her. He did, somewhat, though not in such a way that he wanted to pledge himself.

He set the basket on the floor. The giving required more consideration.

Raking a hand through his hair, he cast his gaze around the room. Reading would allow him a better perspective. After grabbing a book, he went outside.

Absorbed in the text, he turned the pages and walked. He found himself at a bench not far from the wharf. A sea breeze riffled the pages, and a small palm tree afforded the spot some shade, in addition to a peaceful view of the street beyond. The sun crept behind the warehouse and offered more relief. The pages flew by, fast as the minutes. Easing across the bench, he brought a foot to its seat and relaxed.

Wagons creaked by, and a few people strolled. Sam took little notice until a figure caught his eye. He squinted past the pages he read to see Livvie wandering toward him. Gazing toward the sea, she may have been searching for her ship to arrive. She lowered her head, and when she lifted it, met his gaze. Her face alighted in a smile.

A thrill went through him, until he remembered Liam's words. His description of how she looked at him—and he at her—chilled his reception.

"Sam. So nice to see you."

He rose. He always felt he committed a social blunder in her presence, though she never showed any prejudice. "Hello. You're enjoying an afternoon stroll?"

"I suppose. I couldn't stay in the house one moment longer."

"Would you care to sit?" He sat and brushed sand from the seat beside him. "Sorry, I allowed myself to become a little too comfortable."

"Thank you." She perched next to him. "This is a lovely spot for reading."

His hesitation melted in her warmth. "If you need something to read, I'd be happy to lend you a book."

Surprise crossed her face while glancing at the book he held. "I'm afraid I don't have much of a head for legal matters."

"I recently received a new book from my brother. I

was going to begin reading it after I finished this one. You're welcome to it."

"Really? You wouldn't mind?"

"Not at all. We can go get it from my cabin. Or, if you prefer, you can wait here, and I'll fetch it."

"I don't mind walking. I prefer it, actually. I'm afraid patience is not one of my virtues."

"I find it hard to believe you're lacking in any virtues."

A blush colored her cheeks. "You're too generous. I daresay you don't know me very well."

Her honesty stunned him to silence. No one could ever know another person completely, but not many would admit to their faults so easily.

They walked to his home, conversing idly about the heat.

"It's a bit of a mess inside. If you'd rather wait out here, I can fetch it."

"I'm acquainted with the state of your cabin."

"Yes." The memory of that night returned vividly when he opened the door.

****

Sitting squarely against the center of the wall, the bed loomed large in her vision. The first time she'd been inside the cabin, darkness had obscured most details. Not to mention her own blurred vision. And then the second time... The memory caused her cheeks to flush in warmth. Luckily, Sam busied himself searching through his bookshelf. She noted his fine form, how his wide shoulders tapered to a trim waist atop long legs whose muscles showed through his cotton slacks as he bent. His dark hair curled past the collar of his shirt, so white it contrasted his sun-burnished skin. The urge to undo his shirt and push it past his shoulders overcame her, and she stepped toward him without thinking.

He turned and handed her the book. "Are you all right?"

"Of course." To cover her embarrassment, she opened the book. "*Leaves of Grass*? I've never heard of Walt Whitman." Hopefully he hadn't noticed her keen attention.

"It's a new edition. My brother said it's caused quite a stir up north."

Holding it to her chest, she forced a smile despite her onset of nervousness. "I look forward to reading it."

Giving an easy grin, he rested his hands on his hips. "Yes. You can give me your impression after you've finished."

The cabin walls hadn't confined her so before. He stood so near, she feared he'd hear her heart beating, more wildly by the second. Ruminations of what might have happened made her belly flutter, and the fluttering descended to her thighs. A glance told her he'd noticed her awkwardness, so she turned to scour the contents of the room.

Her gaze came to rest on his bookshelf. "You have a great many books. I didn't notice…before." Heated pinpricks swept across her skin. Why had she mentioned it? Oh, she'd often imagined their time together, especially that night. Reliving the warmth of his body against hers, the feel of his touch, the kiss she could almost—but not quite—remember. She wanted to know it all again.

"The mess likely hid them from view.".

To take her attention from the strange effect he had on her, she tilted her head to read the titles. She glanced at him in surprise. "Most of these are law books."

"Yes." He shrugged.

Too hastily, she said, "You needn't be embarrassed. It's admirable you want to improve your station in life."

He laughed. "Improve my station? Why, you surprise me, Livvie."

Frowning, she lifted her chin. "What do you mean?"

Leaning close, he affected a stern expression. "Your snobbery."

His gaze fell to her lips, and she nearly forgot to respond.

"I meant no insult, only that…" The warmth in her face spread to her neck. "Law books are not the easiest reading, so you obviously have a fine mind suited to—"

"I was only teasing," he said. "In truth, I have the best possible station in life. I want no other."

She studied his face, yet made no argument. "Well." To disguise her longing, she held the book to her chest. "I'll make sure to get this back to you before I leave."

He rested his hand on the top shelf, close enough to touch her hair. "Yes. When is your ship due in?" Anxiousness edged his tone, and he narrowed his eyes.

"I haven't yet heard." And she hoped not to. Once she boarded the vessel, she'd never see him again.

Tension weighted the air between them.

Searching her face, his voice turned husky. "There's something else I've been wanting to give you."

"What?" She gazed up at him. Opening herself to him. She wanted nothing more than him, though it seemed the last thing he'd be likely to offer. In expectation, she parted her lips.

Tensing, he set his jaw and bent to the floor. "This."

"Oh." Disappointment weighted her voice. A

basket. Its cold shells would not warm her.

Blinking hard, she straightened, yet couldn't muster a hint of a smile. "It's lovely, thank you."

"It's from Havana," he stammered. "I thought it might make a nice memento. Of your stay here."

A memento! A trinket to set on a table, evoking his face with every glance?

"How thoughtful. I will treasure it." She couldn't stifle her sarcasm. "I should go." She reached for the door.

Hastily, he stepped toward her. "So soon?"

Hope swept her up in its mayhem, and she turned so quickly, her skirt twirled. Meeting her gaze, his eyes burned bright until his brows twitched together, perhaps realizing the mistake he'd made.

"I mean…" He shrugged.

Her chin dropped to her chest. She suspected him incapable of more. "Goodbye, Sam."

He grabbed her arm. "Livvie, wait."

He stiffened as she nestled to his chest, trembling, unable to shield him from the emotions roiling inside of her.

"What's wrong?" He took the basket from her and set it on the bed beside the book.

She clutched his shirt. "I'm afraid to leave. I don't know what awaits me." Or what she would miss by leaving too soon.

He ran his hands across her back and smoothed her hair. "Never be afraid of the unknown, Livvie. Be excited by it. Let it challenge you. You can make your life whatever you want it to be."

"Hold me, Sam. Please hold me." Her voice sounded small as a little girl's, though his touch ignited a fire not to be denied. For too long, she'd yearned for him. This moment might never come again. She must seize it, make it hers forever.

He tightened his embrace. "Everything will be all right. You'll see." He kissed her hair.

She raised her chin and searched his face. Her hands cupped his face and drew his head down. "I want to know you, Sam." Her lips teased his, and a thrill burned through her like wildfire.

"You don't know what you're saying."

Yet he didn't loosen his embrace. She took courage from it.

"I've had nothing stronger than lemonade today." She stepped toward the bed, and fingered his hair. "I know exactly what I'm saying." She ran her hand lightly down his chest to trace his chiseled stomach, its ripples reverberating to her core.

"Livvie." Spoken like a warning, he exhaled a deep breath through clenched teeth.

Why did he struggle to contain the passion she knew to be building within him, the same way it built within her, threatening to burst through her very skin?

"Don't you want me, Sam?" Her lips caressed his neck.

Moaning, he trembled, still holding back. He took hold of her shoulders and peered into her face. "Why?"

She caressed his cheek. "So I won't be afraid of what I don't know." To reveal that she wanted him—and him alone—might cause him to send her away.

He squeezed shut his eyes. "I don't want to take from you what is only yours to give once."

Boldly, she ran her fingertip along his lip. "It's mine to give to whom I choose." His reluctance fueled her confidence.

He sat on the bed and lightly trailed down the curve of her breast. "If we begin, it might not be possible to stop." Although she knew he meant his cautionary words to halt her, his heated gaze invited more.

She eased closer, entwining her fingers in his hair. "For either of us." The words fluttered from her, and she shuddered at his touch. She pressed her lips to his again and again. Entranced, her body followed its own instincts, the need for him so great, it overwhelmed every other sense.

Her pulse pounded in her ears. Her desire equaled his and further fueled it. Her last trace of doubt vanished when he eased away to gaze at her with such intense yearning, she couldn't believe he'd ever look at anyone else that way.

****

He could contain himself no longer. He had to remind himself to go slowly, to take his time receiving her precious gift.

Rising, he turned her away from him. His fingers worked her buttons, his lips following the path they opened down her back. The taste of her exhilarated his senses, heightened each moment. Reaching the last button, he slid his arm inside the warm space between her dress and her bloomers. Using his other hand, he tugged the dress down.

She slipped her arms from the sleeves, pushed the garment over her hips, and turned to face him. Her eyes gleamed bright as amber coals, her face flushed. Fingers deft as a courtesan's, she unbuttoned his shirt, slipping it off his shoulders.

Letting out a ragged breath, he closed his eyes. His

fingers traced along her hips, delving inside the rim of her bloomers.

Her breaths quickened as she fumbled open his pants.

He lightly grasped her waist, touched his lips to her ear and whispered, "Slowly, Livvie," reminding himself too. Had she been anyone else, he'd have allowed his basest instincts to prevail. By the same argument, had she been anyone else, he'd not be so tantalizingly aroused. He wanted to revel in every moment.

Her breath warmed his skin as her nose and mouth slid along his chest.

He lay back and drew her atop him.

She tensed, her golden-brown eyes wide.

He lay still, not trusting himself to move. "Tell me now if you want to stop."

She shook her head slowly.

"It's all right. You have nothing to fear." He untied the front of her bloomers. No corset lay beneath, only her creamy skin. He nuzzled between her breasts to further open it. Probing, he found a hardened rosette and ran his tongue along its outside, luxuriating in the firming pebbles.

She gasped and clutched his head while he suckled. Her legs splayed and tightened around his.

Desire burned in his veins, making him tremble against the urge to push her onto her back and take her right then. Instead, his lips worked down her ribs and along her stomach as she arched above him.

Steeling himself , he held her hips. "Shhh. Easy, Livvie. Slowly."

He waited until her breathing slowed. His hand touched hers, and together they tugged her bloomers down her hips.

Breathless, she asked, "What are you doing?"

He smiled when his lips found the inside of her thighs. "Giving you a taste of what's to come." He soon found the nub he sought.

Moaning, she arched her back. Her hips rocked in rhythm with the flicking of his tongue. She clutched the bedcovers, her head sinking into them, muffling her moans.

Sweet and tangy she tasted, fueling his hunger. He worked his fingers and tongue in delicious concert, bringing her to her virginal crescendo.

Slipping from beneath, he climbed atop her, his kisses moving along her spine. He slid an arm along her belly to her opposite hip, rolling her over. "Are you all right?"

"Are you serious? I'm waiting for what's next." Her legs curled around his hips.

His breath shook. "Careful, Livvie. You'll awaken a beast in me."

"I hoped I already had." She tugged down his half-opened pants, closing her fingers around him. "Ah, yes. There it is." She finished unbuttoning his pants, pushing them away.

The strain of holding back made him tremble. Again he reminded himself this was her first time. The experience must be pleasant enough to make her want more.

And more.

She entwined her legs around his, tightening her grip. When he didn't lower himself fast enough, she raised her hips to meet his. She gasped, "Now, Sam. Now."

He needed no further urging. He guided himself inside her, struggling to quell the furious urge mounting in him.

One small yelp, and she dug her fingers into his back, her teeth into his shoulder. Her breaths eased, and she followed his slow rhythm.

He could hold back no longer. He thrust against her hard, telling himself he'd apologize later, surprised when she returned his thrusts equally. Shuddering in spasms, he burst upon her in an explosion, clutching her close, feeling he could never be close enough.

She laughed, gasping for air, her arms dangling above her head. "Are you all right?"

He leaned away to regard her. "Of course. Are you?"

Her feet sliding along his legs, her mouth curled into a smile. "Oh, yes. I've never been better."

Laughing, he pressed his lips to hers. She was full of surprises. "That was amazing."

She sighed. "Better than I'd dreamed."

Rolling to his side, he pulled her next to him, aware of every inch of her skin. He hadn't taken the time to fully appreciate her naked body before. He took the time now. His hands felt too rough against her softness, but she didn't complain. He followed every curve and narrow of her body.

Her appreciative sighs and moans met his touch, and her hands wandered freely across his body. Her soft touches teased him to hardness again. She rolled on her back, her leg linked around his, her fingers encasing his erection.

He followed willingly.

She opened herself to him, guiding him.

His mouth on hers all the while, he moved slowly

until they both were spent.

Still breathless atop her, he asked, "Won't you be missed?"

"I don't care."

"You're beautiful as an angel." An angel from beyond the realm of his reach, who would soon sail away to a life of comfort, a life she deserved. "You don't belong here."

Her warmth faded to cold hardness. "You're right. I should go." Her expression blanked. Pushing him away, she stood, snatching her bloomers from the floor.

He groaned. He shouldn't have reminded her. "Already?"

"Yes." The sibilance of her response gave him pause. Concern flew from his mind as he became engrossed in watching her.

In the waning light, she looked wildly angelic, her tawny hair mussed, tumbling down her back, falling across her shoulder when she bent to step into her clothes.

She glanced at him while she dressed, her expression unreadable, though she moved hurriedly.

He couldn't stop smiling. Much as he wanted her to stay, her stubbornness would win out, so he sat up to help button her up. "Don't forget the book. And your basket."

Her glance pained, she lifted them from the floor and fingered the shells. "Thank you."

"For what?" He dared not believe she thanked him for taking her virginity.

"For giving me a memory I can cherish, one I can close my eyes and remember after I leave. When someone else's hands touch me, they will be your hands, Sam." Passion and pleading mingled in her voice.

He scrambled upward. "What? No." The very idea flared his anger. He didn't want anyone else's hands on her.

She backed away. "Goodbye, Sam."

"Wait, I'll see you home." He reached for his pants.

"No. It's better if I go alone."

He couldn't argue her logic. If others witnessed them leaving together, someone might mention it to Mrs. Crowell. He would not have her shamed so.

She reached for the door. After one last haunting, accusing glance, she was gone.

Sam lay in the twilight, staring at the ceiling, recalling every moment of the afternoon. He would never be able to erase the memory, that much he knew. The thought of another man's hands upon her, even if they yielded memories of him, gave him no comfort.

To the contrary, the thought tortured him.

Chapter Twenty-One

Blinded by anger and frustration, Livvie strode hard, rehearsing arguments against Sam's proclamation. Didn't belong here? Who did? Everyone on the island had come from somewhere else. The only possible explanation was that he didn't want her to stay. Had never expected her to.

After returning to the boarding house, she ignored Mrs. Locke's prying gaze, fraught with suspicion. Try as she might to comb her hair and straighten her clothing, she could not have looked more different from when she left. No mere walk would produce such a flushed complexion, she knew, nor cause her dress to cling from perspiration. She hoped she could hide the turmoil roiling inside her.

Mrs. Crowell looked up from her embroidery, displaying only the briefest arch of a brow, less a judgment than an acknowledgement. She returned to her task without a word. Florie had the keenest sense for these things and handed her a cool glass of lemonade. The gleam in the cook's wide eyes hinted she knew how strenuously she'd depleted herself.

"Thank you, Florie."

Martha glared accusingly at Livvie. "You missed lunch. It's nearly dinner."

The biddy's haughtiness almost made Livvie laugh. "I apologize, Florie, for any inconvenience I may have caused. I wandered the island too long and became engrossed in my thoughts."

Mrs. Locke arched a brow. "Thoughts?" She made no attempt to hide her skepticism.

"Yes, one of the dangers of being an author, unfortunately. I daydream far too much." A practice she would welcome, after Sam's exquisite touch—despite his protest, his touch would overwhelm any other man's in the future. She wanted to know no other man's touch. Now when she wrote of a woman's love, she would write of the feelings he'd uncovered in her. A true life experience, beyond any invention of her mind. Beyond her expectations. Even if she could never experience it again, she would relive it through her writing.

"Is it a new novel?" Mrs. Crowell asked.

"A book of poetry." Livvie held it up for inspection.

"Oh, lovely. Why not read to us?" She worked her needle through the linen in the hoop.

The proprietress never failed to surprise Livvie; she'd never have guessed Mrs. Crowell an admirer of poetry.

"Certainly." Livvie opened the leather-bound cover, moved closer to the window and read the first entry, 'One's Self I Sing.' "

Mrs. Crowell tilted her head as Livvie ended the short poem and sat lost in her own musings.

Mrs. Locke knit her brows. "It had no rhyme."

Mrs. Crowell returned to her embroidery. "Very interesting language. Very modern. Read another, Livvie."

Interesting, indeed. The "*Form complete*" more than interested Livvie—it invigorated her senses. As did the line, "*Of Life immense in passion, pulse and power*."

Reading these words after feeling Sam's touch instilled an instant recognition of their meaning. She scanned the next poem to learn its contents before reading "*As I Ponder'd in Silence*." Harmless enough, so she gave it voice and paced while she read.

Although Mrs. Locke pressed her lips disagreeably, she made no argument.

Mrs. Crowell paused the needle. "Who is the poet?"

"Walt Whitman," Livvie replied.

"I've never heard of him." Mrs. Crowell waved a finger in the air. "Let's hear more."

Reciting the words to "*In Cabin'd Ships at Sea*," a yearning filled Livvie's breast. The poem referred not to the tall wooden ships, but to his own book of prose: "*Then falter not, O book, fulfill your destiny*."

Destiny. Mr. Whitman believed in his verse, sent it sailing across the country far and wide. Livvie had sent out her own writing, but to what effect? Had the publisher received it? Had Mr. Randall responded yet? Perhaps a letter of acceptance awaited her at her brother's home. The desire to hold her own novel in her hands burned through her, every bit as deeply as Sam's touch.

That he'd entrust to her a book of such deep prose also touched her. Finding a man who respected her intellect was rare. Rarer still was finding a man who engaged her in lively conversation. Embarrassed that her first impression had fallen so far from the mark, she wished she had sufficient time to learn more about Mr. Langhorne. But how much was sufficient? The more she shared his company, the more she learned, and the more she wanted to know.

At Mrs. Crowell's urging, Livvie continued the

reading. Midway through "*Song of Myself*," she faltered. Whitman dared to include *crotch* after *love-root,* following with *light kisses.* Livvie faltered at *Urge and urge and urge*, and again at *always sex.*

Mrs. Locke gasped and fanned herself using her handkerchief. "Outrageous."

Bemused, Mrs. Crowell simply said, "Oh dear."

Livvie closed the book. "Perhaps we should read something else. Some other time."

Martha blinked rapidly. "I should say so. I need a glass of water."

Sighing, Mrs. Crowell went back to her embroidery. "I suppose something else would be more suitable."

Livvie cradled *Leaves of Grass* to her bosom. "If you'll excuse me, I have a bit of a headache." She turned and climbed the stairs.

Livvie noticed she carried herself differently. More freely. Sam's touch had awakened something inside her, a powerful force that had slept while she grew under the protective eye of her father. A force she'd known existed, yet never suspected it held such utter dominance over her. Was she a hussy? Surely other women must enjoy their husbands—and lovers—with as much enthusiasm. None would admit it, though she'd seen hints of it in the way a woman hung on a man's arm, stroked his hair, even a certain look exchanged between them. No, she would not believe herself to be the lone female outside of prostitution who welcomed intimacy with a man.

She would not suffer their judgment, nor indulge them in shame. Her life was no business of theirs. Nor anyone's.

****

The following evening, Sam hurriedly changed his shirt. His hopes to see Livvie earlier were dashed when his work took an unexpected turn. Captain Howe had convinced the captain of the damaged ship to halt salvage of the cargo and attempt to pull the ship from the reef. None had been more surprised than Captain Howe when the attempt succeeded, and they towed the ship to shore for repairs.

An agreeable solution for all, despite keeping Sam from Livvie.

A knock at the door startled him. When he opened it, Livvie stood before him. The sight of her caused a hitch in his chest.

"I've come to return your book."

"You finished already?"

She handed it to him. "I'm afraid Mr. Whitman caused quite a stir in Key West, also."

"What do you mean?"

"You have no idea?" Though her tone sounded more playful than accusatory, it hinted at some guilt. Probably his.

"I told you, I haven't read it."

The door of a neighboring cabin opened. Sam tugged her arm. "You better come in. Now, tell me."

After a backward glance, she entered. "The author describes several…*encounters*, and the ecstasy of two people…*together*."

"Are you joking?" Sam felt his face blanch.

"I believe the encounters were two men." Although she did not smile, her eye held a definite twinkle.

"And this caused further offense." He hated to think of putting Livvie in such a position, and was surprised she showed no trace of embarrassment.

"Mrs. Locke nearly fainted and asked for water."

Had the content not offended Livvie? Or had she looked beyond the surface and recognized the writer's talent? "What was your impression of the prose?"

"It was rather astounding, and stimulating. Mr. Whitman is quite clearly taken with himself, yet he writes with such conviction one cannot help but be taken as well. He uses everyday language to describe ordinary events, yet challenges their very ordinariness. Challenging the reader to make more of each moment." She spoke rapidly, caught up in her own description, and then seemed lost in her thoughts.

"I can't wait to read it." He regarded her in even more surprise. He'd never suspected her to be so open to new ideas. "You weren't offended by the…encounters he described?"

"No. When two people fall in love, I believe it's beyond their control. They give themselves freely to one another."

Liam's words. But Liam's definition didn't include love, only the giving part. On Livvie's lips, the words were akin to a probe. A searching out of the boundaries, something to grasp hold of.

Sam was more accustomed to keeping out of reach. "I see."

If she expected a declaration of love, he wasn't ready to give it. Not even if he wanted to and had practiced different ways of saying it. "Please convey my sincerest apology to Mrs. Locke. I would not have lent the book to you had I known its contents." Damned Edward—probably sent it in jest. A taunt.

"No? Even if I thoroughly enjoyed it?"

He set the book on the shelf. "In that case, I would

have merely warned you against reading it to Mrs. Locke."

"She has very little tolerance for anything out of the ordinary."

"So she must not appreciate her stay at Key West." He sat at the foot of the bed, leaving plenty of room for her beside him.

She did not join him. Instead, she curled an arm around the bedpost.

"She's hardly seen any of Key West. She admonishes me for walking unescorted while there are so many ruffians about."

"Most are harmless. Like Mr. Whitman, they devise other arrangements to fulfill their needs." He ran a finger from her wrist along her arm. Not enough of a distraction to halt the conversation and cause her to throw herself into his arms.

"What other arrangements?"

"Encounters. Or living arrangements. To satisfy their needs because there are too few women on the island." In his mind, he unbuttoned her dress and let it fall to the floor. Her nearness unleashed his desire. He pulled her hand to his lips.

Her lips parted. "You mean…"

He arched an eyebrow in answer.

Some spark caught her eye. "Have you? Ever?" Curiosity tinged her voice, not disgust.

"Me? No. I've no inclination to." If she would lay with him again, he would show her his inclinations. Again and again.

"Aren't you lonely?"

Her words pierced him. He hadn't realized how lonely until yesterday.

"Sometimes." He shifted, uncomfortable about speaking of his personal needs.

"So you seduce shipwrecked ladies?"

He searched her face. "Livvie, if you're implying I seduced you, I seem to remember it the other way around." If she turned this thing around on him, he would never forgive her. Or himself.

Although her face tinged a warm red, her laugh sounded haughty. "Yes, certainly. It was entirely my idea. You wanted no part of it."

"I didn't say that. Of course I—"

"Don't say another word." She stepped toward the door. "I know I shouldn't have…come to you." Her gaze fluttered around the room, refusing to land on him.

He held himself back from going to her, easing her distress. He wanted honesty from her, untainted by his touch. "Do you regret it?"

She set her jaw. "Yes. I always regret acting foolishly."

A cannonball shot through his stomach could not have made him feel more hollow. "What we did was not foolish, Livvie." Much as he forced an even tone, he could not hide his passion.

She turned away. "Stop calling me that."

His eyebrows twitched together in confusion. "It's your name."

"Olivia." She met his gaze, a hardness in her eye. "My name is Olivia."

He stood. "Oh. Pardon me. Perhaps you would prefer Miss Collins."

She lifted her chin, her nostrils flared. "Perhaps it's best, yes."

He stepped nearer. Had he misjudged her? Had she

used him? The irony would be too great to bear. "Did yesterday mean nothing to you?"

She folded her arms across her chest and turned to the window. "Oh, what a question."

"That's no answer."

She whirled to face him, her eyes bright with anger and unshed tears. "How can you even ask me such a thing? When I know perfectly well not to ask you."

He fumbled for words. Was this some sort of trickery?

"It's you who insists on keeping the distance between us, Sam." She reached for the door knob. "I have to go."

If she left now, it might be too difficult—too awkward—to speak to her again. She would leave regretting yesterday. "I wish we had more time."

She paused. "For what?"

Even if the span between them seemed an unbridgeable gulf, he spoke his mind without reserve. "We've only known each other a short time."

"We know one another as intimately as two people can." Her shoulders relaxed, and she half-turned, still averting her gaze.

"Knowing someone intimately doesn't tell enough about them to truly know them." Her youth would not have allowed enough experience for her to learn this, a truth sometimes eluding couples married decades.

She turned quickly, her soft voice full of passion. "You're wrong. I learned much about you from our encounter."

He had not expected such candor. "Such as?"

She searched his face. "I learned you are tender and giving, but you hold yourself back, hold too much inside.

Why? Are you afraid of showing your true feelings, Sam?"

"You don't know what you're saying."

Her intense scrutiny made him uneasy.

"Did someone hurt you? So much that you distrust every other who shares her gender?"

Her face, illuminated by the setting sun, appeared so innocent, so youthful. She could not possibly know of the terrible danger inherent in offering oneself to another. The intricacies of a relationship.

"Yes." The lone word revealed more than he had ever shared with anyone else. He stood rigid, unwilling to display himself further through any action or language.

"Then I am truly sorry, Sam. To close yourself off in such a way that you can never know happiness again. It makes me sad for you."

He laughed, a hollow sound. "You needn't pity me."

Her face hardened, her beautiful lips retreating to a thin, disapproving line. "No. You're right. To choose such a life willingly is your own doing. You deserve no pity."

This was the kind of woman he was used to. Whose tender caresses turned to merciless clawing, so deep his very heart was at peril. "Such harsh words from one who would have me believe—"

"I will not be so pathetic as to cling to false hope. To wait for you to sort out your feelings could take years." She bowed her head. "I hold you to nothing, Sam. Forget yesterday, if you must." She lifted her head to hold his gaze for a moment, perhaps waiting for him to open himself to her. In resignation, she turned and walked out.

Stunned, Sam stood there, staring at the closed door.

She knew him. She knew him completely, her sweet touch had divined his true self, had breathed into his mouth and captured the essence of his soul. Her openness, her honesty, entranced him more than her beauty.

Yet he still could not move, could not will himself to go after her, to confess his feelings.

The sensation of being in Livvie's arms could not be more opposite to his time with Helen. When Livvie looked at him, she exposed herself completely. Nothing else existed in the world. Her giving nature resulted from her feelings, and what she did not feel, she would not give. He knew it to be true.

If Livvie left Key West, he would likely never meet another having near her qualities. Her inquisitive nature inspired him to share his thoughts, his world. He trusted her reaction to be true, not a response designed to please him. Her skills of comprehension and analysis exceeded those of many educated men. Were it not for the constraints of society, Livvie could have risen to great power, if she'd aspired to.

He had never encountered another girl like her. That was perhaps what frightened him most. Yet he still felt rooted where he stood, even as he saw, in his mind's eye, her figure grow smaller and disappear altogether. One thought repeated in his head: *I will never forget.*

Chapter Twenty-Two

Key West buzzed with the news: The *Brilliant*'s Captain Bethel had planned a grand party. Everywhere Sam went, he could not escape it.

Ignoring the commotion proved difficult, especially when Liam took considerable pleasure in reminding him. "Cap'n Bethel's invited all the townsfolk to his house. Oh, and all the passengers from *Elizabeth Rose.* Bit of a going-away party, I'd say."

Sam clenched his jaw. "How generous of Captain Bethel."

"Oh, not generous at all. Bethel likes to stay on the good side of everyone, judges and wreckers alike." Liam's tilted head hovered close to Sam's. "Ye haven't made mention of the invitation."

"Mm." Indeed, he hadn't. Not out of coyness. He simply couldn't make up his mind. To attend the party—where he'd see Livvie, possibly for the last time—might be too ridiculous a pretense to undertake. Too awkward—all those other people nearby. She likely had no desire to see him ever again.

Liam leaned an elbow on Sam's shoulder. "Meself, I think I'll go to the groggery. I'm not one for fancy affairs. Clean clothes. Polite conversation. Ecch."

"Yes, it's a waste because we could be celebrating in a manner more consistent with our lifestyle." Sam held his tongue after realizing his language had taken an upturn from the usual. In his mind, he'd rehearsed speaking in a more casual manner so as not to reveal his background, especially his legal education.

"Eh?" Liam pulled back his chin, his brows knit.

Sam shrugged from beneath Liam's elbow. "The groggery's where I'd rather be too." He might spend more time there than usual in the coming weeks. Or months. He hoped it would take no longer to wash Livvie from his thoughts.

****

Sam and Liam had a table to themselves. The bar held fewer patrons tonight, though not by much. Schooner captains tended not to fraternize amongst their crew. Most were married and returned to their families at night. Many crewmen had wives, also, and busied themselves at home. Like Liam, Sam had refused any ties to person or place. In the past year, Liam's notion of working a farm had gained Sam's favor, and Sam had squirreled away money like never before. He now had more than enough for years to come. When the time was right, he and Liam would buy equal shares of land on another key, and settle down, each in his own way.

Jahner rushed in, his glassy eyes testament to earlier celebration. "Have you heard?"

Exchanging confused glances, Sam and Liam had no chance to answer.

Slapping Liam's back, Jahner said, "Judge Martin ruled for the *Florida.* Tomorrow, we're back to work.*"* His raucous laugh stirred attention, and he moved to the bar to repeat the news.

"Ah, just the news we've been waitin' fer." Liam downed his drink. "Bartender, another round." Frowning at Sam's mug, he clucked his tongue. "Ye haven't even finished yer first."

"Give me one moment." Drinking his ale, Sam tried to steer his thoughts away from the party, where Livvie would surely be dancing, maybe drinking more *camperou*. His stomach clenched; despite her experience at the last dance, she might indulge again. And perhaps another man might try to woo her. Or worse still—succeed.

"Sam." Liam looked at him with a mixture of wonder and disgust. "Ye're as much fun as an addle-brained fool."

"What?" Sam gulped his ale, wiped a hand across his mouth, and stood. "Ready for another refill?"

Liam leaned back. "I'm not stayin' any longer. Ye'll put me to sleep."

"You're leaving? Already?"

"Don't sound so wounded. I've better things to do than coddle ye." He drew some coins from his pocket and carried them to the counter. "Good night."

Sam followed him out the door. "Hold on. I might as well leave too."

Whistling, Liam meandered in the opposite direction he should be headed.

Sam halted. "Where are you going?"

"For a stroll." Liam held his arms wide. "It's a lovely evening, don't ye think?"

"A stroll? Since when are you inclined to stroll?" His friend must be up to something. Sam had no clue what. Whatever it was, he didn't want to miss it.

Liam held up a professorial finger. "A man must follow his instincts, Sam."

Sam guessed more than instinct led him. Still, he'd go along. Following Greene Street to where Whitehead

Street intersected, Sam understood. Every window of Captain Bethel's house glowed, and music drifted merrily from inside.

Liam halted outside the yard and smiled.

Sam stopped beside him, irritated by Liam's smugness. "And what instincts drew you here, my old friend?"

"The oldest instinct of all."

"Mmm." Although Sam had no care to participate in this conversation, it wouldn't stop his friend from continuing it.

Liam lifted his arms toward the house. "Music. Who can resist its siren call?"

Through the tall windows, bodies shifted in rhythm to the lilting melody. Livvie's long gold hair stood out against the rest as she swirled past in the arms of an older gentleman.

Sam wanted to look away but couldn't. "Apparently, no one."

Liam stood shoulder to shoulder beside him. "She's a lovely girl."

"Yes." The lamplight highlighted her hair.

"Feisty, too, eh?" Liam winked.

Sam snorted. "Yes, she's strong-willed."

"The perfect temperament for living in a harsh place such as Key West."

Sam ignored his friend's comment. He couldn't tear himself away from the scene. The more he watched the old goat's hands on her waist, the more he wanted to knock him to the ground and sweep her up in his arms.

Liam sighed. "If I weren't such an old fool, I'd have settled down with a pretty girl like her years ago."

Sam surveyed his friend for a sign of sarcasm.

"You're not serious."

The faraway look in Liam's eyes matched his wistful tone. "It's me one regret in life." He blinked hard, appearing to remember something. "In fact, I believe I'll go find Millie and ask her to marry me."

Sam waved him away. "Now I know you're daft."

Liam laid a hand over his heart. "Ye wound me. Do ye not think me human? In need of companionship?"

"I thought your need of companionship extended only to the groggery."

Liam tilted his head. "I've been contemplating marriage for some time. Millie's agreeable enough. And willing enough."

"She's willing enough, for sure." Sam regretted the comment when he saw Liam's stung look.

Liam clasped Sam's shoulder. "Good night, old friend. Tomorrow, we shall celebrate an engagement."

Sam sat on the curb, and Liam strolled away. His off-key rendition of *My Wild Irish Rose* made Sam wince.

"The bloom's already off that rose," Sam called.

Liam's laugh echoed through the streets. "It's still sweet." His lilting song faded, leaving only the violins and piano to serenade the night.

He should leave too. Go home. He grunted. Nothing but an empty bed awaited him there. Maybe he'd go back to Grohl's.

A rustling of leaves in the yard stirred him to attention. He slipped behind a tree and peered around it. His heart skipped seeing Livvie stroll aimlessly through the garden.

He jumped the white picket fence and went to her, careful not to arouse attention from anyone inside.

Livvie turned, her mouth agape as he approached.

He bowed, giving a flourish of his arm. "Good evening, Miss Collins."

"I didn't think you were coming." Disappointment, and a little anger, tinged her tone.

He would never be able to explain to her satisfaction why he couldn't bear to attend, so he wouldn't try. "I happened to be passing by, and I saw you."

Her gaze flicked toward the street, and back at him. "How long have you been here?"

"Long enough to see you dance with the old goat." He leaned against the coconut palm tree.

"His presence will cause the voyage ahead to quickly become tedious." She stepped around the tree, farther away from the house.

Sam followed, suppressing the urge to press himself against her. "When does the *Excellent* arrive?"

"In a few days, if my brother's letter is correct." She lowered her head.

He couldn't be sure, but he thought he saw tears in her eyes. She pressed her lips together, and a small pulse along her jaw told him she'd clenched back any tears daring to follow.

His chest swelled; the pressure almost too great to bear. The music in the house slowed to a waltz, and he held out his hand, palm up. "May I have this dance?"

She eyed him suspiciously, but relaxed when he tilted his head in a grin. Her breathy laugh mixed surprise and pleasure. "You may." Her fingertips caressed his palm.

Their bodies swayed in perfect rhythm. He was reminded of the day he rescued her, when she stood on the deck of the *Florida*, swaying in time to the schooner's rocking.

Their movements paced slower than the violins playing inside the house. She avoided his gaze, and he didn't allow himself to hold her too close. If he kissed her, he didn't know how he would stop himself.

"You waltz so well," she said.

"You sound surprised." He made his tone light to try to put her at ease.

"Of course, I knew you could dance. The waltz, however, requires a particular grace."

"I thought I'd already proven myself graceful." He'd intended it in jest, but also wished to provoke her memory of their afternoon together. He had been able to think of nothing else.

She drew in a ragged breath, her eyes widened, and she looked away. "You know what I meant."

"And you know what I meant." The scent of her intoxicated him, sent his blood humming through his veins. "Let's leave here, Livvie."

She spread her hand across his chest, bracing against him. "What? Where?"

He linked his fingers through hers, and tightened his embrace. "To my cabin." His lips caressed her ear and he whispered, "To my bed."

Sighing, she trembled against him.

A tumultuous storm rose up and overtook his senses. He smothered her in kisses and drew her into the darkest corner of the yard, unable to hold her close enough to satisfy his need.

She returned his urgent kisses equally, fueling his desire. His caress swept down her back, across her curves.

She pressed against him.

"Livvie, I must have you." He needed her like any other sustenance, as urgently as he needed air to breathe.

She pulled away weakly. "Stop. I can't think."

"Don't think," he whispered. "Feel." He slid his hand up her waist and cupped her breast.

"No." She tugged it away.

"Why not?" His voice shook in desperation.

"No." She pushed hard at his shoulder. "I can't."

He could hardly speak. "What do you mean, you can't?"

She extracted herself completely from his embrace. "I cannot risk another…encounter."

He stood helpless. "What risk?" Did she fear gossip?

"How can you ask such a thing? You know perfectly well." She glared at him. "I'm leaving soon. How would I explain to my brother if I am bearing a child when I arrive in New Orleans?"

He reached for her. "There are other ways, equally satisfying. Let me show you."

"Stop. This is madness." She turned away, lingering uncertainly.

He moved to face her, crouching to coax her gaze to his. "Yes, and I'm a madman. Mad with thoughts of you that come unbidden and won't cease."

"Then why continue?" Her eyes flashed such a mix of emotions, he hardly knew how to respond. Until he recognized one of the emotions as hope. She was frightened, needing reassurance.

"I awake in the night aching to feel you near. I reach for you, but the emptiness is too much to bear." He'd never admitted to any woman the physical need of his feelings. And never in such desperation. Had it been anyone else, he'd have thrashed himself later for such revelations. Livvie had to understand the depth of his feelings.

She withdrew, tears welling in her eyes. "You want me to relieve you of your needs so you can sleep?"

"No, that's not what I meant."

The back door slammed. Speaking in low tones, a man guided a woman to the side of the porch.

Sam froze. When the two embraced, Sam took Livvie's hand, drawing her to the fence. "Come with me."

"I can't." Her eyes held such sorrow.

When he moved closer to embrace her, she turned away.

"Please go."

"Now? Can't we spend a little time together?"

"There's no point." Her voice small, she retreated from his grasp.

Her words stung him. "Oh. I see." He clenched his jaw. "It isn't enough to want to be together."

Her eyes searched his. "For one more night? No. It isn't. You've already told me that I don't belong here." Her statement held a challenge—and a plea.

His stomach clenched. She wanted more than reassurance. She wanted a declaration. A declaration he wasn't ready to give.

From the porch, the man called, "Who's there?"

Livvie swiped her cheek. "Just me," she called. "Olivia Collins. I needed some air."

The woman asked, "Are you all right?"

"Yes." Livvie's face was a mask of disappointment. "I'm just coming in."

He could only watch while she walked toward the house and climbed the steps. He waited in hopes she might change her mind and return, his hopes falling further with each step, until she went inside. The couple stayed on the porch in the shadows.

In one leap, he was on the other side of the fence.

"Is someone there?" the man called again.

Sam strode off. Let them think what they damn well wanted.

He let the darkness swallow him. Before he knew it, he strode to the edge of Conchtown. Three men stood outside a cabin, their identities obscured by shadow.

One stepped in his path.

Jacob Preston tilted his head and sneered, "What's the matter, Langhorne? No luck with the ladies tonight?" The stale smell of ale filled the air between them.

Sam's nostrils flared. "Go home and sober up." He pushed past.

A shove at his shoulder made him whirl, fists clenched.

At first Preston tensed, and then relaxed when Sam made no move to fight. Preston strolled in a circle around him. "You're not very neighborly tonight. I asked a friendly question."

"Maybe it's none of your business, boy." He emphasized the last word. Preston's frame had thickened after a year of wrecking jobs, though not by much. Sam could easily knock the lad cold.

Preston widened his eyes like a madman. "Maybe you're right." He glanced at his friends and laughed. "Maybe I shouldn't worry about it at all. Instead, I should take care of myself."

"Exactly. Good night." Sam took a step.

Preston blocked his way, a gleam in his eye. "I know," he taunted. "I'll go knock on the door of the

Crowells' boardinghouse. There's a pretty girl there. I bet she's lonely tonight."

Sam ground his teeth. He could contain himself.

"Not tonight," his friend said. "I'll wager she's at Bethel's party."

Preston snapped his finger. "Right, I'd forgotten. I'll bet she's thirsty. She does love to dance."

Sam grabbed his shirt. "Careful, lad. You don't want to upset anyone."

His friends stood straight, ready to spring to Jacob's aid.

Although Preston laughed, his voice shook. "Who? You?" He shoved his hands between Sam's arms to loosen his grip.

Sam drew his fist back and sailed it into Jacob's jaw. His eyes rolled back, and he fell to the ground.

Sam turned, ready for the others. "Anyone else?"

They held up their hands and backed away, shaking their heads.

Sam exhaled. "Smart men. Too bad your friend isn't so wise. He might need some help getting home."

They didn't move until he walked away.

He flexed his hand to ease the pain. It was not the release he sought.

Chapter Twenty-Three

An eerie howl awoke Sam. The wind groaned through the shutters in a whisper of doom. Going to the window, he shut it, bolting the shutters. In the pre-dawn dimness, he dressed hurriedly. The gusts soon became a gale. Anything not bolted in place rattled and banged. As Sam stepped outside, a bucket tripped end over end toward him. He stepped from its path, continuing to the wharf, huddling against the driving rain.

The *Florida* rocked in place as waves crashed against the bow. He climbed aboard and then down below.

Liam sat near Captain Howe and a few other men. "Any news?"

"None yet. If any ship's out there, it won't be long before we must go to its rescue."

Two unfamiliar men sat in the corner, their skin darker than the shadows surrounding them. Sam met their gazes momentarily, then sat next to Liam on the floor.

"New divers?" Sam asked.

Liam grunted. "Homer Jackson and Lemuel Smith."

Replacements for Jasper and Isum. The expendable ones. First to be sent to the depths in any weather or situation. Sam's stomach churned, keenly feeling the blinded divers' absences. He couldn't blame these men for taking their places, nor warn them of the dangers.

They already knew. The money more than made up for it, Jasper used to say. Sam wondered what he would say now.

Captain Howe sipped his coffee. "Sleep now, if you can, men."

The crew unfurled their bedrolls on the floor, the schooner rocking like a mad cradle. Sam stared at nothing, his thoughts as tumultuous as the sea.

Captain Howe went up on deck.

Liam stirred, glancing at Sam. "I pity any ship a'sail today."

The captain called from the stairway, "Set sail, men! The lookout spotted a ship." His voice was loud enough for the crew, but not enough to alert wreckers on nearby schooners. If a ship struck the reef, it would need all available hands. Captain Howe obviously intended to arrive first to assume the role of Wrecking Master.

The crew needed no further prompting. Each man scrambled to his feet, rolling his bedroll and stowing it within seconds before hurrying up top.

Light crept through the low, dark clouds, suddenly illuminated by streaks of lightning.

Sam gripped the rail, squinting in the direction of Captain Howe's gaze. A blaze of lightning lit the scene in a surreal light. Sure enough, the silhouette of a tall ship, its sails ragged and torn, rocked a few miles out.

"Quickly," the captain urged. "Get the *Florida* underway."

The men took up their positions. Sam pulled up anchor while Liam freed the schooner from the dock. Using uncanny precision, Jahner guided the rudder to bring the boat clear. The others hoisted sail. The wind favored their destination. The *Florida* skipped across the ragged ocean.

Aided by the force of the wind behind them, raindrops struck Sam's skin, sharp as pinpricks. The rudder groaned when Jahner steered them alongside the ship, lowering the sails so as to keep a safe enough distance to avoid collision.

The wreck creaked, its great moans testament to its gaping wounds wrought by the reef. Aboard, figures scrambled about in a frenzy. By the angle of the stern, the ship was taking on water fast. Their first task would be to save the passengers before negotiating any salvage work.

Captain Howe boomed, "Ahoy!"

The ship's captain appeared at the rail in answer, confirming their assessment. The ship was sure to be a total loss. If not for the storm, the *Florida* might have freed it from the reef to tow it down the Gulf Stream for repairs. The gale battered it against the reef mercilessly, damaging it beyond repair. The great ship tilted at the mercy of the wind.

"Why don't they lower their sails, for chrissakes?" Liam said.

An uneasy feeling crept over Sam. "Maybe the storm surprised them in the night." Even so, someone should have been on watch. These reefs claimed so many ships because most captains only learned of their existence once it was too late, when their ships were caught as surely as an animal in a steel trap.

"The mast won't hold much longer in this." Sam scanned the waters for any sign of life. Rescue would be difficult in these rough waters. Not impossible, but he'd require the crew's expert assistance.

Waves surged against the sinking ship. It responded

in great creaks and groans, its gashes deepening. A sail slumped toward deck, gaining tremendous speed and force. A bolt of lightning shot from the clouds, striking the main mast. A loud crack split the air as it toppled toward the *Florida*. The wreck twisted against the reef, hurling people into the black seas.

Time stopped while Sam stood awaiting his fate. The steepled wood swung from the sky, lowering like the wrathful finger of God. A warning. An omen. An eerie silence prevailed despite the storm. The mast swung down, crashing into the sea within feet of the schooner. The resulting wave swept the *Florida* back toward shore, tilting and spinning like a child's toy. The force of it flung Sam across the deck. He grabbed hold of the first thing within reach, a rope giving too much slack. It allowed him to shimmy up the side rail. Strong hands grasped his leg.

Liam. Sam gripped his extended hand and held tight. Both struggled to hold the rail. The schooner's rocking slowed as the *Florida* righted itself atop the sea.

Sam threw down the useless rope. "I owe you one."

Liam winked. "More than one, but I'm not counting, mate."

Captain Howe yelled orders to bring the schooner back to the wreck. "We've work to do, men. Quickly. People are in need of rescue."

Each man readied for the grim task ahead while they set sail toward the ship. The howling wind echoed with screams. They seemed to bubble up from Davy Jones' locker itself. People had been tossed from the wreck—or jumped. Some bobbed in the waves, while many others had likely already plunged below the surface, struggling for their lives.

Once the schooner came to an uneasy rest on its anchor, Sam leapt with his mates into the choppy sea.

Sharp broken planks and other debris slowed attempts to swim. High waves pounded his chest, engulfing him. Sam gasped for air, his muscles already feeling the strain. He aimed for the nearest person, a woman whose bonnet was stained red along a gash. He took hold of her. She made no attempt to cling to him. He clasped her jaw to look at her. Her eyes had rolled back in her head, though her chest rose and fell with breath. She was alive, but in need of more assistance than Sam knew how to give. He swiveled her onto her back and swam, hauling her along.

Waves crashed over his head almost too quickly to catch his breath in between. He made his arduous way back to the schooner, visible for fleeting seconds between the swells. The harder he swam toward it, the farther away the ocean dragged him, as though Poseidon himself had cursed them all.

This is madness. The shore appeared unreachable from here. He ached to see Livvie, to hold her. Time was too precious, He risked everything here when he should be with her.

Something slammed into the back of his head, sending his face into the water. By reflex he gasped. The sharp taste of salty water stung his nostrils, his mouth. The sea turned black as octopus ink. He felt himself sinking, floating in darkness. In the darkness, a figure glowed—a woman whose hair glistened gold, whose eyes held the hue of dark amber. "Sam," came her watery whisper. "Sam."

Livvie. He fought toward the surface, flailing. A rope splashed on the surface nearby, and he grasped it, holding tight. It dragged him through the rough seas, the clutch of unseen fingers loosening below, begrudgingly. Familiar voices called, yet he couldn't respond. Hands lifted him—more hands, pulling him up from the water, onto the deck. As his eyes fluttered open, faces swam above him.

"Livvie," he moaned. Darkness closed in on him once more.

****

"Nasty blow to the head," a man said. "After a rest, he'll be good as new."

The feel of hardwood beneath him, Sam blinked open his eyes. "What's going on?"

His gaze intently assessing, Captain Howe stood over him. Liam crouched near his bedroll, staring keenly.

Peering through his glasses, Doctor Meade knelt down. "Ah, good. You're conscious. I'll need to clean your wound. I don't think you'll need stitches. Looks more like a surface cut."

"Wound?" Vague recollections came back to him in pieces. Gradually he remembered. "The woman—did you bring her aboard? I don't know what happened; I had hold of her, swimming toward the schooner…" In speaking, he gazed into each man's face, hoping to ease his dread.

Their expressions were answer enough.

"She drowned." Sam let out a ragged breath.

Captain Howe widened his stance. "You made a valiant effort, Sam. Your mates too. The storm grew too violent."

"Where are we?" But he already knew. The doctor could not be aboard if they hadn't returned to shore.

Resolute sadness filled the captain's face. "The risk

became too great. Once the storm subsides, we'll go back. Doctor, we've others to tend to. Please be quick."

Doctor Meade clamped Sam's jaw to turn his head. He dabbed something that stung enough to make Sam suck air through his clenched teeth.

"All right. As I suspected, no stitches. Stay awake until tonight, no matter how tired you may feel. It's very important."

Sam pushed himself to a higher sitting position. "All right. Thanks, Doc."

The doctor moved away, and Sam turned to Liam. "What others? What happened?"

Liam kept his voice low. "We nearly needed a rescue ourselves. The storm became too great."

"Did we bring anyone back?"

The brutal truth in Liam's steely gaze pierced Sam. "Two." He slumped next to Sam and leaned against the wall.

Two. Out of a crew of at least fifteen and who knew how many passengers. Never had they turned away from a wreck.

Never had Sam wanted to, but he did now. He lay against his bedroll, reliving the day's events in his head, trying to pinpoint his mistakes. The doctor needn't have worried. Sam would not sleep tonight, no matter how tired he grew.

Vernon called the crew for dinner, and Liam brought back two plates of fish. His tales of hunting expeditions raised the spirits of the other men. Sam smiled and nodded, even if he only heard half of what his friend said. Never before had a day's events so shaken him.

Upon Captain Howe's orders, the crew slept aboard the schooner. The sounds of snoring in the darkness failed to soothe Sam. Tomorrow could not come soon enough. The earlier they began their work, the sooner they would finish.

****

The men rode in the wagon, too exhausted to walk. Two days of salvaging lumber had taken its toll. The storm had raged another day before the schooner could take up its position again beside the wreck.

Sam pressed his fingers to his weary eyes, wishing he were in his bed already. His head ached less than yesterday, but it ached nonetheless.

At a chinking sound, he opened his eyes to slits.

Opposite him sat Lewis Pinder. His very name irked Sam, compounded by his weasel-like appearance. Lewis' small eyes darted to and fro. He must have thought everyone else too tired to notice when he reached into his pocket and pulled out a chain. It sparkled golden even though the sinking sun hid behind scattered clouds.

Sam straightened. "What have you got there?"

Pinder jerked his head up and cast his gaze wildly to each man's face. Shoving the chain back in his pocket, he glared. "Nothing."

Sam could not abide a liar. "Looked like jewelry. A necklace, maybe?"

"None of your damn business," Pinder snarled. His scowl blistered in his ruddy face.

The damned cheat. He cared nothing for anyone save himself.

Sam could not let the incident pass. "Did you take it from the wreck?"

"I said no." Pinder's tone hardened, and so did his glare. "Bugger off."

Liam nudged Sam, and slowly shook his head. Sam opened his mouth to argue, and Liam arched a disapproving brow.

Sam eased back. Pinder could not escape punishment much longer.

The wagon circled to the warehouse entrance. The men climbed down, too weary to move quickly. Once the final load was secure in the warehouse, they could go home.

Sam's nerves were frazzled. His head hurt, an unusual occurrence, though not surprising given his lack of sleep of late, and ceaseless thoughts. Livvie's impending departure consumed him, and weighing what to say to her tortured him. He should never have taken her to his bed. Whenever he lay there, in the dark, he imagined her next to him. Wanted her there. To hold her, tell her about his day, ask what new thing she'd discovered over the course of the day. Her method of looking at the world opened his eyes to things in ways he hadn't known. She was infuriating, and exciting, and made him wake up every day wanting to see her.

Liam shoved a load of lumber toward Sam. He grabbed one end, and they dragged it inside the warehouse.

Liam bent to stack it atop the other lumber. "Ye shouldn't bother Pinder."

Sam bristled. "He's a thief. And a liar."

"Yer a harsh judge, Sam. I'll wager it's only an occasional crime."

Sam leaned closer, his whisper sharp. "And I'll wager he does it much more often than occasionally. I've seen him take things—expensive things, like jewelry— for the past three wrecks."

Liam shrugged. "He's a lout." He strolled toward the wide doorway.

Sam followed. "I wouldn't mind so much if he would work for it. He's the laziest wrecker I've ever known."

Liam chuckled. "I won't argue the notion."

"When he steals, he steals from all of us. And not from the shipping companies, either. He takes personal items, things meaningful to their owners."

"Aye, he's a slimy scum bucket," Liam said too agreeably, with more than a bit of sarcasm.

The description fit too well, Sam thought. They reached the wagon, where Pinder stood holding the end of a piece of lumber.

Sam murmured, "The first real work he's done today."

Homer shoved the lumber abruptly, causing Pinder to stumble backward. His knee hit the ground, jolting the necklace from his pocket. Pinder reached for it. Not quickly enough.

Sam snatched it up. "What a lovely trinket. Where did you get it?"

"I told you. Mind your own business." Pinder grabbed for it.

Sam held it out of his reach. "It is my business. It's all of our business. Salvaging is what we do. For the *Florida*. Not for ourselves." As much as he wanted to smash the weasel's face, he held back.

Pinder sneered, "Don't be an ass. We're all in it for ourselves."

Bile rose in Sam's throat. "Some more than others." He slammed his fist into the man's jaw.

Pinder hit the ground with a thud and a jingle. A ring

tumbled from his pocket.

Men halted their work to stare and then gathered around.

Sam set his hands on his hips. "Ho, what's that? Another one? What else do you have, you pilferer?"

Pinder scrambled to his feet, lunging at Sam. His punch caught Sam's jaw, knocking him off balance.

The crew jeered, "Get him! Knock the bastard out!"

By their lack of specificity, Sam guessed the men would support whoever won. He intended to be the winner. He thrust his fist into Pinder's soft stomach.

The man doubled over, gasping for air.

"Knock the wind out of him!" someone called.

The lateness of the suggestion made Sam laugh.

Pinder took the chance to ram his shoulder into Sam's chest. They fell to the ground, scrabbling for the upper hand. Pinder managed to overturn Sam, slamming his fist into Sam's jaw.

Hauling out a piece of lumber, Liam whacked it against Pinder's shoulder. Pinder fell to the ground.

When Sam scrambled up, Liam held the lumber threateningly toward him. "End it now. Let the judge settle this."

Sam swiped his wrist against his mouth. It came back smeared blood red. Nodding, he bent to retrieve the ring and necklace. "The clerk can hold onto these until the judge decides. Unless you've anything else to add to them?"

Pinder leaned up on an elbow. Hate glittered in his eyes.

The clerk hurried to his counter inside the warehouse as Sam approached.

Sam laid the jewelry down. "Log these separately.

You'd best lock them up."

The clerk examined the jewelry, noting their descriptions in the register.

Liam leaned against the wagon as two men hauled the last of the lumber from it. "Best go home and get some rest."

"I'm fine." Sam dragged his hand across his forehead.

Liam gave a nod, his tone more firm. "Go on. We'll finish up."

Weariness washed over Sam. He looked into the face of each man watching. No one cheered. No one congratulated him. They drew away, wary and fearful.

Fights between wreckers occurred often enough, ending in a handshake, for the most part. In the wrecking trade, all stood together. They didn't turn on one another.

He turned to his friend, wanting to explain. Sam didn't allow his emotions to control him. He was the first to get between two in a brawl, not the one to start it.

Liam gave a reassuring wink. "Go on."

Sam left, only because Liam asked him. His feet scuffed the ground for the first few steps. At his cabin, he fell into his bed and darkness enveloped him.

****

Sam was not on the crew to patrol the reefs the next morning. He found Liam at the market. "Morning."

Liam glanced around before responding. "Morning. How are ye feeling?"

"A bit sore," Sam admitted. Something in his chest hitched. The talk in the groggery last night must have centered on him. By Liam's careful reaction, their judgment weighed against him, not Pinder. If the others considered him a pariah, Liam didn't abandon him.

"And hungry," he added. "What do you say to breakfast?"

Liam smiled. "Same as I always say. Let's go."

As they entered Grohl's, Sam felt the weight of the glances and the sting as the customers there turned away and spoke in low tones to those sitting near.

"Ah, here's a good table." Liam pulled out a chair by the bar. "Bast, me darlin' man. What have ye for breakfast?" His lilting tones floated above the din of conversation. No one could stay angry long in Liam's company.

Mr. Grohl wiped his hands on a rag. "Ham and eggs. Fresh coconut milk. The usual."

"Delightful. We'll have two."

Sam plopped into his seat. "Coffee first."

A server brought two steaming cups to the table. They lifted their mugs, and Liam cursed its heat for burning his mouth. Within minutes, the server brought two plates. Sam gratefully dug his fork in, replenishing his mouth soon after swallowing, grunting in agreement at Liam's praise of Bast's cooking skills.

Sam pushed his plate away. "You think I was wrong to confront Pinder."

"I'm no judge."

"But you disagreed."

Liam shrugged. "I try to see all sides of a thing."

Sam leaned his elbows on the table. "Even something so obviously wrong?"

Liam's soft voice carried heavy words. "Ye have to understand the motivation of a man. Sometimes he's driven by need, sometimes by greed."

"Pinder's is the latter."

Liam chuckled. "Ye speak like an authority."

Sam could not make light of the subject. "Can you doubt it? He has plenty."

"What seems plenty for us may not be for another." Liam spoke with the authority of a professor. "And I know a bit about Pinder. He has certain methods that make him feel…entitled."

Sam's curiosity piqued. "What methods?"

Liam lowered his voice, as if revealing a secret. "He has a skill for finding objects hidden by their owners. Passengers often fear theft, even from one another, so they stash their most valuable items in places others might not think to look."

Clearly, Liam admired Pinder's ingenuity, if not his ethics.

"All the more reason it's despicable. They're mostly personal things, things having sentimental value. No amount of money can substitute their worth."

"Pinder thinks if he didn't find them, they would stay lost forever. So either way, the owners wouldn't get them back."

"He speculates in favor of himself." The more Liam explained, the more goaded Sam felt. The audacity, to claim someone else's possession on such a flimsy excuse! Pinder himself was a flimsy excuse for a man.

"Perhaps." Liam leaned back in his chair. A signal the conversation had ended.

Liam's penchant for remaining neutral exasperated Sam sometimes. His friend's analytical mind was perplexing and enlightening. Liam had a gift for illuminating a perspective Sam wouldn't have considered. His legal education trained Sam to love a good argument to sharpen his mind. His skill for debate had grown dull from disuse these past few years.

Sam couldn't stop himself. "No judge would pardon his theft based on such a flimsy excuse."

Liam narrowed his eyes a moment. "Ye're right. No judge would."

Maybe his friend's image of Sam had changed. "Still you think I was wrong."

Liam gave an exasperated chuckle. "It's not the being wrong or right, Sam. Ye're missing the point."

"I am. I'm baffled."

His voice a hoarse whisper, Liam leaned closer. "Have ye never done it yourself?"

The question slapped his senses. "Stolen, you mean? No. I've never felt the need." He regarded his friend in a new light. "Have you?"

Liam pressed his lips together. "A few times. Mostly, I saw it as an advance against future payments."

Words escaped Sam, and he struggled to make sense of it. He would never have suspected Liam of stealing.

Liam clucked his tongue. "Don't look so crestfallen, now. I'm human, Sam. We're all weak creatures, capable of anything, given the right circumstances."

"I agree. Desperate circumstances sometimes cause men to undertake desperate measures. My point is: Pinder is far from desperate."

Liam nodded. "He requires more than most. To him, it's insurance against future hardships."

For the life of him, Sam couldn't find sympathy for such a perspective. "None of us know what the future holds. We cannot let possible disaster guide us in our present affairs."

A slow smile spread across Liam's face. "Really, Sam? Now, would that include affairs of the heart?"

Sam leaned back in his chair. "You old sea dog." He

chuckled. "This discussion is not about me."

"And why not? Aren't ye operating under the same principle?"

He'd won. The bastard. "You're right." Sam had tried to ignore his feelings for Livvie because he feared she would injure him. "Why are you trying to marry me off, Liam?"

"Misery loves company, I suppose." A smug smile spread across Liam's face.

Sam cocked his jaw. "You proposed to Millie? Honestly?"

Liam sat straight. "I did."

"And she accepted?"

"She did." Liam leaned closer. "Ye may congratulate me twice. I'm to be a father."

Sam's mouth dropped open in a smile. "You? By God, you are an old sea dog."

He winked. "Plenty of life left in me yet."

"I never thought I'd see the day."

"Ye? I never thought *I'd* see the day." His smile faded, though the happiness in his eyes shone bright. "I want ye to be my best man."

"Of course. When?"

"Soon. She's already beginning to bulge. I have to make an honest woman out of her." His raspy chuckle showed his delight.

Surely Liam knew the baby might belong to another man. Perhaps he didn't care. "Will she make an honest man out of you?"

"I believe she'll try."

"Mr. and Mrs. Liam and Millie Byrne. Imagine." Despite saying it aloud, Sam still couldn't conceive of it.

"And baby makes three."

Sam shook his head in wonder. "I'll miss you, old friend."

Liam's head jerked up. "What do ye mean?"

"Your new wife won't allow you to come to the groggery."

"She'll come with me." He turned pensive. "I have, however, decided to leave the wrecking business."

Sam suspected as much. "So you'll be a pirate?"

Liam laughed. "No, my pillaging days are through. I'll be a farmer."

Sam nodded. "An excellent farmer you'll make."

"I'd be a better one if I had some help." He worked his jaw, regarding Sam, waiting for an answer.

"Me?" he sputtered.

"Why, sure. We're good partners. Ye're a hard worker. And if ye're a terrible farmer, at least I know ye're honest."

Sam chuckled. "I'll think about it. Thank you."

"Once you're a farmer, ye'll be needing your own partner." Liam widened his eyes. "I'm looking forward to having a wife. Someone who'll tend to my needs."

"And you to hers," Sam reminded him.

Liam ignored his taunt. "A warm body to lie beside, her soft whispers lulling me to sleep."

"Or keeping you awake." Annie had complained of Millie's snores after a night of hard drinking. Likely not as loud as Liam's, yet he doubted their chorus would be less than harmonious.

Liam continued, "Someone to make me smile."

"And cry." He wondered if Millie would be able to curtail her flirting after exchanging vows.

Liam slammed his glass to the table. "Dammit, man. Enough arguing. Ye know I'm right."

"I know."

His friend froze; his eyes wide. "What? Ye do?"

Sam inhaled a fortifying breath. "Yes."

"Then go tell her, ye fool."

"I intend to."

"Good man." Giving a long, satisfied exhale, Liam sat back. "For the first time in a long time, Sam, I'm looking forward to the days ahead."

The events of the last week left Sam unsure of which direction to proceed. The past held only heartache, a pain he did not want to repeat in the future. Try as he might to imagine Livvie inflicting such pain on him, he couldn't.

****

After their meal, Sam strode to the warehouse and looked at the posting. Under the large, handscripted heading proclaiming: *Black List, to whom no Wrecking License will be issued, with reason of forfeiture.*

Beneath, Lewis Pinder's name appeared.

The sense of justice Sam expected lasted only a short while. Wrecking was a cruel enough business, and to add to another's hardship brought no satisfaction. If any others committed minor infractions against the law, he wouldn't be the one to bring it to light.

Sam's declaration to Liam came back to him. He should see Livvie. Today. Now.

He walked to Duval Street, within sight of the boarding house. His gut lurched at the thought of approaching Livvie, asking her to stay on in Key West. His veins iced, and he stood unable to move, chilled in the midday sun.

The ship that would carry her away hadn't arrived yet. Maybe he needed to think on it a bit more.

He turned and made his way to the dock to busy himself aboard the *Florida*. By the time he walked home, the moon sailed high in the sky.

****

Sunlight poured through the windows, overheating the front room. From lack of concentration as much as from the humidity, Livvie's fingers slipped along the piano keys. Why hadn't Sam called on her? Several times, she'd walked through town, hoping for a chance meeting. Yesterday, she thought she'd caught sight of him down the street from the boarding house. When she ran downstairs, no one was there.

At the bang of the back door, Mrs. Crowell looked up from her needlework. "Had the mail arrived, Florie?"

The housekeeper's cheerful voice echoed down the hall. "Yes, ma'am." Her lumbering footsteps approached, and she handed Mrs. Crowell a bundle of letters.

Sorting through the stack, Mrs. Crowell lifted an envelope. "Oh, here's one for you, Olivia."

"For me?" The seal on the back caught her eye. Wendell. No mistaking his handwriting. Strolling out onto the porch, she ripped it open and scanned through. Startled to hear of the ship's disastrous end, glad her health was intact... Looking forward to her arrival... Her passage secured on the *Excellent*, arriving at the end of the month... Marianne already planning many festivities.

"Festivities. I'm sure." The words "end of the month" caught her gaze. He'd mailed the letter weeks ago. Clutching the porch rail, dread filled her. "So the ship will be here soon." *Sam, where are you?*

****

263

The sound of thudding footsteps woke Sam from sleep. He rose and went to the window. Faint light rimmed the horizon. Too early for their usual patrol of the reefs. Two men ran through the street toward the wharf.

It could only mean one thing. A wreck. Though the day had been fair, ships caught on the reef in all types of weather.

He hurriedly stepped into his pants and laced his boots.

Outside, Liam called, "Out of bed, ye lazy bugger. We've work to do."

Sam grabbed his shirt and punched his arms through the sleeves. "So I heard." He pulled open the door. "Let's go."

He jogged past Liam, laughing. The older man sprinted alongside, and the two raced to the wharf. The *Florida* drifted from the dock and cast off. Yelling, Sam and Liam leapt onto its deck.

Jahner climbed up topside. "Glad you boys could join us this morning. Haul up anchor."

Homer drew up the chain and secured it, while Sam pushed at the dock post. Jahner steered the schooner toward the wreck. The crew soon had the sails in place.

Sam strained to see in the half-light. "The ship's grounded on the reef?" Another wrecking schooner floated near it, and a second on the way. Captain Howe would not be Wrecking Master of this job.

Captain Howe stood at his side. "Appears to be, though the damage may be minimal."

Liam leaned on the rail. "So it'll be an easy job."

"If it's a job at all," Sam added.

The captain's tone conveyed his weariness. "Aye,

we've had our share of stubborn captains this year."

The *Florida* came to rest behind the *Brilliant*. Captain Bethel had already boarded the grounded vessel. The two men stood together, and the sun crept above the sea in a blinding blaze.

"Wonder how long they've been at it." Liam's mouth angled in deep concentration.

"I'll wager the captain sends him off."

Liam turned toward him. "What do ye wager?"

Sam smiled. "A bottle of rum."

Liam smacked Sam's back. "So be it. One bottle of rum will soon be mine. Ye know my favorite brand, I hope."

"I'm familiar with it." All too familiar. Sam had sworn off it after the last time. Beer would suffice.

"The *Brilliant* found the ship?" Homer leaned on the rail beside Liam.

"'Twould appear so. Must've left early this morning on their rounds."

"Maybe someone caught sight of the ship yesterday and waited for it."

"Could be. I'm not surprised they kept it to themselves."

The wrecking captain climbed from the ropes onto the waiting boat below. The crew gathered around him, listened for a minute, and slowly dispersed. The schooner sat idle. Its men busied themselves tying knots and other mindless ways of passing time.

Sam straightened. "Aha!"

Liam spat over the side of the rail. "Aye, don't rub it in."

Sam grasped his shoulder. "I'll share it with you, my friend. With everyone."

"No, not everyone. It'll do no one any good, at most a shot apiece. Between two of us, a bottle's enough to drown our sorrows."

"What sorrows?"

"The sorrow of sitting useless while we could be making money."

Sam picked up a strand of rope. "We'll have to find useful endeavors to fill our time. The deck could use a good swabbing, if you're bored."

"I'll give ye a good swabbing, if ye're not careful."

Sam chuckled. "The captain will soon come to his senses." He couldn't help but wonder how long it might take. Sam had no wish to be stranded for days on the schooner, away from shore. Livvie's ship could arrive, take her away, and he'd have had no chance to see her. To talk to her.

Three more schooners arrived to await the signal. A crewman on the grounded vessel waved a white cloth in the air. Every man stopped to watch Captain Bethel return to the ship to speak to the captain again. He returned to his schooner in a measured pace. A *Brilliant* crewman shouted, "Passengers going ashore."

Captain Howe awaited the signal. The *Brilliant* crewman signaled another schooner.

The crew watched the wrecker skim easily over the reef, pulling alongside the ship. The passengers climbed down to it. The schooner eased away from the wreck, and then headed for shore.

In the hours that passed, another tall ship sailed into view. The men swept and scrubbed the *Florida* while the tall ship set anchor farther out. Its crew lowered a smaller boat to the sea, and then rowed toward Key West.

Tying knots, Liam glanced at Sam. "The *Excellent*."

Sam's stomach knotted tighter than his nautical rope. "Most likely." Was he doomed to watch Livvie leave while he remained stranded on the *Florida*?

Liam pushed up his sleeves. "Should stay anchored a few days to restock supplies."

"Maybe." A man of action, Sam didn't want to conjecture.

Hours passed. The wait worsened. No more tidying or tasks could be done on the schooner. Sam leaned beside Liam against the rail, the two ships in plain view.

Liam gazed out to sea. "I heard Lewis Pinder set off for Key Vaca. Took all his baubles too. Adam Stroh came across his camp site. Pinder greeted him with a shotgun pellet."

Sam's jaw gaped. "Pinder shot him?"

"Tried to. Told Stroh to turn around, go home if he wanted to live another day."

"The bastard." Talking of him made Sam want to spit.

"He's lost his mind," Liam said matter-of-factly. "All his conniving. For what? To be blacklisted. It drove him mad."

A madness Sam had brought down upon him. But no, each man made his own choices. The judge blacklisted Pinder due to his own bad choices, not Sam's. Pinder had to face his consequences, while Sam had to follow his conscience.

Sam said no more.

Liam turned toward the men. "Perhaps if we sing the *Wrecker's Song*, it'll bring us luck."

"Or at least ease our boredom," Homer said.

Jahner began the tune, his clear baritone echoing through the air. Liam sang in harmony. By the end of the first verse, all had joined in. From the other schooners, the crews' voices rose in concert, the lively tune echoing across the span of ocean.

Come all ye good people one and all,
Come listen to my song;
A few remarks I have to make,
It won't be very long;
'Tis of our vessel, stout and good,
As ever yet was built of wood;
Among the reefs where the breakers roar,
The wreckers on the Florida shore!
Key Tavernier's our rendezvous,
At anchor there we lie;
And see the vessels in the Gulf
Carelessly passing by;
When night comes on we dance and sing,
Whilst the currents some vessel is floating in;
When daylight comes, a ship's on shore,
Among the rocks where the breakers roar.
When daylight dawns we are under weigh, [sic]
And every sail is set;
And if the wind, it should prove light,
Why then our sails we wet;
To gain her first each eager strives,
To save the cargo and the peoples' lives;
Amongst the rocks where the breakers roar,
The wreckers on the Florida shore.
When we get 'longside, we find she's bilged,
We know well what to do;
Save the cargo that we can,
The sails and rigging too;
Then down to Key West we soon will go,
When quickly our salvage we shall know;

When everything it is fairly sold,
Our money down to us it is told.
Then one week's cruise we'll have on shore,
But we do sail again,
And drink success to the sailor lads,
That are plowing of the main;
And when you are passing by this way,
On Florida reef should you chance to stray,
Why, we will come to you on the shore,
Amongst the rocks where the breakers roar.

The last refrain rang out over the water from all boats, and stillness fell across the waves.

Captain Howe took hold of the idle wheel. "We may be here a long while, men. Vernon, prepare some supper."

Vernon popped his head up from below. "Aye, captain. I have venison stew simmering. I'll call you when it's ready."

Sam stood and stretched. "Venison. Who went hunting and didn't invite us?"

Homer glanced up. "We went the other day. We put the word out. You must not have been in your cabin."

Likely not. Sam was not one to sit in his cabin doing nothing. He should have been with Livvie. Damn fool that he was, he'd let time slip away and now he was stuck on the *Florida*, for who knew how long. He looked back toward shore, wondering what she was doing at this moment.

After a while, clanging rang from below. "Stew!" Cook cried out.

The men filed into a line, descending one by one.

"Hot stew on a hot day. He tries to boil us, I

sometimes think."

"Don't take all the meat and leave only broth for us."

"You know Vernon allows no one else to touch the ladle. If you're given only broth, it's because Vernon wants to punish you."

Sam ignored the bickering, brought on by boredom. He filed in behind Liam. "How much longer do you think the wreck's captain will hold out?"

Liam stroked his chin. "Depends on how stubborn he is."

"He has to know the situation won't correct itself. He doesn't appear to be doing anything about it."

Liam aimed an ingratiating smile at Vernon, who filled his bowl with more broth than substance. "Unless the crew is below, moving cargo to the rear in hopes it will ease the pressure."

Sam took the tin bowl Vernon offered, watching the cook ladle the stew. "He risks damaging the hull if the waves continue to push the ship onto the reef."

Liam squeezed slices of bread, selecting two. "I'm sure he's been warned, boy. We can't force our aid on him."

Although arguing wouldn't solve the problem, Sam couldn't stop himself. "His situation can only worsen. Does he have no sense?"

"We can't force good sense upon him, either." Liam climbed the stairs to the top.

Sam grabbed two pieces of bread and went topside. He slid down the side of the boat and ate. Even dipped in the stew, the bread crunched in his teeth.

Liam frowned. "Vernon baked his loaves too long again."

"I heard you." Vernon's voice carried up from

below. "If y'all don't like it, don't take two slices next time."

Sam winced as he ate. Vernon always listened for the crew's reaction to the meal. No one would tell him to his face it tasted awful. To do so risked retribution.

Liam rolled his eyes. "I can't very well starve, now, can I?"

The grumbled response rose, too muffled to decipher. Sam stifled a laugh.

The afternoon wore on, and Sam's small store of good spirits faded. While boredom normally didn't afflict him, his frustration mounted as minutes passed. He could be on shore, doing something useful. Helping Livvie pack. She intended to leave, so he wouldn't stop her. The sooner she was gone from his life, the better off he would be. Since he'd rescued her, he hadn't been himself. He knew better than to think he could make any woman happy for long. Livvie deserved better than him. A man who could give her a fine house, jewelry. All the niceties for which women longed.

His frustration burst from him without thought. "Captain, are we to sit here all day doing nothing?"

The captain swung toward him. "Have you business elsewhere, Mr. Langhorne?"

Liam interrupted. "Business of a personal nature, eh, Sam?"

Jahner snorted. "I saw him with that girl. Miss Collins. She's a pretty thing, Sam. She'll leave you high and dry."

The jests continued, and Sam's anger flared.

"She bats her eyelashes, and he follows her like a hound dog," Jahner said.

"We know what the hound dog is sniffing for,"

another said.

Liam chuckled. "Oh, I believe Sam's done more than sniff, haven't ye, Sam?"

Sam whirled to his friend. "Shut your trap, old man."

Liam's head jerked back. He bowed. "Why, yes, sir, Mr. Langhorne."

Frustration strangled Sam's response. He hadn't meant to snap. Hours of worry had mounted until Sam felt ready to jump from the boat and swim back to shore.

The tension broke when Jahner pointed to the grounded ship. "A flag. They're signaling for help."

Captain Bethel of the *Brilliant* climbed aboard the vessel again to speak to its captain.

"What's goin' on?" Homer asked.

Captain Howe watched the ship with an unwavering gaze. "We'll find out soon enough."

As Captain Bethel returned this time, he moved hastily. He spoke to his men, and they each whirled into motion. A bell sounded on the *Brilliant,* signaling the end of the wait.

Liam winced. "It'll be sundown soon."

Jahner groaned. "Why couldn't he have waited until morning?"

A crewman on the *Brilliant* cupped his hands to his mouth and called, "She's ruptured her side. She's taking on water fast."

Captain Howe strode to the rail of the upper deck. "All right, men. Let's get to work. Two by two, into the hold and hook the first cargo you find."

Sam had noted the shallower waters. All the men would take their turns diving, and the others would stay behind to haul up crates from below.

Jahner said, "And it could have been such easy work. Now we'll have to dive."

The crew set to their duties.

Liam busied himself readying the grappling hook.

Sam stepped near. "Need any help?"

"No." He finished his task without meeting Sam's gaze.

Regret washed over Sam as he backed away. There had been no call to lash out at Liam. The sun had gotten to him. The interminable wait. His own inability to make up his mind.

He'd make it up to his friend later.

"What's the cargo?" Sam asked the captain.

"Cotton. A shipment of rum."

Liam glanced up and grinned. "I know which I'm going after."

The crew's laughter burbled.

Homer's smile filled his face. "Not if I get there first."

Sam checked the line. "Why don't you let me go instead?"

Liam busied himself, repeating the motions he'd already performed. "I'll take a turn first. Ye can't have all the fun all the time."

Homer nodded. "Ready?"

"Irishmen are born ready." Liam followed him to the side, and they lowered their lines. Homer jumped in and landed clear of the hooks.

Liam glanced back at Sam. They held their gazes for a moment, then Liam plunged into the dark water.

Sam strode to the side and watched his friend's shadow dissipate beneath the waves.

Jahner laughed. "I hope he doesn't try to drink it all

while he's down there."

"Eh, Sam?" A hand slapped his back. "What's wrong?"

"Nothing." He couldn't put his finger on it. Couldn't put the strange feeling into words. "Keep a good eye on the line." He began counting.

Laughter and talk mingled while the crew waited. The men said again what an easy job it would be, hauling cargo from a ship that wasn't wrecked, and in fair weather. They discussed ways of helping the captain move the ship from the reef to get it underway again.

A line jerked, and Jahner helped Lemuel crank the winch to haul up the hooked crate. A movement below the waves, and Homer's head and shoulders appeared.

Sam threw him the line. "Any sign of Liam?"

Homer climbed aboard. "No. He should be up soon."

The crate surfaced, and Sam helped pull it in, keeping an eye all the while on the slack second line.

Time stretched like elastic. The wait was too long. Liam had set a personal record of six minutes below the surface, but that was two years ago.

"He should have already been up." Sam moved to the side. "It's been too long. I'm going down."

Lemuel laid a hand on his shoulder. "I'll go too."

Sam nodded. "The rest of you keep an eye out. I may need help. Something must have gone wrong."

Jahner stepped toward him. "Everything's fine, Sam." His expression did nothing to hide his worry.

"I'm going down to make sure." Filling his lungs, Sam dove in, following the line leading to Liam.

It ended abruptly. The line had been severed. He jerked it hard several times, and then swam deep below.

The depths were murky; he had to feel his way to the ship, easing downward. A rush of current sucked him toward the opening, pushing him inside. He pulled himself next to the inside wall, trying to see. While his eyes adjusted to the dimness, a shape flapped in the water's flow. He made his way toward it. The shape became a man, lifeless except for the water's animation. He struggled to turn him around, coming face to face with Liam, open-eyed, his stare a blank.

A burst of air escaped him. He desperately tugged his friend's body. Liam's arm was trapped between the ship and a heavy crate.

Lemuel appeared next to him, hook in hand. In an instant, the other diver appeared to understand the situation. Sam helped him secure the hook on the crate, and then tugged. Once the crate moved, he'd have to be fast to move Liam away or he'd be crushed. The crate lurched. Lemuel helped Sam guide it away from Liam. When Liam sank deeper, Sam grabbed his shirt. Hauling Liam under his arm, he thrust himself upward. He had to get Liam to the surface, get him breathing again. Lemuel took hold of Liam's other arm, His strong strokes soon pulled them both upward.

Sam's legs splayed wildly. Kicking, he thrust himself upward. His chest ached, his lungs burned. He wanted to scream, but tears blinded him. He held tight to Liam, whose weight seemed double.

The shadow of the boat overhead came into view, and Sam reached upward, hoping someone would grab hold. Feeling someone's grip, he tensed his arm to pull up over the surface, gasping. His lungs screamed for air.

At seeing their burden, Homer's eyes widened. Many arms reached over the side to pull them both up.

Sam threw his leg over the side, his chest heaving. Three men took hold of Liam. Their efforts to get him aboard rocked the boat.

Captain Howe hurried down the stairs. "Is he breathing? Get to work on him. Push the water out of his lungs fast. Get him breathing."

The men had already begun their revival attempt. Long after they would have stopped trying on anyone else, the men pressed his belly, squeezing the sea from Liam like a sponge.

Sam sat by the rail watching the crowd of men, as unreal as a scene from the theater. None of it appeared real. He trembled, unable to move.

The men's movements slowed. A silence fell over them. They surrounded Liam, kneeling or standing beside his limp body.

"Why are you stopping?" Sam pulled himself up and stumbled toward them. "Come on, keep at it. He'll come around."

Each man looked up, horror and sadness in their faces.

"What are you doing? You can't just give up."

Captain Howe stepped toward him. "Sam."

"No." Sam pushed past him, dropping to his knees, and pumping at Liam's chest. "Come on, you bastard. Breathe. Breathe!"

The body beneath his hands lay motionless.

Sam pounded his fists into Liam's stomach. "You can't do this. I won't let you." He clenched his teeth, tears streaming down his face.

Someone grasped his shoulder. Sam lurched from his hold. "He owes me a bottle of rum." He sat back and covered his mouth. The last words they'd exchanged had been in anger. Sam could never repair the damage.

Chapter Twenty-Four

The *Florida* returned to Key West after dark. Sam could not shake loose the daze engulfing him. He insisted on carrying Liam's body to the wagon, where he carefully arranged him in the back. Homer drove them to Doctor Meade's house. The examination took less than a minute. The doctor signed the death certificate, while Sam stared helplessly at the man who had been his best friend, more of a brother than Edward.

Sam barely registered it as Doctor Meade bid them goodnight.

Homer thanked the doctor and then tugged Sam to the wagon. "We need a drink."

Every table at the groggery sat full of wreckers from the *Florida*, the *Brilliant*, and other schooners. The men repeatedly hoisted their mugs in rowdy toasts to Liam.

He'd have loved it, Sam thought, a tear escaping down his deadened cheek. In salute, he lifted his ale.

Millie shuffled toward Sam, her hair as wild as her unseeing gaze. "Liam was to be my future. Now I have no future. What shall I do?" Searching his face, she clutched his shirt.

"What we all must do. Carry on." He expected she would throw herself at him, at any man, to fill Liam's absence, to soon forget him, but her glazed eyes and unkempt appearance spoke of genuine shock.

He stumbled to his cabin carrying a bottle of rum,

the bottle he should have shared with Liam. Now he would never be able to. He cradled it to his chest, untying his boots, cocking one foot against the other, readying to remove them. A discreet knock at his door caused his heart to leap into his throat. "Livvie." It had to be her. She knew he needed her and had come to him.

Lurching from the bed, he threw open the door.

Millie swayed on his doorstep.

"You haven't been drinking." His tone accused her without having to speak the words, *While you're carrying Liam's child.*

"No, I'm too sick—in my stomach and my heart." Her mouth curled downward, her lip trembling. "I don't know what to do, Sam." She whispered her desperate plea. "You must help me."

Liam had loved this woman. The law would not provide for her. Sam knew where Liam hid his money. He had to act quickly, before others thought to loot his cabin.

He set the rum atop his dresser. "Stay here. I'll be back soon."

"Don't leave me," she sobbed, throwing her arms around his waist.

He resisted the urge to push her away. "If you want to be able to provide for yourself and your baby, I must go now."

Tears streaming down her face, she released her hold.

He nudged her toward the bed. "Try to rest."

Nodding, she collapsed on his bed, sobs wracking her body.

After quickly re-tying his boots, he slipped from his cabin and down the dark streets. If he could do this one thing for his friend, it would be small repayment.

Liam's cabin sat at the edge of Conchtown, the farthest from any others. The door opened easily; Liam never locked it, despite all it held.

He lit a small lantern, setting it on the floor. Using his knife, he pried up the third floorboard. Tucked beneath, a swatch of fabric tied into a bundle held money. His friend trusted no one but Sam. Even Sam probably didn't know all the hiding places. Still, he would be able to give Millie whatever he could find, so she and the baby could live comfortably.

He lifted every floorboard, finding more cash.

"Where is it, you old bugger?" Somewhere here in the cabin Liam had stowed the grand prize. The one he would have used to buy his plantation on the mainland.

Sam lifted the mattress, feeling beneath. A small bundle lay in the center.

Sitting on the bed, he scoured the room. The rafters. He held the lantern up. A piece of fabric caught his eye. Climbing atop the bed, he plucked it from its perch. More money.

He stepped down, dragged the single wooden chair to the corner, and then held up the lantern. Nothing. He repeated the action in each corner. In the farthest one, a brick-sized object sat wrapped in black fabric.

Sam smiled. "Very smart, my friend." In unwrapping it, the lantern caught the gold and gleamed. A gold bar. This would keep Millie and her baby for a lifetime.

He gathered it all together into a sheet, and then tied it up.

Hushed voices came from outside the cabin. Blowing out the lantern, Sam stepped behind the door. It creaked open. Footsteps were followed by a loud thud, accompanied by surprised cries when Sam tripped them.

Adam Stroh and Jacob Preston scrambled to their feet, crouched, ready to pounce as Sam relit the lantern.

"What are you doing here?"

Stroh looked pointedly at the mangled floor. "We might ask you the same thing."

"I have personal business. You have none." Sam gauged whether he could make a run through the door. His bundle would slow him down.

Stroh nodded at the tied-up sheet. "What have you got there?"

Sam straightened to his full height. "None of your business."

Preston smiled. "We believe it is."

"Step aside. Let me pass."

Stroh stepped closer. "First show us what you have." Preston moved to the side.

"Liam's personal effects." Sam stepped back to keep them both in his line of vision. Further from the door, but he would yet find an advantage.

"Yeah, sure. I bet they're not so personal we all couldn't share, eh?" Stroh glanced at Preston, who nodded.

Sam kept his voice even. "No."

"You crazy bastard," Preston said through clenched teeth. "We know Liam kept his fortune in here."

Sam fought to calm his pounding heart. The boy's arrogance would be his downfall, Sam guessed. "Only one person will have it."

"Not you." Preston lunged, fists swinging.

Sam's foot landed on his hip, sending him backward into Stroh.

He widened his stance. "This is for Millie. Liam was to marry her."

The two exchanged confused glances.

"She's carrying his child. Would you deprive two innocents of their due?" Passion and grace filled his plea. If they set upon him, he could not stop them.

Grumbling, they stood slowly.

Stroh wiped his mouth. "No."

Preston pointed at Sam. "If you're lying to us, we'll take it out of your hide."

Sam met his glare, knowing full well why Jacob Preston wanted a piece of him. It had nothing to do with Liam's money, and everything to do with Livvie.

"I've no reason to lie," Sam said. "I owe a debt to Liam. I intend to make sure it's paid in full."

Stroh jerked his head toward the outside. The men shuffled out of the cabin.

Shouldering the bundle, Sam turned out the lamp again, closing the door behind him. Approaching his cabin, the cries from within shook him to the core.

Millie lay on the bed, still sobbing inconsolably. She rolled toward him when he walked in. "Where have you been?"

"Retrieving this." He laid the bundle on the bed beside her.

She blinked, pushing her hair off her face. "What is it?"

"Liam's savings. He would have wanted you to have it."

She gasped through her tears. "I—"

"You'll need to spend it wisely." He would not abide an argument from her. He guessed she wouldn't argue much. "There should be plenty for you both."

Her lip quivered. She threw her arms around Sam. "I don't know how to thank you."

He knew how. By not betraying Liam's memory. He extracted himself from her embrace. "Use it to take good care of yourself."

She nodded. "I'm going home. To Virginia. The baby will have a good home there."

"You should go rest. I better keep this for tonight. Two men showed up at Liam's. They may show up at your place." He moved to the door. "I suggest you stay with Annie tonight. Come back in the morning for the money."

"All right." Before leaving, she kissed his cheek. For once, her look held no invitation, only gratitude and sadness.

Sam dropped to the bed. Images of Liam swept through his mind. Most vivid was the final look Liam gave him before diving to his death. A look of such weight, it nearly suffocated Sam.

He'd have no sleep tonight.

****

Dishes clinked in the kitchen as Florie finished cleaning up for the night. Since her neighbor's visit this afternoon, she'd fallen unnaturally quiet. For Florie not to sing or even hum must mean terrible news. For several hours, Livvie had wanted to seek her out, yet Mrs. Locke always managed to hinder her.

Livvie hurried down the hallway into the kitchen. "Florie," she whispered.

Turning abruptly, Florie's eyes flew wide. "Goodness, miss. You startled me."

"I'm sorry. I've been dying to know—have you heard any news?" She searched the woman's face.

As Florie dabbed at her eyes, Livvie's insides went cold. Something awful had happened, then.

Hanging her head, the housekeeper leaned against the table. "Oh, Miss Livvie, it's too terrible to speak of."

"Tell me, please! Don't keep me in agony. Is it Sam?" Moments stretched to infinity waiting for the woman's reply.

Flashing a tearful smile, Florie patted her arm. "No, miss. His friend Liam Byrne."

Gasping, Livvie clutched her hand. "Is he…" She couldn't say the word.

A sob escaped Florie, who nodded. "Drowned. Poor, poor man. Poor Mr. Langhorne too. They say he tried to save him. It was too late. Too late." Her shoulders shook with her tears.

"Oh, no! Sam. I must see him. Have they returned?"

Raising her head, Florie's expression blanched.

Livvie turned to see Mrs. Crowell in the doorway.

"You'll go nowhere tonight, Olivia. A letter from your brother promises payment for your stay upon your safe passage to New Orleans. You won't want to miss the ship's launch tomorrow morning." Her soft expression contradicted her cold tone.

"Mrs. Crowell—"

"I'll abide no argument, Miss Collins. I wouldn't want to have to call my dear friend Captain Howe, to report Mr. Langhorne's unsavory behavior."

"How dare you suggest—"

"Now, Olivia, I'm not *suggesting* anything." Her tone indicated a knowledge rather than a suspicion.

Feeling her cheeks flush warm, Livvie held her tongue. No, an argument would do no good. Neither would a boardinghouse proprietress stand in her way.

She'd find a way to see Sam.

****

Morning dawned slowly, diffused by clouds. Sam had drifted in and out of sleep for what had been left of the night. By the time Millie knocked on his door, he'd had enough of his bed. He leapt from it, throwing open the door.

Dark rings hung beneath Millie's eyes. She stood dazed, not truly seeing what was before her.

"Millie. Come in."

No one appeared to be following her. A good sign. Maybe Stroh and Preston would leave her alone.

She sat on the bed. Her voice had no tone, only breath. "I tossed and turned all night. When I awoke this morning, I thought it a terrible nightmare." Her gaze met Sam's. She sobbed, "It's not. He's really gone."

He circled his arm around her and sat. "Shh. Now, now."

She burrowed her head into his shoulder.

He let her cry until she had no more tears.

She pulled away, sniffling. "I'm sorry, Sam. I know you loved him too."

"He was like a brother." He crouched to retrieve the bundle beneath his bed. "Here it is. I didn't count it. You should, though."

"He'd be so proud of you." Her lips twisted into a crooked smile, and tears rimmed her eyes.

"Do you have a safe place for it?" Though he didn't want to alarm her, risks always existed regarding such a large amount of money.

She nodded. "I think so. Liam showed me a place to hide things. I had nothing to put in it until now."

Just like Liam. "Good. Put it there right away."

She lifted the bundle.

He walked her to the door and opened it.

She turned and laid her palm against his chest. "You're a good man, Sam."

He lifted her hand to his lips to kiss it. "Not as good as Liam."

On tiptoe, she pressed her mouth to his cheek. "I'll miss you."

"You haven't arranged passage yet, have you?"

"No, although I hope to soon. I'll say a proper goodbye before I go."

"I hope so." He was surprised to realize he meant it.

Closing the door, he rubbed his hand across his face. Livvie.

He had to see her. He had so much to tell her. This time, he would make sure she understood how much she meant to him.

****

Livvie's insides seemed abuzz, her nerves on edge. She dressed quietly, then crept down the stairs. If anyone saw her, they would try to stop her. Today, of all days, she couldn't let that happen. Her future hinged on what happened next.

The front door creaked as she eased it open and pulled it shut.

She waited a moment for any commotion inside the house.

Nothing.

She hurried down the steps and onto the street, following the most direct route to Sam's cabin. By the time she reached his street, she labored for breath. She stopped to calm herself. She didn't want him to see her like this.

His door opened, and her heart leaped. Did he see her coming? She took one step, and then froze at the sight of Millie emerging from within. What was she doing there so early in the morning?

Livvie's skin chilled. She hadn't seen Sam for days. She'd assumed he worked the wreck, same as the others. Assumed he'd been too tired, too busy to see her.

Now she knew what had occupied him.

Millie laid her hand on Sam's chest. When he brought it to his mouth and kissed it, he might have shoved a knife in Livvie's heart. The pain made her gasp.

Millie stood on tiptoe to kiss him. Sam smiled down at her. The traitor!

Livvie bit the back of her hand to keep her strangled cry to herself. How could he betray her so? And Liam not even buried yet?

Blinded by tears, she ran all the way to the Crowells'. A buggy sat out front.

Livvie wiped her cheeks and ran up the stairs.

On the sofa, Mrs. Locke's head snapped toward her. "Where have you been? The carriage is here to take us to the ship."

The ship. Livvie's stomach lurched. Another journey in Mrs. Locke's company. She would endure the torture to escape this place.

"I'll only be a minute." She hurried upstairs to her room. She already wore the clothes she owned; she hadn't much to pack. Some of her writing. Two letters from her brother. The seashell basket sat on the table by the bed.

She lifted it, running a finger over the delicate whorls. Perhaps she should leave it for the next occupant of the room. No, she needed it. Not as a memento. As a grim reminder to guard her heart more carefully.

After one last look around, Livvie shut the door and went downstairs. Florie stood in the hallway, dabbing her eyes. "You take care, miss."

Livvie hugged her. "I shall miss you, Florie."

Martha clutched Livvie's arm. "Hurry, Olivia. We must get to the docks."

"They will not sail without us, Mrs. Locke." She turned to Mrs. Crowell. "You have my address in New Orleans, if any adjustments are needed to the balance."

Mrs. Crowell took her hand. "Take care, child."

Her unexpected kindness, even so small a gesture, brought tears to Livvie's eyes. Nodding, she went outside to the buggy, where Martha struggled to climb inside. Livvie steadied her, following behind. The driver clicked to urge the horse ahead, while Livvie bit back her tears.

Mrs. Locke patted her arm. "There, now. You can write Mrs. Crowell. I hope you will write me also. I will be sure to give you my address before we make port."

Forcing a brief smile, Livvie turned away. Yes, she would write. She had so much to write about now. She could do so with authority. Sam had helped her experience every possible emotion since she'd arrived.

The ride to the docks took only minutes. The buggy jerked to a halt. Livvie's heart caught in her throat at the sight of the *Florida*. Of the two men visible aboard, she recognized only one. No sign of Sam. Relief and sorrow mingled inside her. She steeled herself. The buggy driver led them toward another schooner. Maybe Millie hadn't left his cabin after all.

The driver helped them climb aboard, preparing to sail to the *Excellent,* waiting beyond the reef. Five other schooners floated near the wrecked ship, their crews working industriously to retrieve crates from the deep.

Livvie's vessel pulled alongside the *Excellent*. Two crewmen helped them board a lifeboat, latched it to the hooks, and signaled the men above to haul up the lines.

While the crew guided the lifeboat upward, a schooner raced toward the *Excellent*. Livvie froze, her throat thick. The *Florida*'s flag flew on its mast, and Sam stood at the helm. Was something wrong? The schooner swerved away within inches of striking the *Excellent*.

Sam yelled up, "Livvie, you're taking my heart with you."

She gripped the edge of the lifeboat. "It's a fine time to be telling me!"

His smile flashed from below. "Come back down, and I'll tell you again."

Her heart swelled in her chest, near to bursting. Sam prized his freedom above all else. After what she'd seen this morning, she couldn't go back to him.

The boat lurched. Mrs. Locke cried out, "You'll tip us over."

Livvie sat back, her gaze locked on Sam's. The crewmen hauled the boat alongside the deck.

"Come back, Livvie!" Sam called. "Stay with me! Every night we can share what we had together."

Mrs. Locke gave a horrified shriek. The crew urged her to climb out. Her feet touched the floor, and she let out a great gasp.

They waited to help Livvie out. Still, she sat in the boat, unable to unlock her gaze from Sam.

One of the men extended his hand. "Take hold, miss."

Mrs. Locke hissed, "She's holding up the entire

ship."

Sam stood unmoving. Watching.

Why didn't he say something? Anything. Of course, he had no clever argument today, did he? His guilt must be silencing him.

Livvie drew in a ragged breath. For once, Mrs. Locke was right. No need to hold the ship hostage to her wayward emotions. Clutching the basket to her breast, she moved toward the waiting crewman, took his hand, and climbed down.

The captain called for crew to hoist the sails, haul up the anchor, and make way. The sails billowed, and the ship cast safely off the reef, its rudder set hard toward the sea.

The *Florida* followed in its wake. Wind filled the great sails, and the ship picked up speed. The schooner fled along the top of the waves and came alongside.

"What are they doing?" asked a crewman.

Glancing at Livvie, another answered, "It would appear they're racing us."

Livvie ran to the side.

On the *Florida*, Sam waved a white cloth. "Livvie!"

Mrs. Locke held her hand to her mouth, her face a mask of horror. "He's a madman."

Livvie clutched the side. She shouldn't have come aboard. Too late now. The captain wouldn't lower sails for her, he'd likely sooner have her jump overboard. To do so at this speed would mean certain death.

Sam cupped his hands around his mouth. "You've wrecked me, Livvie Collins. I want no other than you!"

Tears stung her eyes. The fool, to wait until too late to speak the words she so longed to hear. Maybe that was his plan. He knew she could not act on his confession, so he was safe. He'd go back to his life, and she'd sail on to her new one.

"Livvie, come back to me!"

His persistence made her blood boil. "You're only saying it because you know I can't leave the ship!"

"What?" The schooner cut dangerously close.

Her frustration burst forth in a roar. "You coward!"

Mrs. Locke tugged at her arm. "Come away from the side, Olivia. Come below." Her quaking voice and clinging hands felt more like drowning than falling overboard.

She whirled toward the whining woman. "You go below. Leave me alone." She turned back to Sam. "You leave me alone too!"

"Only if you say you don't love me."

Tears streamed down her cheeks. "I—" She bit back sobs.

The winds weakened his voice. "Stay, Livvie!"

Stay? Stay at home while he sailed away across the glittering seas? Or worse, into every passing storm? She'd end up bearing ten babies, owing as much to her own passion as his. And alone, no better off than Millie. Worse, in fact, letting her feelings overwhelm common sense.

"Livvie!"

In a blind fury, she picked up the seashell basket and hurled it at the schooner. It fell into the waves between the two boats. If only it could have been herself, falling into Sam's arms.

By the look on his face, she might well have ripped out his heart. A crew mate called something to another, and the *Florida*'s sails shifted. It fell away, and anguish welled within her. She ran along the rail, watching the schooner become smaller, Sam rooted to the same place like an accusing statue.

Chapter Twenty-Five

The carriage halted outside a large wrought-iron gate set in an adobe wall the color of apricot. The driver, whose crisp white shirt, in sharp contrast to his dark skin, reflected the sun's brightness, jumped to the cobblestone street and opened the door.

Livvie stepped down. "Thank you."

He gave a nod, opened the gate, and rang the bell. Livvie followed the flower-lined stone path to the interior porch. The house, of apricot-hued adobe, wrapped around an inner courtyard, overlooked by the second-story balcony which skirted its length. White columns stood out against black wrought-iron rails and black-shuttered windows. Tall palm trees anchored the courtyard at the exterior corners, spreading their fronds across the end of the balcony, shielding it from public view.

Entranced by the home, Livvie strolled slowly toward the door. It opened, and Marianne stood in the doorway, flanked by two girls—one a toddler with golden curls, the other a dark-haired beauty a few years older. Marianne's smile faded when she took in Livvie from head to toe.

Embarrassment crawled across Livvie. Shame halted her, realizing how ragged she must appear. Marianne, by contrast, exuded the epitome of class and womanhood. Her French accent had amused Livvie at their first meeting. At the time, Livvie had met Marianne's wholehearted approval. Six years had since passed. It seemed such a long time ago.

Marianne froze a smile on her face and held out her arms. "Olivia, darling sister. Welcome." Wendell's letters boasted of Marianne's established reputation as a gracious hostess for the constant dinners and balls he held for partners, associates, clients, and would-be clients, and anyone else in the upper social climes. If Livvie had disappointed Marianne, her sister-in-law would not disgrace her brother by showing it.

Wary of her welcome, Livvie stepped onto the porch. "Thank you, Marianne. I'm most grateful for your hospitality. I apologize for my appearance."

"Nonsense. You've had quite an ordeal. You must be exhausted."

Livvie exhaled a breath she hadn't known she held. "Yes. Quite." The truth of it hit her. Her very bones ached. Oh, for a bed! A real bed, having a mattress and pillow.

Marianne stepped aside. "Come in, dearest. We'll get you settled in your room. Where are your bags?"

Livvie dropped her chin to her chest. "Gone."

"Oh, you poor little thing." Marianne's wide-eyed daughters clung to her billowing skirt.

Livvie crouched to their eye level. "Hello. I'm Olivia. And who are you?"

The older girl's French accent sounded thick like Marianne's. "I'm Amelia."

Marianne lifted the younger girl to her hip. "This is Claire. Say hello to your Auntie Olivia, my sweets."

Amelia curtsied, apparently schooled in formal introductions. Claire laid her head against her mother's shoulder. Marianne whispered something in her ear, and she clung tighter.

"I'm sorry. It's close to nap time. Come along. I'll take them upstairs to their nanny and show you your room." She closed the door behind Livvie and continued talking, gliding up the wide staircase. "We'll have Nanette draw you a nice bath, and I'll find you some new clothes until we can take you shopping. Oh, you'll love the new fashions."

"Have any letters arrived for me?"

Marianne paused on the stairs. "Letters?"

"Yes. I'm expecting a reply from a publisher."

"A publisher?" Marianne's gaze fluttered to the house, then back to Livvie.

"Yes, Mr. Kenneth Randall. From New York City."

"I'll have to ask Wendell. I'm not aware of any such letter, or any mail at all having arrived for you."

"Oh." If nothing had arrived yet, she doubted it ever would. Her best option was to finish the adventure novel she'd begun while en route to New Orleans, and send it off as well.

Livvie held onto the banister and took in the high-ceilinged entrance boasting an elaborate glass teardrop chandelier winking in the sunlight. A huge room lay to the left, its polished floor suggesting a ballroom. Likely it served to accommodate—and perhaps elevate—their social standing. To the right lay a large drawing room, beyond which a servant walked, probably between the kitchen and dining room. All the accoutrements of a well-appointed house. Everything in its place, shined to perfection.

"Olivia?" Marianne waited on the curved staircase, the perfect portrait of a lady.

"Sorry. Coming." She hurried behind her sister-in-law.

She missed Key West already. This place would never be home.

****

Dinner, Marianne had informed Livvie earlier, was always at seven-thirty. Livvie understood it to mean she should bathe and make herself presentable well in advance.

At seven o'clock, Livvie descended to the drawing room in a dress borrowed from her sister-in-law, hair swept back into a barrette and curled. By seven-thirty, she'd tired of waiting and grew restless to return to her room to write.

Marianne preened Claire's hair and sent her off to play with Amelia. "He'll be so excited to see you."

"I'm excited to see him as well." If the situation were reversed, she'd have rushed home early to greet him.

At quarter to eight, the clop of a horse's hooves sounded outside the courtyard. Marianne glided to the window. "Here he comes now."

She rushed to the door ahead of the servant. Hushed voices echoed in the foyer.

Livvie remained on the sofa, pretending to read despite the awful feeling that something was wrong. Horribly wrong.

Wendell's form filled the entryway. "Olivia." At his booming voice, Amelia and Claire ran to him. He lifted one into each arm and strode to Livvie.

"Hello, Wendell. It's so good to see you." Even if he was barely recognizable. Though he was nine years her senior, his hairline had receded as far as his belly had protruded.

"And you. Are you well? You've had quite the journey."

She leaned forward to receive his cheek on her cheek. "Yes, quite."

"Marianne and I worried about you so."

"How sweet." She began to tell him there was no need for worry, so he'd call for the food.

He turned to his wife. "Where's dinner? I'm starved. I'm sure Olivia must be, too."

"It's ready, dearest. We were waiting for you." Marianne swept into the kitchen.

Wendell ushered Livvie into the dining room. After setting the girls in their cushioned high chairs, he pulled the next chair out.

Livvie sat on it, feeling a bit like Alice in Wonderland. The wide seat could almost accommodate two people, and the high back was gilded and ornate.

Three uniformed servers carried silver trays heaped with lidded silver dishes.

"Soup?" Wendell winced. "I want no soup. Bring the main course. And a bottle of wine."

Marianne appeared at the opposite end of the table and waited for a servant to seat her. "Now, darling, don't be grumpy. Cook made your favorite gumbo."

"I'm not grumpy. I'm hungry. My little pumpkins can eat it all. Give me my steak." He grabbed the bottle of wine from the servant, sloshed it into his glass, then into Livvie's.

Marianne visibly gathered herself. "As you wish."

Livvie sipped. She had a feeling she might need to refill her glass before the end of the night.

Another servant delivered Wendell's main course of

steak and potato, which he ate with gusto.

Livvie found the gumbo a tad spicy, but delicious, as was the fish. The others ate mostly in awkward silence.

Toward the end of the meal, Livvie could bear no more. "Marianne tells me your law firm's doing very well."

He eased back in his chair. "That's what I tell her." He flashed a strained smile.

Out of the corner of Livvie's eye, she caught the bow of Marianne's head. How odd. "So it's not doing well?"

"Of course it is. But you women shouldn't worry about such things." A stern reprimand directed mostly at his wife.

The last thing Livvie wanted was to cause trouble. "I wasn't worried, Wendell. Merely making conversation."

"It's rather complicated."

"I'm well able to fathom the inner workings of a business, brother." Equally well able to understand her brother controlled her father's estate.

"Yes, you always were very…bright."

Livvie barely held back a laugh. "You make it sound like an affliction rather than a compliment."

"No, merely a waste."

"Because I'm a woman?"

He regarded her with care. "I suppose you have grown into a woman. I shall have to start thinking of you that way instead of the scrawny little girl astride her horse."

"Speaking of which." Livvie leaned forward. "Are you able to transport Sir Galahad to New Orleans?

Safely, I mean?"

"Transport him?" Wendell waved her off. "Out of the question."

"But Father said—"

"I am not responsible for Father's deathbed promises, likely made in a hallucinogenic state."

"Father was lucid to the end. You'd know that if…" She wouldn't say it. Wendell hadn't visited, but Livvie attributed it to work pressures. He simply couldn't spare the time after launching a new law firm.

Wendell sighed heavily. "Marianne, isn't it time for the girls to go upstairs?"

Marianne held out her arms. "My sweethearts, say goodnight to your daddy."

Livvie rose. "I'll say goodnight as well."

"Olivia." Wendell drew out her name in a strained tone of annoyance.

She wouldn't let him claim victory. "I'm exhausted from the journey, that's all." She bent to lift Claire. "Oh, by the way, I was expecting a letter. Marianne said you might have intercepted it."

Wendell's sharp gaze flicked to his wife. "A letter?"

The atmosphere in the room grew to a palpable thickness.

Marianne's eyelids fluttered the same way they had earlier when Livvie inquired about it. "I merely said he may have seen it, Livvie dearest. Not that he had intercepted it."

Wording it that way wouldn't have evoked such a strong response. Livvie forced a pleasant tone. "Have you seen it, Wendell?"

He rolled his tongue inside his cheek. "No, I have not. But I'll ask Francois. He collects the mail."

Manners could hide many emotions, and Livvie smiled her thanks but made note to ask Francois herself.

****

Since sailing from Key West, Livvie doubted the oddities of any other place could charm her. To escape her sister-in-law's dismay, Livvie wandered the streets. Not only did New Orleans charm her, but it seeded her fertile imagination. Who cared for the flowered vines flowing from the wrought iron balconies, sometimes cascading from the third story to the ground? Stopping to peer through a shadowed, enclosed alleyway leading to a courtyard, she wondered who might meet there on a sultry evening. What seductions took place behind the curtained second-story balconies? Penning new stories, Livvie took delight in describing the wrought iron angels atop a gate, metalwork delicate as lace, and the lion's head gushing water into a half-circle fountain set in a wall.

Having no constant ocean breeze, New Orleans could hold oppressive heat. Or perhaps it wasn't the heat so much as the atmosphere within Wendell's house. Although Marianne graciously welcomed Livvie, she sensed her sister-in-law's keen awareness of the disruption to her household. Marianne valued order and schedule. Livvie could abide neither.

So she found herself disappearing more frequently. Sometimes she borrowed Wendell's spare buggy and drove it around the city on the excuse she needed to learn its layout. In truth, she loved to ride to the Mississippi River and pause to watch the vessels skidding past, especially the paddleboats.

She found it ironic she should find herself in yet another port city. What must it be like, she wondered, to live inland? Somewhere out of sight of a departing vessel, away from the temptations of a ship about to set sail?

New Orleans had a definite flair and flavor unique unto itself, she had to admit, though Key West held her heart.

And her heart's desire.

Livvie poured those thoughts into her writing, which she endeavored to do every night after dinner. She suffered the evening gathering in the parlor for only as long as necessary. When Marianne told her daughters to kiss their father good night, Livvie volunteered to bring them upstairs. The girls giggled as she scooped them up in her arms and whooshed them up the long staircase. After delivering them to their nanny, Livvie retreated to her spacious bedroom. It offered access to the balcony overlooking the lush courtyard, fortuitously situated to capture the light of the moon while it traveled across the night sky. As the first full moon lit her room in a blue haze, Livvie dragged her writing table and chair closer to the French door.

She wrote until her hand cramped and tears stained the pages filled with lush descriptions of the island and its inhabitants—especially one in particular. As the moon crept from view, she crawled into bed. A lovely four-poster bed with fresh sheets, and a soft pillow, yet its comfort paled in comparison to the safety of Sam's arms. To think she would never again experience such feelings made her weep long into the early hours of morning.

A knock at the door startled her awake. Marianne said, "Olivia. Are you awake? Olivia?"

Livvie pushed the hair from her face. "Just a

moment." She shuffled to the door and opened it.

Marianne made no mention of Livvie's unkempt state. "Hurry downstairs."

"Why? What's wrong?" Fear clutched at Livvie.

Marianne smiled. "You must have breakfast before we can go shopping."

"Shopping? No, I…." Her mind wouldn't function properly. She could think of no reasonable argument. Marianne would not understand when she said she had no interest in fashion beyond how she would clothe the characters in her mind.

Marianne took her hand. "Of course! You need new clothes. Especially now we are planning a ball." She squeezed.

A ball. Of course. She must be properly adorned if she was to be showcased for the local gentry. Held up for public admiration, available to the highest bidder.

"Marianne, it's not necessary, honestly."

"Nonsense. Now hurry." She shooed her away.

Livvie stifled a groan. "I'll be down soon. I must change first."

Marianne's eyes shone in victory. "I'll be waiting."

Livvie closed the door and leaned against it. "And so it begins."

Perhaps she could feign an illness. Some sort of food poisoning. Or perhaps she could act the part of a giddy know-nothing. No, such behavior would only attract more would-be suitors. Her best chance at avoiding marriage appeared to be acting as herself.

****

Livvie enjoyed the excursion with Marianne only because her nieces exuded excitement. Claire had taken to Livvie within days and now ran to her as she came in sight, arms wide, begging to be held. In the carriage, Claire rode on Livvie's lap.

"Really, you will spoil her," Marianne chided. "She must learn to hold herself, like a lady."

Livvie had no intention of releasing her. "Claire has many years until she's a lady. She's not even three."

"Next month she will turn three. Amelia knew how to act like a lady at her age."

"She's a baby." Livvie placed her cheek against Claire's and rocked.

Marianne pursed her lips. "Perhaps you should marry and have your own babies. Wouldn't it be lovely, girls? Cousins for playmates?"

Amelia inched closer to Livvie, prompting Marianne to cluck her tongue. "You're a terrible influence on my daughters."

Livvie didn't want to be the cause of punishment for her nieces. "Sorry. We'll all behave while we're shopping. Won't we, girls? And when we get home, we'll have a tea party in your room to entertain Mademoiselle Annette and Monsieur Julian."

Marianne rolled her eyes. "You indulge their fantasies too much."

"Every girl's fantasies should be indulged once in a while." A pang hit Livvie as the memory of Sam rushed back. The feel of his skin against hers. His lips trailing to…

The carriage hit a bump and brought Livvie back to her surroundings. She shifted the baby to the seat beside her and folded her hands in her lap. Fantasies were wonderful, but she needed to face her reality.

They arrived at the boutique, and as promised, Livvie, Amelia, and Claire were perfect ladies while

Marianne ordered three dresses made for Livvie for everyday, and a beautiful indigo silk gown for the ball. "The color complements you so well. You'll be the most beautiful belle at the ball."

"Your generosity is excessive, especially regarding my looks." Some women stared at Livvie's tanned skin, the mark of a commoner. Their haughty glances made Livvie hold herself taller and speak with more conviction. No wife of a banker or lawyer would define her by her appearance. Livvie intended to define herself in her own right.

On the ride home, Marianne prattled on about the guests. "All of society will be there. Plenty of handsome men, Olivia, who will instantly be smitten." Her smile waned. "Of course, you must be careful not to believe everything a man—even a gentleman—tells you."

"What do you mean?" Livvie stifled a smirk. If Marianne thought her innocent of worldly ways, Livvie wouldn't shatter the image. She did, however, envy her nieces, sound asleep on the seat, their heads each in a lap—hers and Marianne's.

"I don't mean to intrude, dear. Wendell has said many times he wished your father had sent you to boarding school after your mother's passing. Without her womanly knowledge, you had only your father to guide you. I'm sure he meant well. Wendell has secretly worried that being headstrong might tarnish your innocence."

Wendell should have kept his thoughts to himself. "I appreciate Wendell's concern, but you really shouldn't worry about me."

Her sister-in-law was well-meaning enough; perhaps she even liked the terrible politeness of society

Livvie found so constraining: the smiling women who made a blood sport of back-handed comments, the leering men who believed they could escape any punishment if they had enough money. Key West had shown her a freedom she'd never guessed at, people living their lives without restraint, their days joyful.

"Of course we worry because we love you. I promised to speak to you. Certain delicate matters should be discussed among women."

If her sister-in-law could not be dissuaded, Livvie would pretend to listen. "Such as?"

Arching a brow, Marianne's eyes brightened. "It's absolutely vital not to let any man have his way with you before your wedding night. Not only will it sully your reputation, the man will then abandon you."

"I quite understand." More than her dear sister-in-law would care to know.

"Men will say anything, act desperate to love you and only you. Don't doubt that they say the same thing to every woman they see. Men are insatiable beasts. Even Wendell. Every other night, *mon Dieu*." Marianne fanned herself.

"You don't enjoy it also?"

Marianne smiled slyly. "Of course I do. It's very important not to let him see your desires. Act like it's your wifely duty. And it is, but it's much more than that."

"Oh?"

"It's power. And you must keep that power in your control. If the man thinks you enjoy it, he will do whatever he pleases. You'll have no hold whatsoever on him. However, if you make him beg and plead, you retain the power. Do you see, *ma chère*?"

Livvie did see. Had she gone about it all wrong?

She'd gone to Sam instead of waiting for him to come to her. Yet if she'd waited, she knew in her heart he'd never have come to her.

Oh, of course. He wouldn't have come to her because he could go elsewhere. To Millie. Such a fool! She'd taken an enormous chance and had been lucky not to have conceived. Emotionally, Sam was little more than a child himself; he would close his door on her if she showed up bearing a baby. He'd claim she seduced him and must have seduced any number of other men, so therefore the chance was so slim as to be nonexistent that he'd fathered the babe. Sam loved to argue, and he had every weapon in his arsenal on this account. Oh, how foolish she'd been. Never, never again.

To disguise her despair, she forced a pleasant tone. "Marianne, if I can aid you in any way…"

Marianne knit her brow. "No, no, Olivia. The servants shall take care of everything. Your only task is to wear your new dress and make the men swoon."

Not exactly the challenge she wanted. "I make no promises regarding the swooning."

Marianne tilted her head. "Dearest, I assure you. There will be swooning." She sighed. "And now you can burn that old blue dress of yours. You must be terribly sick of it."

"No," Livvie said too hastily. Burn her blue dress? Every time she buttoned its buttons, she imagined Sam's fingers alongside her own. "I want to keep it."

"Whatever for?" Marianne appeared truly puzzled.

"A keepsake of the journey." And of her past life, which had slipped through her fingers like grains of sand.

****

Guests overflowed through the Collins household.

A string quartet played in the main hall.

Descending the staircase, Livvie's stomach churned. So many people crowded the great hall, and the air closed in on her when she entered. Her breathing grew shallow while Wendell introduced her to too many people to remember. Her dance partners consisted of a long succession of men whose close inspection made her long to flee. Talk of their successes made her mind wander from boredom. Each competed for her approval.

Wendell's stern looks cautioned her to be polite, so she imagined herself dancing in Sam's arms, him sweeping her along in a jig, calling the gentleman from the captain's ball an old goat. The memory brought her pleasure until she recalled their bodies swaying together in the waltz. His strong embrace, keeping her safe, exciting a fire within her she'd never known.

Oh, what had she done? What might have happened if they'd had more time? Tears threatened, and she excused herself, feigning a headache. She went up to her room, stood on her balcony, as distant from the partygoers as one of the stars blazing brightly overhead.

"Sam, you've wrecked me too. I will always remember the way you made me feel." The woman she'd become in his company: strong, confident, intelligent, unafraid to speak her mind. "From now on, your memory shall help me to be that woman." She whispered her fervent oath like a prayer to the stars.

****

At breakfast the following morning, Livvie hardly listened to Marianne's nonstop chatter about the ball. The event had galvanized Livvie's resolve. She had to act now on her predicament, or she would end up wed to one of the goats, old or young, paraded before her.

Marianne prattled on between sips of tea. "So many of our guests were quite taken by you, Olivia. I wouldn't be surprised if you have a few gentleman callers very soon."

Despair overtook her. "Oh, no. Do you think so?" She realized too late her sorrowful tone.

Marianne steeled her gaze but otherwise didn't change her pleasant expression. "Why, yes. You object to the idea?"

Livvie stammered, "I've only just come here. I need some time to adjust to New Orleans, to get to know its rhythms and styles. It's very different from New York, you know."

Marianne's smile brightened. "Why, any of the gentlemen would be happy to escort you around the city so you could experience its charms. Once you become familiar, I'm sure you'll find New Orleans most agreeable."

"Oh, yes. I'm intrigued by so many aspects of the city. I'm sure you can understand how unsettled I am, after all I've been through. It's all so overwhelming, you know." If Mrs. Locke had taught her anything, it was how to play the part of a weak female. To pretend so was against Livvie's nature, but if it were her only defense, she would use it.

Marianne reached for her hand. "My poor dear. You have had a time of it. First your father's death, and then having to endure a terrible shipwreck." Her eyes widened. "Oh! And the ruffians in Key West. I can't bear to think of you in their hands. Thank goodness for civilized people like Mr. and Mrs. Crowell."

"Yes, the Crowells have a lovely boarding house. And their cook is excellent." She couldn't hold back from adding, "The wreckers aren't ruffians. They're hardworking and honest."

Marianne withdrew her hand and dabbed a napkin to her lips. "Olivia, you're such a generous soul. You never speak ill of anyone."

"It's the truth, Marianne. I never met more generous souls, so willing to risk themselves for others." Coolness met her impassioned plea.

"As Wendell says, my dear, there is good reason the wreckers are who they are. If they didn't live in Key West, they would labor elsewhere. The world is in need of laborers."

Wendell says. Marianne no longer offered her own perspective. Before marrying her brother, she had, but women deferred to their husbands' opinions as though they had none of their own.

Livvie had no husband—and no intention of obtaining one. Since leaving Key West, she'd often imagined Sam as her husband. She could abide no one else.

She calmed her voice. "They are more than laborers. They are guided by their consciences."

Marianne arched her brows and straightened her shoulders. "Why, Olivia, I hardly know what to say. You have had quite a shock, and your gratitude is well-founded. For your own good, it's time for you to think of your future and forget the awful experiences of your past." The personification of propriety.

No use arguing further. "I apologize. The remnants of last night's headache caused me to over-speak."

Marianne's expression softened. "No need to apologize." She rose from her chair. "If you'll excuse me, I must go ensure Josephine has dressed the children properly." She swept from the room, leaving Livvie alone at the oversized dining table.

Awful experiences—if Marianne only knew how Livvie had cavorted with the so-called riffraff in Key West, she would surely faint. Perhaps Livvie should recount the town hall celebration, which had led her to Sam's bed.

Her breath came ragged at the thought of his hands on her, his sweet lips on hers. Tears welled, remembering how the *Florida* had raced after her. Why had he ruined everything by spending the night with Millie? Of course Livvie had rebuffed him after what she'd witnessed. She'd never be able to trust him again.

Now, Livvie was left with only dread for what lay ahead.

Chapter Twenty-Six

Christmas approached rapidly. Marianne planned a holiday ball and insisted on ordering a new gown for Livvie once again. Off to the dressmaker's they went, without the girls, to Livvie's dismay. Her nieces would have provided a welcome diversion. Marianne's conversation centered on society gossip and fashion, subjects of which Livvie knew little and cared less.

The coach approached the dressmaker's shop, where a crimson silk gown hung in the window.

Grasping Livvie's hand, Marianne beamed. "You must let me buy it for you—you will be stunning in it. Men cannot resist a woman in red, especially one so beautiful." She rushed her from the carriage into the store.

"Marianne, I cannot impose on your generosity any further." Resistance had proven a problem only for herself, not for men, no matter what color she wore.

"Nonsense. It brings me great pleasure. It's like dressing my grown daughter; you are such a dear sister-in-law. And I know you won't spill milk on your dress like Amelia or Claire." She turned to the clerk. "Excuse me. The gown in the window, my sister-in-law will try it on now."

The girl nodded and scampered to fetch it. Bonneted heads turned in Livvie's direction, and the women made no disguise of appraising her. Since she'd arrived,

Livvie's skin had paled, though not to the extent of Marianne's luminous porcelain complexion. A blush crawled across her cheeks when other customers inclined their heads together, whispering.

Marianne took Livvie's hand and followed the clerk to a back room. She undressed as if readying for the gallows. The girl helped her try on the dress, buttoning the back. To Livvie's disappointment, it fit almost perfectly.

Marianne clapped delightedly. "Wonderful. We'll need just a few adjustments." She circled Livvie. "Take it in a bit here." She pinched the waist. "And the shoulders." Her gaze met Livvie's. "You are perfection in it. Wendell will be so pleased."

Wendell! Livvie had liked her brother well enough growing up, even if he'd never paid her much attention, being always busy with schoolwork or his friends. Now, she didn't want his attention, nor his charity.

Since arriving in New Orleans, she'd written every night, so that her novel of her adventures was nearly finished, and she had already written to several publishers inquiring of their interest. One would print her story, she was sure of it.

On the coach ride home, Livvie tried to muster some enthusiasm for the upcoming party, yet couldn't help feeling she would be little better than a slave on the auction block, going to the bidder her brother and sister-in-law deemed best fit to improve her place in society. She blushed to think of the remark she'd made to Sam about improving his station in life, when she had no more desire to do so than he did.

Marianne boasted about the guest list. "Wendell has invited an attorney new to New Orleans. Very debonair,

Wendell said. Mrs. Farley said he was most handsome. And single." At the last remark, excitement shook her voice.

Livvie forced a smile. How lovely. Another one to fend off.

Marianne's face turned somber. "I do hope you don't suffer one of your terrible headaches again."

"I'm sure I'll be fine." She had to at least make a show of it this time. Marianne had been nothing but kind, and she couldn't shame her sister-in-law.

"Good. It would be such a shame, after all the planning and preparations we've done." She sniffed. "And all the gentleman callers you were unable to see."

Livvie's only defense was to feign another attack of femininity. "It's all been so overwhelming since I've arrived. And after the terrible ordeal of the shipwreck…"

Marianne's tone sounded less sympathetic than usual. "Yes, I'm sure. However, it's time to put things in the past, dear. Time is of the essence."

The hiss in her sister-in-law's voice hinted Livvie wasn't getting any younger. Men viewed her as the prime age for breeding, producing heirs for their estates.

Suitors be damned. She would attend this ball, but afterward she would declare her intention to remain single. Until the publisher responded, perhaps she would seek employment as a nanny. A live-in nanny.

****

The dress cut lower across Livvie's bosom than she would have preferred. She supposed Marianne thought she had to show her wares if she wanted bidders to up their ante.

Marianne instructed her servant to take special pains fixing Livvie's hair. Livvie sat without complaint for almost two hours while the woman washed and curled it, scenting it with a spicy-sweet fragrance.

When Livvie finally looked in the mirror, she gasped. "Oh, Nanette—it's lovely. Thank you." Swept up to one side, her long tresses cascaded down her shoulder.

Marianne burst through the room. "Olivia, are you nearly ready? Guests are beginning to arrive." She halted at the sight of Livvie, and rushed to her, took her shoulders and embraced her. "My, my! If you are not engaged by evening's end, I will be amazed. Now hurry downstairs."

"I must finish dressing." Livvie hoped her sister-in-law didn't hear the defeat in her tone. Now the night was upon her, her devil-may-care attitude had abandoned her.

Marianne hurried away, and Nanette helped Livvie into her dress.

Nanette stepped back to assess her. "You are a beauty, miss."

Livvie flashed her a grateful smile. "Due to your magic touch. Thank you, Nanette."

In a curtsy, the girl blushed and then went out the door.

Music floated up the steps, conversation accompanied by waves of laughter. Each minute, more coaches sounded outside, bringing more guests. Tonight, if Livvie told her sister-in-law she felt overwhelmed, she would be speaking the truth.

Livvie sighed and strolled to the balcony. A group of men and women stood in the courtyard below. Their animated chatter made her lonely. She couldn't continue isolating herself, waiting for something to happen.

"Time to move on, Livvie. Take hold of the rudder

of your life."

When one of the men looked up at her, a chill went through her. He hadn't been at the other parties, she was sure of it. The soft glow of the lanterns provided too little light to see him clearly, though from what she could see, he was a man of means. Well dressed, his dark hair swept back, reaching to his collar, so he must not be so old, at least. Perhaps this was the new attorney in town, here to join in the gathering fray of suitors.

She might as well go downstairs. The sooner the night began, the sooner it would end.

Descending the stairs, heads turned in her direction. Mr. Orville smoothed his mustache, his gaze sweeping over her, leaving an invisible trail of slime across her skin that made her want to run to wash it off. Mr. Orville ogled her outwardly. The crimson dress acted as a beacon for attention. She wished she hadn't worn it.

She fixed a polite smile on her face, no more nor less, strolling into the main room. Marianne stood with Wendell near two gentlemen, Mr. Orville and another man whose back was toward her. Marianne smiled at Livvie, an encouragement to join them. Returning her smile, Livvie sighed. In a few more steps, she would soon enough be in their midst.

Mr. Mitchell stepped toward her. "Good evening, Miss Collins. May I have the next dance?"

Dancers swirled past, two by two. She would have to muster up the energy for dancing—particularly for Mr. Mitchell, whose toes frequently landed atop hers on the dance floor.

She smiled sweetly. "Thank you, sir. I'm afraid I'm currently expected by my brother's group. Perhaps later."

A dejected look crossed his face. He gave a curt bow, and then walked off.

Her gown continued to draw glances, men indicated their approval by arching a brow or with a leering smile, while their women indicated their disapproval by their cold glares.

Marianne stepped forward, taking her arm. "Here is our lovely Olivia now." Linking arms, she pulled her to the group.

Livvie fortified herself with a breath. "Good evening." She smiled at Marianne, followed by Wendell, and Mr. Orville.

Marianne gestured demurely to Livvie's right. "Olivia, this is Mr. Langhorne. Wendell is trying to woo him into his firm. Perhaps you can help convince him what a wonderful opportunity it would be." Marianne's laugh rang through Livvie's head.

Langhorne? An electricity traveled across Livvie's skin. She turned to the gentleman next to her. His outstretched hand was sleeved in an ecru linen jacket and a white cotton shirt. Time crystallized, moments stretching to infinity. She lifted her gaze to the smiling face of Sam Langhorne.

"Miss Olivia." His dark eyes sparkled as he extended his hand. "I'm delighted."

She slipped her fingers into his instinctively. He brought them to his lips in a lingering kiss.

Her voice escaped in a breath. "Mr. Langhorne."

His brows rose in amusement.

Unable to hide her astonishment, she asked, "You're an attorney?"

Wendell rocked on his feet. "One of the foremost experts in shipping law. Graduate of Harvard University.

Isn't that right, Mr. Langhorne?"

"Yes. Harvard." While he held her gaze, his eyes taunted her with his secret.

Livvie seethed in anger. She tugged her hand from his grasp. Harvard! Why had he pretended to be nothing more than a wrecker?

Nervousness edged Marianne's laugh. "Olivia, are you well?"

The tight dress dug into her ribs. She couldn't breathe properly. "Yes. No. I need a drink." She could not restrain her agitation.

"Some punch, perhaps?" Sam teased, his expression innocent as a boy's.

Only he knew that the last time she'd had punch—too much—she'd sickened herself, and in plain view of other wreckers. The evening haunted her still. Not because of the humiliation, but the heated memory of Sam's mouth upon hers, his body wonderfully heavy atop hers.

Sam turned to Marianne. "Mrs. Collins, would you have any?"

"Oh, dear, no. We have a wonderful selection of wines."

Livvie said, "Yes, I'd love a Sangria, please."

He fetched her a glass and one for himself. "Excellent." He smiled at Wendell, and turned to Livvie. "Don't you think?"

She gulped it down to quell her quaking nerves. "Yes. Very fine. I believe I'll have another."

He lifted the glass from her grasp. "First, would you care to dance?"

Her teeth clenched. She couldn't very well refuse him in front of her brother, and Sam knew it full well.

"Certainly."

He extended his hand, and she allowed him to lead her to the dance floor.

He pulled her to him. "You don't seem pleased to see me."

She knew he meant his tone to convey confusion and disappointment. She would only acknowledge his amusement.

"What brings you to New Orleans, Mr. Langhorne? The temptation of a law firm position?"

His gaze bored into hers. "Other temptations take precedence." His low voice curled around her spine.

She feigned ignorance, but knew all too well what other temptations he succumbed to. "Such as?"

The playfulness left him. "Must you ask, Livvie? You left without even saying goodbye."

"Oh, I did endeavor to say goodbye, Mr. Langhorne. When I went to your cottage that morning, you were otherwise engaged, so I thought it best not to interrupt."

"What are you talking about?"

"Millie," she hissed. "She was in your cabin, not more than a day after poor Liam's death." How Livvie had wanted to comfort Sam, hold him close. Until seeing that hussy at his doorstep first thing the following morning.

He gave an incredulous laugh. "Is that what you think?"

His cavalier attitude stung. "It's what I saw." Livvie blinked away her frustration at sounding like a lovesick fool. She could not think straight when he looked at her like that. Such yearning in his eyes. Such love. False admiration.

"She was distraught, Livvie. She needed

comforting."

"Yes, and you were more than capable of providing it."

"You must have come early. She left soon after she arrived, and I went to the Crowells to find you. You had already boarded ship."

The missteps of that fateful day came back fresh as a bee sting. She held her head high. "Really, Mr. Langhorne, I would think an attorney of your measure would be able to devise a more plausible excuse."

His tone sharpened. "It's no excuse, Miss Collins. And as an attorney, I recognize my right to remain innocent until proven guilty."

She kept her response light and airy, though her insides churned. So many unanswered questions remained. "Your innocence does not exist." A great yearning filled her. If only he'd exonerate himself, prove worthy of her trust.

"You are a harsh judge." His disappointment this time sounded real.

She couldn't let him use it to his advantage. No longer would she allow herself to be weakened by his pretended affections. "Only in reaction to the harsh truth. I know what I saw." How many other females had he fooled with his warm smile and tender whispers?

The violins screeched to a halt, and the song ended.

She stepped back, out of his embrace. Wobbling, she steadied herself. "Excuse me. I must take my leave." She held a hand to her mouth; tears burned her eyes. If she revealed her despair, she did not care.

"Livvie." He sounded in anguish.

Racing up the staircase, she heard no footsteps behind her. Of course not. Mr. Langhorne appeared the soul of virtue and grace. He would not betray society's rules by making a show of himself.

No matter what promises she'd made to Marianne, she would not suffer through another minute of being in the presence of Sam Langhorne. The imposter.

****

Sam rented a horse and buggy at the livery. Livvie would hear him out, if he had to tie her to a tree. If she still rejected him afterward, he would return to Key West, to his life of owing to no one for his actions. The life he'd intended when he'd first chosen to stay there.

The horse's owner assured Sam it knew what to do without instruction. It had been years since he'd held reins, and even longer since he'd navigated a buggy. Boats were much more predictable, and not given to protesting commands. Horses, on the other hand, had minds of their own, sometimes too little mind to make them worthwhile. He had no use for skittish animals unable to follow a command. Better to yoke an ox to a cart than a skittish horse.

This one appeared old enough to know what was expected of it, though Sam suspected animals smelled his own skittish nature around them and took advantage. He held the reins taut enough to assure the horse he was in control. The horse, however, took no notice as he pulled back to avoid another carriage in their path.

Sam yelled, "Whoa!" as the horse threw his head. He jerked the reins tighter. The other driver veered the carriage away within inches of a collision, saying something just loud enough for Sam to hear, but not his passengers. From inside the carriage, a man glared at Sam out the window. The lady arched her brow, smiling.

Grinning, he nodded an apology. "Sorry, folks.

Temperamental horse." To the horse, he muttered, "Another similar misstep, and you'll be sent to the slaughterhouse."

He drove to the Collins residence without further incident, halting the horse successfully, even if several feet beyond his target. Not trusting the beast to stay put, he called on a servant in the yard to hold the nag.

He placed a coin in the servant's hand, and then strode the stone path to the front porch. His slacks and jacket had wrinkled during the drive, so he attempted to smooth them, finger-combing the hair falling across his brow.

No use in prolonging the suspense. If she wouldn't see him, he would leave.

His loud rapping on the door brought a wide-eyed servant within seconds.

"Good afternoon. I'm Samuel Langhorne, come to call on Miss Olivia. Is she here?"

The woman pulled the door open wider. "Come in, sir. Take a seat in the parlor, please, while I fetch her for you."

Voices echoed through the hallway and dining room, probably the cooking staff. Up the curling iron-railed stairway, little girls' laughter sounded from a room.

The servant gestured toward the front room, sweeping noiselessly up the stairs.

Sam paced across the parlor rug. Its Chinese design lured his eye across pagodas to females in geisha attire, carrying petite umbrellas. Such rugs had been cargo on several doomed ships, hauled up only after great effort.

Outside, the servant stood holding the reins, looking toward the house, still as a statue. The formality of the city's residents struck Sam as odious. Too similar to Philadelphia.

A swishing of fabric sounded. Marianne walked past the parlor entrance, her skirts hoisted to accommodate her hurried pace. She halted so abruptly, her skirts swung like a bell.

"Mr. Langhorne. I had no idea you were here." Her surprise appeared severe enough to be akin to an ailment.

He bowed his head, affecting an airy tone. "Good afternoon, Mrs. Collins."

She swooshed toward him. "To what do we owe the pleasure of your visit?"

"I am hoping to entice young Miss Olivia out for an afternoon buggy ride."

Her open-mouthed surprise shifted to delight, and she turned as Livvie descended the stairs. "Did you hear, Olivia?"

"Hear what?" Her gaze snapped from Mrs. Collins to him.

His pulse quickened when her face softened with longing. Quickly she pressed her lips into a thin line, her eyes glittering hard as diamonds.

"Mr. Langhorne is here to bring you for a buggy ride. Isn't it delightful?"

If Sam had doubted the outcome of his proposal, he no longer feared it. The lady of the house had removed any decision from Livvie in no uncertain terms.

Livvie's voice fell flat, and she glared at him. "No. I hadn't heard." She held the rail and directed her question to her sister-in-law. "We planned to take the girls shopping this afternoon. I can't let them down. They'll never forgive me."

Mrs. Collins conveyed her disapproval in her tilted

head. Her light tone could not disguise the weight of her words. "Nonsense. We can go shopping tomorrow. The girls prefer to play in the yard anyway. You and Mr. Langhorne can go for a nice, long ride." She emphasized *long,* smiling at Sam.

Livvie's shoulders slumped. She pulled herself straight and descended. "Well, Mr. Langhorne, it seems I have no excuse not to accept your offer."

Sam tried not to smile. Although Livvie might be an unwilling partner, she'd be a partner nonetheless. All his. He stifled his pleasure.

Mrs. Collins bustled to the steps. "Let me get you a hat, Olivia. The sun is unkind to fair young skin."

"No, please, Marianne. I detest hats."

"The surrey has a roof, if it's any assistance," Sam offered. Livvie's sharp glance told him it was not.

"A shawl, then," her sister-in-law said.

Livvie groaned. "It's too warm for any coverings. I need nothing else, thank you."

Mrs. Collins' thinned lips and sharp exhale conveyed her dismay at her inability to control her inherited relative. She turned to Sam. "I know you will look after my dear sister."

"Exerting the utmost care." His tender tone drew a fiery glare from Livvie.

"Excuse me a moment while I get ready." She strolled slowly up the stairs, her head held high.

Mrs. Collins gave a breathy laugh. "Please excuse her, Mr. Langhorne. The impudence of youth still affects her."

He smiled to reassure her. "It only sweetens the wait, Mrs. Collins."

Sam had spoken too soon. The wait extended longer

than he anticipated. Upstairs, women's sharp voices hinted an unpleasant exchange.

He stood at the window. The servant tasked with holding his horse looked no better nor worse than before. The horse shook his head, the expressionless servant holding fast to the reins.

Mrs. Collins descended the stairs, gliding toward him. "I'm sorry to keep you waiting so long, Mr. Langhorne. Olivia will be down momentarily. I wondered whether you had dinner plans for this evening?"

"None whatsoever." The one meal he'd ordered at the Arcade Hotel had left his stomach roiling. He'd endeavored to eat out since. He could not claim to enjoy the hot spices in New Orleans food.

Mrs. Collins grasped his arm. "Good. So you must join us. We have a lovely dinner planned, and I know Olivia would welcome your company as much as Wendell and myself."

Sam doubted it. If anything, it would raise Livvie's ire, though perhaps it might provide the needed push to an outburst—one in which she would speak her mind. Or, he should say, another outburst, judging by what he'd already heard. Women were more apt to speak their minds in such times of heightened emotion.

"I would be happy to join you. Thank you for the kind invitation."

Footsteps on the stairs signaled Livvie's descent. Her flushed cheeks gave away her indignation. "I'm very sorry to keep you waiting so long, Mr. Langhorne." She kept her gaze lowered.

"You are worth the wait, Miss Collins. I take it you're ready now?"

Her jaw clenched, but her voice was sweet. "Yes, I am."

Sam smiled at Mrs. Collins. "I shall return her safely." He strode to the front door and held it open. Livvie swept through without a word.

Mrs. Collins followed them onto the porch. "Have a lovely time."

Sam took Livvie's arm, and she stepped up into the surrey.

She smacked at his hand. "I'm perfectly capable of entering a buggy of my own accord."

"I don't dispute it." He stood by while she settled into the seat. Crossing in front of the horse, he gave another coin to the servant. "Sorry for the long wait."

The boy's eyes widened. "Thank you, sir."

Sam climbed in the surrey and unwound the reins from their hitch.

Livvie gazed ahead. "If you're trying to impress me with your generosity, you needn't bother."

He would have to work at loosening her stiff attitude. "Not at all. He did me a favor, and I rewarded him. I don't believe you have any reason to be impressed by such a small gesture."

Not otherwise moving, she narrowed her eyes. "I thought you didn't like horses."

"I don't." He snapped the reins across the horse's back, and the surrey jerked forward when the horse jolted ahead.

Livvie grabbed the front of the surrey. A loud gasp came from the porch.

Sam waved to Mrs. Collins. "He doesn't like me, either, unfortunately."

Livvie clutched her seat. "I hope you handle horses

better than you do females. You do know how to drive a buggy, don't you?"

Sam grinned. "I'm learning. On both accounts." He eased the reins back, and the horse slowed from a trot to a fast walk. "You see? I'm mastering a new skill."

She turned away. "I cannot quite guess at your motives, Mr. Langhorne."

"I thought my motives were most obvious, Miss Collins." Nothing was ever obvious enough for any female. No, apparently he was in for a long session of groveling and apologies.

Her laugh sounded haughty, so unlike her. "You show up in New Orleans, transformed into a dandy—"

"I couldn't very well wear my wrecker's clothes, now, could I?" A dandy indeed. He despised such self-absorbed men.

She continued as though he hadn't spoken. "The toast of high society, and you scheme with my sister-in-law."

"I am not scheming with Mrs. Collins." He couldn't let her turn everything against him.

She snapped her gaze to his. "You never told me you were a lawyer."

Hurt lay beneath her harsh features.

"I wasn't a lawyer in Key West. I lived the life I chose, not the life forced upon me by my father. I thought you, of all people, would understand such a position." To win an argument, one had to use the offensive. To aim for the opponent's soft underbelly. And oh, how he'd missed that side of her.

"What am I supposed to think, Mr. Langhorne?" Desperation edged her tone, and she sat rigid.

If only he could find a private place. Damned

buggies allowed everyone in the street to hear their conversation.

He lowered his voice. "You are supposed to see me, Livvie. *Sam*. The man who traveled from Key West to New Orleans to be with you. Because you didn't give me a chance to speak to you before you left."

"What could you possibly have to say? That you haven't already said to Millie, I mean?" Her voice broke at the last.

Anger billowed inside Sam like a full sail. He loosened the reins, and the horse's jog quickened to a trot with the new leeway. Sam angled toward Livvie. "Will you never stop bringing up that woman? I told you what happened. She was distraught—"

Livvie's eyes widened. "Look out!"

The horse whinnied and threw its head. A man pulling a handcart across the street increased his pace to get out of the way, but too late. The horse's hoof caught the end of the cart, and the surrey wheel smashed into it. The cart overturned, spilling fruit across the street.

Sam yanked the horse to a stop and handed the reins to Livvie. "Hold this monster." He jumped from the surrey.

The man held up a fist and yelled something in what sounded like German. Passing carriages and wagons smashed the fruit.

Sam dashed into the street to gather what fruit he could from the path of destruction. The man stood at the side of the road and cursed while Sam righted the cart and scooped up the scattered apples and bananas. "I'm very sorry. My horse is to blame. I'll shoot him later, if it makes you feel better." He'd shoot him now, except they'd have no way to get the carriage back.

The man continued his rant. Sam turned in dismay to the roadway. A useless exercise. The fruit lay ruined beyond salvation. He dug in his pockets and pulled out some bills. "Will this cover it? Is it enough to pay for the damage?"

The man furrowed his brow, his response unintelligible except for the anger. Money acted as a universal language.

Sam dug for more bills and presented them. "Is it enough? I have no more." He shrugged in apology.

The man swiped the money from Sam's palm and muttered ill sentiments.

When Sam looked at Livvie, she hid her face behind her hand, though her smile was evident beneath. His spirits lifted, and he strode to the buggy as though walking on air.

He climbed in. "This is becoming a most expensive trip." He reached for the reins.

She held them away. "You'd better let me drive."

He sat back in the seat. "Are you sure?" He wouldn't mind. He could ignore the outraged glares of passersby. He touched his finger to his forehead and smiled at an old man who stared.

"Oh, yes. Quite sure." She snapped the reins and whistled, and the horse walked.

Riding was a much more pleasant experience. This way, he could watch Livvie. Her torso inclined toward the horse, the curve of her back an alluring line Sam's fingers ached to trace.

"Where are you taking me?" he asked.

She clicked to the horse, and it trotted. "To the river."

"Will I be returning? Or do you plan to dump my

body there?" He rested his hand on the back of her seat, yet dared not touch her. Not yet.

A trace of a smile lightened her glance. "We'll have to see."

They drove along the Mississippi. A paddleboat steamed by.

"I'd love to have one of those. I fear, however, it wouldn't last long on the sea."

Livvie sighed. "I'd love to get on one and float away." As if she'd revealed too much of herself, she straightened. "We'd better get home before Marianne sends the cavalry to search for us."

"Oh, I wouldn't worry." Sam suppressed a smile.

Since his arrival, Mrs. Collins had been nothing but gracious and done everything to ingratiate Livvie to him. Livvie's suspicions had been correct. Her brother and his wife would have her married off in no time. And Sam intended to be the groom.

****

The excellent brandy helped Sam endure Wendell's lengthy discussion of the legal affairs of New Orleans.

Wendell opened a cigar box and pulled one of its contents beneath his nose in a long sniff. "These beauties are Cuban, the best of the best. And quite expensive. Would you care for one?"

"Certainly. If I'd known your preference for Cuban cigars, I could have brought you ten boxes."

"Oh?" Wendell's amused tone riled Sam.

"We frequently sailed to Havana. Cigars are easily obtained there, and for a reasonable price."

Wendell held a match to the cigar Sam held to his mouth. "What a shame. For me."

Sam puffed the cigar. "They are excellent."

A knock at the door, and Wendell said, "Enter."

The maid peered around the door. "Mrs. Collins said to tell you dinner is ready, sir."

Wendell stood. "Shall we?"

Sam followed him to the dining room. Livvie trailed Marianne, who suggested Sam sit across from Livvie. Sam held her chair, and Livvie strained to say thank you.

Looking pleased with the arrangement, Marianne sat and straightened a napkin across her lap. "Tell us, Mr. Langhorne, what brings you to New Orleans?"

Livvie set her gaze on Sam in mock interest.

He suppressed a smile. "I have a number of pursuits here, Mrs. Collins."

While the maid set their plates before them, Marianne asked, "Will you be staying long?"

"It all depends, ma'am, on how long it takes me to conclude my business."

Wendell said, "I hoped I could persuade you to stay indefinitely."

"I wouldn't rule it out entirely, Wendell. As I said, it depends." On the host's sister, though Sam would not say it aloud. Not yet.

"New Orleans could use a top attorney. The shipping business will increase in the coming years, and you'll never want for work."

"A desirous position, to be sure." Desirous to someone else. Sam choked at the thought of being cooped up in an office drowning in paperwork.

"Enviable, among our profession. Your expertise is needed here. New Orleans is a major trade port, you understand."

"I'll certainly give it serious consideration." He hoped he reassured the man enough to drop the subject.

Wendell narrowed his eyes. "You have other prospects elsewhere?"

"Several, yes." Sam flicked his gaze to Livvie, who feigned sudden disinterest.

Wendell grunted. "We'll have to sweeten our deal somehow."

Sam's intense gaze burned into Livvie. After several irritated glances, she pushed away her plate in favor of wine.

Marianne leveled a disapproving gaze as Livvie drained her glass.

Marianne touched her husband's sleeve. "Wendell, why don't you offer Mr. Langhorne a nightcap? We could all adjourn to the courtyard. The cool evening air is so refreshing." She smiled at Sam.

Wendell rubbed his stomach. "Excellent idea. Shall we?"

Sam flashed a grin. "Sounds perfect." More perfect if he could be alone with Livvie again. They had much to discuss, and time did not favor him. Livvie appeared to grow more irritated by each passing moment.

Wendell opened the wide doors to the courtyard. Sam's attention wandered from his chit-chat to observe Mrs. Collins speak in hushed tones to Livvie in the dining room. Their conversation was barely audible, but the hostess appeared to be scolding her houseguest, who brandished an envelope like a sword. Livvie finally tucked it away, perhaps inside her sleeve. Sam couldn't quite tell.

As Livvie stepped toward the courtyard, Marianne blocked her path and took hold of Livvie's hands. Sam thought he heard Mrs. Collins ask Livvie not to disappear to her room, not to insult Mr. Langhorne; tonight was too important to Wendell.

Mrs. Collins could not have been more pleasant when she approached the men. Livvie's eyes flashed in a glare.

****

In the courtyard, Livvie stood at one end of the stone bench where Marianne sat. Sam stood at the other. She would prefer more than a bench between them. For now, it would suffice.

Wendell puffed his chest like a rooster. "How about a brandy?" he asked Sam.

"Absolutely."

"Excellent." Wendell strode to the door.

"Might I have a small glass?" After the discovery she'd just made in the dining room, Livvie needed something to loosen her tight nerves.

Marianne laughed nervously. "Perhaps a glass of wine instead, sister?"

Livvie knew she couldn't weaken her sister-in-law's resolve by arguing. "Of course." Though she might be tempted to dump it over her brother's head. Another liar.

He returned carrying the drinks and two more cigars. Sam declined the cigar and gulped the liquor while Wendell droned on about business matters.

Livvie clenched her fist and touched the envelope in her sleeve. Opened, though not by her. By Wendell. Never would she trust him again.

At a break in the conversation, Marianne stood. "Please excuse me. I must check on the children."

Sam gave a courteous nod. "Certainly."

Glancing at Livvie, Marianne arched a brow and discreetly held her hand to her side in a command for her to stay.

Livvie watched as Marianne flitted inside. At the sounds of girlish laughter, Livvie gazed up to the second story with undisguised longing. She loved the nighttime ritual—reading to her nieces in bed, tucking them in. After tonight, she would leave this place and hated to think she'd never see them again. Maybe once they'd grown into lovely young women, they would visit her, attend one of her readings.

Marianne appeared on the balcony. "Dearest, come say goodnight to your darling daughters."

Wendell grunted. "Pardon me. Duty calls." He, too, disappeared inside.

A blatant attempt to leave her and Sam alone. Livvie crossed her arms over her chest and turned away.

"I neglected to tell you. I have a dog."

"What?" She spun to face him.

He brightened. "Yes. William Whelan—you remember, he owned the dry goods store?" He set his glass on the bench. "His dog had a litter of seven. He's holding a pup for me."

"So you intended to return all along." The realization deadened her enthusiasm.

"Actually, I told him if I didn't return within three months, to find it another home. However, it would be a shame to lose such a fine dog. You'd love him. Light brown fur, not too long to make a mess. He'll be perfect on the farm."

She blinked. "What farm?"

"I have my eye on a plot of land. Liam found it, actually. We'd planned…" His voice choked.

"I was so very sorry to hear about Liam. I know you loved him like a brother."

He nodded, and took a sharp breath. "The farm's on

the mainland of Florida, within miles of the sea. A perfect distance for short sailing trips. Doesn't it sound lovely?"

Confused, she moved away as he approached. Grief could ravage a person, send him whirling out of control, make him do and say things contrary to his nature. Losing Liam must have left him unmoored. Who knew better than she how a person in mourning could reach out to grasp someone, anyone, desperate for sympathy? She'd nearly been tempted to look for a husband to remain at home in New York. The allure of a travel adventure equaled the thrilling opportunity to seek publication of her novels. To make her own way in the world. Now, her dream was within reach. Her fingers itched to hold the letter she'd discovered hidden in a desk drawer, re-read each word, but especially Mr. Randall's glowing praise of her latest novel, which he wanted to publish. Why, he'd asked, had she not responded to his offer to publish her other novel?

Why indeed. Livvie would be sure to ask Wendell.

"Yes, it sounds lovely." Why did he tease her so? He'd come to New Orleans to work for her traitorous brother, hadn't he?

"How long do you intend to punish me, Livvie?" he asked calmly.

"I am not punishing you," she said over her shoulder. Being with him was torture with both of them pretending to be other than their true selves. As much as she wanted to believe Sam had decided he loved her more than Millie, could she trust him? Was he in league with her brother against her?

His footsteps sounded closer. "Then what?" His voice shook.

She turned and folded her arms. "I don't know." Since his unexpected arrival, her thoughts flowed through her head too quickly to make sense. Her emotions swung from hate to love, relief to anguish. She didn't know what to think, or believe. And then, finding Mr. Randall's letter by accident had threatened to unnerve her completely.

She glanced up at the house, praying for salvation in the form of interruption. Time—she needed time to sort it out. To confront Wendell. She already guessed at his response: she was a female in need of a man to guide her. No wonder Father and Wendell never got along.

Sam stepped in front of her. "What don't you know? Ask me anything. I will tell you."

She spat a laugh. "Really, Sam. And you'd speak the truth?" Her question sounded more of a plea.

"I have never lied to you."

His insistent tone reminded her. Now she knew why he'd always been so well spoken, always had such a ready argument, had such an interest in legal texts. He'd been schooled for legal matters. Trained to present his argument to his best advantage because he wanted to win it.

She wouldn't let him outwit her. "You never told me the truth outright, either."

He stood in her brother's house, transformed. The peasant-like Sam Langhorne of Key West now appeared a prince, more handsome than ever. If he thought himself irresistible, she would prove him otherwise.

His brow furrowed. "You're angry because I was schooled to be an attorney?"

"You told me you were a thief in Philadelphia."

A twinkle lit his eyes. "I said I was little better than

a thief, so I spoke only the truth."

"Yes, I should have guessed by your love of argument, I suppose, what you truly meant." Her insides churned, twisting in on themselves. She had no idea what to believe.

"I didn't tell you about my past because I chose to leave it behind."

Was he trying to make himself seem a kindred spirit to her? "Why? If you're so intent on revealing yourself, tell me everything."

"All right."

His soft voice twisted her anger into desire. Walking toward her, heat filled his gaze. "I never wanted to be a lawyer. I went to school because my father wished it. I joined my brother's law firm. A very successful firm. So profitable that the woman who ensnared my affections endeavored to become my wife."

He had a wife? His revelation singed her gut and left her too weak to breathe. This was too much in one evening. Livvie turned away.

He grasped her arms so she had to face him.

"No. You asked, and now you will listen. To all of it." His grip tightened, and his tone hardened. "I was engaged to a woman. Helen. I bought her anything and everything she wanted. And she wanted a lot." Bitterness tainted his laugh. "I was such a lovesick fool I set aside my suspicions while she spent time in the company of other men. What man wouldn't want to court her? She was beautiful, born to a well-connected family, an asset to any man."

An asset. How typical. Yet supremely disappointing, coming from Sam.

"And?" she prompted. "What happened?"

His depth of emotion conveyed the answer.

His gaze drifted. "A week before our wedding, I found her in the company of someone else." The wound she'd inflicted appeared to reopen, if Sam's pained expression were any indication. He released her.

"How awful."

His idle gaze grew more focused as if coming out of a trance. "I couldn't stand the thought of having to attend the same social gatherings as Helen and John."

"So you left it all behind." She couldn't blame him. She'd escaped an awful marriage herself, though it hadn't damaged her heart in the least.

"I'd read of Key West and been intrigued. Going there was the best thing I could have done. I should have done it years earlier, instead of wasting my time at Harvard."

Her lifelong frustrations bubbled forth. "Only a man would say such a thing. If only I could have gone to school." Although her father had been sympathetic to her desire, he'd gently denied her again and again. Yes, it would benefit her writing, but it held no guarantee of success like other occupations.

"I'm sorry. I understand."

"How can you possibly know what I feel?" She fought back tears.

"Oh, yes I do, Livvie. I know exactly what you feel." He moved behind her.

She tensed, expecting his touch. The fine hairs along the back of her neck prickled with his warm breath when he spoke, he stood so tantalizingly close. Closing her eyes, she steeled herself.

"You feel trapped living with your brother and his wife, who expect you to marry into society. A life you don't want. You long for freedom, to do as you please."

She glanced back, yet didn't turn to face him. She walked beneath the balcony, out of view of the prying eyes surely watching from above.

He followed, and moved closer this time, his whisper like a silk ribbon reaching within her, twining itself around her heart. "You think of me as often as I think of you. Throughout the day and night. You dream of me, and awake in a sweat, aching for my embrace. I know because I feel the same ache for you. An unrelenting yearning."

Her breath quickened, and she searched for something indefinable. She couldn't think straight. She needed more air. She stepped away. He gripped her arms, and she gasped.

"You are afraid of what you feel for me. Afraid I will have nothing to offer you."

"No, it's not true." She wanted nothing from him, nothing but himself. But if she couldn't have all of him, she wanted none of him.

"It is. I'm here, Livvie." He turned her toward him. "I will do whatever is necessary to win you. If you want me to stay in New Orleans and join your brother's law firm so you can live in a pretty house, I will. It would be worth it to come home to you every day. To be able to hold you all night. I would endure silly gatherings of mindless men and prattling women if it meant you were mine."

Her stomach clenched at the thought. Had Wendell lured him though she could not? "No. You don't want that life." She'd never wanted that life, either. Its pretenses and falsities sickened her.

His fingers drifted along her arm. "Yes, Livvie. I see

myself through your eyes and glimpse the man I could be. You make me want to be that man."

She laid her hands against his chest, wanting desperately to know if he really was that man, or the mere illusion of him. "It's no use. I don't want such a life." She'd left New York to escape it, and would not succumb to it here. She could not let him sacrifice his freedom, either, whatever the reason.

"It would be a good life if we were together."

God, what was he saying? How could he suggest they live a life he'd gratefully escaped? She pulled away, and he tightened his embrace.

"What do you want, Livvie? Tell me. I will do anything in my power to give it to you."

His urgent tone arrested her. She searched his face.

"I will not be trapped into asking for your freedom. And if you gave it to me, however willingly, you would hate me later for accepting it."

"What about your freedom? Isn't that a fair exchange? Yours for mine?"

Unshed tears burned her eyes. She had to ask him about the letter. If Wendell had told Sam about it, asked him to keep it a secret, she would be able to tell by his reaction. The sole reason she feared to ask.

"Livvie, I know your soul yearns for freedom as much as my own."

She steadied her hands against his chest and pinned him with her gaze. "Did you know about the letter?"

"The letter? The one you spoke to your sister-in-law about earlier?"

Oh, God. "You knew, then."

"I saw you with her. Is it significant? I don't understand."

Significant? She wanted to laugh. And cry.

His soft voice plied her so deeply, and he looked at her with such yearning. Marianne's words came back: *Men will say anything, act desperate to love you and you alone, but don't doubt that he says the same thing to every woman he sees.* Did anyone in this house speak the truth? Her emotions roiling, tears burst forth and she covered her face.

When he encircled his arms around her, she twisted away from his embrace and ran into the house. Once in her room, she slammed the door and locked it.

Tomorrow, she would leave this place. First, she would write Mr. Randall to inform him her address would change, and not to trust her brother with any news.

****

Sam's heart deadened in his chest. He leaned against the wall and heaved a long sigh.

So that was her answer. An offer of his freedom in exchange for hers wasn't good enough.

He went inside. The dining room lay in darkness, as did the hallway. A lantern burned in the parlor, but its silence amplified its emptiness. Spying some paper on a desk, he sat and wrote quickly. From his pocket, he removed several items and wrapped them inside another page. Using a ribbon he found inside the drawer, he tied it. After scrawling Livvie's name on the outside, he left it on the desk, went to the front door, and slowly pulled it open, hopes mounting that Livvie would come back to stop him.

"Mr. Langhorne?" a woman said.

His heart leaped and he swiveled around.

Marianne stood on the staircase. "Is everything all right?"

He strained to keep his voice steady. "I'm afraid my business here is concluded, Mrs. Collins." He ducked his head. "Thank you for your hospitality during my stay."

Concern etched her features, and she descended. "You're not leaving, are you? You've only just arrived."

"I'll be returning to Florida as soon as I can arrange passage."

"I'm very sorry to hear it. I'm sure Olivia will be too."

He gave a bitter laugh. "No, I'm afraid she'll greet the announcement joyously. I would ask a final favor of you. Please deliver the package on the desk to Livvie for me?"

She reached for his arm. "Of course. But—"

He pulled away. "I must say goodnight. And farewell." He bowed.

She curtsied. "Goodnight, Mr. Langhorne."

He strode through the courtyard, the burden of his despair a leaden weight that would not allow him to glance up to the balcony. He knew Livvie would not be there.

****

Livvie lay in her bed. Tears flowed until her eyes burned and her stomach ached.

When he'd taken her in his arms tonight, she'd felt as though she were drowning all over again, this time in deceit and indecision. She'd wanted nothing more than for Sam to fill her arms, to open herself to him as she'd done that night in his cabin. The roar of her passion mixed with her confusion and allowed no rational thought. Since her father's death, she'd blocked so much from her mind and railed against the unfairness of her gender.

Damn her brother for concealing the letter, and damn Sam for aiding in the deception. Why should she be controlled by a man, any man? How dare either of them attempt to rob her of the only dream she'd ever had?

Why had Sam revealed he'd chosen a dog? That part of the conversation made no sense. And that he'd bought a farm.

Such an idyllic life had haunted her dreams since she'd sailed away from the island. The constraints of society were a distant thing in Key West, something the *Key West Enquirer* might report on, yet seldom followed by the islanders. While the wreckers might live reckless lives, they were honorable nonetheless. Unlike New Orleans, where people were murdered in public without protest, and thieves stole into houses and pilfered valuables, Key West residents left their doors unlocked from morning until night with little consequence. Although some islanders might behave rashly, even harshly toward one another, every man there would lay down his life for another.

Farm life meant hard work, but if her novels sold well enough, she could afford to hire help for both Sam and herself.

She walked to the balcony. The crescent moon hung low over the house. It looked so close, Livvie might have reached up and grabbed it and climbed aboard to sail off into the night.

He'd spoken tonight about her desires as though he'd looked inside her mind to see her thoughts. He was right about everything, including her yearning for him. At times, when she thought of him, the images appeared so vividly in her mind she could almost feel his presence.

No matter the distance between them, he was always near, as warming as the sun.

Yes, even now, she would forgive him for straying with Millie if he swore he'd never see the woman again, and if he swore he held no allegiance to her brother.

Foolish thoughts. Useless, now.

****

The sound of little girls' laughter greeted Livvie as she awoke. Sunshine poured through her window like a ray of hope. She arose and stretched in its warmth.

Her novels would be published! Two of them! She could barely contain her excitement.

Or her fury. She hoped Wendell had already departed. If not, she would simply inform him she was moving out. Today.

A new life awaited. She could not stay rooted in a past that no longer existed, fearful of her future. Sam's encouragement for her to live life as she deigned fit exhilarated her beyond measure. She would follow his advice, though it hurt to think of a future without him.

She dressed hurriedly and flew down the stairs. Amelia and Claire sat at the dining room table, the nanny between them.

"Auntie Livia!" they cried.

"Good morning, my sweeties." Livvie kissed the tops of their silken heads. How she loved their exuberant smiles and unbridled joy.

"Join us, please?" Amelia kicked her feet in anticipation.

"I'm sorry, I can't this morning. I have urgent business to attend to."

Marianne strolled in. "What business?"

Livvie's cheeks warmed in a blush. "I must seek an

attorney."

Marianne set a glass of juice before each of her daughters. "If you're referring to Mr. Langhorne, I'm afraid he thinks your business is already concluded."

Livvie's senses snapped to attention. "You spoke to him? What did he say?"

"He's arranging the earliest possible passage back to Florida. He might have already departed." Her sister-in-law's sorrow—and accusation—showed plainly in her face before she turned away. "He did leave this for you." Marianne handed her a crudely wrapped package.

Livvie ripped it open. Out fell her mother's pearl-and-sapphire necklace, and a sapphire ring. She unfolded his handwritten note—and her pages.

Dearest Livvie,

I should have returned this necklace to you upon my arrival. I had to bribe Pinder for it. From your description, I knew it to be your mother's.

I hoped you would accept the ring and wear it as my bride. Not as a means to ensnare you, but as a small token of my immeasurable love. Now that I know you will never accept me as a husband, I give the ring to you freely. Use it to sustain you until you make your fortune through your writing career. For I know you will, dearest. Reading your pages thrilled me as no other to believe you might have been thinking of me when you put pen to paper and described your deepest longing. Foolish of me, I know. Your brilliance shines through on the page, and readers will fall in love with you. Not nearly to the depths I have.

I shall never forget you, Livvie. You've wrecked me for any other woman. I intend to return to mainland Florida and live out my days on a farm alone. Except, of course, for my dog.

Try to remember me with some fondness.

Sam

Livvie turned her mother's jewelry in her hand. Sam truly had worked a wonder in retrieving them for her. *Because he loves you.*

She pierced Marianne with her glare. "Tell me now. Did Sam know about Mr. Randall's letter?"

Momentarily flustered, Marianne then met her gaze evenly. "Wendell wanted to protect you. He wants you to have a good, secure life."

"Tell me, Marianne. Did Sam know anything at all about this? That Mr. Randall offered to publish my novels?"

"Mr. Langhorne sought out Wendell. Now we know why, of course—to find you."

Her thoughts raced. She must find him. Talk to him. It couldn't be too late to right things between them.

After carefully folding the letter, she fitted the ring to her finger. She fastened the necklace around her neck and then bolted for the door. "I'm borrowing the buggy."

"You cannot be thinking of following him."

She paused only long enough to say, "I can. And I am." What had happened to the vibrant girl who married her brother?

She rushed to the stables and enlisted the aid of a stable boy in readying the buggy. His slow movements agonized her. "Please hurry. It's very important."

He increased his pace only slightly. Livvie rushed inside the stable, threw open the stall door, and led the horse to the front of the buggy. She clucked her tongue and backed him up, speaking soothingly while the stable boy connected horse to wagon. Once he'd finally finished, she thanked him and climbed in.

After she slapped the reins against the horse's back, the buggy lurched forward. She negotiated the streets leading to the Arcade Hotel and steered the buggy to its entrance. A valet held the reins while she ran inside.

The man at the desk looked up in alarm as she rushed toward him.

"Is Mr. Sam Langhorne here? What room is he in? Can you get him for me?"

The man ran his finger down the ledger. "Mr. Langhorne's no longer a guest at this establishment."

Her veins chilled. "No. When did he leave?"

"An hour ago."

She clutched the counter. "Where did he go? Did he tell you?"

His stare questioning, the clerk drew away. "No, miss."

She rushed outside to the buggy. The wharf—he had to be headed there.

She thanked the valet and climbed back inside. The reins struck the horse's flank. It threw its head and jerked forward. The wheels rattled along.

The bustle at the wharves lent more confusion to Livvie's plight. Leaving the horse tied to a hitch, she spied into every boat she passed, whether big or small. A large paddleboat steamed away. She ran to the end of the pier, shielding her gaze against the blazing sun.

Passengers crowded the boat's upper and lower areas. One man caught her eye. He leaned against the end of the lower deck, gazing out over the water.

Her heart jumped against her ribs. "Sam?" she called. "Sam!"

His head turned. "Livvie?" came his distant call.

Laughter bubbled through her throat. "You can't leave! Come back, I need to speak to you!"

He leaned over the rail. "What? I can't stop the boat."

She held the wharf post, straining toward the vessel. The growing distance between them brought back harsh memories of Key West, when she'd stood on the bow of the ship to watch him fade into the distance. "How many times must this happen to me?" This couldn't be the cruel end.

Clenching her teeth, she vowed, "I won't let it be."

She scanned the river, and then the dock. A rowboat floated nearby that might bring her to the paddleboat. With surprising efficiency, she untied it from the dock, stepped inside, and took up the oars. Although she rowed hard, she couldn't make much headway.

"Livvie!" Sam dove from the paddleboat, swimming toward her.

"Sam." Fear shot through her. *He'll be fine. He swims the ocean in storms, and he can navigate the muddy Mississippi.*

"Hang on, Livvie." His powerful strokes brought him to the boat. He gripped its side and laughed, water streaming down his face. "Will you save me?"

"It depends. Tell me again why Millie was at your cottage."

"I was the only one who knew where Liam hid his money. She stayed there while I retrieved it. She's now on her way to California."

"And you knew nothing about the letter?"

"What letter?"

"From the publisher. My novels will be published, Sam." She reached for him, and the rowboat rocked perilously.

He steadied his hold on the side. "They will? That's wonderful."

She must look a fool, with this ridiculous grin on her face, but she couldn't stop.

"Now that you're wealthy and successful, will you have pity on me and let me in the boat?"

The boat seesawed as she reached over to tug him inside. Once he was seated across from her, she kneeled and wound her arms around his neck, all her misgivings melting away. This was where she belonged. In his arms.

He nuzzled his cheek to hers. "You've salvaged my heart from the depths."

"I'll pay you a fair price." She drew back to appraise his reaction. "My heart for yours."

The gleam returned to his eyes, the same light that had shone there in Key West. "Done. Now, can we continue our negotiations on land?"

"Anywhere, Sam."

As he rowed them toward shore, she knew she could go anywhere with him, and it would be home.

Thank you for purchasing
this publication of The Wild Rose Press, Inc.

For questions or more information
contact us at
info@thewildrosepress.com.

The Wild Rose Press, Inc.